SELECTED STORIES

J. KAROLEWSKI
APRIL 21, 2020

by Jack Karolewski

D1602615

KINDLE DIRECT PUBLISHING

2020

This special edition is dedicated to my family and friends.

TABLE OF CONTENTS

BRIMSTONE

Walter Brimley was a haberdasher in a popular store in downtown Philadelphia called Johaan's. He sold men's shirts, suits and neckties, but mostly he was obsessed with tales of the Old West. He avidly read the exciting and popular Beadle's New Dime Novels about tough cowboys, hero sheriffs and dastardly desperados, and he yearned to see that wild frontier for himself before that way of life vanished forever. The year was 1879, and Walter had just turned twenty-four.

Three years earlier, Brimley attended the city's 1876 Centennial International Exposition, along with ten million other curious visitors. With exhibits from thirty-seven countries, Walter marveled at the new technological inventions and consumer products. He saw Bell's original telephone, Edison's automatic telegraph, and Remington's typographic machine – the first typewriter. He tried a new snack called popcorn, sipped a Hires Root Beer, and sampled Heinz Ketchup. For fifty cents, he climbed to the top of the right arm and torch of the Statue of Liberty, a gift from France which was shipped to America in pieces, to eventually be built in the harbor of New York City.

All of his experiences at the Exposition, however, convinced Walter that the future was rushing up to meet him, inconveniently at a time when he only wanted to savor the vivid but fading past. Wild Bill Hickok had been killed while playing cards in Deadwood just this year. Wyatt Earp had left Dodge City with his brothers James and Virgil for Tombstone, in the Arizona Territory. But Jesse James and his gang had recently robbed two stores in western Mississippi, netting a haul of over $2000. And Billy the Kid was still roaming around. Thrills and adventure were still alive, thankfully! The germ of a plan of action was thus formed in Walter's mind. He started saving his money at that point. He figured he would wander out West for a minimum of one year. He even imagined he would write up his adventures and sell them to Beadle's, and possibly become rich and famous!

Now, in 1879, he was ready. Walter quit his haberdasher job, and bought a one-way train ticket to Fort Smith, Arkansas, located on the river opposite the border of Indian Territory. He carried a single cardboard suitcase with his belongings. The five-day rail ride took him through Pittsburgh, Indianapolis, St. Louis, and Joplin. Once in Fort Smith, he went directly to a hotel near the train depot, checked in (oblivious to the bemused clerk's raised eyebrows), and soon found a nearby bath house to wash up and shave. Next, he went to a Western clothes outfitter on Garrison Avenue and purchased two cotton Drover shirts (one tan, one brown), a light gray felt 'Boss of the Plains' Stetson hat, a pair of Levi's XX blue denim waist overalls with suspenders, a red bandana, and a pair of dark leather cowboy boots. Admiring himself in the store's full-length mirror after changing, Brimley felt he was transformed from a greenhorn city dude into a real Man of the West! The fact that he had never fired a gun or rode a horse had not yet entered his thinking.

Fort Smith was famous for its merciless town District Judge, Isaac Charles Parker, who was dubbed "Hanging Judge Parker." He had every apprehended outlaw dragged before his bench, and then dispensed swift, heavy jail sentences, or even the death penalty by public hanging for the worst – often repeat – offenders. Walter Brimley saw his first real hanging the following day, August 29, having been tipped off to the spectacle right after breakfast by the hotel clerk, a skinny, red-haired man named Rufus. "You'll get to see 'em dance for the Devil, 'cause the Judge never has their legs hog-tied," Rufus explained. "It's really something to see, young fella. You ought to go."

The hanging itself was a shocking and sickening display for Walter to witness. A crowd of about two-hundred people had formed – men, women, even children. Two downcast-looking men were marched out -- William Elliott Wiley, alias 'Colorado Bill,' and Dr. Henri Stewart, both earlier convicted of murder -- then placed on a six-man platform in an open courtyard area adjacent to the large, multi-storied Army Barracks/Jail/Courthouse building. After the rafter nooses were slipped over the men's heads and partly tightened around their necks, a weary-sounding minister read aloud from the Bible. A sheriff next read the charges and proclaimed the death sentence. At his concluding signal, a large hand lever was pulled by the County executioner, and the two hapless criminals dropped through the floor. Their faces first turned red, then bluish-purple, as they slowly strangled to death, making hideous gurgling sounds in their throats. In their final throes, Brimley saw what Rufus was referring to when the hanged pair 'danced' until they departed this life. Frontier justice had been served. But what would the folks back in Philadelphia think about this grisly spectacle? Walter wondered. It wasn't anything like the dime novels at all. Yet the crowd seemed unemotional, and slowly dispersed, once the gruesome act was over.

But Texas, not Arkansas, was what Walter really wanted to see, so he left by train the next day and headed south and west to Denison, the nearest Texas town of any consequence. Population: 3,842.

Anxious to see some local Texas 'color,' and also being thirsty on this hot, humid, late August afternoon, Brimley saw he had a choice of at least six saloons on Main

Street. He picked one called the Cattle Pen and entered its cool, darkened interior. He was still clutching his cardboard suitcase.

Walter walked with feigned confidence up to the long bar -- remembering how it was done in the dime novels he so admired -- put his right boot on the brass foot rail (narrowly missing a spittoon), and said, "Bartender, I'll have a beer." He gazed around the room at the other dozen or so patrons who were either further down the rail or seated at tables of four, drinking and playing cards.

"Ain't got no beer left, sonny. Just rye whiskey," the grizzled barkeep replied, peering curiously at the newcomer.

Not knowing what else to say, Walter ordered a whiskey. When it arrived and he sipped it out of a less-than-clean glass, he almost gagged. The drink was fiery but foul, tasting unlike any liquor he had ever tasted. When he started coughing, two rough-looking men at the rail slid over, so that there was now one on each side of Brimley. They were filthy, with blood-shot eyes, and stank like an overflowing latrine.

"Where you from, stranger? You look new to these parts," the first man asked. He looked about ten years older than Walter, his face scoured from sun and wind and dirt. He coolly noted Walter's smooth, clean city hands and even fingernails.

When Brimley cordially replied to the query, the other man angrily said, "See...I told you he was a Goddamn Yankee, Chet! And I bet he's a nigger lover too. How about it, boy? You a nigger lover? Lots of good Southern men died on account of those black bastards."

"Look, mister...I don't want any trouble," Walter carefully replied. "And if this has something to do about the Civil War, keep in mind that I was only six years old when Ft. Sumter was shelled," he further explained, beginning to get very nervous and uncomfortable.

The first man, Chet, then replied, "Well...that being the case, I don't think you'd object to buying us both another drink and toasting the honored Stars and Bars right here," the drunk offered, indicating the tattered Confederate flag on the wall above the bar's backdrop mirror. "You know...to show your respect for all our fallen Rebels."

Walter awkwardly declined, saying, "Sorry, friend...but I don't know either one of you well enough to be buying any drinks. Maybe another time," he added, moving away from the stench of booze and the fetid breath of the pair. He went towards the saloon exit, holding his cardboard suitcase.

"Why you son-of-a-bitch! Don't walk away from me when we're talking to you!" the second man -- who was named Dunk -- crudely side-stepped and blocked Walter's escape path. Then he threw the remains of his clutched whiskey glass in Brimley's startled face. "There...now you can go. You've been baptized, Texas-style! And don't come back!" he roared, then laughed along with Chet at the newcomer's cruel shaming.

Walter wiped his face with his shirt sleeve once outside in the harsh sunlight. He felt humiliated and angry and embarrassed, but didn't know exactly how to react. He decided to check into the nearest hotel, wash his face, and have some lunch while he did some serious thinking.

Later that afternoon, Brimley felt that he couldn't hide and be seen as a coward, so he visited three other saloons to try his luck to be accepted as a Westerner. But at the Shady Lady, the No Chance, and the Black Bull, he met with similar rude distain: first, he suffered a bruised jaw from a drunk's punch who claimed Walter stepped on his foot; next, a pre-arranged tripping when a cowboy playing cards stuck out his leg as Walter was trying to leave; and finally, the remains of a mug of beer deliberately spilled on his new shirt as an 'accident.'

The former haberdasher from Philadelphia was ready at this point to leave Denison forever. In somewhat of a daze, he slowly walked through more of the town. But when he peered inside the Last Call saloon at the far end of Main Street, and noticed it was empty except for the barkeep, he decided to take one last risk and step inside.

"Howdy, pardner! Come on in. My thirsty regulars won't be along until later tonight, so it's nice and quiet now. You must be the dude everyone in town is talking about, seeing as you're wearing those new duds. I heard you ran into Chet Carver and Dunk Webb. Webb's real first name is Duncan, but he hates being called that. They're two worthless skunks, if you want to know my opinion. The dirty secret about that pair is that they hide behind Confederate patriotism even though they were both deserters in the Rebel Army. Say, how about a beer, on the house? Tell me how you wound up in Denison, of all places, if you feel like talking. By the way, my name's Clem...and you are...?" the friendly bartender inquired.

Walter shared his basics. In return he learned that Clem Harper was fifty-five, a widower and father of four, and a veteran of Shiloh and Pea Ridge. He took a ball in his right knee, which still caused him a slight limp. He was originally from Alabama. He moved to Texas three years ago, looking for a fresh start, like most folks.

"Well, Walter, I can give you a crash course in bar room habits and etiquette, such as they are here in the Lone Star state. First of all, never sip your drink. It is considered unmanly. You need to knock it back down in one gulp. Next, always offer to buy the person next to you at the rail a drink. It's being friendly and polite. Third, never refuse a drink, even if you don't want one. That's considered very rude," Clem advised.

When Brimley asked why the whiskey tasted awful, Harper had to laugh. "It's because most saloons cut their liquor with turpentine, ammonia, chewing tobacco, burnt sugar, or black pepper. If you notice a tin funnel behind the counter, you can guarantee the bartender is thinning his bottles. Of course, further west of Texas, they even soak their 100-proof rotgut in barrels with rattlesnake heads, cayenne pepper, hot chilies, even gunpowder...you name it. Anything to give the drinker a burning throat and belly bite. Whiskey out here is also called snake piss, coffin varnish, red-eye, ol' tanglefoot, or tarantula juice. Now you know why!" Clem chuckled.

Harper continued. "Saloons won't serve Indians or Chinamen. Negroes aren't particularly welcome, unless they are working a cattle drive with a crew of white cowboys. Mexicans are mostly tolerated, except by those who are still bitter about the Alamo. Anyone new in a saloon is asked their first name only, and you won't ever learn their last names or life history unless they offer it. There are many types of saloons too: although every one serves alcohol, some are mostly set up for billiards, or as a dancehall/restaurant, or as a gambling den for games like Faro, Stud poker, Three-Card-Monte, or Chuck-A-Luck."

Thinking back to his reading of dime novels, Walter asked about women in bar rooms.

"The ladies there are almost never whores. Those 'soiled doves' have their own particular section in every town. The women in saloons are paid to keep company with the spenders by asking for drinks while they provide conversation and attention, or sing songs, or encourage gambling. But they drink only cold tea in their special shot glasses -- although their clients are overcharged for whiskey. In dance halls, the women charge per dance, with the house keeping half the cash at the end of the night," Clem explained.

"The bottom line out here, Walter, is: shoot first, and ask questions later. You need to buy a pistol and holster and learn how to use it right. You also need to learn to ride a horse. And you need to always fight back. That is the only law out West. Sure, some towns have sheriffs, but they can be away when you need them most, or out drunk. So if you don't heed my advice, young man, you're going to wind up deader than ol' Abe Lincoln. You're going to encounter every manner of saddle tramp, drifter, outlaw, ex-soldier, drunk, cowboy, and mental defective. You need to decide right now if you want to stay, or if you want to go back home to Philadelphia…while you're still alive." Clem Harper gave Brimley a serious stare.

Walter said he would stay. "My Pa was a drunkard who beat me regular when I was a boy, and I have lots of repressed anger," Brimley confessed. "He never taught me any of the manly arts, particularly in self-defense. So I want to learn everything I need."

"Good, Walter. I like your grit. Now, I have a friend in Waco who can help you out. His name is Ben Steed. Just tell him Clem Harper sent you. He's a bona-fide Texas Ranger. Don't know if he's retired yet. Haven't seen him for several years. The last I heard, he helped track down and kill Sam Bass after that outlaw and his gang robbed the Round Rock Bank near Austin. I believe that was on July 21 or thereabouts, last year. Bass was only twenty-seven years old when he met his Maker, but he was a murderous thug, and the world is better off without his sort," Harper remarked.

The two men warmly shook hands, as Walter gratefully thanked the first man out West who was sincerely friendly to him. Brimley then checked out of his hotel the next day and took the train, via Dallas, south and west to Waco.

Walter had no difficulty finding Ben Steed. He had retired as a Ranger, however, and was now living safe and comfortably with his wife, Anabelle, on a modest ranch spread just outside of town. Brimley walked the four miles from the train depot to the homestead. Steed was sixty-years old, tall and trim, with black hair streaked with gray and a thick salt & pepper moustache. He had dark, observant eyes. Ben exuded a no-nonsense aura of command and control. The couple had twin daughters who had both recently married and moved with their husbands to Oregon.

"Glad to hear that old Clem is still doing well, Walter," Steed remarked. "I need to visit him one day soon, now that I have the time." The men were enjoying sitting in the shade on Ben's porch. Anabelle had served them glasses of cold lemonade. The weather was even hotter here than it was in Denison, and still humid. But there was a nice breeze coming off the Brazos River. Waco itself, in the distance of heat haze, was twice the size of Denison, Walter had earlier noted when he arrived at the train depot.

"I was one of three brothers, and we all became lawmen," Ben began. "My older brother, Hank, was a deputy who was killed at the Long Branch Saloon last year in Dodge City. Shot in the back by a coward who himself was later caught and hung. When I went north for the funeral and burial, I met Wyatt Earp and two of his brothers. Wyatt was tall and dignified, with blond hair and a long, tawny mustache. He used a pistol with an extra-long barrel, I remember. He shook my hand and gave me his condolences. Nice fella, highly respected. Piercing blue eyes. Moved with his brothers to Tombstone by now, I heard. My younger brother, Ted, is sheriff down in San Marcos, a ways south of Austin. His town badly needs a new deputy. The last one up and quit. It a lawless town of 1200, just getting started – or trying to. Lots of killing going on down there." Ben looked off silently to the far horizon for a few moments, the sound of the cicadas in the heat shrill and insistent.

Steed continued. "I'm going to make a bargain with you, Walter. I'll teach you how to ride and how to fight and how to shoot. We will devote eight months together to accomplish this task. You will room and board here with me for free. You'll need to buy your own gun and holster and horse and saddle, of course. But in return for my training, you must promise me to go down to San Marcos and help out Ted by becoming his deputy for a minimum commitment of one year. That's our deal, Mr. Brimley. No negotiations. Can we shake on it?"

Walter realized his good luck in these unique circumstances. To be trained by a real Texas Ranger! Maybe his dime novel fantasies would turn out all right after all.

"Yes, sir, Mr. Steed. When can we get started?"

"You can call me Ben now, Walter. We are going to be friends," Steed smiled. "Can I call you Walt? I'll let Anabelle know about our new arrangement, then we'll go into town and get you your necessaries. Let's put your suitcase in the guest room, then I'll hitch up the buckboard."

The four-mile ride to Waco took under an hour. They went first to a gunsmith shop.

"I suggest the Colt .45, Walt. The Remington 1875 is a reliable weapon, but the barrel is a might long for quick draws. Plus, the Colt is easy to load and dissemble for cleaning. Cartridges and parts are widely available too. As for a holster, you need to pick one that sets low on your hips. I notice that you are a right-hander like me. Good. It will make training simpler. And I'll show you how to wax the inside of your holster back at the house. You want your pull to be fast and smooth. Every second counts when you have a showdown, I'm sure you can imagine, when life or death are on the line."

Next, the men went to a livery to trade for a horse. Walt ultimately selected a good mount and saddle with Ben's help. It was a spirited tan and white Paint mare, four years old, whom Walt named Lucky. They harnessed the horse to the back of the buckboard and returned to Steed's homestead.

Over the next eight months, Brimley gradually learned everything he needed to know -- beginning with riding, then progressing to fighting (bare-knuckle and buck-knife), and finally to shooting. Lucky proved herself smart, dependable and obedient, with a steady temperament. Ben led Walt on horseback out on various local trails, then showed him how to camp overnight under the stars – first together, then Ben let Walt try it alone. Steed also taught the urban newcomer how to fish, and how to hunt for fresh meat, and how to dress the carcass, and explained which wild plants were edible or poisonous. For fist-fighting practice, Ben demonstrated various techniques in slow-motion, then had Walt try his moves out in actual speed with two, part-time 'hired help' men (Rory and Taggert) at the ranch, who were about Brimley's height and weight (5'6" and 150 pounds – average for the time). "And in a knife fight, remember: there are no rules. Watch out for kicks or dirt thrown in your face. Try to slash the arms or cheeks, or go for an eye. If you have to kill, twist the blade sideways once you plunge it deep in the belly. This will have your opponent weaken by bleeding out faster," Steed gravely advised.

Gun practice with the Colt began with aiming and blasting stationary bottles and tin cans on rocks and fence posts, then graduated to moving targets. "Slide your piece out smoothly and cock it on the pull. Shoot from your hip level. If you draw, you draw to kill, because the other man will too.

Always watch his eyes. You'll know when to kill or when to just maim. Shoot first and ask questions later. Aim dead center. Give a man a fair chance to surrender, but if he won't, then you'll know what to do," Ben explained. Next, Steed showed him how to 'fan' his revolver for multiple shots – "Hold the trigger down and flip the hammer back repeatedly with the side of your other hand. That'll give you six quick shots." He also had Walt practice with a sawed-off scattergun ("Always good for hitting anything without fail at close range.") and with a lever-action rifle. The men went through dozens of various boxes of ammunition every week. Walt practiced hour after hour with fierce seriousness and deadly focus. His confidence was soon solidified. And Ben Steed was impressed with his earnest pupil.

At mealtimes and in the evening, everyone got to know each other better. Anabelle was a lively and interesting conversationalist and a wonderful cook. Meanwhile, Walter added noticeable muscle to his trim frame due to all of his new activities and exertions. His face and hands were burnished by the outdoor elements. Fall, winter, and spring came and went. Christmas and the New Year – 1880 -- had been happily observed and celebrated. Walt also marked his twenty-fifth birthday on February 15.

By the end of April, Walt was ready to leave Ben Steed for San Marcos and begin his new partnership with Sheriff Ted Steed.

As Brimley said his goodbyes, Ben offered him some parting advice.

"The first time you have to kill a man, Walt, it won't be a pleasant experience. You will probably feel remorse and maybe regret, even if the outlaw totally deserved your lethal punishment. But always remember my favorite Bible verse. It is from Genesis 19:24, in the Old Testament. It goes like this (Ben spoke from memory):

'Then the Lord rained upon Sodom and Gomorrah brimstone and fire from the Lord out of heaven.'

So you see, Walt, sometimes we must do God's work here on Earth. We are entrusted to do so, backed by the laws of civilized men, to bring justice and retribution to the wicked people that still sour our frontier. That being said, I want to give you a gift, my friend, as a reminder of our times together and as re-assurance of your new authority once you are sworn in as a legal deputy." He handed Brimley a compact leather-bound Bible. "Go now with God, Walt, and bring fire and brimstone down upon any sinner, whenever and wherever you need to." Ben solemnly shook Walt's hand ("You were like the son I never had, Walt, these last eight months..."), then

Anabelle hugged him. She also gave him a generous poke filled with food (he could smell the ham and the fresh corn dodgers through the sacking) for his journey on Lucky to San Marcos. It would be about a five-day ride of some 135 miles, passing for a stop through Austin, the Lone Star capitol. "Write us from time to time if you can," Anabelle urged, as Walt waved his light gray Stetson adios and rode off south under the bright, mid-morning sky.

Brimley hoped to finally see some real Indians somewhere along his journey, but didn't. He did note, however, that more Mexicans were working about in the tiny hamlets and settlements that he passed through on Lucky. He recalled a few Spanish phrases from his dime novel readings, and called them out where appropriate, such as 'Buenos Dias,' 'amigo,'or 'Buenos Noches.' Such words were always returned with a friendly wave and a toothy smile. Walt had never even seen a single Mexican when he lived in Philadelphia. He made camp each night, tired but contented, and cooked his meal using mesquite wood, often while listening to coyotes yipping somewhere in the distance. He had since bought a Winchester rifle and a large Buck knife with a leather sheath to compliment his Colt. He gazed at the vast, clear field of stars overhead, and figured that his dime novel fantasies were at last coming true. He thought, too, again about what Ben had said regarding Genesis 19:24. He got out his Bible and read it for himself. I can be God's instrument of justice, he vowed -- an avenger against any and all evil! Turning in, he always arranged his saddle rope in a circle around his bedroll on the ground as he had been taught, to keep away the snakes. In the morning, he remembered to carefully shake out his boots, because scorpions and other such critters liked to burrow in them overnight for warmth. Such was Walt's routine, until he arrived in Austin, where he treated himself to a nice hotel bed, a hot bath, and a shave. And that's when he decided to grow a good, manly moustache like Ben's.

When Brimley arrived in San Marcos, however, he was stunned to learn that Sheriff Ted Steed lay dying in the town doctor's house, having been bush-wacked earlier that very day while on routine patrol.

Walt went directly there, and was allowed to quickly tell Ted -- who was bleeding out from three bullet wounds -- who he was, and why he was there as the new deputy, and about Ted's brother, Ben.

Steed grabbed Walt's arm and pulled him close and whispered, "You've got to be sheriff now, Walt...there's no one else. Take my badge. And bury me back in Waco, on Ben's spread..." Ted then took a final, sighing breath and died. He was fifty-two years old.

Doc Leighton explained that San Marcos didn't have a telegraph office yet, but that he would transfer the body by horse and buggy to Austin tomorrow afternoon and inform Ben Steed by wire from there, after loading Ted's casket on the train to Waco.

The town gathered for a brief but touching funeral service -- with several fitting tributes -- the next morning, then Walt Brimley was sworn in legally as the new lawman by the local Justice of the Peace, Stephen J. Bishop. "The Territorial U.S. Marshal usually swings through here every eight weeks or so, and he'll probably check up on you, and give you any pertinent information regarding your new position," Stephen explained. As to exactly who killed Ted Steed, there were unfortunately no clues and no witnesses. "Not unusual out here," Bishop remarked. "It's a rough world. Just watch out for yourself at all times, Sheriff."

Walt set up shop in Ted's former office, a tiny room with an adjoining two-man jail cell. Lucky was fed and comfortably stabled across the street. All was quiet in San Marcos for about two weeks, but suddenly there was a reported disturbance at one of the four saloons on Austin Street, called the Watering Hole. Gunshots were heard.

Sheriff Brimley walked in with his Colt drawn, and saw two ragged muleskinners attempting to rob the panicked, unarmed, elderly bartender of his cash box.

"Drop your guns, boys...slowly," Walt ordered, His mind was awash in adrenaline, but he steadied his nerves by trying to remember everything that Ben had taught him, especially,' Watch the eyes,' and "Shoot for dead center.'

"So you're the law in this piss-ant town? Why, you're nothing but a kid," one of the men scoffed. "Go away before you get hurt. We're taking the money here and leaving."

"Can't let you do that. I'm asking you and your companion one more time to drop those hog legs and come with me," Brimley commanded. "Or there's going to be some killing, here and now." Walt was suddenly flushed with clear-minded courage and determination. So he added, "Ever read the Bible, mister? Maybe you know Genesis 19:24. It says: 'Then the Lord rained upon Sodom and Gomorrah brimstone and fire from the Lord out of heaven.' Well, I'm ready to do God's will and bring brimstone down upon you both if you don't do as I ask right now," Walt directed, his Colt in position.

The filthy pair darted side glances at each other, then the heavier of the two barked, "The hell, you say! We's two agin one! You ain't got the sand!"

The novice sheriff somehow knew what was coming, as he saw the muleskinners' eyes and their pistols turn towards him and cock, ready to shoot. This was it.

As he had practiced many times, Walt held down the trigger on his pistol and fanned the hammer with the butt of his left hand, blasting off one shot into each man, then another in each, for a total of four fanned shots. The saloon filled with the sight and acrid smell of gun smoke. The barkeep was startled but safe now, as the other three saloon patrons crouching in a far corner rose to their feet. Along with the sheriff, they walked towards the inert bodies of the two would-be thieves. Nobody recognized them, or knew their names. Their blood was leaking and pooling into the thin layer of sawdust covering the bar's wooden floor. Lawman Walt was understandably shaken up by what he instinctually had to do, but he also felt a kind of elation at serving God's justice of right over wrong.

From that fateful day onward, Sheriff Walt Brimley became known as "Bible Brimley," or more simply (and lethally) as "Brimstone." He carried the compact, leather-bound Bible that Ben Steed had gifted him, and he displayed it publicly whenever making a point about doing God's work of good vs. evil. Then he vowed to go after wickedness with a single-minded vengeance. But unlike the actions of a common vigilante, this would all be sanctioned by the law, and was encouraged by the grateful community.

Several days later, the U.S. Marshal, Ross Argent, rode into to San Marcos and introduced himself to Sheriff Brimley. Ross was a large man with cheek whiskers and a worn face reddened by the sun. He read Walt's report about the killing of the two muleskinners, who had since been buried in unmarked graves on the barren prairie outside the town limits.

"You did a good job, Walt. I have to commend you with how smartly you handled your first killing in the line of duty," Argent remarked, putting aside the report and lighting a cheroot. "Some skinners have been known to turn to crime in desperation, now that most of the buffalo herds are fast disappearing." Ross then asked if the sheriff needed a deputy.

"Thanks, Marshal, but I think I'm ready to tackle my duties alone at this point. Of course, if overwhelming circumstances arise, I'll ask for help. I've received messages from New Braunfels, San Antonio, and Austin offering any assistance I might require," Brimley explained. The telegraph had finally been connected to San Marcos, and the train line was expected to be here, too, by year's end.

The lawmen shared supper that evening in the cafe, then Ross left Walt with a stack of wanted posters and script from the State which allowed him to draw his pay and trail expenses from any bank. "We've got to clean out the territory of all its lowlifes, and help make Texas a fit place to live for decent folks, Walt. So use every legal means at your disposal to finally rid our great State of such scum. I'll check back with you from time to time. Good luck, Walt...or should I call you Brimstone now?" the Marshal winked and smiled as the men shook hands.

Brimley didn't smoke or chew, and when he wanted a drink, he chose only beer because he never trusted what unknown might have been laced into the whiskey. Often, when visiting a saloon, he would simply order a cup of black coffee. And if he was hungry and on the move, he would enjoy a quick, cold glass of buttermilk instead, if it was available. Walt was also popular with the ladies, for he was careful in public to display a clean, confident appearance whenever possible – trimming his moustache, bathing and shaving once a week, getting regular haircuts, and brushing his teeth. He often took Sunday dinner in the afternoons -- after church at various households with eligible daughters -- when he was not on the trail tracking down outlaws. The town of San Marcos trusted and admired their young sheriff, and the 1200 inhabitants felt safe from lawlessness for the first time in a long time.

Over the coming months, Walt learned that nine out of ten men would quickly obey any command from a lawman. But that left one out of ten that wouldn't obey the man with a star. Forcing justice on that sort always led to fists, a knife-fight, or a shooting. Brimley always gave the stubborn sort a fair chance and a strict warning before escalating the trouble to the next, sometimes lethal level. During his first year as sheriff, he was forced to kill four men. He also arrested sixteen wanted criminals, and was in seven fist-fights and two knife fights. Folks would murmur by now when Walt Brimley walked into a room, or a saloon, or was seen on the street: "That's Brimstone…" or "Isn't that Bible Brimley?" Most of the lawless would come peacefully when ordered, for Walt had earned a reputation for swift, fearless action – always making note of Genesis 19:24, like an Old Testament prophet. He would kill like an avenging angel and later sleep without guilt, but bad men saw him as a devil out of Hell, and they wanted him dead. Those that tried to put out Sheriff Brimstone's fire, however, wound up six feet under, with their boots off, to a man.

Meanwhile the West continued to change. Billy the Kid was gunned down in New Mexico in 1881. He was only twenty-one years old. And Jesse James was assassinated in St. Joseph, Missouri, the following year.

Over the next few years, Sheriff Brimstone's pronouncements became somewhat legendary. Here were some of them, verbatim, from eyewitness accounts:

"You must be real stupid to want to die today."

"I've dealt with trash like you my entire life. I'm sick and tired of the likes of you and your ilk. Aren't you ashamed of yourself before the Almighty and proper, civilized society? Surrender, pay the penalty, reform your ways...or I'll shoot you down like a rabid stray dog."

"It's time to face a fair trial with a judge and a jury, mister...it's jail or the hangman...or you'll die here -- right here and right now, so help me God. Genesis 19:24."

"Come peaceable, or I'll send you to Hell."

Ten years after he began his lawman career, Walt continued to fight crime in San Marcos, as well as on the trail searching for wanted men, or while helping out other sheriffs and deputies in New Braunfels and San Antonio. At this point, he had gunned down seventeen men and arrested forty-eight. He had been grazed by bullets six times, but luckily nothing serious. He had earned several facial scars from fist-fights and knife-fights, but he was still formidable at age 35. He burst into saloons and outlaw hideouts, brandishing his Bible, which he slammed on the bar or on a table before quoting

Genesis and going into action. "Brimstone is gonna be coming down!" he announced. "Anyone not involved with the law had best leave right now..."

In 1891, while in San Antonio on business, Brimley learned that his comrade, U.S. Marshal Ross Argent, had died at age 62 of natural causes. (Ben Steed had previously died the year before in his sleep at age 70, Annabelle informed Walt in a long, sad letter.) In a deathbed plea to the Texas governor, Ross recommended Walt for his job vacancy. But before he could either accept or decline, Brimley was approached by an imposing Texas Ranger while walking past the mission ruins of the Alamo. The tall, lean Ranger introduced himself as J.R. Jackson.

"You must be Bible Brimley...or Brimstone, if you prefer. I surely recognize you from your picture in the newspapers. You've got quite a reputation, my friend. Plus you are specially blessed by not getting killed yet in our hazardous line of work. It's funny that we should meet, Walt, because I wanted to speak with you, either in person or through a telegram. I wanted to offer you a job as a Texas Ranger," Jackson declared.

The sudden, twin offers took Walt by surprise. The pair went to a nearby restaurant for pie and coffee. They exchanged career stories in a casual manner, as only real lawmen could do. After more than an hour, J.R. announced that he had to go. Brimley told him he would give the Ranger his answer soon, after careful consideration, via telegram to Jackson's office in Dallas. Then the men went their ways.

However, as Walt mounted his faithful horse, Lucky (now fifteen years old but still full of pep), to head back home, he saw two familiar faces enter a saloon down the street. The memory of shame from twelve years ago in Denison came rushing back like a bad toothache. Chet Carver and Dunk Webb!

Brimley dismounted and re-tethered his mare, then removed his gun belt and star badge and secured them in a saddlebag. This was going to be done with fists, he decided. But he kept his Buck knife in its sheath on his waist belt, just in case.

The Rebel louts appeared unchanged, though perhaps they were even dirtier and smellier. They were lined up at the bar, ready to quench their need with some cheap, bottled rotgut. Their backs were to Walt so they didn't notice him come in. The saloon was packed with customers, close to fifty men.

Brimley walked casually up to the motley pair. Several patrons happened to identify Walt as he strode in, and they said to each other, "Hey, isn't that Bible Brimley?" or

"That's Brimstone! Get ready for a show!" Walt slapped both men on the shoulder in a chummy way.

"Well, if it isn't Chet Carver and Duncan Webb! Remember me? I was the city dude you boys shamed in the Cattle Pen saloon back in Denison some twelve years ago. Glad I ran into you again, because that will give you both a chance to apologize, and buy me a drink."

"I hate that name," said Dunk. "And I'll be damned if I'm buying you anything." Chet, meanwhile, peered at Walt in confusion, his eyes blood-shot and his brain pickled.

"That's a pity, Duncan, because if you ain't going to be friendly-like, we'll have to settle matters outside. I'm not heeled – he opened his coat to show that he was unarmed – so it will have to be fists or knives. What's your pleasure?"

"Jesus Christ, Dunk, don't you know this man? He's Sheriff Brimstone from San Marcos. He'll bust your head so bad that your mother won't even be able to recognize you. That goes for you too, Chet," the bartender warned. "You better apologize right proper, and fast!"

Chet had enough sense at this point to stagger, then run tail out the door, mount his horse and gallop away. Dunk stood staring at Walt, unmoving. So Brimley grabbed the man's whiskey glass and threw the contents in Dunk's startled face. "There now. You're baptized. We're even. You want any more, you lousy, low-down, yellow-bellied Rebel deserter?" Walt stepped back, his brutal fists at the ready, his eyes like smoldering coals.

"No sir," Dunk meekly mumbled. "It's done." He looked down, ashamed, staring at the collection of old tobacco chew juices that had missed the nearest spittoon and had splattered on the floor.

"Alright then, Duncan. Just remember that I've got my eye out for you and Chet. Should you get into any mischief anywhere in Texas, I'll be there. Genesis 19:24. You can count on wrath like you've never even imagined. Good day." With that promise, the sheriff turned and left the bar. The saloon immediately buzzed with comments relating to what they had just witnessed, once Brimstone was out the door.

Walt ultimately decided to take the Texas Ranger position, rather than that of U.S. Marshal. After meeting with J.R. Jackson in Dallas, he next informed the mayor of San Marcos that he was resigning as town sheriff.

Over the next decade, Walt Brimley chased down outlaws across West Texas, from Laredo to El Paso to Lubbock and then Amarillo. He adapted to the heat and dust, the desolation between towns, and to living on the three Texas food staples: beans, beef, and biscuits. His growing reputation was such that he was personally invited by Theodore Roosevelt to join his Rough Riders to fight in the Spanish-American War in 1898, but Walt declined.

In 1901, Ranger Brimstone found himself back in Waco on business, serving an arrest warrant. Stopping by to visit his old friend Anabelle Steed, he was later introduced to the local school teacher, Lola Revere, an attractive brunette with blue-green eyes who was twenty-eight years old and ready for marriage and children. Brimley surprised himself by falling in love, so after courting for six months between his lengthy, state-wide Ranger duties, the happy couple got married on May 12, 1902. Walt was forty-seven, and still in fine health.

Anabelle attended the wedding, but soon fell ill shortly afterward and died. She was seventy-nine. The new couple were stunned when they learned that she bequeathed her entire homestead to Walt and Lola in her will, explaining that Ben would have wanted it this way. So Mr. & Mrs. Brimley now had their first home in Waco.

Walt worked for three more years until 1905, when he turned fifty. Coincidentally, Walt's loyal horse, Lucky, also died that year at age twenty-nine. She was deeply mourned by her master. Brimley saw it as a sign of sorts that his lawman days were indeed meant to be over. He had been a lawman for twenty-five years, and he figured he had earned a rest, and that his place was now at home with his wife. Over time, they had two sons and a daughter. During his career, the former haberdasher from Philadelphia had killed twenty-two outlaws, and arrested seventy-four men, in the line of duty. He had only been seriously wounded once, in the left shoulder, while taking on two tough desperados simultaneously. The Texas Rangers gave Walt a retirement plaque and banquet in Dallas, and even Governor Lanham sent him an official proclamation of thanks, praising Walt for his devoted service to the People of Texas.

In 1912, Walt discussed with Lola the possibility of moving from the Lone Star state to the exciting, golden promise of Southern California. He carefully researched the fast-growing fruit industry there, and finally focused on buying a mid-sized orange grove. Later that year, the Brimley family made the move to Riverside, and purchased a fifty-acre spread with mature Valencia trees and a farmhouse, which had recently appeared on the market after its former owner retired and sold out.

The ex-lawman took to his orchards with determination and vigor, enjoying its new challenges. He carefully hired his Mexican work crew and oversaw all aspects of his investment. Over the years, he kept an eye out for any affordable lands for expanding his holdings, and he also dabbled in the nearby lucrative Los Angeles-area real estate market. Lola and their children – Joe, Paul, and Ava -- likewise loved the healthful, moderate Southern California climate, and the proximity to the Pacific Ocean for relaxing day-trips. Walt's favorite place to visit was the enormous, red and white deluxe Hotel Del Coronado, on Coronado Island off San Diego. The family always had lunch there (with Walt usually trying new vegetables and fruits like artichokes, avocados, and Chinese gooseberries – things he never even knew existed when growing up in Philadelphia), then they all went swimming off the beautiful, broad stretch of sand beach behind the hotel.

The horrors of World War One and the deadly, global 1919 Spanish Influenza epidemic fortunately bypassed the Brimley family with minimal disruption. The California orange business was booming, the fresh fruit demand from the Eastern U.S. and elsewhere seemingly insatiable.

But now, the Old West that Walt had lived through was virtually gone. Except on farms, horses were not really needed anymore. One might see a few weary dray horses still pulling delivery wagons in the cities, but that sight was becoming rarer and rarer. Motorcars and electric trolleys were filling the streets instead. Aeroplanes were now flying overhead in the clear blue skies. Tall brick and steel buildings were regularly going up. And everyone either had (or soon intended to buy) a radio, for entertainment and information.

In late June of 1926, when Walt Brimley was seventy-one, he decided to visit some friends and do some necessary banking business in Los Angeles. While there, he was also curious about the new motion picture industry expanding in Hollywood, so he decided to pay a visit to a real movie studio. Walt had previously seen several silent films with his family, starring famous Western actor William S. Hart, so maybe he would be allowed on an actual movie set to observe the process if he identified himself as a former Texas Ranger.

Hart had basically retired from films the year earlier, after having made a feature called "Tumbleweeds." The most popular Hollywood cowboy star was now Tom Mix. Brimley learned that Mix was currently working on a new Western called "No Man's Gold" at Fox Studios, owned by the Fox Film Corporation. Charlie Chaplin's silent film "The Gold Rush" had been spectacularly popular the previous June, so Fox thought that having the word 'Gold' in their title might bring them extra recognition and hence success at the box office.

When Walt introduced himself as a former Texas Ranger eager to visit a Western film set, the guard at the studio gate called in his request, and it was approved. Brimley was given directions to Studio 8. When he walked in from the bright afternoon sunlight, it took a moment for his eyes to adjust to the darkened interior. The room was huge, with a thirty-foot high ceiling. In a section of a far corner, Walt saw a flood-lit, Old West-style painted backdrop, with artificial tree and cactus props, and lots of electric wiring on the floor. The minor actors were being 'blocked' for various camera angles, while make-up was being applied to their faces. The director, Lewis Seiler (who had replaced the original director, Tom Buckingham), stopped and greeted Brimley, exclaiming, "I know you...you're Ranger Brimstone! I read about your exploits back in Texas in the newspapers, what was it...maybe twenty or thirty years ago? Well welcome, pardner!" They shook hands. "Pull up a chair, and watch us go to work."

The movie's main stars, Tom Mix and his blond co-star, Eva Novak, strode onto the set a few minutes later. This would be their tenth silent picture together. The director introduced them to their visitor, who had also seen several Tim Mix movies before. But it was a bit disconcerting for Walt to see a Western cowboy hero like Tom Mix wearing lipstick and eye shadow! Mix was forty-five years old, and make-up was also applied to hide some of his facial wrinkles.

The filming of the picture's next scene was fascinating to the newcomer. Walt noted that setting up the scene took much longer than the actual filming action. The actors had a lot of waiting between shots, so they killed time by talking among themselves, or skimming the Los Angeles Times, or smoking, or closing their eyes and taking a nap. Brimley also noted that facial close-ups had to be shot again and again until the director was satisfied with the lighting and the actors' expressions. The whole experience looked less than fun and not very glamorous. The one-hour silent movie, when completed, was scheduled to premiere in theaters at the end of August, Seiler announced.

That was when a tall, distinguished stranger -- who had been sitting in the shadows, away from the action -- got up and walked towards Walt. The man was a bit older than Brimley, but his gait was proud. He wore a finely-cut, pearl-gray, lightweight wool men's suit over a spotless white shirt. He had a neatly combed full head of white hair and an impressive white moustache. His blue eyes were clear and steady.

"I hear that you're Ranger Brimstone -- formerly Sheriff Brimstone -- out of Texas. I read about you. Tell me, are all those stories about your exploits true?" the stranger asked in a cordial way, with just the hint of a smile.

"Well, sir, there's a common saying not to believe everything you read in the papers," Walt Brimley replied with bemusement.

"Ain't that the truth," the stranger agreed. "We both know that...And there aren't many of us old-timers left now to tell folks the story of what really happened."

"By the way, friend," the stranger extended his right hand, "I'm Wyatt Earp..."

THE END

by Jack Karolewski

January 25, 2020

THE TOWN YONDER

Adam Taylor, age 64, had waited a long time to buy a new car. His old brown Ford Explorer had lasted seventeen years, so after almost 200,000 miles, it was time to upgrade. Adam had his sights on a new burgundy Kia Optima. He and his wife, Sara, had saved up, so he was able to write a check for just over $23,000. They were looking forward to saving money on the new, better gas mileage of the Kia.

He had the new car for just over six months when the accident occurred. He had been driving home to his house in Santa Rosa, CA from his community college job, where he taught history. It was a drizzly Friday afternoon in February. Suddenly, a huge semi-truck blew a front tire, lost control, and careened into the Kia. Adam had never been in so serious an accident before. His airbags deployed but he was still crushed in his car. He was barely conscious and covered with shattered glass when the paramedics arrived and used the "Jaws of Life" to cut into his crumpled vehicle and extract him. He was rushed by ambulance to the hospital emergency room. Using his wallet with its identifications, the nurses contacted his wife. The police also came to fill out the accident report. The truck driver had been instantly killed when his semi flipped over after striking Adam and had burst into flames.

Adam had suffered massive internal injuries and multiple broken bones. As he lay on the operating table drifting off under the anesthesia, he thought of his wife, his son (Phil), and his daughter (Terri), and of his life. He felt disbelief and disorientation, and grew weaker and weaker. Then he fell into inky darkness...

Adam soon heard some birds singing, and he next realized that he was lying in a comfortable bed. The sun was up, and golden sunlight was peeping in through the edges of closed window blinds. He gradually opened his eyes and looked around a room which appeared to be a bedroom.

He looked down at his arms, and saw that he was wearing blue and white plaid summer pajamas. He also noticed that his wedding ring was oddly gone from his left hand. He slowly swung around to the side of the bed and got up. He instinctively reached for his eyeglasses on the bed stand, but they were not there. Hmmm. There were, however, brown leather slippers on the floor and he thought it a bit strange when they fit. He left the bedroom and turned right, where he noticed a simple bathroom with tub, shower and toilet. He went in. Above the sink was a mirror. When Adam saw his reflection, he gasped. The face he saw was him, but it was him probably forty years ago! His hair was thick and brown again, yet cut short. No sign of wrinkles. No saggy skin on his jawline, or bags under his brown eyes. No sign of his greying moustache. I must be dreaming, Adam thought. He took off his pajama top and saw that his once firm and muscular torso was back. He squeezed his eyes tight, rubbed them, and opened them again. His image was unchanged. He ran some cold water in the sink and splashed it on his face and dried off with a towel. He took a long, needed pee in the toilet and flushed it.

Just then, he heard a soft thump from somewhere in another part of the house. "Hello, anyone there?" he called out. No answer. He put his pajama top back on, then left the bathroom and walked past a dining room (noticing a kitchen on his left) and a living room. A wall clock noted it was 6:55. He found the front door area, opened the screen door and stepped outside. Adam looked left and right. He was in a town of some sort, probably somewhere in the Midwest. He looked down and saw a folded newspaper at his feet. Maybe this caused the thump sound when it landed, he surmised.

He went back inside with the newspaper and opened it up. The banner proclaimed: The Journal, New Ulm, Minnesota. But Adam was stunned when he saw the date: Monday, June 15, 1959! Adam was born on May 12, 1951, so he would be only age eight, but he looked to be in his mid-20's when he had gazed at himself in the mirror.

This can't be right, he panicked. This is either a dream or a bad joke. He went outside on the porch again. He heard a church bell in the distance toll the 7 a.m. hour. The blue sky was sunny with a few white fluffy clouds, and the air felt like it was warming up quickly. He noted tidy Victorian-style houses, carefully painted a variety of colors. Some had white picket fences, others metal fences painted black. Some of the green lawns had sprinklers running already. Then he recognized the automobiles. It was like being in a car museum, seeing the old 1950's Buicks, Oldsmobiles, Dodges, Chevrolets, and Fords. I know, Adam thought. This is some sort of movie or TV set that they saved from "Father Knows Best" or "Leave It to Beaver." But everything seemed so real and genuine, he mused, and that was unsettling to say the least.

Adam went back indoors and explored the kitchen. He found an opened glass quart bottle of milk in the refrigerator along with eggs, iceberg lettuce, and other perishables. In wooden cabinets, he found a box of Post Toasties and noticed a store of canned and packaged foods. In another cabinet, he saw plates, bowls, glasses, cups and saucers. Near the sink, he found the pots and pans. In a drawer, he found the silverware, a can opener, some carving knives, and a bottle opener. He was suddenly hungry, so he decided to have a bowl of cornflakes before the owner of the house showed up. Adam munched his cereal and pondered.

Almost an hour had passed, but still nobody showed up. Adam decided to explore the house some more. In another unused bedroom, he found a closet with men's shirts, pants and jackets hanging in it (with three pairs of shoes on the floor), and a dresser with men's underwear, socks, and undershirts. When he checked the clothing sizes, he realized they would fit him, so he got dressed in a yellow cotton short-sleeve shirt, white chinos with brown belt and tan Hush Puppies suede loafers with white socks. He then went to bathroom again to shave (Burma-Shave and a safety razor) and brush his teeth (Ipana), hoping the home's owner would not be too upset when he or she returned. Oddly, he saw no female toiletries. Adam continued to check each room, noting the furniture, the books on the bookshelves (Reader's Digest Condensed Books, many literature classics, and American history mostly), the art hanging on the walls (Western landscapes), the other furnishings and knick-nacks on the end tables under the lamps. There was no computer, no wi-fi router, no flat-screen TV, no microwave oven, no Smartphone – just a heavy black, Bakelite dial telephone, a 21" Philco wooden console TV (no remote control), a phonograph record player with 33 1/3 rpm disks of Frank Sinatra, Connie Francis, and Elvis Presley nearby, and a dial-tuned portable radio. Adam also found a stack of Life and Look magazines from 1959 and a few from late 1958. One cover featured Alaska as our newest 49th state (Hawaii rumored to be added in August, the article hinted), and another showed a bearded Fidel Castro in Cuba, after his successful revolution there. If this is a movie set, Adam thought, the attention to detail is amazing!

Next, he went out the back porch into the back yard. A woman next door was in her garden, weeding, and she wordlessly smiled and waved, so Adam hesitantly returned a wave. Feeling nervous, he quickly ducked into the garage. The tool bench was well-used and carried an assortment of tools. And the garage also held a nicely waxed 1957 blue 2-door Chevy Bel-Air.

Adam returned to the house and turned on the television. It took several moments for the inside vacuum tubes to warm up. First he saw a commercial for Nestle's Quik — "try it with cold milk in the summer to cool down fast!" — then came an episode of "I Love Lucy." (All broadcasting was still in black & white -- until NBC first showed "Bonanza" in color in 1960, Adam remembered.) He also noticed that there were only three TV channels to choose from! He turned the set off. Next, he tried the radio. It had been tuned to a pop music station coming in from St. Paul, so he enjoyed "Venus" by Frankie Avalon, followed by "Dream Lover" by Bobby Darin. Listening to these two familiar tunes relaxed Adam somewhat, until he heard footsteps coming up the from porch steps. He turned off the radio and quickly went to the front screen door.

"Hi Adam! Looks like another sizzler today. Oh well, better this than Old Man Winter," a man in a light blue uniform chuckled. Adam was startled when the mailman spoke his name. He knew me? How?? Adam, caught off guard, responded with a weak, "Ain't that the truth." The mailman smiled and handed him a small stack of mail. "Must be nice to have the summer off. You teachers have all the luck. See ya!" the mailman said as he turned away and continued down the sidewalk. A dog barked in the distance, and a green Ford rolled down the street. The male driver yelled "Hey Arthur!" to the mailman, who waved back.

Teacher? What was that about? Adam wondered. He checked the names on the various pieces of mail, which were mostly bills. Adam Taylor...Adam Taylor...Adam Taylor. Then he looked at the addresses. All were marked 505 Maple Lane, Sunrise, Minnesota. The newspaper I saw was from New Ulm, so Sunrise must be a smaller town near there without its own newspaper, Adam assumed. But it must have a school if I was referred to as a teacher. Maybe I should go outside and walk around the town and find it, he decided.

He left the house and closed the door behind him but couldn't lock it because he didn't notice any keys lying around while exploring the residence. Once outside, he marveled at the little town. It was attractive and peaceful. He saw several children playing hop-scotch, stickball, or tag. He saw other boys and girls riding their bicycles. One boy even cried out, "Hi, Mr. Taylor!" as he zipped by on his green Schwinn, its colorful plastic streamers jutting out of the handlebar grips. The men were most likely away at work, Adam surmised, for all he saw were women watering the lawn, or hanging laundry, or beating dust out of rugs or airing bedding. He did, however, notice a few older men dozing on their porch swings or reading a newspaper while puffing and chewing on their pipestems.

       Adam passed the town square, a large green park where the war memorials and a band gazebo were located. He also saw on Main Street: Gowen's Drugstore, a First Minnesota bank, three churches (Catholic, Lutheran, Presbyterian) , Snappy's Diner, two taverns, a Dairy Ripple (burgers, sodas, and ice cream), a Sinclair gas station (gas @ 25 cents/gallon), a firehouse, a doctor's office, Bud's Car Repair shop, a small Woolworth's, a SaveMore supermarket, Danny's Barbershop, a classic Carnegie library (established 1910), the police station, the City Hall, and a sign that bragged "Sunrise, Minnesota – population 8776 and growing!" The Prairie Theater was showing the Disney animated movie "Sleeping Beauty" on Friday and Saturday nights – one dollar for adults &

fifty cents for kids. Adam was pleased to find on his stroll that the whole town was generously shaded by stately elm and maple trees. Meanwhile, Arthur the postman was proven right: it really was getting hotter and more humid by the minute.

Near the western outskirts of Sunrise were two athletic fields which indicated that schools were nearby. Sure enough, Adam found a sturdy brick elementary school and a somewhat newer high school near the town's silver water tower, which proclaimed: "Go Sunrise Spartans". In the far distance were vast wheat fields and farms, but no movie trailers or television equipment. This place was not a TV or movie set, Adam realized with growing puzzlement and some unease.

He walked closer towards the elementary school front door. Suddenly, a faint voice called out: "Hey, Mr. Taylor! You work over here, remember?" It was probably the janitor, Adam thought, as he headed towards the man standing in front of the adjacent high school. As he approached, the janitor said, "Well that was a fast summer vacation! You just got out on Friday. Did you forget something in your classroom?"

Adam had to think fast. "You must've read my mind. Can you let me back in for a minute?" The janitor smiled and took out a wad of keys. He opened the front door, then walked with Adam to a classroom, and unlocked that door too. "Gonna be another hot one today. I'm gonna take my lunch break now, so just pull both doors shut when you're done and they will lock themselves. See ya later!"

Adam was alone now in what appeared to be an American History classroom. The blinds were closed, but there was still enough light to look around. There were posters on the walls referencing the American Revolution, the Civil War, and World War II. There were neat stacks of a thick textbook entitled "My Country 'Tis of Thee – American History, 1492 to the Present." And the U.S. flag hanging in the corner next a framed picture of President Eisenhower had only 48 stars on it. (The school must be waiting to order the new flags, Adam surmised.) At the teacher's desk was a 1959 calendar, a grade book, and a cup with assorted pens and pencils. Adam was disturbed to see his name written on the grade book cover, in his familiar cursive handwriting. He felt dizzy and disoriented again. I guess then that this really is my class, he realized. The grade book was for U.S. History – Grade 11. That would be juniors in high school, Adam knew. Twenty students were neatly printed in alphabetical order inside the grade book, and twenty identical desks were also arranged in straight rows in the room.

Adam was tired from all the new information taxing his mind since he awoke, and he was getting hungry, so he decided to head back to his "home." On the way, he stopped in the Sinclair gas station to look for a state map.

"Hi Adam," said the middle-aged attendant. "Enjoying your break from the teenagers so far this summer?"

Adam noticed his nametag "Chet."

"Sure am, Chet," Adam replied. "Say, do you have a state map I can look at?"

"Sure thing, Adam...Here's a free one you can keep," Chet said, grabbing a Minnesota map from a nearby stack. "Stay cool!"

When Adam got back to the house he woke up in that morning, he went to the kitchen to make a sandwich. He found sliced bologna, a jar of Miracle Whip, and the lettuce in the refrigerator, and grabbed the Wonder Bread and a bag of potato chips from a cupboard. He poured a glass of milk and proceeded to eat at the dining room table while he scanned the state map.

Adam quickly found New Ulm, then looked in a fifty-mile radius around that city. Due west of New Ulm was Sleepy Eye, Springfield, Sanborn, Lamberton, then the town of Walnut Grove -- made famous by author Laura Ingells Wilder's

"Little House on the Prairie" book series. A few miles further west of Walnut Grove before Tracy was Sunrise. So it does exist, Adam now knew.

He thought about the impossibility of his being in Sunrise on June 15, 1959. He now eliminated the possibility that he was dreaming. He was not on a TV or movie set façade. He was convinced he was not dead, nor in some kind of heaven or afterlife. People knew his name here. He had an address here and had received mail, so probably the house and the blue Chevy were both his. He had a teaching job, and had been on summer vacation for three days. He had somehow previously purchased food and clothing. Maybe he was in some kind of bizarre "alternate universe" time/space warp? Was a duplicate Adam Taylor still with his family in Santa Clara in 2015? He vaguely remembered being in a serious car accident with a truck, and being wheeled into surgery at the hospital. Where were his wife, Sara, and their grown kids, Phil and Terri?

Adam decided to explore "his" house more thoroughly. He found a thin telephone book under the heavy black dial telephone and looked up his name. There it was: A. Taylor, 505 Maple Lane, Sunrise, 938-8559. Other names he saw at random while flipping through the pages ended in the letters "sen" or "son" – an indication of probable Scandinavian ancestry, which made sense in a state like Minnesota.

Next, he found a wooden bowl on top of the fireplace mantle with a wallet, some house and car keys on a metal key ring, a Bulova wristwatch, and a few loose coins. He opened the wallet and discovered that all the currency was pre-1959. There was a photo of an unknown but attractive young blond woman in the top clear plastic sleeve. The wallet also contained his Social Security card (with the actual numbers he remembered) and a Minnesota driver's license. He saw that he was born on August 22, 1932 -- whereas he knew in 2015 that he had been born in 1951 in Mt. Carroll, Illinois! Hence he was 26 years old here now, and would turn 27 in about two months. The coins were likewise all pre-1959. And there were no credit cards in the wallet.

Adam then found a thick photo album on the bottom shelf of a bookcase. When he opened it, there were photos he immediately recognized as those of his parents, assorted relatives, his two sisters, and of his own childhood in Mt. Carroll. Yet next to the photo album were three Sunrise Spartans high school yearbooks, and when Adam leafed through them, he saw his picture several times in all three volumes – both as a staff member and in scenes interacting in student activities! Furthermore, in a drawer in a desk in the living room, Adam found a roll of four cent first-class stamps and a bank account passbook from First Minnesota with a balance from of $1787.35 dated 6/12/59. So I have money here as well as a job and a home, he realized with relief. He wasn't sure if he was renting his house or whether he was paying a monthly mortgage.

By now it was late afternoon, and the heat was on. The house had no air-conditioning, but Adam turned on two box fans to help stay cool. He took a cold shower first, which felt great. He could hear cicadas making their screeching noise outside. Exhausted, Adam laid down on the couch, closed his tired eyes and dozed off.

When he awoke, Adam saw the day's shadows lengthening through the windows. The wall clock said 6:37. He was hungry again, so he went to the kitchen to look for some dinner. The top freezer section of the GE refrigerator was a bachelor's paradise – Swanson's frozen TV dinners and frozen pot pies and frozen pizza and some Eskimo Pies. Adam chose the meat loaf dinner, and heated the oven and put it in. In the bottom of the refrigerator, four cans of Old Style beer were resting, so he used a can opener and drank out of one of the cans while his meal cooked.

He took his food to the living room and found a TV tray and set himself up in an easy chair in front of the Philco. He warmed up the set and watched an episode of "Rawhide," starring a very young Clint Eastwood. He flipped through the other two channels afterwards for a while (more

Westerns), then went outside to sit on the front porch swing. In 2015 at this time of day, he would be checking emails on his laptop, doing a Google search, going on Facebook, or texting messages on his iPhone. But none of that existed in his current era. It was dusk and the town was cooling off slowly. Crickets started chirping and fireflies blinked on and off in the fading light. Parents called out for their children to come back inside, and dogs barked when screen doors slammed. It was a safe and secure feeling being in a small town in the heart of America, despite the continued Cold War with the Soviet Union. Adam knew all the major events in world history from this moment up to the year 2015, but he deliberately put those facts out of his mind for now. Would he be stuck here – in 1959 again – for a "second" lifetime, he wondered? He also recalled seeing no blacks, Asians, or Latinos on his walk through town, so unlike multi-ethnic California in 2015. Sleepy again, Adam went into his bathroom to brush and floss his teeth before climbing into bed, but there was no floss in the medicine chest. (It had not been invented yet, he realized with amusement). He did see a bottle of Aqua Velva after-shave lotion, however, along with a bottle of Bayer aspirin, a box of Band-Aids, and a small bottle of mercurochrome next to the Ipana toothpaste, the BurmaShave, and a metal tube of Brylcreem.

That night, Adam Taylor dreamed of his life back in Santa Rosa. He was explaining in his dream to a dis-believing Sara his newest theory of space and time traveling.

But the following morning, he woke up back in Sunrise, Minnesota. The familiar thump soon sounded on his front porch, indicating that the daily New Ulm Journal had landed. Adam got up to fetch it and took it into the kitchen.

June 16, 1959. George Reeves, who played the Man of Steel on TV's "Adventures of Superman," had been found dead of an apparent self-inflicted gunshot wound. Boy, the kids of America will be stunned at that news, Adam thought, remembering when he first heard the news at around age 8 in Mt. Carroll. Why didn't the bullet just bounce off his head? they will ask, and their parents will weakly try to explain. The weather was going to be similar to yesterday, the newspaper forecasted. High: 88. Possible tornados by Friday.

Adam made scrambled eggs, fried up some bacon, and put two slices of Wonder Bread into the toaster. He craved some Starbucks coffee, but all he found was a bag of ground Maxwell House and a percolator. He wracked his brain trying to remember how his own parents used this classic coffee-brewing device when he was a lad. After three attempts, he finally figured it out.

Just then, the telephone rang. Adam was startled. The clock on the wall said 8:20. He walked to the phone in the living room.

"Well, hello stranger!" It was a woman's voice. But who's? he wondered.

"Still recovering from teaching those pesky Juniors? I haven't heard from you since Friday. Did you forget all about your poor fiancé?"

Fiance? Adam had to think fast. "No, um...I've just been really busy. You know how it is." How lame, he winced.

"Well, I can be over by 9, because we have a lot to do before August 8. Our wedding is less than two months away, Mr. Taylor, so the future Mrs. Taylor really needs your help." Before a shocked Adam could reply, the voice said a cheery "Good-bye" and hung up.

Adam's heart was pounding, and he felt dizzy. But I'm already married, he thought. Yet someone was going to knock on his door soon, so he had to get washed up and dressed and ready.

The doorbell rang at 9 o'clock sharp as Adam just finished combing his hair and brushing his teeth.

"It's me, Pam!" a pleasant voice called out through the screen door. Adam walked over to the front door with a mixture of curiosity and dread.

She was an attractive, petit woman about 5'3" in her early 20's, with sparkling blue eyes and a few cute freckles on her nose. Her nice white teeth were visible in her gleaming smile. She wore a coral-colored sleeveless top with a small brown-beaded necklace and yellow shorts, and she had brown sandals on her feet. Her blond hair was pulled back in a smart ponytail. She smelled freshly showered. Short fingernails with no polish. Tanned, smooth skin. She glowed with health.

"Come here, handsome..." she said as Adam opened the door. Pam rushed in and gave him a huge, mushy kiss (he tasted her...was it Pepsodent?) and a big hug. Adam was speechless. Then he knew where he had seen her before -- she was the girl in the photo in his wallet.

What am I going to do now? Adam panicked. I can't handle all of this. This is going to lead to a nervous breakdown. But then he realized that if he was stuck here in the past and might never get back to 2015, he needed to accept and adapt to all of these new realities. So he simply smiled and played along as if he was doing summer stock.

He let Pam do most of the talking over the next few weeks whenever they got together, trying to piece together both his past and present. They went to Snappy's Diner and the Dairy Ripple on dates in his blue Bel-Air. They saw movies at the Prairie Theater. He met her friendly family, the Conners – her mom, dad, and younger sister. The engaged couple (he now noticed the ring he "gave" her) drove into New Ulm to look at furniture, appliances, and draperies. (They had discussed moving into his house after the wedding.) Pam Conners was 22, and she worked as the assistant librarian at the Carnegie Library. At First Minnesota, Adam discovered that his house was mortgaged, and how much he paid per month on the $9,898, 1000 square foot home. He listened to and talked with "friends and neighbors" and some of "his" students around town, trying to keep their names and all the facts he was learning straight in his over-taxed brain. He went with Pam to St. John the Evangelist Catholic Church every Sunday, where the marriage would later take place. He learned that he had been born in Sunrise, and that he had gone to school here, and that he went away to college in Minneapolis and earned a teaching degree but came back, and that his parents moved to St. Paul four years ago, but had both been killed in a tragic car accident there (even though, in 2015, both were still alive in their late 80's). Slowly, sometimes awkwardly, Adam made sense of his new life in the little town of Sunrise, Minnesota.

It was less a surprise when Adam found himself growing physically attracted to Pam. Her affectionate ways – the hand-holding, the kissing, the close warmth and fresh smell of her -- and her bodily charms were rapidly ramping up his testosterone. While not in love with her yet, Adam was disturbed and felt guilty that he dreamed less and less about his wife Sara and more and more about having sex with Pam. Pam obviously adored him, and that was not bad. Or was it? Adam was torn, confused, alone in his struggles. Of course, sex before marriage was out, Pam insisted, after an hour of heavy petting on Adam's couch one humid night.

The summer went by in its usual lazy manner. Because school was out, Pam worked at the library on a reduced summer schedule. So on her days off, there were barbeques and picnics, swimming and canoeing in nearby lakes, the organizing and sending out of wedding invitations, music concerts at the town's band gazebo, and many moonlight walks. The weather was sunny and hot most days. There were a few violent thunderstorms – one even with hail – but luckily no tornados that summer. The pair talked about everything "normally" -- except about what Adam most wanted to ask and have explained: How did I get here? How long will I be here? How can I tell people that I came from 2015 -- where I was a married 64-year-old family man living in California -- without them thinking I'm completely insane? Can I ever get back?

By now it was August. The wedding on the 8th was coming up fast. Will I be compelled to marry Pam even though I'm still in love with and married to Sara? Adam wondered. The moral ethics here were cloudy and uncertain.

The night of August 7 was sheer agony. Adam felt he had no alternative but to go through with the wedding. Pam was a wonderful person, and he was fortunate that she had chosen him. Perhaps over time, his physical desire would lead to love. It was weird to think that he apparently had the chance to live forty years over, only in a different time and place. Who else could claim such an experience? He knew the upcoming events in U.S. and world history, and could mitigate them somewhat as to their effect on him personally, and he would know which events ultimately needed no fears or worries. He could also undo mistakes he had made in his "first" life. He could have new children with Pam, whom he knew wanted babies. Such thoughts had his mind ablaze as he tossed and turned again and again in bed. Finally, blessedly, he fell into a deep, dreamless sleep...

When Adam awoke, he felt dull pains in various parts of his body, and realized that parts of him were heavily bandaged. There were tubes in his nose and tubes coming out of his arms. He slowly turned his head towards an unfamiliar bed stand and saw his eyeglasses resting there, next to a glass of water and some medicine bottles. A nurse hurried out of the room and brought back a doctor and Sara.

Sara had tears of happiness coursing down her cheeks as she stood beside Adam's bed. The doctor checked Adam's vital signs and appeared relieved. "We thought we lost you there a while back," he announced. "but you'll be fine now." He briskly stepped out of the room.

Sara gently held Adam's hand. "Phil and Terri are in the waiting room, dear. They flew in from Atlanta and Boston last night, but without their families. We were all so worried, Adam, when we heard about the truck accident. Then you went into cardiac arrest after surgery. You were clinically dead for just a moment, but the doctors brought you back to us. Oh Adam, I was so afraid!" she confessed, and her tears resumed.

Adam was in the hospital for ten days, then spent an additional four months in recovery at home. He would have a limp in his left leg where the bone had been badly broken, but apart from that, he healed well. He was unsure whether to tell Sara and his family about his weeks in Sunrise. Maybe someday. Yet he had to tell someone! Maybe he needed to see a psychiatrist. Was it all some sort a hallucination? But it was so real, and I was "away" for all of those weeks, he remembered.

When his physical therapy sessions were completed and he could walk again without a cane, Adam resumed his teaching job at the community college. One day, at the campus library, Adam grabbed a U.S. atlas and quickly flipped to an enlarged map of Minnesota. He found New Ulm and the other small towns on the main route going west. But when he looked between Walnut Grove and Tracy, he was shocked to see that Sunrise was missing! He then checked the atlas town index for Minnesota under the letter "S." But Sunrise was nowhere to be found.

Adam went back to his office, did a fast Google check on his laptop, and then called the Minnesota Tourism Bureau. They were polite but they had never heard of a town called Sunrise. They offered to email him back after checking with the Minnesota Historical Museum archivist, to see if Sunrise had undergone a name change over the years. The reply the following day was negative. There was never a town named Sunrise anywhere in the state, they definitively declared.

Next, Adam searched the name "Pam Conners." He came up with 33 finds in the state. Over the next several days, he called each one. If Pam was still alive and living in Minnesota, she would be around 78 years old (if she had actually existed, Adam reminded himself). In each phone call, he asked if he was speaking to Pam Conners, daughter of Sid & Mary Conners and sister of Debbie Conners, who used to live in a town called Sunrise back in the late 1950's. No luck. Plus, nobody had ever even heard of such a town name.

Adam was running out of options while still keeping his experience a secret from his family. Across the nation, there must be tens of thousands of "Pam Conners" (a rather common name), so looking beyond Minnesota was unfeasible. As a last ditch idea, he contacted the New Ulm Journal, which thankfully was still in business. He asked to put an ad in the newspaper for a full month, inquiring if anyone knew the whereabouts of a Pam Conners from Sunrise, and leaving his email address. Never heard of town called Sunrise, the receptionist remarked, and the editor soon tried to dissuade Adam from "just wasting your money." But Adam was insistent, so he gave the newspaper his credit card number to pay for the ad. The month passed, and nothing was reported.

The date was now June 14, 2015. Summer vacation at the community college had recently started. When Adam went to bed that night, lying next to Sara and listening to her soft and contented breathing, he thought back, back...to Pam, to the house on Maple Lane, to Sunrise. To somewhere...

Suddenly startled, Adam remembered that, on a whim during his search for Sunrise, he compared calendars for the years 1959 and 2015. They were identical.

And tomorrow was June 15th.

Adam Taylor prayed, and waited until dawn...

The End

by Jack Karolewski

4/26/15

TRUSTED

Mark Canfield was a fifth grade teacher in Streamwood, Illinois, a middle class suburb northwest of Chicago. It was his eleventh year in the profession at Meadowview Elementary School, and he had already seen "the good, the bad, and the ugly" in terms of students, colleagues, parents, and administrators. Overall, however, he had retained his optimism and idealism and his love of teaching. He was convinced that he made a difference. Mark was happily married and had two daughters, Suzie and Janie, who were not yet of school age.

Carl Forster was Mark's principal. One day after school, he called Mark into his office. It was a mid-November day, with a chilling wind, gray and drizzly.

"Mark, I've got a problem," he confessed. "The district office is pressuring me to take a boy with serious social and developmental problems. He's transferring in from out-of-state next week. He has been bounced from school to school repeatedly. I thought you would be the man who could help straighten him out."

Mark was getting tired of this pattern. Why do the few men on staff at elementary schools always get the real troublemakers? It wasn't fair to the other students in class, and it wore down the teacher's energies overall. But Mark kept these thoughts to himself.

"Well, Carl, if you think it is for the best…,"Mark replied, avoiding eye contact. He knew the decision had already been made.

"Great, Mark…I knew I could count on you," Carl announced. "I'll bring him to your room on Monday. The boy's name is Kevin Winters. Thanks." The office secretary, Mrs. Hunnicut, poked her head in. "I have a parent on the phone for you on line one, Mr. Forster, if you are finished with Mark, "she said. Mark got up and returned to his classroom to finish grading some remaining science tests. Any transfer in the middle of the school year, he knew, was always bad news…At least Thanksgiving break was coming up soon. Suddenly, Mark felt very tired. It was dark outside and time to gratefully go home to his family.

The Monday before Thanksgiving, Carl brought Kevin to Mark's classroom door, Room 5-A. Kevin was rather small for a fifth grader, with blonde hair and pale skin. Maybe some Scandinavian blood? Interesting that the boy's parents were not there to see him get settled in, Mark thought. Kevin had pale blue eyes, but he looked past you rather than in your eye when asked any questions. The other 28 students stared at the new pupil when Mr. Canfield introduced the new boy. Mark had an empty desk and the necessary textbooks ready for Kevin, positioning him close to the front of the room near the whiteboards.

Nothing unusual happened in class for those three days before the 4-day turkey break. The other students basically avoided Kevin, and there was no bullying or confrontations. Upon returning to school after Thanksgiving, Mark scheduled a 5:00 p.m. conference on Tuesday with Kevin's parents. In preparation, Mark asked Mrs. Hunnicut for Kevin's file. It was heavy and thick, another bad sign. Mark leafed through it with a sense of dread at what he might discover. Yep. It was all there. Suspensions galore. Violent outbursts and tantrums. Caught with bringing knives to school. Threats to other students. Psychological testings. Social worker visits to the home. Poor grades. Excessive absences and tardies. Refusal to eat lunch. Counseling sessions. Incomplete grades. "Social promotion" just to move him up from grade to grade and get him out of the public school system. "Red flag" reports from past teachers and school districts. Kevin was a living disaster, a ticking time bomb. And Mark was the latest recipient.

When Mark met Kevin's mother, Audrey, he was surprised to learn from her that the father was not coming because he had recently packed up and abandoned the family – something not yet noted in Kevin's file. Kevin was an only child, his mother said, and it had been a difficult birth, ultimately a C-section. As he grew up, she had tried everything to turn Kevin's increasingly shocking behaviors around, but to no avail. Mrs. Winters spoke in a soft, pained voice. Her eyes were reddened, as if she cried a lot or didn't get enough sleep or more likely both. Kevin had a bizarre fascination with knives, she confessed, and once she had awoken in the middle of the night, only to find Kevin hovering over her bed with a steak knife from the kitchen in his hand and a strange, vacant expression on his face. She screamed and her husband awoke and beat Kevin mercilessly.

"Are you a religious person, Mr. Canfield?" Mrs. Winters asked. "I actually went to a priest once and asked if Kevin was – God forgive me -- possessed by the Devil." She started crying softly. Mark offered her the box of Kleenex from the table's far corner. "The priest shook his head no, and we held hands and prayed together for a few moments, and he agreed that Kevin had to see a psychiatrist, a doctor, and a school psychologist as soon as possible. Before my husband left us, we took Kevin in for testing. Nobody seemed to have an answer on why Kevin was so strange, so anti-social, so withdrawn. Mr. Canfield, I'm ashamed to admit that I am afraid for my only child. And I am really afraid of my only child. I found some drawings once that he had hidden in his closet. They were filled with demons and knives and squirting blood." She was shaking now and crying again. "I'm begging you to try and help him. Please don't write him off. Give him a chance, a fresh start. He needs a father figure now, Mr. Canfield. Mr. Forster told me that you have two little girls of your own, so you know how important and difficult good parenting is."

Mark listened earnestly to Mrs. Winters for another ten minutes or so, then the parent conference wrapped up. When Mark got home for dinner, he hugged his two smiling daughters, then told his wife, Carol, all about his experience with Kevin's mother. "Honey," he told Carol, "I've been thinking that maybe – just maybe -- I can try and turn this strange kid around." Carol cautioned Mark not to let the attempt ruin his relationship with his other students, and not to let it deplete all his time and energies. He agreed as he hungrily dug into his mashed potatoes and meat loaf with ketchup. He replayed the parent conference in his head a few times before he drifted off to sleep that night.

December went by with no unusual Kevin incidents. The other students still avoided him on the playground, and whispered about him, and refused to sit by him at lunch time, but there was no teasing or bullying. Things began to look to Mark like maybe Kevin could have a productive year for once. Mark gave Kevin some extra jobs around the classroom to encourage him to fit in. Kevin had to promptly catch the afterschool bus home each day, so Mark had few opportunities to talk with him in private or to casually ask him how he was doing at home. Meanwhile, his grades on quizzes and tests were still, unfortunately, quite low. Kevin was pulled from class for half-hour slots throughout each week to meet with the school social worker, or the school nurse, or the district psychologist or other support services specialists. But before long, it was time for the class Christmas party and exchanging grab bag gifts and singing carols before the long holiday break.

A few days after January classes resumed, Kevin was caught by the playground supervisor carrying a large sharp folding knife, which he used to nick off some wood from the large wooden school playground structure. Under the district's "no weapons on campus" policy, Kevin was immediately suspended for five days.

When Kevin returned, his mother Audrey walked him to the doorway of the classroom and made him apologize personally to Mr. Canfield for bringing the knife to school. Mark accepted, and sent Kevin to his seat with a folder of make-up work that Kevin missed during his suspension. After school, Kevin waited until the other students left the room, then shyly muttered to Mark, "Mr. Canfield, I like you and I hope you like me too" before running out to catch the bus.

After that, Kevin followed Mark around on the playground whenever he had supervisor duty, just to talk a little about anything. Mark was impressed by Kevin opening up, and he said as much to the school specialists and to Audrey Winters. Mark even thought he saw Kevin smiling at him once during a math lesson.

Mark was eating a typically hurried lunch at his desk one Friday afternoon when a lunch supervisor rushed in and said that Kevin had cut another boy's arm with a knife on the playground near the monkey bars. Mark rushed outside and saw Kevin running away through the school parking lot, clutching some kind of knife. Mr. Forster was running with a first aid kit to the injured, bleeding boy, while other lunch duty staff keep the curious crowd of kids back. Mark ran and caught up to Kevin about a half-block from campus.

"Give me the knife, Kevin!" Mark yelled. Kevin hesitated, then slowly surrendered what appeared to be some kind of switchblade. "Why did you bring another knife to school, and what made you want to hurt another student?" Mark demanded. Kevin stood silent, his blonde hair tussled by the wind.

The School Superintendent and even Mr. Forster thought that moving Kevin to yet another building with yet another teacher would be the best solution when they met with Mark during Kevin's indefinite suspension. An official police report had to filled out for the assault as per district policy, but fortunately the boy who had been injured by Kevin was not deeply cut (no stitches), and his parents were not inclined to sue or make any demands other than urge the district to immediately get Kevin out of Meadowview School.

But Mark was not convinced that Kevin should go. "I know what he did was horrible and shocking, but I think I am making some good progress with him, and if he can just stay with me a few more months until June, I think maybe I can break through some of his problems and get him to trust another human being, maybe for the first time in his life. He has faced nothing but rejection from others. He deserves another chance. Please. Let's not quit on him again. Didn't we enter this profession to help young people grow past their problems into educated, well-adjusted, and capable adults?" Mark pleaded. The Superintendent and Mr. Forster said they would consider Mark's offer after they discussed the case in detail with the District's legal advice team.

The class in Room 5-A was surprised to see Kevin re-appear at school the first day in April. Mr. Canfield asked his other 28 students to try their very best to make Kevin feel welcomed and part of the group again. Incredibly, they helped out as much as possible, talking with him before class started, helping him with in-class group assignments, and even sitting by him during lunch. But at recess, Kevin was required to play within arm's length of an extra playground supervisor, who was specially hired by the district to monitor him and him alone as a way of appeasing many concerned parents. Audrey Winters came in or called to thank Mark on several occasions during the remaining weeks of the school term. "You are all he talks about at home now," she gushed, "and he says that his nightmares aren't as bad anymore. Plus, he is eating more and he seems less moody."

Before long, the last day of school came. Report cards would be distributed, informal class yearbooks would be autographed, and the farewell class party would be held. But first the final awards assembly had to take place in the multi-purpose room.

Mr. Canfield had invented a special certificate just for this occasion, to be awarded to the student who he had learned the biggest life lesson from during this school year. "I learned how important it is to trust other people," Mark said, "because nobody gets through life without trusting others and being trusted in return." Kevin looked down as he walked to the stage podium for his certificate, and he looked down on his way back to his seat too.

As the school day ended with the bell at 3:00, Mark shook hands 28 times, wishing each of his students a wonderful summer vacation and good luck next year in sixth grade. As was now kind of a routine, Kevin Winters stayed behind until all the other students had left. Now it was just him and Mr. Canfield.

"Well Kevin, you made it...I am sure that your life will turn out better from now on. So keep up the good work in sixth grade! And don't forget your certificate. Now, before you go, how about a little hug good-bye?"

As they hugged for a few seconds, Mark suddenly felt an odd, sharp pain in his stomach. He winced and stepped back in surprise, staring at Kevin's oddly blank face with its pale blue eyes. Then he noticed with horror the knife in Kevin's hand, now bloodied. He looked down with disbelief at the red stain slowly soaking his shirt as Kevin ran out the door...

The End

by Jack Karolewski

12/27/14

FAR SIDE OF THE MOON

[Although our moon spins on its own axis, we on Earth only see its front side. This is because its rotation is synchronized with its simultaneous orbiting around our planet. As a result, we never get to see the moon's dark side from our home. For centuries, humans have wondered about what mysteries could exist on its far side.]

The United States had last visited the moon in December, 1972 during the Apollo 17 mission. Now, forty-nine years later, America was once again drawn by necessity to our nearest neighbor in space. Because the year was 2021, the mission was named Apollo 21. Sensors on earlier unmanned probes had detected frozen water just under the surface of a lunar area named Mare Undarum, "The Sea of Waves." This mare was located in a central, far eastern area near the zone where the brightness of the moon's face met the darkness of the moon's back. Astronauts were needed to ascertain how much water lay hidden underground, for a colony could then be established there to be used as a launching post for a manned Mars mission, tentatively planned for 2030.

The trusty NASA Saturn 5 rocket had long since been retired, so Apollo 21 used the new, powerful Saturn 500. It incorporated a special chemical fuel additive which caused its five massive engines to burn hotter and faster with less fuel. This provided more thrust and yet permitted more payload because the rocket itself was lighter in weight. Also, the new, larger Lunar Module -- nicknamed "The Bus," because it was about the length of a typical school bus, although twice as wide -- would directly jettison from the Saturn 500 booster once in space and be able to land itself on the moon, as well as blast-off from the lunar surface when it was ready to return home. Instead of taking three days to make the 240,000 mile journey to the moon, now it would take only two.

The seasoned NASA crew of four for this important mission were all Ph.Ds in their early thirties: Commander -- John Riley; Pilot/Navigator -- Derek 'Deke' Conners; Communications/Medical Officer -- Kenji 'Ken' Sakura; and Science Officer/Geologist -- Valerie "Val' Gibbs.

As Apollo 21 approached the moon, all was well and running smoothly. Soon, the 150 mile-wide Mare Undarum area came into view. Various shades of grey -- rocks and boulders and mountains and craters, and their dark shadows -- were crisply visible through the ship's observation ports. The moon looked utterly desolate, lifeless, and forbidding. Awe and exhilaration in the crew's minds mingled with the reality of the challenges which lay ahead.

"Houston, this is 21...all systems look good and we are preparing to land." Sakura reported.

"Roger, 21...your signal is strong and clear...you have permission to land. Now go find us a lot of ice. Good Luck," Mission Control replied.

"O.K., Deke, let's park this bus," ordered Commander Riley. "Everybody buckle in. Here we go..."

Conners fired the craft's retro-rockets to center and slow their descent. "Steady, steady...easy does it," he said aloud. "Ah... we are getting too much drift, Commander...I need to fire the main port lateral thruster to move us more to the right."

"Go for it then, Deke, she's all yours," Riley replied.

The pilot pushed the required button sequence on his control console. A correction that should of taken just a few seconds incorrectly continued without stopping. That was when malfunction alarms flashed, then echoed throughout the cabin.

"The thruster appears to be jammed in an 'on' position, Commander," exclaimed Gibbs. "Deke, I'll try to override it for shutoff." Each crew member had been cross-trained for just such an emergency. She flipped a nearby emergency toggle switch. "Anything, Deke?"

"That's a negative on the shutoff. Our descent is skewed, and we are continually drifting miles away to the right of our landing zone every second," Deke said in frustration. "Dammit!"

Riley quickly ordered Sakura to inform Houston of the problem. "Tell them we are coming in hot and heavy and going off course. If we drift into the dark zone, we will lose all communications with Earth. Keep relaying our position coordinates as they change. Deke, fire your starboard lateral thruster. Maybe that will neutralize and compensate for the drift. Then land us anywhere safe and flat as quickly as you can. And try and keep us in the sunlight."

"Copy that, Commander...here goes..." the Pilot replied, pushing another pair of square buttons. The module lurched and tilted, then seemed to stabilize somewhat. "That did some good, but we have to watch our fuel consumption during those extra maneuvers. Remember, we need enough gas to get home," Conners added.

Meanwhile, The Bus had drifted into the dimming twilight zone between the lighted front and the dark backside of the moon. The craft was coming down too fast, now at 15,000' and 178 mph.

The radio crackled. "21, this is Houston...we copy your problem and have your last reported position...request you emergency jettison your port fuel tank. This will stop the port lateral thruster from firing. You will still have enough fuel for return home. Acknowledge."

"Roger that, Houston. Engaging emergency jettison...mark!" Deke replied, throwing a switch. The procedure worked as the faulty thruster quit, but the momentum inherent in Newton's Law continued to push the craft sideways into utter blackness. They had crossed the barrier and had now entered the unknown and mysterious far side of the moon. All contact with the earth ceased. The Bus was coming down hard, now at 250' and 48mph.

"Activate landing legs. Turn on all external flood lights. Rig for collision!" the Commander ordered. Gibbs flipped her nearby switches. The retro-rockets kicked up plumes of thick grey dust, caught in the glare of the landing lights.

BOOM! The Bus was down, and appeared intact. But it was resting somewhat at an odd angle.

"Is everyone O.K?" asked Riley. All four astronauts looked around and nodded affirmatively to each other. "I need a quick damage report, and I need to know our fuel status."

"Commander, we are obviously not resting level. Did we land in a crater, or strike a boulder?" Sakura asked.

Valerie unbuckled her safely harness, got up, and looked out a viewing port. "No, Ken, but it looks like one of our landing struts has collapsed on impact." Everyone else also unbuckled and got up to look at the external damage. Internally, upon examination, the craft was secure and undamaged, but the fuel supply stood at only 57%. They needed a minimum of 52% to get back home.

"Alright then," Riley spoke. "Here's where we stand. We have enough food and water and oxygen for eight days, plus an additional six hours of air each in our EVA suits. If we can fix the external landing leg damage, we can launch level and go right back to earth. If the leg is irreparable, we can try at least to launch the Bus up low and laterally back to the sunlight side again so that we can reconnect with NASA and wait for rescue in about two or three days. You are all probably now like me -- too tense to sleep yet. So I suggest we eat a meal, then I'll suit up and go outside and check the damage up close and report. We have experienced the unexpected, but we are all well-trained and I am confident we can work out this dilemma and get home safely to our families. And Deke, don't blame yourself. It was not your fault, and you did everything possible, right down the line. I am very proud of each of you."

Deke spoke up next. "Thank you, Commander. I'm sure that we can get out of this mess. I estimate we are only about 20 miles from the sunlight side. Now, let's keep calm and clear-headed and grab some hot food."

After they ate some reconstituted NASA chicken and rice, peas, peaches, and a piece of carrot cake with coffee, Gibbs reported that the outside temperature was a deadly minus 280 degrees F., whereas on the sunlight side it had been a blazing 260 degrees F. Gravity now registered at 17% that of Earth. "Obviously, Commander, we cannot use our solar panels for recharging our electrical systems, but our batteries are fully charged at the moment, so we can maintain our internal and external lights. Our environmental life support and other systems will likewise last us about eight days," she announced. The module's batteries were inside the 60' x 15' x 10' Bus, and were thus protected from damage from the extreme cold of space.

Commander Riley donned his white EVA suit and exited the module's double airlocks. The remaining crew members listened to him on the com, and watched his helmet cam video on their monitor screens.

"Dust is about an inch deep here. I can see the damage to the right rear landing leg. It appears that the 4' titanium stabilizing bar was thrown off when we hit. I can't see it anywhere nearby, but in the one-sixth gravity, it could have flown or bounced more than a half-mile away in any direction. If we could find it, I think we can fix the leg and get out of here. In this lower gravity, we can slowly lift the corner of the Bus together and brace it with rocks, then re-drill and reattach the strut. So I need all of you to suit up and meet me outside with your flashlights. We can spread out and look for the missing strut." Riley gave a 'thumbs up' signal.

The crew quickly obeyed the order. Once outside, they peered into the vast, unknown darkness past the craft's floodlights. Each astronaut was briefly lost in their own thoughts (I'm actually walking on the moon!), but then it was back to work. They shuffled and bounced a bit in the low gravity as they moved, just as they had been trained on earth.

"O.K., now each of us will be responsible for a 90 degree arc of search area," Riley ordered. "That will give us a complete 360 degree search zone. Remember to stay in constant communication. I'll take the northern quadrant. Go no further than a half-mile from the Bus. Valerie, you take the western section. Deke, you take the southern. Ken, you take the eastern. Let's find that strut."

The flashlights of the crew swept left and right as they slowly combed their assigned quadrant. Because the moon has no atmosphere, there is no sound, so all the astronauts could hear was their own breathing inside their helmets.

After about twenty minutes, Kenji called out, "Hey everyone, I think I see the strut...it glinted when my flashlight hit it...it's appears undamaged, but it's at the bottom of a small crater, down about 50'. The angle down to retrieve it looks to be about 30 degrees. Not too difficult to get."

"Nice work, Ken! Set your suit's locator beacon so we can find you. Everyone, head for Ken's crater," Riley directed.

The crew soon met up with Kenji. The crater appeared to be about 250' wide. Such enough, the strut was at the bottom, the track of its skidded entry path clearly visible and fresh in the dust.

"Commander, with your permission, I'd like to retrieve it, alright?" Kenji asked. Riley agreed. "Just be careful," he added. Sakura slowly descended down the crumbly crater's slope with his flashlight.

When he got to the bottom, he picked up the titanium piece and waved it back and forth in triumph. It was then that his foot struck something unusual. He stopped and bent down, and used his fingers to push aside some of the accumulated moon crater pebbles and dust. He was shocked to find what appeared to be the corner of a huge metal door or some kind of hatch. "Commander... everybody...you all better come down here right away and see this!" Kenji exclaimed.

The crew carefully made its way down to Astronaut Sakura. Once there together, they were equally amazed.

"I assumed that we were the first beings to explore the far side of the moon. I guess I was mistaken," Commander Riley admitted. "Turn on your helmet cams and leave them on. I want to record everything from here on out. Let's clear off the rock debris from the edges of this thing and see what we're dealing with."

When this was quickly done, the four saw the revealed outline of an approximately 50' x 50' metal square.

"What the hell...?" Deke Conners muttered. "Is this from earth, or is it extraterrestrial?"

"Commander," Gibbs interrupted. "I think I found a small entranceway over here." The group assembled by Valerie. Such enough, a tunnel was noticed. It appeared to be carved directly into the grey lunar rock, on the side lip of the crater, near the large metal square.

"I doubt there is any way we could budge that big hatch open, so I think we should investigate this tunnel. Everybody, stay together and communicate anything unusual or dangerous," Riley commanded. "Our helmet cams will record and relay everything we see and say back to our ship's computers. Ken, bring the strut."

The four astronauts followed their flashlight beams into the mysterious tunnel. It was luckily just tall and wide enough for them to fit, walking single file. The passageway led downward on an easy angle. After several minutes, the tunnel opened up into a large, cavern-like chamber. Strangely, the team felt a regular 'thump, thump, thump' pulsing coming from somewhere, which they felt bounce off their spacesuits.

"Look!" cried Conners. "I see some kind of mist coming out from the far perimeters of this chamber. I know that seems impossible at these temperatures, but there it is." The others quickly noticed the same. "Commander, we have four hours and forty-three minutes of oxygen left in our suits. And you have about fifteen minutes less," Gibbs then reported. "Temperature is now at minus 131 degrees Fahrenheit." Somewhat less extreme but still lethal, everyone realized.

Riley verbalized what they all had concluded: "This definitely indicates intelligent design, but not of our planet. Has to be alien."

Sakura's flashlight beam next discovered a long neat row of clear, coffin-like pods. "Oh my God…"he exclaimed. The crew cautiously stepped forward.

Incredibly, the astronauts beheld naked young male and female human beings, in pairs from each racial group – European, African, and Asian. The bodies were perfectly preserved, and looked to be simply asleep. Next to them were specially-sized clear pods containing a horse, a cow, a dog, and a cat. But this domesticated animal display was different, in that their internal organs had been removed and placed along side their bodies.

"Over here!" Deke shouted. He had spied another row of four pods. What the crew saw inside the containers left them speechless. A perfectly preserved young white unicorn, complete with a spiraled silver horn protruding from its forehead. A minotaur, with the head of a bull on the body of a very tall, muscular man. A perfectly preserved young milk-white winged horse, a Pegasus. And finally, what appeared to be an infant dragon, reptilian with teeth and claws and brownish-green scales, yet also winged.

"So, these were not just the fanciful imaginings of Earth's mythology," Gibbs said breathlessly. "Wait until NASA reveals this to the world!"

Commander Riley was next. He said just two words: "Flying saucers…"

The astronauts immediately focused all of their flashlights on the far wall of the pitch black chamber. Lined up were several models of used spacecraft – rectangular, triangular, cigar-shaped, and saucer-shaped. Riley counted six in all. "Looks like U.F.O.s were real too, after all," he declared, clearly puzzled and more than a little unsettled. "That big metal hatch above us must be somehow moveable so as to allow these in -- and out."

The crew spread out a little and continued to explore the chamber, their helmet cams recording all that they said and saw.

Kenji then discovered a clear, flat type of large display case on a kind of metal stand in a corner. "Is this what I think it is?" he wondered aloud. The others quickly joined him.

Deke spoke first. "I know this sounds crazy, but I think we are looking at some kind of blueprints for building the Great Pyramids of Egypt. And the other seems to be a detailed map of a continent in the middle of our Atlantic

Ocean back home...could it possibly be Atlantis?" He was completely bewildered and amazed, as were the others, with the ramifications for Earth's history of this latest discovery.

But it was Commander Riley who had the final announcement regarding their exploration, after the group continued to wander and observe in the strange underground chamber. "I can't believe my own eyes, yet here sits the Soviet space capsule, Luna 15. It was said to have crashed, unmanned, just a few hours before our Apollo 11 lifted off from the moon back in July, 1969. Just look at the markings...C.C.C.P., hammer & sickle, everything...and..." He peered inside the viewing ports with his flashlight. Two dead cosmonauts were eternally resting there, buckled in their seats, perfectly preserved in their now antiquated spacesuits.

"That's it...we've seen enough here...maybe even too much to absorb objectively," Riley decided. "Let's head back to the Bus, repair the landing leg, and get out of here. NASA is going to go crazy when we download our recordings once we get back in the sunlight...Val, how's our oxygen?"

"Good, Commander...we have been here a little over an hour, so we still have a more than three hour supply. That's more than enough to walk the half-mile back to our ship and initiate repairs."

"Alright, it's back up top side through the tunnel," Riley ordered. "Keep in single file: Val leads, then me, Deke, and Ken brings up the rear. Don't forget the strut, Ken. Let's go."

When the team exited the tunnel and climbed out of the crater, they saw their distant Bus module to the west, its floodlights welcomingly visible a half-mile away. The astronauts were tired and somewhat overwhelmed, but sleep would have to wait until they were aloft and out of danger. They were moving on pure adrenaline reserves now. They were, however, able to drink some needed water from a water bladder tube inside their EVA suits, which helped them stave off dehydration.

It was as dark as being in the belly of a black cat at the bottom of a coal mine at midnight. Only the astronaut's flashlights, and the floodlights of the Bus, gave any semblance of familiar reality.

The group was about half-way back to their base when Kenji Sakura was killed. Neither he -- being the last in line -- nor his comrades saw the ominous dark shape that grabbed him from behind before he could cry out, as his helmet was brutally ripped off his spacesuit and his head immediately vaporized in the moon's vacuum of space.

A few moments later, Deke Conners dropped his flashlight and screamed, "OH NO!" just once, before dying.

Riley and Gibbs both turned around, and were shocked to see that both Deke and Ken had simply vanished. Only their flashlights remained, abandoned, in the grey lunar soil. Riley yelled, "Get back to the ship, Val! NOW!"

Gibbs moved as fast as she could in the moon's one-sixth gravity, trying not to stumble, which would cause even more difficulties. She made it to their floodlit Bus module and its first airlock and opened it. But when she looked back, her flashlight beam showed nothing but inky blackness past the nearby grey rocks and dust beyond the floodlights.

"Commander...come in! Commander...where are you? I'm at the Bus, ready to go in. Acknowledge! Commander, please respond!" Valerie pleaded. But there was no response.

Gibbs had no other choice but to seal the first airlock shut behind her. After re-pressurization, she opened the second airlock and entered the ship's main cabin. After removing her EVA suit, she rushed and grabbed a com console microphone which was also linked with Riley's helmet. She loudly called again and again for him to respond. "If you are hurt and can't move, just wave your flashlight back and forth. I'll come get you, John," she urged.

Silence. No light beam wobbles. Nothing.

Astronaut Valerie Gibbs was alone on the far side of the moon, in a crippled spaceship, possibly stranded, without being able to communicate with Earth. Plus, someone or something unknown had killed her three companions.

Val buried her face in her hands, rubbing her facial skin and her eyes over and over again in exhaustion, and then scratching her short blond hair with her fingers. She knew that with Kenji gone, so was the titanium stabilizer strut. Even if she had it, Valerie realized that it was unsafe to go out and attempt any repairs until she knew exactly what killed her friends. She went over and checked the electrical systems and the fuel gauges. Battery power was good, but what was this...? The fuel level was at 57% when they landed, but now it was only at 22% and slowly falling! Christ! Probably a tank puncture due to a micro-meteor strike when we were gone. Still leaking too. Shit! Gibbs knew she needed 52% fuel to get home. She was doomed...

Overwhelmed and in a daze, Valerie wandered over to her private bunk area where each astronaut was allowed to display a few personal effects and photographs. She picked up a picture of her and her family vacationing at Glacier National Park in Montana last summer. Blue sky, sunshine, mountains, fluffy white clouds. Everyone so relaxed and happy!

Her smiling husband, their son, and their daughter...even their golden lab, Boomer. My hair was longer then, she briefly mused. Funny, but she could still smell the exhilarating, fresh cedar and pine air in her mind...if only I was there now...

That was when Gibbs realized that she could either give up and pathetically die there on the moon when her oxygen and food and water ran out, or instead, figure out a way to survive and be rescued on the sunlight side. It was only about 20 miles away, she remembered.

Valerie's body absolutely craved sleep, but she couldn't allow it in her current emergency situation. Her energy was also lagging, which made her thinking sluggish and potentially mistake-prone. So she decided to eat a high-carb NASA meal of spaghetti with marinara sauce and crackers to help pump up her blood sugar. She also made and drank two large cups of strong black coffee, and used the toilet. Val soon felt more alive. Plus, she had decided what needed to be done. She had a plan that might possibly work. And she was now 100% determined to get home to see her loving family again.

Gibbs decided to use all of her remaining fuel to get back to the sunlight side of the moon. She had one shot, but it was a logical gamble. If she succeeded, she would be back in contact with the earth, which would send a rescue craft, arriving in two or three days. She had enough food, water, electricity, and all-important oxygen to last until then. She could deploy the solar panels on the Bus again. She could download to NASA all the footage of their startling underground discoveries. The deaths of her three comrades would not be in vain or ever be forgotten.

It was now or never. Fuel registered at 19% but was still gradually dropping. Gibbs buckled herself into Deke's pilot chair and powered up the instrument panels. She would fire the ascent thrusters, instructing the engine computers to level off at just 2000'. Then she would fire the starboard lateral thruster manually, to push the ship to the left, west into the sunlight zone. With luck, Valerie would just make it before all remaining fuel was depleted. If she was unlucky, and the craft fell short, she knew she was finished. No possibility of walking any distance outside to safety or rescue.

Suddenly, Val was startled to hear an odd scraping noise from somewhere outside the Bus. Her first thought was that it was Riley...John was still alive! He was trying to come back inside! But cold logic quickly convinced her that Riley was dead. Then she heard a pounding of metal on the metal hull of the Bus. Something wanted to get inside and get her, she realized with horror...

Without hesitating, Valerie Gibbs flipped off the craft's outside floodlights, engaged the navigation computers and fired her ascent thrusters. The engine roared to life. The craft shook roughly as it tried to right itself on its three good landing legs, but slowly it ascended. Valerie kept a cautious eye on her fuel gauges. The percentages kept falling, alarmingly.

At 2000', the Bus leveled off as programmed, and Val manually fired the starboard lateral thruster. The craft responded and began to veer to the left, as expected. Now if only the fuel will hold out for the twenty miles, she prayed. Meanwhile, the gauge showed just 9% of fuel remaining. The leak must be enlarging due to the ship's acceleration and vibrations, Valerie realized. "Hang in there, Bus!" she said aloud..."you can do it...just a little farther...come on..."

The seconds went by excruciatingly slowly. The fuel dropped to 6%. But soon, Valerie could see the sunlight zone -- there, on the horizon! She was now in the dim twilight zone between the light and dark sides of the moon.

At 3%, low fuel warning lights and alarms went off. Valerie's fingers were white because she was gripping her control stick so hard. "Come on...come on, baby...she urged the craft onward to the west.

The full glare of the sunlight side temporarily blinded Gibbs as she realized she had arrived at a possible flat landing spot. She immediately shut off the starboard lateral thruster. She had a dangerously minimal fuel level to fire the retro-thruster to land, but had no other choice. It was all or nothing. Valerie hit the necessary buttons, and the craft began its descent. Now I just need about 60 seconds more of fuel to slow and land without crashing, she grimly realized...

Apollo 21 ran out of fuel at 33' above the moon's sunlit surface, but it had slowed sufficiently to crash land very hard yet safely and intact.

Val unbuckled her pilot's harness and got up and quickly checked every system on the Bus. She was relieved to find that all was well. She then went to the main NASA communications console and switched it on.

"Houston...Houston...this is Apollo 21...Houston, do you read me?" After only a few seconds, NASA responded.

The emotional strain she was under all this time finally burst through her professional self-control. "Houston, this is Astronaut Valerie Gibbs of Apollo 21...request emergency rescue at these coordinates...other crew members lost..I'm all alone...please help me...tell my family I'm alive," she repeated the last words again and again, tears streaming down her face...

THE END

by Jack Karolewski   November 9, 2017

TEXAS JAILBIRD

My name is Cameron Wells, but most folks call me Sonny because I was the last of ten children. I was named after my Daddy. I grew up in Carthage, Texas, in the northeast part of the state not too far from the Louisiana border. Carthage is the county seat of Panola County. The word 'panola' means 'cotton' in the Redskin language. Like most of our neighbors, Daddy grew cotton, and I did my share of chopping and picking the stuff before I left home at age 26. I went to the same grade school as country singer Tex Ritter. Because of him, most people know the name Carthage.

In October, 1930, the Daisy Bradford #3 oil well finally hit a gusher at 3500' down, in a field about six miles north of Henderson, which was 28 miles west of Carthage. Like many other men in the area, I left my family to learn a new trade by trying to find better paying work in the oil fields.

As luck would have it, I landed a job. Maybe the boss thought I had an honest yet determined face. I started at the bottom of the totem pole: as a ginsel, a 'worm's helper,' a 'worm' being another name for a leadman. After so many months, you could work your way up to being a chainman, then later a derrickhand. But the work was brutal, dirty, and exhausting – much, much harder than farming cotton. The good pay was very welcome, however. The Great Depression was now in full fury, with one-third of able-bodied men wandering and out of work nationwide. So I was glad to be earning some cabbage.

Sadly, it was there at the oil fields that my troubles began. I was cocky and stupid and picked up several bad habits from the other veteran roughnecks: drinking, gambling, fighting, cursing. I started visiting cathouses on Saturday nights with my buddies. I stopped going to church, and forgot about all the lessons my Mama taught me from the Good Book. I was ashamed to tell my parents about my sins, so I said nothing, although I did send a goodly chunk of my paycheck home every week. Then, one day, I got into a dumb, stubborn argument with my job foreman. I refused to be lowered head down by rope into a drill bore to retrieve a busted drill bit. He let me go then and there, so suddenly I was out of work. Other unemployed men who were eager to take my job without complaint were already lined up outside the company fence.

So I drifted, hitch-hiked, rode the rails. Gradually, I took on the demeanor and appearance of an ordinary bum, one of millions it seemed. I was too proud to go back home and fess up. When hunger became too much, I begged at churches, or at folks' back doors, or lined up with other down and outers at soup kitchens. I learned to avoid policemen and railyard bulls. I became an expert liar and deceiver. Then I started stealing -- first items when there was no one around, later mugging other weaker bums and drifters for a dime or a hunk of food. I felt pathetic, but helpless to change.

My worst mistake was trying to rob a filling station in Silsbee, near Beaumont. I just wanted the cash drawer, not to hurt the attendant. But the old timer drew a hidden pistol, and as we struggled, the gun unexpectedly fired. The man was mortally wounded by his own hand, but who would believe that? I ran, but was later picked up and identified in a police line-up by a witness who happened to be exiting the filling station's men's room at the time of the shooting. I was made, and no mistake.

I later went before Hardin County Judge Sammy Reston, and was sentenced to fourteen years hard labor without parole at Huntsville Penitentiary for involuntary manslaughter. (I would have gotten only seven years in the Can, but I had a folding jackknife in my pants pocket when I was caught. That counted as a deadly weapon that I might have brandished during the hold-up, even though I didn't.) My descent into Hell commenced from that point. In the courtroom, my Mama cried after sentence was passed, and my

Daddy just looked away, ashamed. Needless to say, I was the first of my brothers and sisters to go to prison. I was a sorry case. And now I was just a common, ordinary jailbird.

Huntsville is the oldest penitentiary in Texas, built back in 1849. It was made of red brick with high walls, so it was nicknamed "The Walls" by its former and current inmates. The death penalty was carried out there by hanging rope until 1923, then the prison switched to the electric chair -- "Old Sparky." Huntsville once housed the famous outlaw John Westley Hardin, but I wasn't impressed by that fact, because I really didn't want to be there anyway. I broke the law and now I had to pay the price. I figured I would rot in Stir until I turned 40.

I don't mind admitting that my first day in prison was awful. First you strip naked, then they check your mouth, your hair, and up your ass for any contraband. Then they take your civvies and issue you a black and white striped jailbird suit and a cloth cap. Next, they give you a thin wool blanket, a towel, a comb, a toothbrush, a cake of soap, a set of drawers, a pair of socks, and a cheap pair of work boots. Then they read you the rules. You get to shave once every three days, and you get to shower once a week. Clean clothes come once a week. Visitation time is one hour a month -- family and relatives (or your lawyer, if you have one) only. You can write up to three letters a month. You can read the heavily-screened (nothing sexy) prison library books and magazines, or the Bible. You rise at 6 and have lights out at 10. You get three squares a day, but don't expect your mama's cooking. Grits, eggs, fried bologna, okra, cornbread, collard and turnip greens, black-eyed peas, beans, fruit, fried potatoes, and fatback mostly. Greasy and starchy -- you get the picture. Rusty-tasting water and lousy black coffee to drink. The State of Texas wants its prison meals filling enough to keep you alive, but they want to do it on the cheap. Nary any milk or desserts. No candy or soda pop or even sugar for your joe.

Next, you get a con number and a cell assignment. I'm con # 4277, cell # 323. My cellmate was Vernon Mitchell. When I first met him, he said to call him "Taters" on account of his favorite food is potatoes. He was in for nine years for an armed robbery he tried down in Galveston. He was about twelve years older than me, and he'd been inside "The Walls" for two years so far. They kept all the niggers in another cell block, so we never saw them unless we were on a big outdoor chain gang job. But even then, whites and darkies were kept separate so no fights could break out. Made sense to me.

I never saw the Warden, Willard Stillman, but Taters told me that Stillman was a washed-out rummy that kept his door closed and a bottomless bottle of hooch hidden in his desk. As a result, the guards could pretty much do what they wanted to the inmates. My #1 problem was the senior guard on my block, Dewey Drummond. "Call me Boss D, new meat! And always answer me with Yes, Boss," was my introduction to this balding, beady-eyed, 300-lb. mountain of blubber, as he pointed at my face with the mean end of his billy club. Taters told me Drummond was probably queer, by the way he eyeballed the younger prisoners in the weekly shower room. Probably had a pecker the size of a peanut, I figured. I once heard that those kind usually did. I learned fast to stay wide and clear of Boss D, but he must have had it out for me, because he kept getting in my face.

When Boss D got a chance to read my file about a week after my arrival, he must have learned that I had once worked in the Henderson oil fields. "Well, look at what we have here, boys...an oil millionaire gone wrong. I think I'll call you 'Oil Wells', boy!" he guffawed one morning during roll call. As usual, Boss D was red-faced and sweaty merely from the exertion of dragging his bulk around. His sadistic smile showed a big gap between his two stained front teeth, and he usually had flecks of white spittle parked in both corners of his mouth.

My first experience of off-site chain gang work was not pleasant. You get shackled with heavy ankle chains, then they load you up in a twenty-man flatbed truck. They drive you away for the day to chop weeds and briers alongside county roads. You get a double-edged sling (kaiser) blade to sweep back and forth as you cut the brush. The guards watch you with their shotguns and rifles and dogs. Prisoners get a water break every hour for five minutes, and a fifteen minute lunch break for some sandwiches and fruit. If you have to piss or crap, you have to ask permission. On a typical hot and humid summer's day, the work is torturous and mind-numbing. Soon, you are soaked with sweat. No talking except during breaks and on the drive there and back.

Whenever it rained, we were shackled again but taken instead to private nearby factories to haul and size burlap cloth and then machine-stitch it into sacking. It was free labor for the plant owners, through some prior payback arrangement with the State of Texas. The work was boring as hell but not too sweaty, and days like that went by rather quickly.

But the very worst work detail was the rock quarry. In addition to the ankle chains, each prisoner was attached to a twenty-five pound ball. You were given either a pick, a sledgehammer, or a shovel. The job was to break large rocks into smaller gravel pieces for road constructions, then load the pieces into trucks. The sun's glare off the white rocks always hurt my eyes badly. Sunglasses could only be worn by the guards. You had to hoist and move your ball with you all throughout the day -- even to take a piss or a crap, either of which had to be done a sizeable walk away at the upper ground level of the quarry. The relentless labor was muscle-aching and back-breaking! And if you didn't keep moving and working, a guard would gladly whack you with his trusty Ugly Stick to set your mind back on business.

The weeks slowly turned into months. How could I ever endure this nightmare for fourteen long years? Nights in Stir were especially unsettling, because inmates would often yell out or even scream in the dark when having bad dreams. My cellmate, Taters, and I had many long discussions about how best to serve our time in the Slammer. Meanwhile, Boss D stepped up his harassments on me and other hapless prisoners. Once, in the mess hall, he slyly but deliberately tripped me while I was taking my food tray over to a table. "Oil Wells, you clumsy son of a bitch, clean that mess up right now!" he bellowed. Another time, while I was mopping the dull green floor on the center aisle of the Main Hall of our cell block, Boss D came over and spit a huge gob slowly right next to my foot. "You missed a spot, Oil Wells. Do it over again, and make it right this time, you hear me boy?" I grew to hate him more and more by the day. I fantasized about shoving his fat face down a filthy toilet bowl and holding his head underwater while I flushed it. Then I would take his billy club and beat him all over his stinking body until he begged for mercy.

Later, I found out that Boss D was stealing some of my letters to and from my family. I learned of this from my parents when they came to visit, when they asked why I hadn't written, or asking if I had received such and such letter from them. Sure enough, I would catch Boss D openly smirking while he was eavesdropping on my conversations from across the visiting room. The dirty bastard!

Prison is a rough world, a place you never want to wind up in, trust me. I kept my nose clean going into my first year behind bars. But now I really wanted Boss D dead. I knew that other prisoners had secretly made shiv knives to stab, cripple, or even kill other prisoners who had ratted them out, or had gotten in their face for one reason or another. Sometimes they got caught and had their sentences increased, or were punished by being locked away in Solitary for a time on bread and water. Yet sometimes there were 'no witnesses' and the attacker got away scot-free. I asked Taters if he had ever seen a guard get what was coming to him by getting stabbed by another prisoner.

"Sonny, don't you ever even think about doing it. If you stab or kill a prison guard -- or a cop on the outside, for that matter -- you're a dead man. They take care of their own, understand? You won't make it to trial. You will have a fatal 'accident' on the way to the courtroom, or you will be found hung in your cell as a 'suicide,' or you will get shot 'trying to escape,'" Taters warned. "Best thing is to lay low and take the abuse and wait out your time. It ain't right, and it ain't justice, but it's all we can do when we're stuck in the Big House. The Man holds all the cards, and he knows it."

Boss D continued, however, to zero in on me, especially during chain gang work details, cracking me on the back or shoulders with his wooden club when I least suspected it, snarling, "Get back to work, you lazy prick," or "What are you staring at, Oil Wells? Daydreaming about pussy? You won't be drilling for any of that stank for thirteen more years!" The fat bastard always laughed in the same sick way, while scratching his overhanging belly as it strained against his uniform shirt buttons.

Another year dragged by. I was now 28 years old. How could I stand this torment for another dozen years? Then I came to the ultimate realization that all convicts eventually come to: There just has to be a way to...ESCAPE!

I talked over the matter at length with Taters. "Four have tried to escape in the time I've been here, before you came, that is," he replied. "Nobody made it. Two were shot dead trying to flee a roadside weed detail. Another one tried to steal a truck at the quarry, but he was caught and beaten to a pulp by the guards. His sentence was then doubled. The last guy tried to sneak out of the laundry room by breaking through a ventilation shaft. They flushed him out using a hot steam hose when he got stuck in the shaft. Spent four months in the prison hospital, he was burned so badly on his hands and face. Then they transferred him out to another prison. I suppose a large cell block riot, with guards taken hostage, might allow a few cons to escape in the chaos. But that requires a lot of planning and trust and organization. I really can't see it ever happening. So my advice, Sonny, is to forget about getting out of here, and just ride out your time as best you can, like I'm doing. You'll be older, sure, but you'll be wiser too, and at least you'll still be alive."

I might have taken my cellmate's advice, except for the fact that Boss D kept riding me. One day, I was using a push broom during cleaning detail on the second tier of my cell block. While I was finishing sweeping, Boss D wheezed his way up the stairs on some errand. But as he tried to squeeze past me in the end stairwell, he tripped on my broom handle and awkwardly fell down a few steps at a bad angle and busted his ankle. "Goddammit, Wells, you pushed me on purpose!" he wailed. "Guards, take this son of a bitch to Solitary! Of course, his lie was believed, and it was one month in The Hole on bread and water for me.

When I finally got out of Solitary, there was Boss D, still wearing an ankle cast and leaning on a cane. "Oil Wells, one day we are going to have a reckoning. It might be inside, or it might be outside, or it might be after your release in 1944. But I mean to have your hide – once and for all -- for what you did to me," he hissed menacingly. "Doc said I might have a limp for the rest on my life once this cast comes off. If that turns out to be the case, you're a dead man, boy, and make no mistake."

Arguing is useless when you're in prison. You have no real rights, and no one cares about truth and justice. You're just a con with a number, like me -- #4277. So instead, my thoughts went back again to planning an escape. I simply had to get out of Huntsville before I went crazy!

New Year's 1933 came in without any joy or celebration. The nation was still stuck hard in the Great Depression. We followed some of the bad news in the old newspapers that some of the guards shared, or sometimes we got to hear FDR on the radio. But on February 1st, our cell block got a new guard by the name of Rufus Lemont. He was about my height and age, not married yet, and seemed at first to be largely innocent of the cruel ways of the world. Rumor had it that Rufus' father was a friend of Texas Governor Sterling, and that's how he got the lucky job. The most interesting thing about Lemont was that he had his own motorcar -- a new, dark blue Ford Coupe with real whitewall tires that his big shot daddy got him. Rufus always proudly talked about his car as he chatted with and got to know the cons on my block. Of course, Boss D was immediately suspicious, then jealous, of this new guard. Whereas Dewey Drummond was despised by every con, Boss Lemont related to the men more like normal human beings instead of animals. So Boss D set out to change that.

When the weather warmed up, we resumed our outdoor chain gang work – both on the roads and in the quarry. Boss D ordered that Boss Lemont had to beat any prisoner with his billy club who was caught 'eyeballing' -- that is, daydreaming, or silently staring, and thus not working. Bullying, kicking, and punching the cons was also promoted. After six months or so, Boss Lemont slowly gave into the pressure from Boss D and the other guards and became just another soulless prison enforcer. But he was still green enough to make small mistakes in his duties. I carefully observed these, and thought of how I could somehow use this flaw to my advantage.

Eventually, an idea formed in my mind. I promised myself that I would one way or another escape this lousy lockup by the end of the year. I bounced my plan off of Taters to get his opinion.

"If you can lure Lemont close to our cell bars with any kind of distracting conversation some night -- near the end of his regular shift -- I can try to grab him fast and knock him out, then lift his keys and open our cell. I'll drag him inside and switch into his uniform. Then you can help me dress him in my stripes and put him in my bunk. I'll relock our cell from the outside, and leave the keys out of reach on the ground. Boss Lemont is just about my size, so if I pull his guard hat down low over my face, I think I can walk outside in the dark like he would, carefully find his car, and -- calmly as I can -- drive off. What do you think? I know you don't want to run with me, Taters, so you'll just stay safe behind in our cell. Tell the Screws that I knocked you out too, and confess that you knew nothing about my plan. That'll keep you out of any trouble."

"Well, Sonny, it's very risky," Taters admitted. "And you're right in thinking that I don't want to go with you. I'd rather ride out my time, like I've been doing. But I'll do my part to help you because we are pals. Who knows? Maybe one day on the Outside, we will meet up again somewhere and you can do me a big favor in return. All I ask is that you really knock me out too after you give Lemont his lights out. A nice lump on my noggin will give my side of the story some good, solid credibility," Taters grinned.

Soon it was December. A week of blustery, miserable, heavy rain arrived. As luck would have it, Boss D had called in sick with a bad chest cold, so a different guard – old and tired -- from Block G was substituting. He promptly fell asleep in a far corner chair down the Main Hall. I felt it was as good a time as any to make my move. Boss Lemont's shift would end at midnight. It was about 11:40 p.m. on Wednesday, December 13th. I knew it was now or never!

"Psst...Boss Lemont..." Taters called out in a low voice from Cell 323. "I can't sleep, Boss...I have a pain in my mouth, like maybe something sharp is stuck between my teeth...I know it's late, but do you think you can take a quick look in my mouth with your flashlight? Or maybe even take me to the sick ward?" begged Taters, still in a low voice. "It hurts real bad, Boss."

Lemont checked his watch, sighed, then said, "Alright, Mitchell, but let's make it quick before my shift ends." Rufus walked over to the cell while I pretended to be asleep in my bed. Under my blanket, I clutched a badly worn-out baseball I had earlier lifted from the discard can in the sports yard.

Taking out his flashlight, Boss Lemont peered inside Tater's mouth close through the steel cell bars.

"Hmm...I can't see anything...but, man, your breath sure stinks," Rufus observed ruefully.

That was when I boldly made my move. Leaping up from my bunk, I put my left hand over Lemont's mouth while simultaneously ramming his skull backward toward the bars. In my next motion, I clobbered Rufus squarely on his crown with my right hand clutching the hard league ball, holding him as he silently slide down then to the dull green block floor. I quickly grabbed his flashlight, then his keys, then slowly unlocked the cell door. Next, I quietly dragged his unconscious body into 323 and, with Taters' help, switched into the guard's uniform. Lemont's uniform shoes were unexpectedly tight and uncomfortable, but they only had to be worn for a short time. We placed Rufus in my bed wearing my stripes and covered him with my blanket. Finally, Taters and I locked eyes and I solemnly shook his hand in thanks and goodbye. He turned his back dutifully towards me. I whispered, "Sorry, old pard, but I've got to do this," and he answered, "I know...Good luck." I clobbered him out cold with one shot of the baseball -- surely giving him a real goose egg -- and then placed him gently on his bed. I checked left and right down the Main Hall of the cell block to be sure that all was clear, then I locked the cell door from the outside and placed the keys on the floor. With as much confidence and calm as I could muster, I pulled Lemont's cap down over my face as best I could and made for the block's exit. I was routinely buzzed out through a security gate by a bored guard leafing through a sports magazine who mistook me for Lemont. It was pouring rain and dark outside, which helped obscure visibility from both the guards at the main gates and the armed guard towers. I looked in somewhat of a panic for the dark blue Ford Coupe, but thankfully found it just as Lemont's shift replacement came running by, dodging muddy puddles. He gave me a quick wave in the downpour. I silently waved back without raising my head. I knew that Lemont always kept his car keys under his passenger-side floor mat (an inmate had once asked him what car keys looked like nowadays, and he revealed that useful little detail), so I found them fast with my dripping wet fingers and fired up the engine. I hadn't driven a car for three years, but the skill returned fast -- like riding a bicycle, you never forget. I turned on the headlamps and took off calmly and carefully, smoothly shifting the gears. I checked the rearview mirror as the massive red walls of Huntsville Penitentiary receded in the distance. I was out, but not out of danger yet!

I knew I had to make as much distance between myself and the prison as possible, because once they found me missing, and Lemont was discovered and recovered, the manhunt for me would begin in earnest.

My plan was to drive -- fast but not too fast -- south using back roads, then ditch the car and the guard uniform somewhere in Houston. From there, I would skip the obvious route to Galveston and instead head for more obscure Port Arthur. Once there, I hoped to hitch a boat ride into Mexico, maybe to Tampico or even Veracruz if I was really lucky. True, I had no money, but I could always beg, or roll a drunk outside any back-alley honky-tonk for a few coins. I was a wanted man, and desperate. Circumstances were dire, and I was sorry in advance. I wanted to go straight for sure, for I never wanted to go back to prison – any prison – ever again. I promised myself that I would try and become a model citizen and start a fresh, new, clean life somewhere, anywhere! If only God could give me a second chance...

I drove in the rain until I spied a railroad worker's equipment shed near a rural crossing just outside of Houston. It was perfect. I broke in through the window, and found some stained overalls that fit, a ragged cap, and an old wool jacket. I quickly got out of my prison guard uniform and swapped outfits. I also found a floppy pair of work boots to replace Lemont's tight-fitting uniform shoes. I looked around for any food to take, but found none. (Truth be told, my adrenaline was so high that I wasn't even hungry yet.) I drove about a mile, then ditched the Ford, with the uniform inside, in some thick brush. Meanwhile, the rain had stopped and the sky was beginning to lighten in the east. Suddenly, I heard a distant train whistle. Maybe it was heading east? I ran back the mile towards the train tracks in my floppy stolen boots. I got back just as I saw a long freight, mostly, but not all, oil tanker cars, heading into the rising sun...east! Watching for any railyard bulls, I gingerly found an empty box car and hoisted myself aboard. Fortunately, it was empty, so I settled in and immediately fell asleep from exhaustion. I dozed fitfully until I awoke to the sweet salty smell of the Gulf. Was I still in Texas, or had I slipped into Louisiana? I peered out of the boxcar's door and saw we were indeed near Port Arthur. I decided to jump when the train slowed down for a curve and then started off again on foot into town. I could hear the screeching of the seagulls already in the distance.

I went into the first open diner I saw down by the docks. Its worn wooden shingle said: FINLEY'S. Inside was a small counter with six stools, and an arrangement of four tables with chairs. There were no other customers this early, so I asked the fry cook scraping his grill if he knew of any boats that needed crewmen. "I need a job, any job, badly," I confessed.

"Got your seaman's papers, son?" the fry cook asked cordially.

"Sorry to say, no sir, (I almost slipped and said, "No, Boss") but I've worked in the oil fields as a roughneck and I'm no stranger to hard work," I admitted.

"I reckon you're broke then too," the cook remarked, sighing. "So many are today...Well, seeing as you're the first customer for the day, and Christmas is almost here, how about a cup of joe and a donut, on the house?" he offered. "My name is Ephram Finley. I own the joint. Used to be a shrimper back in the day until I got too old for the work. I'll ask around down by the docks while you eat and see if any boats need an extra worker. Are you particular as to what kind of job, or to where the boat's heading?" Finley asked.

"I'll do or learn anything – fishing, crabbing, shrimping, loading, even dry dock repairs -- but my real goal is to make it down to Mexico for work in the oil fields near Tampico or Veracruz. I hear the cost of living is cheaper South of the Border, so I thought I'd give it a shot until things improved here in the States. By the way, my name is Travis," I fibbed. "My family's from San An-tone." We shook hands. "So you were the one who fought at the Alamo, eh?" Finley chuckled. "Promise not to rob me while I'm gone, O.K.?" he added good-naturedly. He poured me a hot mug of coffee and put a nice big donut on a little plate for me. Then he headed out the door. I immediately poured a ton of sugar into my joe, stirred it in, and sipped. Ah!

About ten minutes after Finley left, a tall brunette smoking a cigarette walked in, attractive (especially to me, having not gazed at a live dame for three years), shapely, probably in her late 30's. She introduced herself as Finley's sole waitress, Florence. "You can call me Flow if you like," she winked in a flirty kind a way, as only someone who works mostly for tips learns to do. "Everybody does." I could easily still smell the soap she used for her morning bath, and her light touch of perfume, even over the smoke from her cigarette. Sexy woman smells I had almost forgotten! I instantly liked her breezy, smiling manner, and told her my fake name and what I was doing there, and where Finley had gone, while I ravenously ate my donut and drained my extra-sugary coffee.

Finley returned shortly afterwards with some good news.

"Travis, I found you something going to New Orleans. Your job is retrieving crab pots in the waters between here and there. It's about a five-day job at sea. Pays $7 plus your meals. Skipper's name is Tall Tom. The boat's called The Chanteuse. Leaves right after she fuels up, so you better get a move on. From The Big Easy, you might later catch a boat headed for the Mexican Gulf Coast and those oil fields," Finley explained. "One more thing, Travis. I hope you don't object to working for a nigger. Some whites won't, which is why he's short-handed on this run. But I know Tall Tom and I trust him, and so can you," Finley added.

"Ephram, I don't know how to thank you for all of your kindness to a stranger like me, but I'll never forget you," I said, shaking his calloused hand goodbye. "Bye too, Flow!"

I found The Chanteuse straight away. She was a beat-up but sturdy-looking tub, and I immediately spied the Skipper, a very tall, muscular buck in a stained white undershirt and blue dungarees.

"You must be Tall Tom. Ephram Finley just spoke to you about your needing an extra hand with the crab pots on a run to New Orleans. Well, I'm your man," I added, extending my hand in greeting. "My name is Travis." We shook.

Tall Tom must have been 6' 4" and 250 solid pounds if he was an ounce, and was probably in his mid-30's. His dark eyes looked me over in a quick, appraising glance. "Ever done any crabbing, Travis?" he asked, smiling, showing strong white teeth.

"No, Skipper, I'm afraid all I know is oilfield work. But I can learn real fast, believe me," I replied. "I'm honest and uncomplaining and ready right now to give you my best work."

"I bet you are, so I'll give you a shot," Tom agreed. "If you follow my orders, we'll get along just fine. I have two other crewmen who'll come with us. They're out getting food and other supplies. Once we gas up, we're ready to cast off. Pay is $7 and your chow. You'll be the only white man aboard, seeing as my other man is off drunk somewheres. Got a problem with that?" he asked with raised eyebrows.

"No sir, Skipper," I replied. "No problem at all. Happy to be aboard."

"Now Travis, I would guess that you are flat broke. I think I'll pay you $4 in advance and have you get a new set of working clothes and some better shoes. There's an Army/Navy surplus store down the street that'll fix you up fine. And I bet you're hungry too. So when you get back, I've got some beans and cornbread with molasses and coffee down in the galley, and you can have your fill," Tall Tom generously offered.

I did as he asked -- naturally keeping a careful lookout for any cops -- and when I came back and was finished eating, I met the other two crewmen of The Chanteuse. Leroy was 16, and Nathaniel ("Natty") was around my age. Both were easy-going and good-natured.

Before long, we shoved off, going east. Keeping close to the shoreline in waters no deeper than twenty feet, we reeled in the crab pots which were marked by small floating yellow buoys, then emptied the catch into barrels filled with fresh seawater. Leroy and Natty then showed me how to re-bait each pot – which was actually a square or circular metal cage – with either chopped up raw chicken legs or something called 'beef melt,' which was like chunks of beef liver that the crabs went nuts for. (Going for the bait, the crabs would enter the pot trap through a one-way opening and get stuck inside.) The re-baited pots were finally tossed back into the warm Gulf waters. The blue crabs we caught would eventually wind up on the plates of hungry diners in fancy restaurants in New Orleans and elsewhere. But Tall Tom made sure we enjoyed plenty of the sweet crabmeat ourselves, for our catch was bountiful during our five-day run. They were mighty good eatin' too, especially with some spicy hot sauce!

All of us crew worked hard, ate well, and slept soundly. The rhythm of the routine, the steady drone of the boat's engines, and the refreshing salt air was all a balm to my formerly prison-battered soul. (One night, I found out that the boat was named on behalf of a special nightclub singer that Tall Tom had fallen in love with, but she ran off with some rich guy from the big city.) I still had to be careful, however, in sharing any details of my life with the rest of the crew. A lot I had to make up, then remember, so as not to slip-up in a string of lies. But the chief lesson I learned on this voyage was that niggers were not as bad as other whites – even me, too, once -- seemed to think. They were just folks like us, with the same problems and the same glories. All men are born, live for a time, and die. Skin color doesn't make any difference.

We pulled into New Orleans on schedule, and unloaded our crab barrels onto waiting wagons at the docks. The catch was repacked in wooden crates filled with layers of ice to keep the blue crabs fresh. When our work was finally finished, Tall Tom walked us down to the nearest saloon and bought us each a cold bottle of Jax beer (my first taste of suds in over three years, and believe me, it went down like heaven) and then gave us our pay. "You did a real good job for me, Travis," Tall Tom admitted. "You're more than welcome to become a regular on my boat. Leroy and Natty like you too. We go back and forth between here and Port Arthur pretty regular in season. I'll never get rich, but it pays the bills, and it's a good life -- especially being your own boss. What do you say?"

"Skipper…Leroy…Natty…I swear that you guys were some of the best men I ever worked with. I thank you all from deep down and sincerely. But I must move on. I'm going to look now for a bath, a shave, and a haircut, then I'm going to try and find a freighter heading for the Mexican Gulf.

I've got to try my hand again in the oil fields and try and save up a nest egg. Maybe find a nice senorita and get hitched. Maybe even have a few *ninos* of my own! I hope you all understand. So I reckon it's adios now, my friends." I smiled and warmly shook each man's hand, wished everyone good luck, then turned and left the bar.

After getting cleaned up, I used some of the remainder of my pay to buy two new work shirts, two new pairs of socks and a new pair of drawers. Then I went to a Chinese laundry and had my crabbing outfit washed and dried while I waited. I was still fearful of the police, but I felt much more like a free man. Being away from Texas and spending five days at sea helped me clear my mind and refocus my life.

The rusty Mexican freighter I eventually found at the Port of New Orleans cared little for any kind of official documentation such as seaman's papers or a passport. (U.S. Customs and other authorities must have been on 'the take,' because I never saw them; they never inspected the ship- - "El Yucatan" -- or its cargo.) I was just one of twenty-three men from anywhere and nowhere willing to load and unload whatever cargo was being delivered or collected in various ports along the Mexican Gulf Coast. In port, we took on a cargo of cotton, lumber, machine parts, coal, and cinder blocks to be used for building construction. The pay was $1 a day, in Mex pesos, plus my grub. I would have my choice to get off in either Tampico or Veracruz. It looked like my ultimate escape plan would finally be coming true! Soon, I was in Mexican waters. Free at last from the horrors of Huntsville! It was December 25 – Christmas Day – when I made my momentous realization. It truly was a *Feliz Navidad*!

After three more weeks of work and travel -- mostly loading and unloading lots of bananas and mangos -- I wound up getting off in Tampico, and soon found work there as an oil chainman at the Ebano site for a year. I made my way overland the following year to Veracruz, where I also stayed for a year. I worked hard there as a derrickhand in the oil fields at the Poza Rica site. Naturally, by now, I had learned the basics of the Spanish lingo. I saved my money and stayed out of bar fights and avoided any trouble. I dated plenty of fine Mexican ladies too on my time off -- avoiding Mexico's infamous cheap whorehouses and their curse of The Clap. I also remember that year reading in the Mex newspapers about the deaths of the bank-robbing outlaws John Dillinger and Bonnie & Clyde, back in the States.

When 1935 arrived, I heard from the other roughnecks that better money could be earned in the Orinoco Belt oil fields of Venezuela, down in South America. My Spanish was very good at this point, as were my oil field skills, so I felt I confident that I could get a new job there, even as a 'Norte Americano gringo.' This time, I could afford a regular ship's tourist's passage from Veracruz to Caracas. I obtained a phony American passport with yet another alias ("Walter C. Dobbs"), and off I went.

After two years working as a tool pusher -- a top position in the oil field ranks -- outside of Caracas, I was now thirty-three years old. I had found a beautiful Venezuelan wife with long, raven-black hair, Consuela, who was ten years my junior. Together, we had a new baby boy that we named Roberto. The three of us were thriving, and I was very, very happy. We hoped to have more children too.

One day, alone in town, while buying some supplies, I heard an almost forgotten voice behind me say clearly, with menace: "Hey, Oil Wells...I finally caught up with you..."

My mind reeled and my stomach dropped. I automatically balled up both of my fists, and slowly turned around to face my destiny...

But instead of the dreaded Dewey Drummond, I saw that it was my old pal and cellmate, Taters Mitchell! He had fooled me with a convincing imitation of Boss D's voice.

Taters went on to tell me over a glass of beer in a nearby cantina that he had recently finished his sentence and that he had been formally released from Huntsville two months ago.

"I remember you telling me about wanting to go to Tampico and Veracruz, Sonny, so I went there first looking for you. Nobody knew the name Cameron Wells, so I described your features and they said that it sounded like an American guy named Travis, and that he went to Caracas to try his luck in the oil fields there. So here I am," Taters explained. "I wandered around town this whole last week hoping I'd eventually bump into you."

Taters went on to say that Boss D was dead -- "just keeled over from a heart attack last year on The Block...some cons actually applauded" -- and that a bunch of Texas Rangers had searched for me for about six weeks before they gave up on my escape. "They did find Rufus' Ford and his uniform, however, right outside of Houston where you dumped it," he added. "And you might like to know that Boss Lemont was transferred to a different prison too."

I then proceeded to tell Taters every detail of my life from the last four years.

"You could write a whole book on all of those adventures of yours, Sonny," Taters remarked. "Oh, by the way, I visited your family back in Carthage. They are all doing fine. They admitted that they sensed you were still alive somewhere. But they said that you must never go back to Texas or you'll get arrested and sent back to Huntsville. They said if I ever found you, to give you their love. I'm going back to the States anyway, so I'll drop by their place again and tell them you're O.K."

I took Taters to my house to meet my wife and baby son, and he stayed for dinner (*"Voy a tener un poco mas de esas papas por favor, Senora,"* he asked in halting Spanish) and was given a guest bed for the night. I tried the following morning to persuade him to remain in Venezuela, but he had "other big plans...but don't worry -- they are all legal! Plus, I have a nice gal waiting for me back in the U.S." So I gave him $200 in bolivars, plus another $200 of the same for my parents. "You can exchange this for Yankee dollars at any major bank in town," I explained. "And please tell my family that I love them, and that one day, somehow, we'll all meet again."

As we said our final, emotional farewell at the docks later that day, I realized that Taters -- Vernon Mitchell -- had been the best friend I ever had...

THE END

by Jack Karolewski

June 26, 2018

FLORIDA REDEMPTION

It was a cold, snowy, miserable March in 1972. I was attending Northern Illinois University in DeKalb, IL. This college town is located about 65 miles west of Chicago, out among vast flat farmlands. Its historic claim to fame is the patented invention of barbed wire by a local, Joseph Glidden, in 1874. DeKalb is also known for its hybrid corn, whose universally-recognized logo is a golden ear of corn with two flying wings. All I wanted to do that gray and windy day was to fly down to sunny, warm Florida over our two-week Spring Break – specifically to see for myself the supposed non-stop college kid party scene in Ft. Lauderdale. But because I lacked anywhere near the airline fare, my trip would have to consist solely of hitch-hiking. I roughly planned on taking Interstate 65, then I-75, and finally I-95 which hugged Florida's eastern shore. I filled my aluminum-framed green Kelty backpack with assorted cold and warm weather clothes, a towel, some toiletries, a plastic water bottle, a sleeping bag, a few snacks, and some free gasoline station road maps. I had $50 in cash, which my 20-year-old brain thought was enough.

In those days, hitch-hiking was still common, but it was now beginning to wane from its popular heyday during the free-loving Hippy/Flower Power Movement of the late 60's.

Still, I figured it was a safe and reliable mode of transportation for impoverished young students such as myself. What could possibly go wrong?

At the time, I was living in a rented house near campus with five other guys and four gals -- our "Glidden Gang commune", as we liked to call ourselves, because the house was located off of Glidden Avenue. It was a large, two-story white frame house, with five bedrooms and three bathrooms. One of the women, Marty, was in the kitchen doing her rotation of dish-washing. It was just after breakfast. I told her of my travel plan, and that I would try to be back sometime before Easter, which was April 2nd. She wished me a good trip, and said she would let the others know that I had gone South, for everyone else was either out or on their way home for the holiday.

I walked to the main road out of town -- Lincoln Highway -- and put out my thumb. Quickly, I was offered a ride all of the way to Chicago, which I saw as a good omen. I asked to be dropped off near an interstate clover-leaf, and before long I got a lift to I-65 after about an hour freezing by the side of the road. Illinois state troopers didn't bother hassling hitch-hikers as long as you stayed on the entrance ramps. Soon, after a few different rides with mostly families in station wagons, I had completely traversed Indiana, and was now over the border of Kentucky at Louisville. I had to briefly connect to I-64 to merge with I-75 here.

It was getting dark by now, when an old, 2-door dark green Ford Thunderbird pulled up. The driver must have weighed 300 pounds. I smelled that he had been drinking. He was a smoker too. I thought about refusing his ride, but I figured I would take it just a short way to get into better position for a long haul lift which would let me safely fall asleep for the night. The weather was still chilly, but it was getting better. No more snow!

We made the usual small talk, but then he suddenly put his hand on my left leg. This was unexpected and frightening. I quickly moved my leg away. I then asked to be let out at the next interchange. I grabbed my pack, thanked him for the ride and automatically shook his hand, but I really should have skipped that last polite gesture. He looked sad and hurt. Very creepy. I was so relieved to be out of there.

Fortunately, my next ride was just the opposite: a safe, friendly group of five hippies – three gals and two guys -- around my own age in a kind of old camper vehicle, with a mattress set up in back to stretch out on. They had upbeat, popular music on their sound system, and offered me various snacks to eat. I shared some of my food too, and I told them about my previous ride experience. They were sympathetic to my scare. "Always need to be alert when you're on the road," they cautioned. "There are a lot of weirdos out there!" After more conversation, I told them I had to get some sleep, and they were fine with my request. They turned down the music while we drove southeast into the night through Tennessee and Georgia. I had a nightmare about the Louisville man.

When I awoke, we had stopped for gasoline somewhere in Georgia, and my group asked if I could chip in ten dollars for gas. I happily complied. They were going all the way down to Florida too, so I could continue to ride with them. Good luck for me, and a good ten-dollar investment! The weather was continually turning milder, and the sun came out. Its warmth striking my face through the window was an eager tonic.

About two hours later, right outside of Valdosta, GA, huge thunderstorms suddenly erupted. It poured like a monsoon, and traffic on I-75 was surprised by the heavy rain and tried to slow down on the slick and flooded pavement. Then it happened: a chain-reaction car crash! Our driver slammed on the brakes, but it was too late. We were going about 45 m.p.h. then, and we smashed into the car in front of us as several cars in front of us likewise collided into each other. A moment later in our shock, we in turn were rear-ended, and our rear window shattered. Glass shards filled our vehicle interior. The rain storm passed and the sun quickly returned. It was actually hot and humid outside when we climbed out of our wrecked vehicle, shaken but unhurt. The old camper car was totaled. We heard sirens from police cars and ambulances. There were injuries in other cars. I went back to our wreck and grabbed my backpack, which was now bent and torn. My road friends conversed for a few minutes in private, then told me that they would just abandon their vehicle there rather than have to pay for a tow truck, do a police report, etc. They each picked up their belongings and stuck out their thumbs. I did the same, as we said good-bye. I was on my own again.

I eventually got a ride from a middle-aged salesman who wanted to discuss the "generation gap", and why young people were challenging The Establishment, and why we needed to win the Vietnam War. I listened more than talked, as we crossed over into Florida. After the salesman dropped me off, a Florida highway patrolman pulled up and asked to see my identification, how much money I had, what I was doing, where I was going, and so on. I was not long-haired or bearded, but I needed a shave and a shower. He told me that Florida routinely arrested hitch-hikers, but he would let me go if, when he came back in an hour, I was gone. I prayed for a quick ride!

I was picked up by two men in a beat-up, dark 4-door Chevy. They were both sloppily dressed and unshaven and had bad teeth. I got in the back seat with my busted backpack. They said they had to exit off of I-75 for a while. I was starting to get that creepy feeling again in the pit of my stomach as we got on a secondary county road. We exchanged some small talk, then I was alarmed when the man in the driver's seat said, "Show it to him." The man on the front passenger side reached under his seat and pulled out a nickel-plated revolver. He casually pointed it at me. "Don't worry, it ain't loaded...yet," he laughed. The driver laughed too. By now it was getting dark, and we were driving through some swampland, by all my reckoning somewhere in the middle of nowhere. I was completely panicked. I tried to carry on a more normal conversation by changing the subject away from that gun and by trying to keep my voice calm.

The Chevy abruptly pulled over to the side of the road. The two men said, "Wait here," indicating that I should stay in the car. There was nowhere for me to run, so I sat tight. I could hear them whispering to each other and looking over in my direction for a few minutes. One seemed to want to do something, but the other didn't and he seemed to win out. Then they came back to me and announced, "OK, you can get out now, and don't forget to take your pack. We have to turn back, so you'll have to wait here to get another ride. See ya later, buddy!" They got in the car and sped away back in the direction we came from. I was alone in a swampland in the dark, smelling fetid vegetation in the humid, still air, listening to croaking frogs and wondering if alligators attacked lone hitch-hikers in the moonlight...

I was seriously fearful now. What if they came back and killed me? Why was this happening to me? Then I heard a pick-up truck with a bad muffler coming towards me. Would this ride be good or another disaster? The truck slowed down and my heart sank. It was two very drunk teenaged boys on a joyride in the middle of the night. When they got close enough, I could hear their country and western music blaring from their radio. One boy threw an empty beer bottle at my head – just missing me in the inky darkness -- and they both laughed and spun the truck around and peeled out. I was alone again with my fear. I was too shaken up to sleep, so I sat down and ate some food and then hung my head and prayed. There were no more rides until morning. Eventually, a farmer picked me up and got me back to I-75, and another ride took me the rest of the way on I-95 to Ft. Lauderdale.

By this point I was exhausted and starving for a real meal. I had made it to the warmth I had sought and the beaches and the palm trees and the salty Atlantic, but there was no real joy inside. Ft. Lauderdale was swarming with police cars and police patrols, trying to keep the thousands of college kids under control. It was pandemonium! Not what I expected at all. I walked until I found a public restroom off the beach where I gave myself a wash and shampoo in the sink after changing into shorts. Then I spied a Denny's restaurant and had a huge platter of food which somewhat restored my spirits. It was hot and I was already getting sunburned in the tropical sun. My pale winter skin felt flushed, but I wanted to swim in the ocean in my shorts so I did. The water was strangely warm, unlike the cold fresh- water lakes in the Midwest. The beach sands burned my feet and shade was hard to come by. Finally I found a grove of bushes near a smelly public restroom. I climbed a chain-link fence into the grove and hid there until dark. I unrolled my sleeping bag and had yet another fitful sleep that night – especially after I heard policemen walking around nearby, arguing with and threatening small college crowds, actually arresting some for public intoxication.

The next morning I went back to Denny's for breakfast. Stopping first in their bathroom, I was disturbed by my badly sun-burnt face reflection in the mirror. My primary motivation after having gotten all of the way here was now just to get back home. But how? And did I have enough money?

For three more nights I returned to my concealed bush-lair to rest. By now, my severe sunburn was starting to peel, and I badly needed a shave. I tried to stay clean with soap and fresh water. I found a beach rise-off shower down the street and used it each day. During daylight hours, I tried to stay out of the sun as much as possible. I thought about the best options for returning to Illinois. I had about $20 left. I struck up casual conversations with other college students, sharing tips and advice. I met other hitch-hikers my age too, from other parts of the U.S., and we traded road stories. But I avoided the rough-looking, older, homeless lone men who hung around my area. They survived by panhandling, picking useful items out of garbage cans, and looking for edible food refuse in dumpsters behind restaurants when the police were out of sight.

With my facial stubble, peeling skin, and less-than-clean clothes, was I starting to look like them? I used the public restroom near the beach and carefully shaved, using my bar soap and my safety razor. Then I washed my hair in the sink and combed it neatly. It was time to get out of here!

I gathered up my gear and started walking north out of town. After an hour, I stopped at a Union 76 gas station and started asking the customers one-at-a-time for a free ride. No takers. After another hour or so, I was starting to get worried. Would I be stuck here?

It was then that I noticed that a nice, shiny tan Jaguar had been parked under the shade of some trees at the far corner of the gas station lot. There was a man sitting inside, but neither he or his car had moved all during the time I was there. On a whim I slowly walked over. The driver side window was cranked down. The driver was wearing a white, long-sleeved shirt and grey slacks. He had a gold-colored wristwatch and a gold (I presumed) wedding ring. He was fair-haired -- thinning on top -- and looked to be in his mid-30's. He resembled the actor-singer Noel Harrison, son of the famous Rex Harrison.

I shyly greeted the man and asked if he was willing to give me ride north. He said he would like to, but his car was out of gas and he didn't have any cash. He was trying to get to West Palm Beach to close a big real estate deal. He was from London -- his first time in America -- and he had underestimated the amount of dollars that he needed, and although he had some British pounds, no one would accept them. It was Sunday and all the banks were closed until tomorrow. If he could get to a Barclay's bank on Monday morning, he could get a cash wire-transfer from his London home office. Then he extended his hand and said, "By the way, my name's David Clark."

I introduced myself and we both smiled and shook hands. Then he said that he had an idea. If I had some money for gas and for a meal, we could fuel up and drive to

West Palm Beach and wait until the Barclay's opened at 9 a.m. in the morning. Then he would reimburse me my money. At first I was suspicious with his suggestion. I would only get a few miles north at the waste of most of a day. I told David that I needed to get back to Illinois as soon as possible.

"Well, in that case, don't worry. We'll go to the bank first, then I'll drive you to the West Palm Beach Airport and buy you a one-way plane ticket back to Chicago. Now, how's that?", he offered.

This was either the biggest con I ever heard, or the luckiest thing that ever happened to me! It was a huge risk...but I agreed. I took out my $20, and David used half of that for gasoline. The rest we would use for dinner, after which I would likely be broke.

David headed us out on I-95. The Jaguar had leather seats and David was sporting some kind of light cologne. Could I trust him? Would he try to grab my leg like the Louisville man? Could he be some kind of kidnapper or murderer? I forced myself to relax and think more positive thoughts.

We wheeled into West Palm Beach at around 5 p.m. It was time to look for a place to eat. We found a Best Western motel that had an adjacent restaurant. We looked over the menu after being seated. We had to order what we could afford, so we both had club sandwiches, french fries, and iced tea. We talked while eating, he about his family (a wife and two daughters) and their life in London, and I about life at college. He asked about student protests in America and said that similar activities were happening among the young in England. After settling the bill and leaving a tip, we had 58 cents left.

We stopped at a gas station for directions to the bank. When we got to the Barclay's, David parked the car in a far corner of its lot behind the building. Hopefully the police wouldn't notice us and think we were bank robbers. Then, both being exhausted, we each tilted our bucket seats backward and tried to sleep. At first, this was rather awkward -- two adult men, largely strangers, basically sleeping next to each other. But soon sleep took over.

We woke with the dawn, sore-muscled and stiff. We got out and stretched. I had noticed a Dunkin' Donut shop a few blocks away on our drive in the previous evening, so I told David to wait with the car while I discovered what 58 cents would get us. I returned about 45 minutes later with one frosted donut and a medium cup of coffee with cream and sugar. We split this meager breakfast while waiting for the bank to open.

At 9 a.m. sharp, David grabbed his briefcase and entered the bank while I waited outside by the car. It was already starting to get hot and humid. After about 30 minutes, David came out with a big grin, waving a small wad of greenbacks gleefully. "Next stop," he triumphantly proclaimed, "the airport!" He told me that after giving me my ticket and dropping me off, he would find the closest motel to shower and change clothes before heading on to lunch and his real estate appointment.

We went into the airport lobby together and walked up to the Eastern Airlines ticket counter. The next available flight to Chicago was the following morning at 9:30 a.m. David paid cash for my ticket, then turned and handed it to me, put out his hand and said, "Good luck, Jack, and thanks" as he hurried out the door. Still in a state of disbelief at my incredible good fortune, I weakly asked ticket agent, "Are you sure this is a real ticket?" She laughed and said yes it was.

I had a day and a night to kill, and the wolf of hunger set itself upon me. I had a pauper's 8 cents to my name. I noticed that there was a restaurant located in the far corner of the airport lobby. I walked over with my broken and torn backpack. I asked the waitress quietly if I could wash dishes or do anything else in exchange for a meal. She called for the manager, who was also the owner. His name was Charlie. I told him my story. He looked me hard in the eyes for a long moment. "OK," he said, I'll give you a chance. Order what you want off the menu, eat up, and then we'll see what kind of jobs we can find for you around here."

I quickly ordered a large bowl of chili with crackers and a large, fresh-squeezed glass of Florida orange juice. When the waitress, Elaine (who was also Charlie's wife) saw that I was still hungry, she added a large slice of peach pie and some chocolate chip cookies to my feast with a smile.

Charlie basically serviced all of the big airliners that landed and took off here, between running his restaurant. He stocked the planes with pre-made meals and beverages from another nearby facility, and also cleaned out the toilets and trash on each plane. These would be my duties for the day, because his normal helper had called in sick at the last minute. Charlie drove a specialized truck that lifted itself upward so as to be level with the back service doors of each aircraft. The truck was fitted with racks, carts, and shelves to hold our supplies. The job had to be done fast -- about 20 minutes per plane -- while the newly landed aircraft was being fueled for its next flight. Sometimes the planes came in one right after the other. Other times, Charlie and I rested for a half hour or so, and drank frosty cans of soda to rehydrate ourselves in the steamy heat, and munched candy bars while we talked about this and that. I could tell he liked me, and he said I was a good worker.

When day was done, I was awarded a free dinner, so after cleaning up, I sat down at the counter and chose fried chicken, mashed potatoes, salad with Thousand Island dressing, rolls & butter, iced tea, and butter pecan ice cream. I was stuffed but satisfied as I chatted with Elaine. She said I could later unroll my sleeping bag in the back stock room and bed down there for the night. Then she and Charlie turned out the lights, locked up, and went home. I was really pooped and fell right asleep.

Morning came fast, bright and sunny. Elaine and Charlie came in to get the breakfast shift up and running with their black fry cook, Johnny. He smiled at me and said, "You look like a scrambled eggs and bacon kind of boy. How 'bout it?" I got a big platter of just that , with hash browns and toast with grape jelly and a large orange juice.

My 9:30 a.m. flight was almost ready to go, so it was time for good-byes. Charlie and Elaine both shook my hand and wished me a great life. Then Charlie opened his wallet and gave me $15. "I know our agreement was just for meals, but you worked so hard that I feel you earned this too," he said and smiled. Johnny waved so long from his cook's station. Elaine gave me a hug, and said I reminded her of their son when he was my age. He had been killed in Vietnam three years earlier.

When my Eastern Airlines flight landed at O'Hare, the weather in Chicago was about twenty degrees warmer, and all the snow had turned to slush. I had been gone for ten days. It was March 29th. I took a series of city buses to the Loop downtown, then headed over to the Greyhound bus station. I bought a ticket for DeKalb. Almost home! I slept on the bus.

When I walked in the door of the Glidden House, everyone was still gone except Marty, who ironically was washing dishes yet again. She welcomed me home with a big hug, asked me how the trip went, and remarked at my red sun-burned face. I recounted my adventures for about twenty minutes.Then she offered to sew the large rip in my backpack after I straightened its bent aluminum frame.

I took a long, hot shower and changed clothes. Then I sat down and wrote a letter to Charlie and Elaine, thanking them again and telling them I got home safely.

And that was the last time I ever hitch-hiked...

The End

by Jack Karolewski

12/10/14

HOUSE OF HORRORS

In 1953, Maxwell was an all-American kind of small town in Nebraska. It was built on the Union Pacific rail line in 1908 about a mile north of the Platte River, and had 2514 residents. Located in central Lincoln County, Maxwell was eleven miles east from the county seat of North Platte (population 15,523), and nine miles west from the next closest town, Brady.

Maxwell had a small K-8 school, a post office, a filling station/car repair, a cozy diner, a library, a one-man police station, a volunteer fire brigade, an evangelical Christian church, a simple food market, and a modest weekly newspaper – The Chronicle. There were a half-dozen empty stores on Main Street, yearning for businesses to set up shop. Most folks drove the eleven miles to North Platte to purchase clothing or furniture or hardware or to see a movie.

Perry Duncan was nine years old, the youngest of three brothers. His older siblings were named Terry and Jerry, so the unofficial town jest was to mix up the boy's names, especially at school. Perry's mom, Mary, was a housewife, and his dad, Fred, sold ranching equipment in North Platte. The Duncan family also had a collie named Larry.

It was early October, that golden month when the weather was still favorable before the brutal harshness of a Nebraska winter settled in like an iron claw. Wary local cattle ranchers were always prepared even at this time of year, however, because winds in this state could swing temperatures wildly up or down, even day-to-day, depending on their direction of origin. Ranching was a fickle business, but not as risky as farming, due to the irregular annual rains on the Great Plains.

Because his brothers were several years older than him, Perry often found himself either exploring his surroundings alone or with his best school friend, Matthew. Lately – although his mom discouraged him repeatedly – Perry liked to visit the scariest place in town, an old, two-story, abandoned house on Plumer Street. Rumors around town said the house was haunted, so naturally it was a magnet for curious youngsters.

The Plumer House was at the end of a long gravel driveway, the road lined with living and dead gnarled trees. One afternoon after school, Perry rode his bike there from his house. The house had peeling, faded grey paint. Several windows were broken, and the porch was collapsing. Its red brick chimney was likewise crumbling onto its dilapidated roof. The doors were padlocked, with a large DANGER – DO

NOT ENTER sign out front. But Perry already knew how to sneak in the back kitchen window.

Once inside, the pungent smell of the house was disgusting -- a mixture of dirt, dust, and pellet turds from various small mammals. Busted glass shards littered the floor, along with torn, ancient newspapers and magazines. Ripped curtains covered some of the windows. Broken chairs and distressed tables were strewn here and there. Upstairs, a teen 'make-out' den was artlessly arranged for amorous couples -- consisting of a dirty bare mattress on the plain wooden floor, some old pillows tossed on a torn green couch with some dark springs sticking up through its upholstery, and a solitary soiled blanket. Empty beer and soda bottles lay scattered about, along with discarded snack food wrappers, cigarette butts, a candle with a pack of matches, and a well-thumbed nudie magazine. But Perry didn't trust the rickety stairs, so he usually confined his explorations to the ground floor.

He found some Life and Saturday Evening Post magazines and casually flipped through them in the dim light, focusing on pictures advertising the new 1954 cars. Perry heard the wind moaning through the broken window panes, and knew he would never visit here at night, even on a dare! And Halloween (coming up soon) was absolutely out of the question, though his brothers Terry and Jerry bragged that they had once spent a midnight hour here. Were there really ghosts in this place? Perry wondered. It was certainly creepy enough to house more than a few.

On Saturday, Perry invited his best friend Matthew to accompany him on a visit to old man Vickers's house. Clem Vickers was a widower and the town's oldest man at age 89. He had been in the merchant marine, and had traveled to many exotic foreign ports. How he wound up in Nebraska, thousands of miles from any ocean, was a bafflement. His favorite hobby was whittling and carving, using various-sized knives. His specialty was making a linked chain out of a single block of wood. If asked, he would recount his memories of such famous events as learning about the Wright Brothers first flight, or about the sinking of the Titanic, or of the Great Flu Epidemic of 1919, which took the lives of millions worldwide, including his brother, Alfred. But today, Perry wanted to know all about the Plumer House. Clem was on his porch in his rocking chair, whittling as usual.

"Were you here when people still lived in the old Plumer House?" Perry began. Matthew likewise perked up his ears.

Mr. Vickers put his knife aside, pondered the sky a moment, then responded. "Well, Perry, six different families lived there long ago in the years before you were born.

I think the house was built sometime in the late 1880s. Legend has it that some kind of witch came to town and moved in and started luring children inside and wound up murdering three of them. She also killed two infants in the same house after kidnapping them. That was about fifteen years ago, just before World War Two, I think. The witch woman disappeared or died or moved away, nobody can say for sure. She was never caught, and the bodies of those poor innocent children were never found. As the years went by, folks once again moved back in the house, unaware that such killings had occurred. That's when the stories about haunted night time events began to run wild. Night wails and cries of tortured infants. Thudding sounds. Flickering light bulbs. Stomping on stairs. Rumors of secret passageways. The ghost of a silent woman in a rocking chair holding a dead baby. Naturally, the families moved out, and the house fell into disrepair. Nobody has lived there since The War ended."

Clem paused to clear his throat and spit a gob off his porch railing onto his lawn. "If you want to know more, boys, go see Miss Fischer at the library. She probably has old copies of the Chronicle for you to look at. I recall that no photo was ever taken of the witch woman, so we don't know exactly what she looked like. But it is said that she always wore a black shawl whenever she ventured out of the house. Well, boys, I hope this stuff won't keep you up tonight and give you any nightmares! I'll catch the dickens from your folks if it does." Mr. Vickers picked up his whittling knife again. He was currently carving the antlers on a small buck deer, his hands still remarkably steady for his age. "Next time, I'll show you boys the secret trick to putting a model ship in a bottle. Oh, one more thing...they say that every criminal feels compelled to return to the scene of the crime one last time, so keep a sharp eye peeled," he nodded sagely. "Y'all run along now."

Perry and Matthew popped on their bikes and quickly pedaled to Maxwell's modest public library. Miss Fisher smiled as the boy's walked in. "Well, if it isn't my two explorers, Daniel Boone and Davy Crockett," she quipped. She stopped her book processing and let her silver eyeglasses drop down so that they hung on the thin metal chain around her neck. Her white hair was pulled back into a tight bun. Nobody seemed remember a time when she had not been town librarian. When once asked casually why she had never married, Miss Fischer smiled and had cleverly answered, waving her hand expansively towards the tall stacks of library bookshelves, "Look around...I DID get married...and these are ALL my children!" Now, she looked at the boys and asked, "What's it to be today, gentlemen? More Jules Verne? The Adventures of Tarzan? Or perhaps you'd like to read about rocket ships to Mars?"

"None of those...thanks, Miss Fischer," Matthew replied. "Perry wants to know more about the haunted Plumer House. Mr. Vickers said you might have some old newspapers about the murders. I want to know too."

"Hmm...crime is really the department of Officer Merrill, you know," Miss Fischer offered. Mike Merrill was the town's only policeman. He was on duty in Maxwell six days a week. One day a week on rotation he went to Brady, because that neighboring town of 203 people was too small to have its own full-time lawman. (Perry had a running gag going with Officer Merrill: every time he encountered the policeman, he always asked the same question – "Did you catch any bank robbers today, Officer Merrill?" The answer from the lawman was always, "Nope, not today." Then they would both laugh, because there was no bank in Maxwell! The closest bank was in North Platte.)

"But let's go in the basement and see what we can dig up," Miss Fischer directed.

Down the stairs the trio went. The library basement was rich with the musty smell of old books in storage. It was also where the town archives was kept. Miss Fischer opened a flat, black file cabinet tray. "Here...let's look back about fifteen years in the Chronicle." She leafed through several back issues, circa 1938. "O.K. Here we go...I hope you are both mature enough to handle this material."

Together they read under a single high-intensity lamp. They learned that indeed three children and two infants had been killed there, as well as one adult. Motive unknown, disappearances/murders never solved, bodies never found. A strange woman wearing a black shawl was reported living in the Plumer House. Next, the trio examined newspapers up through the years: 1942 – A nine-year old boy, supposedly fleeing the house in fright, fell down the stairs and broke his neck, dying instantly; 1944 – A woman cradling a dead infant is found sitting in a rocking chair alone in the house, and is committed to the state mental institution in Lincoln; 1948 – A 12-year old boy is found dead, hung from a ceiling light fixture in the front parlor of the now abandoned house. And more: strange sightings reported of floating lit lightbulbs in the house at night, terrifying midnight screams, eerie supposed ghost encounters, even dogs afraid to approach the building -- night or day. When they were finished, the trio looked at each other, their faces partly obscured in shadows where the lamplight missed them. "Awful...just awful," Miss Fischer sighed, getting up and placing the newspaper stack slowly back into its flat black file cabinet tray. "We're done here, boys. Let's go back up. That's all we have. Enough dark thoughts for today." They ascended the library basement stairs and returned to the front circulation desk by the main entrance. After thanking Miss Fischer, the boys rode home, splitting off when they came to their own houses.

The next day was Sunday, so Perry dressed up and went with his family to worship. About 300 of Maxwell's residents were there at the local evangelical church, including Perry's fourth-grade teacher Mrs. Jeffers, whereas other Maxwellians attended different churches in North Platte.

The minister at The House of the Risen Lord was the Reverend Malcolm Beck. He was in his late 40s, tall and imposing, with piercing black eyes and a swept-back mane of salt and pepper hair. He had been a widower since arriving in Maxwell five years ago from Montana. Today's special announcement at the beginning of the worship service was the surprise introduction of his new bride to the congregation. Her name was Lilith. She was plain-looking and somewhat shy, also in her late 40s, and she hailed from Massachusetts. The minister asked that the community help make her feel welcomed. The reverend then grabbed his Bible and began his service with relish after the rousing opening hymns were completed. Mary and Fred Duncan both liked the preacher because they felt that he helped put the fear of God in their three growing boys with his imaginative, fiery sermons.

Monday after school, Perry ran into Officer Merrill as he was getting into his patrol car. "Did you catch any bank robbers today, Officer Merrill?" Perry asked innocently. "Nope, not today," the policeman responded, likewise straight-faced. Then they both started smiling. "Hey, Perry, did you hear about the new store opening on Main Street? It's an antique shop. Lots of interesting old stuff in there. You should have a look. The owner is a lady named Mrs. Magillacutty. She just moved into town over the weekend. I think she came from Kansas. Well, I'm off to make my rounds. Stay out of trouble. And good luck with your homework. I hear Mrs. Jeffers can really pile it on, but it's for your own good. See you later!"

Because he was close to Main Street and wasn't overly anxious to tackle his latest math assignment just yet, Perry decided to stop in the new antique shop and browse a bit. The new store name stenciled on its front window in fancy lettering said: Past Times.

Mrs. Magillacutty came out from somewhere in the back of the store once Perry entered. She was holding an old-fashioned candlestick telephone. From afar, she was ordinary-looking and modestly dressed, the kind of woman that could blend into a crowd such as you would never notice or remember her.

Her voice was cool and appraising as she approached. "Can I help you, young man?" she inquired. Perry found himself staring at her eyes and her face. Although he couldn't put his finger on it, she made him distinctly uncomfortable. She seemed to look into his deepest soul and was maybe even taking notes. Perry was the only other person in the shop. "No, thank you. I'm just looking," he replied. His eyes saw, over her shoulder, shelves full of bric a brac. He also spied an Edison phonograph with its large listening horn, displays of antique toys and glass bottles, some heirloom furniture, several stacks of old books and magazines, and more.

"Halloween is just around the corner, so maybe a book about ghosts and goblins?" Mrs. Magillacutty suggested. "Or how about a book on witchcraft and magic spells?" She arched her left eyebrow, ever so slightly.

"Sorry, but my folks would get very upset if I ever brought home anything like that," Perry replied, somewhat nervously. "They are very religious and read the Bible a lot... Well, I got to be going. Thanks anyway."

That night, over dinner with his family -- macaroni and cheese, baked ham, salad, and cherry Jell-o with fruit cocktail in it -- Perry kept mum about his encounter at Past Times with its owner. But the next day at school, he told Matthew all about it during recess. "She gave me the creeps," he confessed. "I'm never going back in that store. And you should stay away too."

Five days later, a Maxwell child went missing. Eight-year old Jessica Perkins was last seen playing alone in her backyard. When her mother called her in to dinner, she was gone. Officer Merrill was immediately alerted. The town was thoroughly searched, and frantic phone calls were made, but little Jessica was nowhere to be found. Merrill then searched neighboring Brady without any luck, so he next notified the police in North Platte. They, in turn, also notified the Nebraska Highway Patrol. The local Maxwellians were in a panic, and naturally the Perkins family was devastated as the days dragged on with nothing new to report.

A week after Jessica disappeared, none of the frightened townsfolk allowed their children to play outdoors after dark. On that particular day, Perry and Matthew had a half-hour left before the sun set and dinner would be ready at their homes. They decided on a lark to visit the Plumer House again, having grown restless after playing catch for an hour. That old place was never boring for them.

The boys crawled in the back kitchen window, as always. But this time, they noticed a strange smell. Probably a dead raccoon or opossum, they figured. They looked around both downstairs and up, but found nothing new.

Matthew then suggested they look in the crawlspace under the house. As they approached, the smell grew more intense. They both noticed that some of the dirt there seemed recently disturbed, so they found some broken pieces of wood to dig with and began excavating, to satisfy their boyish curiosities.

Perry was the first to find a small, somewhat discolored human hand. Its tiny fingernails had traces of chipped pink nail polish. The hand was connected to an arm, and then, assuredly, to an entire dead body, the boys realized. Now terrified and nauseated, they boys dropped their digging implements and fled the crawlspace. They rapidly biked to Officer Merrill's office. It was closed, and it was getting dark fast as cold autumn winds whipped up, swirling the season's last fallen leaves. Rather than go home, however, the boys went directly to the policeman's house. The lawman was relaxing out of uniform, and getting ready to sit down and eat dinner with his family.

After getting all the details from a frightened Perry and Matthew, Merrill told the boys to go right home as he strapped on his revolver belt and grabbed his jacket and Stetson, along with a large flashlight. As the boys jumped on their bikes, the policeman stepped into his patrol car and sped away.

A sizeable crowd of sympathetic townspeople attended little Jessica's funeral two days later at The House of the Risen Lord. The girl's casket was closed. Her parents sat in stunned disbelief as the Reverend Mr. Beck intoned the eulogy, his wife Lilith sitting beside him, dressed somberly in black. Jessica Perkins was in a better place, the minister assured his congregation, for she was now in the eternal bosom of Jesus. The whole Duncan family was there, and Perry also noticed that old man Vickers and Miss Fischer were there too, but he saw no trace of Mrs. Magillacutty. And oddly, a mysterious woman had also attended the memorial service, yet no one knew who she was. When the Perkins' were later asked if the woman was a distant relative, they admitted they had never even seen her before. The Reverend Mr. Beck was similarly baffled.

According to the Lincoln County coroner, the Perkins girl had been murdered by having her throat slit. Forensics at the crime scene were still ongoing but were inconclusive at this point. The Chronicle ran extra editions for several successive days, because the public couldn't wait week to week for news updates on the vicious, shocking crime that rocked the community. Some residents even demanded that the old Plumer House be torn down.

At school, the boys were rather famous for having discovered the corpse, and they were repeatedly asked by their classmates for the step-by-step details of what it was like to find a genuine dead body of someone everyone knew. Yet like most sensations, life gradually resumed its routine as the initial rush of publicity tapered off. Meanwhile, Halloween came and went. It was a bust, because traditional trick or treating was cancelled due to safety concerns. The school, however, provided cake and ice cream, and the kids could wear their costumes in class for the afternoon party. But nobody wanted to be cheerful. Nobody was in the mood to be scared, even for pretend.

Another month went by without the authorities finding Jessica Perkins' killer. A week after Thanksgiving, the weather in Maxwell got really frigid, with snow and brutal winds coming from the north, and plunging temperatures. Winter was coming in early.

That was when Matthew disappeared.

He had been shoveling snow on a gloomy, grey day for an elderly neighbor down his street. Just before 11:00 a.m., when that same neighbor yelled out the front door with an offer of a break for some hot chocolate, Matthew didn't answer and seemed to have vanished. His snow shovel had been left stuck upright in a snow pile. Soon, Officer Merrill was at the scene, a sickening, familiar feeling of dread in his stomach. As it had some six weeks earlier, word rapidly spread through the town after Matthew's family was notified. When Perry found out the horrible news that evening, he locked himself in his room and repeatedly punched his bed pillow in frustration, his face red and his eyes watery. His brothers, Terry and Jerry, eventually calmed him down. Then his parents tried to reassure him that his best friend would probably be found safe -- somewhere and soon.

But nothing positive happened, even after 72 hours. Matthew was still missing. The entire town of Maxwell was on edge. His family was understandably in shock, and feeling helpless. Naturally, Officer Merrill checked the Plumer House thoroughly as part of his investigation in searching the town, but the derelict structure offered no clues. Meanwhile, Matthew and Perry's teacher, Mrs. Jeffers, even called in sick one day because she was so upset.

It was then that Perry had the awful feeling that Matthew was dead and buried under the Plumer House, just like Jessica Perkins, and that somehow Officer Merrill had missed something. Perry even had a vivid and disturbing nightmare about finding his friend's corpse, with Matthew's eyes still open in death. He decided that he would sneak out of his house the following night and try and find out the truth. He knew he would surely get a punishment beating from his father later -- because his parents had expressly forbidden him to ever enter the Plumer House again -- but he had to do everything he could for his best friend, no matter what.

The next night, Perry put on his boots, then bundled up with his thick winter coat, his red wool hat with earflaps, and his scarf and mittens. He had also remembered to bring his trusty Boy Scout flashlight with him. It was about 1:20 a.m., according to the clock on the living room fireplace mantle. Larry, the family collie, woke up and thought that Perry was going to take him outside for a non-routine walk, but the boy pushed the dog back away from the door. "No, Larry, not now. Go back to bed...be a good boy," he whispered. Perry then carefully tiptoed out the back door without getting caught.

The skies were clear and the moon was full in the bitter, crisp night air. Perry decided to walk because getting his bike out might make too much noise. It took about fifteen minutes to get to the gravel road at the end of Plumer Street, then another five to get to the abandoned house, down its lane of dead and dormant trees. Perry's breath made huge huffs of steam as he trudged through unshoveled snow and piercing west winds. His exposed nose and cheeks were stinging and red, and his nose was runny.

Using his flashlight, he awkwardly climbed in the usual back window by the kitchen. Because of the Plumer House's many broken windows, the inside of the house was still cold, but blessedly not very windy. Perry scanned the downstairs area first with his flashlight, then chanced the rickety stairs leading precariously up to the second floor. He got halfway up when he heard a sound like someone running in the snow outside the house! He slowly descended and retraced his steps and went to the nearest main floor dirty window – a rare one because all of its glass was still intact.

The wind moaned like a banshee as Perry swept his flashlight beam back and forth and approached the window. He could see shadows of tree branches, cast by the full moon. Suddenly, for just a split second, he saw a woman's face staring at him mere inches away from the other side of the window outside! Her eyes glared at him in hatred and evil. She was wearing a black shawl, which covered most of her head. Perry was startled and dropped his flashlight. Then the mystery woman disappeared. Perry picked up his flashlight again and pointed it out the window. Peering through the grime on the glass, he saw that no one was there. But there was a clear trail of strange footprints in the snow. He knew that the face had not been his imagination. Yet it all happened so fast that he couldn't tell if he had ever seen the woman before or not. Her eyes, though, he could never forget...

The boy thought about running home then and there, but something compelled him to finish his search upstairs first. When he got to the second floor, he saw some recently used food dishes near the soiled mattress on the floor. No mice or rats had disturbed the remains yet. Perry then tripped on a loose floorboard and made a loud crash as he fell, knocking over some empty beer bottles casually stacked on an old cardboard box. After he got back on his feet, he heard a muffled noise coming from behind a closed closet door. Next, he heard a kicking sound. He cautiously went over to the door and shined his flashlight upon it. Then he opened it. Matthew was inside! His hands and feet were tied with hemp rope and his mouth was gagged with a ragged cloth. He was wearing blindfold too. He was alive but weak, his body loosely covered by an old blanket. Propping his flashlight against the door on an angle for light, Perry carefully removed his friend's blindfold. Matthew's eyes appeared bloodshot, as he looked at Perry first in surprise, then quickly in recognition, and finally in sheer relief. Perry next removed Matthew's gag. "Get me out of here," Matthew begged with hoarse voice. Then he started to cry.

Perry quickly untied the ropes binding his friend, then helped him to his feet, which were unsteady. "Let's get to the first house we see and have them call Officer Merrill," he offered. "I'll help you walk."

The boys climbed slowly out the old kitchen window. Perry saw no trace of the horrifying woman in the black shawl, so they moved as quickly as Matthew could walk through the snow and cold, the tattered blanket his only protection from the biting winds.

When the gravel driveway ended, they were at the far end of Plumer Street where the regular row of homes were. They banged on the first front door they saw, while repeatedly ringing the doorbell and yelling, "HELP! HELP!" Mr. and Mrs. Ramsey soon answered the door in their bathrobes and got the boys safely inside. They immediately called the police and both boys' parents. All five additional adults arrived within minutes.

Over mugs of hot milk with Ovaltine and some pound cake, an exhausted Matthew told Officer Merrill and the others everything he could remember about his terrifying abduction and captivity.

"I was shoveling snow when something hit me over the head. The next thing I knew, I was tied up and blindfolded and gagged and stuck in the back seat of a car. I heard a woman's voice. She was humming some kind of chant. Then I heard crazy words like: Lucifer, I give you my soul...Only the Devil will triumph...The Prince of Darkness must have fresh blood... Weird stuff like that. We would drive for a long time, then stop at what sounded like abandoned houses out in the country. She un-gagged me only when she fed me bread and some pieces of baloney and gave me water to drink. She unbuckled my pants and dropped them when I needed to pee. Then I would sleep. We did this for a few days, until Perry rescued me. I was sure she was going to kill me soon. But I never saw her face." Matthew stopped and began to cry as his mother rushed forward to comfort him. Perry then relayed his part in the rescue, including his seeing the woman's face in the window and her footprints in the snow. Officer Merrill soon realized that the day when he had searched the Plumer House immediately after Matthew's disappearance and had found nothing, it was because the boy was actually being held by his abductor at a different abandoned location.

Matthew was taken to the hospital in North Platte for examination and observation. Other than exhaustion and shock and a touch of malnutrition, he would be O.K. again with plenty of food and bed rest. He was released and went home after two days, much to the relief of his family and the rest of the town of Maxwell, not to mention the Duncans. Matthew later thanked Perry profusely for saving his life, and gave him his favorite pocket knife as a sign of everlasting friendship.

Eight days later, Perry was asked by Officer Merrill to come by the police station afterschool. "I already told your parents. I need you to identify a suspect for me. I think I have the woman who kidnapped Matthew."

Perry was very nervous as he entered Merrill's office. Sure enough, there was a woman there in handcuffs, but her back was to Perry so he couldn't see her face.

Officer Merrill angrily turned the shackled culprit around. "Alright, Perry, take a good look. Was this the face you saw in the window at the Plumer House that night?"

Perry was shocked to see Lilith Beck, the minister's new wife, looking blandly back at him.

"Ah...ummm...I'm not positive, Officer Merrill...it all happened so fast..."Perry was hesitant.

"That's O.K., take your time. Take another look, Perry. I have to know," the lawman said calmly.

Lilith Beck was stock still, staring at the boy.

"How about now, Perry?" the policeman asked. He quickly produced a black shawl and wrapped it over Lilith's hair. "I found this in her car trunk."

The shawl had the instant effect of changing the woman's facial features into those of a deranged monster.

Her contorted eyes became filled with pure hatred and evil. Just like that freezing night at the window at the Plumer House...those eyes!

Perry was stunned at the transformation. "It's the woman!" he gasped. The boy instantly recoiled and instinctively tried to run away, but Officer Merrill quickly grabbed his arm. "You're safe here with me, son, don't worry...I didn't catch a bank robber today, but you helped me catch a killer." Perry began to relax a bit when Merrill pressed his shoulder in a fatherly manner.

Lilith Beck suddenly screamed, "Satan...save me!" But Merrill dragged the handcuffed suspect and locked her in the only jail cell in the station. She moaned and chanted a few unintelligible phrases, then fell silent. Perry was thanked and sent home. Mike Merrill quickly got on the phone to the District Attorney's Office at the state capitol in Lincoln...

****

In the weeks to come, Lilith Beck -- under rigorous cross-examination and psychiatric examination by experts from the state of Nebraska -- confessed to the five murders going back to the Plumer House in 1938, and to the killing of Jessica Perkins, and to one recent kidnapping with the intent of murder. But she denied ever killing an adult, so that case remained unsolved. She had fled Nebraska in 1940 for Salem, Massachusetts. She met and later married the Reverend Malcolm Beck while he was attending a national church conference last year in Salem on the modern dangers of witchcraft.

As for further evidence of her more recent crimes, Matthew definitively identified a tape recording of Lilith's voice as his abductor, and her shoes matched the footprints in the snow that Perry had noted. She had lied to her minister-husband about her absence when she had killed and buried Jessica Perkins, saying that she was visiting some sickly out-of-town relatives overnight. The same excuse was made to explain her days missing during the Matthew kidnapping incident. After his wife was convicted, her husband divorced her. The Reverend Mr. Beck later left town and his ministry after suffering a nervous breakdown.

Lilith Beck was judged criminally insane and sentenced to life without parole in early 1954. She was spared from the electric chair, but the state's worst mass-murderer, Charles Starkweather, who killed eleven people over a two-month spree, was given the chair in 1959 at age 20. Beck died in the Nebraska Women's Correctional Facility near York in 1972. She was 66 years old.

So what became of the House of Horrors at the end of Plumer Street?

Neither the town of Maxwell nor Lincoln County could ever appropriate enough funds for its demolition and removal. A person or persons unknown tried to burn it down with kerosene one night in 1961, but the volunteer fire department quickly put the blaze out before it did much damage. For years, it was infamously considered one of the most haunted houses in all of Nebraska. The Plumer House still stands, though continually rotting and collapsing, surrounded by a chain link fence that a sympathetic contractor in North Platte donated. Thus, anyone can see it even today, but no one can ever enter it again...

THE END

by Jack Karolewski

November 28, 2017

KILLING KIM

The bedside alarm went off at 7:00 a.m.

James Bond was not by nature an early riser, but he had a 10:00 a.m. appointment with M, so he knew he needed to be extra alert. Bond had been on a two-week leave to rest after concluding some nasty business near the Syrian border. He quickly climbed into his sweats and trainers and went out for a vigorous hour jog. The day was overcast, but for late September, the temperature was still comfortable.

Bond lived in an attractive Regency-style neighborhood in the Notting Hill area of London these past four years, at #1 Stanley Gardens, W11, 2ND. His second floor flat balcony faced west onto Stanley Crescent. He chose it because it was only five miles from MI6 headquarters – a short ten-minute drive in good traffic – and because any bright rising sun in the morning would not disturb his sleep.

At the end of his run, Bond stopped at the Farm Girl café, which was just a block from his flat. Run by a chipper young couple from Australia, it served breakfast all day. He ordered three scrambled eggs, Greek yogurt, and a large black coffee to take away. As usual, both the wait staff and clientele were twenty-something Millennials, with their colored hair, facial piercings, and tattoos. The food was all 'organic' this and 'naturally sustained' that, but it was always tasty. On other days if he had more time, Bond would walk to Portobello Market down the street and buy his own groceries and cook for himself. Or more commonly, have his latest girlfriend cook for him.

Being a bachelor, James Bond was not concerned with decorating his flat in any harmonic manner. The few artworks he had acquired (mostly framed prints of historic sailing ships) were still resting on the hardwood floors against the walls. Furniture was sparse, and used laundry was in a casual pile in one corner of the bedroom, to be sent out. The dishwasher was full. Books rested in a stack near the sofa. He had a laptop computer and a mobile, but Bond didn't own a television. Once a month, when he was not on assignment abroad, he had a regular housecleaner come and tidy up.

Bond hungrily ate his take-away, took first a quick steaming hot then a longer icy cold shower, shaved, carefully applied a nicotine patch to his left upper arm, and dressed in a dark tan suit with cream shirt, black knit silk tie, and black oxfords. He glanced at his copy of The Times – endless problems and strife worldwide – and fleetingly wondered how much longer the planet could keep going like this.

At least he could depend on his company car, a beloved magnetic silver Aston Martin DB11. The V-8 engine roared to life, then purred contentedly as he headed to Vauxhall. MI6 headquarters – dubbed Babylon on the Thames or even Legoland by cheeky staff members because of its rather peculiar architecture – soon loomed ahead. Bond eased his car into the company underground parking garage, then took the lift up to his office. After checking his phone messages and reading some inter-office memos, Bond walked down the hall towards M's office. It was 9:55 a.m. when he saw Ms. Moneypenny.

"Good Morning, James. How have you been? Did you enjoy your break?" Moneypenny was 27 years old, a Jamaican with a pearly smile, cocoa eyes, and flawless café au lait skin. She'll make some lucky bloke very happy someday, Bond mused.

"I'm glad to be out of that Syrian mess alive, Penny, and yes, I had a pleasant leave, thank you." Bond replied. What made Moneypenny especially exciting was not just her beauty, but her calm intelligence. Professionalism, however, precluded anything beyond mutual admiration and the business at hand.

"He's ready for you now, so you can go right in," she indicated, as the room's clock chimed the hour. The sound of Big Ben echoed similarly outside in the distance.

M was busy reading a thick file when Bond walked in. The Section Chief removed his eyeglasses and motioned Bond to the chair opposite the large mahogany desk. "Have a seat, 007. Nice job there in Syria. Your action saved the lives of several of our undercover agents. Feel rested and fit?" M's real name was Ajit Thakur, from Mumbai, age 47, married, with three sons. He had been Section Chief for five years now. As Bond had heard it, the name 'Ajit' meant 'invincible.'

"Thank you, Sir. I believe I am ready for my next assignment."

"Good. I understand that you have given up your smoking habit. How is that going? I believe you were up to three packs a day until last month."

"Frankly, Sir, the craving is still there, but my Section Physician Dr. Hawley has me on the patch and on nicotine chewing gum. Both are very helpful. I believe I'm getting better every day." Bond had smoked a special Turkish blend of Morlands, with its three gold bands, for many years. Now at age 38, they were starting to hurt his endurance, so Bond was determined to quit.

"What about drink, James? What did Hawley say about that?"

Bond was embarrassed by M's directness, but answered with honesty. "I have cut back, Sir. Probably half of what it once was."

"Sorry to put you on the spot, 007, but I wanted to hear it from you. As you know, you are one of only three agents in this department that are licensed to kill. You are also the oldest. Most 'double 0' men here quit by the time they hit 35. Just burn out, living on the edge 24/7, so to speak. The muscle reflexes go, the eyes lose their 20/20, it's only natural. It's a hard, hazardous, and lonely life, I don't have to tell you. So I need to know if my top man is still up to par, especially with possibly the most important job of your career before us now."

M paused and moved through his stack of files. "I just got off the phone with the Foreign Secretary, who was in touch with the Russians, the Americans, and the Chinese. The current situation with Kim Jong-Un and his nuclear threats is increasingly alarming and unacceptable. Putin, Trump, and Xi Jinping are all on board with having Kim removed with extreme prejudice. The three major powers claim they cannot get directly involved due to political constraints. That leaves us. They have offered to share intelligence, then look the other way. Her Majesty's government has directly authorized us to kill Kim Jong-Un. What do you think, James? You don't happen to speak any Korean, do you?"

"No, Sir – just French, German, Spanish, and Russian. But if you could specifically tell me what you have in mind..."

"No problem, 007. Kim went to school in Switzerland, so he can read, write, and speak in English, French, and German. Here's our plan: We will fake your death and provide you with a new identity, but it will mean this will be your final assignment. Once you are gone, you are gone. Your twelve years here were exemplary, James, and as a reward for taking this possible suicide mission, Her Majesty's government has authorized MI6 to grant you a double service pension for the rest of your life -- 98,000 Pounds Sterling per annum."

Bond remained attentive but unexpressive. Yet in his mind, he knew he would accept. He knew deep down that he was secretly psychologically tired of his work – the tedious desk work, the stressful and exhausting field assignments, the lonely lifestyle of always being on guard and of being able to trust almost no one, with no time for a normal life of marriage and children. Plus he had to live with the memory of killing fifteen people in the line of duty. Those he killed surely deserved it. But like a battlefield soldier, nightmares crept up, and peace seemed never to come. Bond concluded that it was time to go before he completely burned out. So this was an 'out' with honor and with justification, for killing Kim would be worth Bond's final official action. Then the freedom to enjoy a regular life afterwards, if he survived! That would be the true reward.

M continued and hence Bond's focus returned to the present. "Here are the specifics, 007: You will be killed by an imaginary female named Kimberly Abbott. Her photo will be a computer composite. She was jilted by your refusal to marry her after a long relationship. Then she commits suicide. You will have an official obituary in The Times, a Royal Navy Commander's funeral for your four years of service, and even a grave plot with headstone. Meanwhile, you will secretly be here in our company hospital, undergoing a change of appearance. Your blue-grey eyes will be injected with a new, permanent dye which will change their color to brown. A chemical injection will change your black hair and eyebrows – indeed all of your body hair -- permanently to a greyish-white, 'silvery' color. That takes about a week. Then you will undergo a further chemical injection which will aid in making you look ten years older, with facial blotches and some wrinkles. But that third effect will wear off in about two months, so don't worry. We'll do some dermal abrasion on your 2 " vertical right cheek scar, and of course alter your fingerprints with laser. Your new identity will be as a black market arms dealer from Vienna named Klaus Rybeck. You will take the Chunnel to Paris, fly to Moscow, board the Trans-Siberian Express to Vladivostok, where one of our Russian friends will meet you and transport you to Khasan, which is on the border with North Korea. We have a long-time mole in Kim's inner circle, a general named Woon Ha Lee. He will escort you to Pyongyang, and later to Kim Jong-Un's Presidential Palace and private residence. There you will meet Kim and offer to sell him a black market 28 kilogram, two kilo-ton, suitcase-sized nuclear bomb for $15 million U.S. After you conclude the deal, you will shake the Supreme Leader's hand. On your right hand will be a signet ring, specially designed by Q Branch, which will painlessly inject a lethal nerve poison into Kim's body. You will have about thirty minutes before Kim suddenly dies, as if from a heart attack. By this time, General Lee will have you spirited out of Pyongyang on your way to coastal Nampo, where a fishing boat will sneak you out of North Korea under cover of darkness into the Yellow Sea. There you will be picked up by one of our submarines and taken to Gibraltar, and then to your choice of anywhere in the world you would like to live, as a retired Royal Navy officer on a pension. Naturally, you can select your new name and country of residence. All of your belongings in your Notting Hill flat will be delivered to you over time. Unfortunately, you cannot keep your company motorcar. You will surrender its keys, and your office keys, when you leave London. Our Armorer also will collect your Walther PPK and your shoulder holster from your flat. There you have it, James. It is all outlined in this file." M handed Bond a dossier stamped EYES ONLY in red block letters. "Finally, you are required to sign our standard non-disclosure document – to never reveal anything you have done for MI6 over the last twelve years. Well, James, this is the Big One, and a bit of a grand finale for you and your career. I'll give you 48 hours to think it over. If you decide to proceed, you have five business days to put your financial affairs and other personal details in order, before we alter your appearance in our private company hospital ward. Think of a new name and where exactly you want to live. Any questions, 007?"

Bond gazed briefly over M's head at the large oil painting of the Battle of Trafalgar. Life and what one did for one's country was surely clearer in those days, he imagined. One directly knew one's enemy, his strengths and weaknesses. Yet there was still honor and dignity and patriotism, on both sides back then. Today, all was an endless, complicated muddle, often with no real winners or losers. Just politics, and the dirty grubbing for money and power.

"I won't need 48 hours, Sir. I'd like to volunteer for this assignment now."

"I had hoped you would agree, 007. Here is the latest file on Kim." M handed Bond a hefty file. "Take it home and study it. Stop at Q Branch on your way out now and get a briefing on the use of the poison ring. Good luck, Commander. That is all." M looked down, picked up his Waterford, and busily began scribbling some notes onto yet another manila folder.

"Thank you, Sir. I estimate my odds at 1-4 in succeeding in this scenario, but I will do all I can to accomplish my mission."

"Unfortunately, our simulation experts give slimmer odds of just 1-5 here, James," M replied, looking up. "But if anyone in Britain can pull this off, it's you...so good hunting. Your country and the world will be better off for the elimination of this deranged megalomaniac."

Moneypenny met James' glance as he exited M's office. "How did it go, James? Off to save the world again?" she asked cheerfully.

"I think I should get 'Korean for Dummies' and learn a few basic phrases," Bond quipped, waving his thick folder. "Well, I'm off to see Q. I'll tell you more later, Penny -- if I can."

In the vast basement of the MI6 complex, Bond was instructed in the use of the poisoned signet ring by its designer, Alistair Thwaite, known simply as Q. Thwaite had been Section Quartermaster for the full dozen years Bond worked here.

"This is rather straightforward, James. The ring has one dose of fatal nerve toxin." Q took out a small case, revealing a gold signet ring. "It is completely safe to you, the wearer. By pressing the front 'KR' initials of your new name three times..." he demonstrated by casually draping his left hand over his right and pressing them with a finger "...a micro pin is activated on the underside. When you shake Kim's hand, the pin will painlessly and undetectedly touch his skin, rapidly releasing the poison in under two seconds, then retract. You have thirty minutes to leave before Kim suffers what will appear to be a heart attack. He has gained an enormous amount of weight over the last 14 months and probably weighs close to 21 stone, so his heart giving out will not be much of a surprise to either his nation or the world. Only if he is given a full autopsy will the truth ever be detected. But you will hopefully be long gone by then, 007." Bond thanked Q and headed for his Aston Martin parked in the company garage.

Bond needed a drink, but he needed a clear head too for reading Kim's file. However, he was also hungry, so he drove to Claridge's in Mayfair for an early dinner. There, at its Fera restaurant, he had a fresh grilled sole with new potatoes, seasoned Brussel sprouts, and a half bottle of vintage

French Muscadet. Afterwards, over coffee but no dessert, Bond thought about how over the years his life was slowly transitioning from one of pure action and adrenaline to one of more relaxed contemplation and a surprising desire for -- with lack of a better word – 'domestication'. Could he someday soon make the switch to becoming a husband and a father? He felt he could, but he abruptly snapped himself out of his reverie to focus on the difficult reality of the deadly job ahead. At least he was convinced that his acceptance of the mission was undoubtedly the right choice. The last time, and he had to make it work. Plus, he had to survive!

His nicotine patch having worn out by now, Bond chewed some nicotine gum as he drove back to his Notting Hill flat. Once inside, Bond changed into casual clothes, then poured himself a neat tumbler of chilled Latvian craft vodka. He sat at his living room desk, and opened the file on Kim Jong-Un.

It read in part:

"Age -- estimated 33-35 years old.

Height -- 5'7".

Weight -- current estimate at 21 stone (almost 300 pounds, U.S. measurement).

Psychological -- a delusional paranoid sociopath (Bond paused and thought back, recalling Dr. No, Goldfinger, Scaramanga, Drax, Ernst Stavro Blofeld, Zorin, Le Chiffre, Largo, and other twisted personalities bent on world domination and destruction whom he had killed...Kim was more of the same, like all the sick scum in SMERSH and SPECTRE);

Habits -- smokes Yves St. Laurent cigarettes, prefers Johnny Walker Black Label whiskey, drives a custom supercharged Mercedes, and is fanatical about American basketball (and is publically a 'friend' of Dennis Rodman).

Politics -- Supreme Leader and Chairman of the Communist Party of North Korea since the death of his father on 28 December, 2011.

Health -- probable diabetes and hypertension, ankle problems due to excessive weight, prone to gout due to fatty unhealthy diet and alcohol consumption.

Family – Kim had his exiled half-brother killed with VX nerve agent on 13 February, 2017 at Kuala Lumpur International Airport. Thought to be married to young model Ri Sol-ju, and to have a daughter, Ju-ae. Never photographed together. May have additional illegitimate children.

Residences -- Kim is believed to have several heavily guarded palaces across the country. In addition to the Presidential Palace in Pyongyang, satellite images show another large palace on the eastern North Korean coast in Wonson. Compounds usually include horse stables, a swimming pool, a private airstrip, and an underground train station. Coastal palaces would also include boat docks.

Additional -- Kim suffers from an inferiority complex, and is trying to outdo both his dynastic father and grandfather in bending the population to his will and ego. Wants to go down in history as Korea's greatest leader.

Summary – Unpredictable, unstable, unreliable, corrupt, with a dangerous ever-growing arsenal of nuclear weaponry. Likely determined to start World War III.

Her Majesty's government official suggested course of action = complete elimination of Kim Jong-Un with all possible dispatch."

Bond put down the file and finished his drink. He went out on his balcony and gripped the black wrought-iron railing, lost in thought. The street lights were on now, and all the white Regency buildings around and including his flat shown with a soft glow. He knew he could and would kill Kim Jong-Un without hesitation, when the time came. Then he went back inside, undressed, and went to bed naked, as was his habit.

Morning arrived with clear skies and a cooling north wind. After a late breakfast and The Times, Bond took out his world atlas to help himself visualize where he would like to live. After an hour of eliminating several possibilities, he finally decided on the island of Mallorca – specifically the sunny northeastern coastal town of Alcudia. He had been there years ago and had found it both attractive and peaceful. Pleasant year-round weather, and not far from the international airport at Palma. Plus, the language was no problem because he spoke Spanish. As for a name, Bond flipped through the telephone directory, choosing a new first and last name that he could live with. Hence, after he became black market arms dealer Klaus Rybeck for his upcoming mission, he would retire as a Royal Navy Commander named Alec Weston in Alcunia, Mallorca.

Over the next few days, Bond attended to his necessary financial and legal needs, but this was done in a careful manner so as not to tip off any suspicions of a major life change or upcoming catastrophe. MI6 was expert at doing everything else in making anybody disappear and then re-appear as a completely different person with a new passport and driver's license, a new personal history with all prior documentation and records, and even – as in Bond's case – an altered physical appearance. Bond was ready. He glanced at himself in the hallway mirror and pushed the careless comma of black hair (which always seemed to fall over his right eyebrow) back from his face for what was probably the last time. Goodbye, James and Hello, Klaus, he thought ruefully as he walked out the door. It was Tuesday, October 3rd.

****

The one-week transition surgery at the MI6 clinic went off without any complications. Bond had earlier cleaned out his office, and had turned in both his car and all personal keys (but was allowed to keep his trusty Rolex). Next, he said goodbye to a tearful Ms. Moneypenny, signed M's non-disclosure release and bid a rather somber farewell to his stolid, 'invincible' boss. Finally, he informed Personnel of his new residence choice and his new selected name, and opened a new Swiss bank account where his pension would be secretly deposited every month. All computer and hard copy evidence of the existence of a certain Commander James Bond was then scrubbed. The announcement of Bond's death and memorial service and burial was carefully choreographed and made believable. Because Bond had no family or living relatives and no close friends apart from his MI6 coworkers, his 'vanishing act' was simple to accomplish. 007 himself was rather amused when he read his own obituary in The Times!

Next, he was given a new Austrian passport as Klaus Rybeck, new credit cards, and a new mobile, along with a lengthy dossier on his new 'past' to commit to memory. In the file were photographs of the suitcase-sized nuclear bomb that Bond would attempt to sell Kim Jong-Un. There was also a photograph of his Russian contact, "Boris," who would meet him at the Vladivostok Station. The biggest surprise was when Bond saw himself in the mirror for the first time, now with brown eyes, a somewhat puffy-blotchy-wrinkled complexion, and silvery hair and eyebrows. He looked ten years older (What would the ladies think? he immediately wondered), but inside he felt exactly the same. It would take some getting used to, so Bond was grateful for six days on a train to gradually adapt to the transition. And so it was done. No turning back now. 007 went to the company gymnasium for the last time to work out for two hours, and finished with thirty-eight fast laps in the staff swimming pool -- one for each year of his life.

Going from London to Paris to Moscow was routine. When Bond arrived at Yaroslavski Station, his trained espionage eyes immediately detected the various Russian Mafia drug dealers, drug addicts, pimps, prostitutes, vagabonds, drunks, businessmen, youthful backpackers, and other tourists in the milling crowds inside. He carried a leather Gladstone, a briefcase, and a folded garment bag containing a tan trench coat. The clothing selected for this assignment was less-tailored and more drab than 007 would normally wear, but that was that. He was already wearing the tarnished -- so as not to appear new -- poison signet on the ring finger of his right hand. (Q had repeated the importance of a good, firm, two-second handshake with Kim so as to completely discharge the ring's toxin. "Remember, James, Kim doesn't ordinarily like to shake hands with strangers, so part of your job is to get him to like you and trust you so he will not decline at the crucial moment.") And, as a parting good luck surprise gift, the MI6 staff had included a large tin of 007's favorite Beluga caviar, and a bottle of his favorite Latvian craft vodka, under his clothing folded in the Gladstone. He was wearing a rather ordinary medium grey suit, pale yellow shirt open at the neck, with brown loafers. 007 missed wearing his Walther, and felt somewhat odd having no weaponry of any kind on his person for this mission.

Bond found his way to the Trans-Siberian Express platform. He would be riding the Rossiya #2, which ran every other day to Vladivostok, 6000 miles and six-days away. It was the world's longest single-service railway, stopping at fifty-nine stations over its 144-hour run. It was Thursday, October 12th, and the train would depart Moscow that evening at

23:45. If the train ran on time, he would arrive at Vladivostok on Wednesday, October 18th at 23:55.

        His train was luckily one of the newer TSE versions, painted two-tone grey with red accents. A first class LUX room for a single passenger cost 1205 Pounds Sterling, which equaled 90,993 Russian Roubles or 1326 Euros. The room had two sofas which converted into beds, but Bond would have the tastefully wood-paneled room all to himself. There was a small fold-down table near a picture window with drapes. Air-conditioning/heating controls, a fan, a mirror, and LED wall-mounted television, various lighting and electrical outlets, and storage areas completed the layout. All meals were included in the tariff -- to be eaten either in the dining car or delivered free to one's room. There was a shower car for first class, and a sink/toilet at the end of each car. Each car also had a matronly female car attendant, a throwback to the Soviet days, whose job was basically to keep an eye on her charges and attend to any extra passenger needs while also making sure there was always plenty of hot water in the car's samovar for preparing tea. Although the room window itself could not be opened, the multiple hallway windows outside one's room could be lowered for fresh outdoor air. The train also offered two other, less-expensive rooming options: Second Class, a private room with two upper and two lower beds; and Third Class, which was a large, unisex dormitory-style room with fixed bunk beds and no privacy. Neither of these two options included meals or a shower car, so people either brought their own foodstuffs (bread, cheese, hard-boiled eggs, sausage, fruit, tomatoes, cucumbers, nuts, crackers, beer, bottled water, liquor) or purchased edibles and beverages at any of the 10-20 minute (up to 30 minutes at the larger cities) station stops. They could also purchase meals in the dining car, to be paid for in roubles only. As for washing, most used baby wipes or took wet cloth 'sponge baths' in the cramped toilet areas.

007 was escorted to his Room #4 by his Provodnitsa car attendant (Irena, who smiled, flashing a silver incisor, when he addressed her in fluent Russian and tipped her five Euros), and then he unpacked. He stowed his clothing items and toiletries, and exchanged his dress shoes for more comfortable calf-skin moccasins after changing into casual black slacks and a burgundy polo shirt. He had also brought his Smart mobile (perfect for accessing Korean language lessons) with charger, a portable shortwave radio (for music and the BBC), a small magnetic chess set, a deck of playing cards, his Swiss Army knife, and a selection of four paperback books (mostly history and biography). Wrapping up the inventory was an adequate amount of nicotine patches and related chewing gum. Luckily, there was no smoking on the train at all, only outdoors at each station stop. He checked his Rolex as the train moved out, pleased that it was on time. The TSE would stay

strictly on Moscow time for the next six days as it crossed seven time zones from Russian Europe into Russian Asia and the Far East, all the way to its terminus.

Rossiya #2 rolled eastward, the land flat and monotonous, punctuated by groves of the national tree, the birch. Bond stayed mostly in his room the first two days, reading, thinking, and relaxing while gazing out his window. He got out for a stretch at most of the quick daylight station stops. His room was compact but comfortable and it was just wide enough for him to be able to do some push-ups and sit-ups to help maintain fitness. His meals were filling and nourishing, but certainly not gourmet. Still, he enjoyed his meat or fish dishes, his potatoes and cabbage, his borscht and blinis. Plus, he had his stash of craft vodka and caviar! By now, the train had crossed the Volga River, sped past Kirov and Perm and the white obelisk at Mile 1777 marking the official boundary between Europe and Asia. Then came Yekaterinburg -- the town where the last Tsar, Nicholas II, and his entire family were butchered in the Ipatiev House by the Bolsheviks on July 17, 1918. Omsk soon came and went.

The problem began on Day Three, when the TSE crossed the Ob River and stopped in Novosibirsk. Bond had decided to eat his lunch in the dining car for a bit of a change-up, rather than in his room. He was finishing a slightly stale eclair with his black coffee, when an overly made-up, overly perfumed, mini-skirted woman in her mid-twenties shyly ask in Russian if she could join him. He instantly knew she was a whore, but thought it harmless to engage in a little conversation in the local tongue. "Tanya" ordered tea, and asked him where he was from and where he was going. 007 immediately and professionally concocted another alias and went on from there, making up lies as he went along. They chatted for about twenty minutes.

"Forgive me, Eric, but I noticed you are not wearing a wedding ring," Tanya observed.

"Sadly, my wife died in a motorcar accident when we were skiing in the French Alps last winter," Bond replied.

"Don't you ever get lonely, Eric? Those are too many months to be alone, especially for a strong, handsome man like you," Tanya cooed, smiling. "Perhaps you would like to come to my room sometime? I'm in Second Class room #9."

Bond laughed inside, clearly finished with the charade. "Oh, you are very nice to offer such comforting companionship, Tanya, and you are very attractive, truly. But I'm afraid I am still in mourning and not really in the mood. I hope you understand."

Tanya quickly looked over Bond's left shoulder with a sudden look of fear. "Excuse me," she said abruptly, "But I must go now. Goodbye." Bond turned as she walked away, noticing a swarthy man in his early 30s near the dining car exit door. Probably her pimp, he surmised. 007 got up, paid for Tanya's tea, and started back to his First Class car.

Before long, in the corridor, he felt a man's hand roughly grab his arm from behind. Bond turned slowly around, instantly analyzing the situation. "What is the matter, my friend?" the swarthy man hissed in Russian, reeking of garlic. "Don't you like the girl? Trust me, she is clean. Only 200 Euros, thirty good minutes. A bargain, eh? Come on...you aren't gay, are you? Or maybe you want to buy hashish or coke? How about some heroin? I need you to do some business with me today," he smiled sickly, showing bad teeth, squeezing 007's arm more tightly.

The two men were alone in a corridor of a Second Class car. "Not today, comrade...Now, if you'll be good enough to release my arm?" Bond offered, with a bland expression.

"Look, you son-of-a-bitch, I'm tired of playing games. Give me 100 Euros first, then I'll let you go. I have bills to pay. All you businessmen can afford it. Write it off on your expense account. Let's have that money. Now!" Mr.

Garlic Breath flipped out a switchblade knife and held it to 007's throat.

James Bond always had trouble controlling his anger. Just before he would explode, his mouth would set itself into a thin, cruel line, and his jaw muscles would tighten. Like now. He spoke low and direct in Russian. "You are making a big mistake, comrade. Now put the knife down and walk away."

"Nyet, comrade. I'm giving the orders here. Let's have the hundred before someone gets hurt."

In a blinding flash, 007 spun around and grabbed the man by his oily hair and crashed his face into the thick glass window in the corridor. Then he neatly broke the man's arm -- which was still holding the knife -- on the metal sill of the nearest open window, sending the switchblade flying away outside. This was followed by debilitating body blows and paralyzing kicks until the stranger crumpled unconscious on the corridor's blue carpeting. A single door in the hallway opened, and Tanya's head popped out of #9.

"Oh my God! What happened? she wailed.

007 dragged the inert body into Tanya's compartment, then closed and locked the door behind him. He took out Garlic Breath's wallet and emptied it of about 1600

Euros. "Look, Tanya. I'll take him off at the next station stop and leave him there. Then I want you to take this money and get off at the best next stop. Disappear. Go back home to your family or friends or whatever. This is no life for a nice girl like you. Now, did either of you have any luggage or any drugs?"

Tanya produced a single purple backpack. "This is everything. Sergio and I had been working just the Novosibirsk to Irkutsk segment. I was a runaway from Smolensk. He took me in and took care of me -- at first. Then he changed and started beating me. He forced me into being a whore. He threatened to kill me if I ever tried to quit or leave him. I think he is Russian Mafia. I am glad he is dead."

"Well I didn't kill him, Tanya, but he will be hurting for weeks when he wakes up. I need you to take the backpack to the toilet room down the hall and flush away any drugs that were in it. Then flush his wallet with all of his identification too. The metal toilets empty their water and contents out under the train onto the tracks. Can you do that without being seen? Then come back here. I'll check the train schedule to see where and when the train stops next. Now go!" Tanya quickly obeyed.

Bond pulled out his mobile, and saw on the TSE schedule page that the next stop was Yurga, coming up in about 20 minutes. That was where he would stand up and half-drag off and dump his "poor, drunk friend...he fell...too much vodka!" (if anyone asked) in a toilet stall in the station's men's room. Tanya would then stay alone in her room for another 600 km until Krasnoyarsk, where she would get off, head for the airport, and vanish. When she returned to the room, she agreed with Bond's plan. She thanked him profusely and kissed him tenderly on his cheek after Sergio's removal was completed in Yurga. "Remember, Tanya, we can't be seen together anymore now, so this is goodbye. Good luck." Bond quietly left Room #9 after checking that the car hall attendant was not visible. He returned to his own room, poured himself a tall Latvian vodka, and chewed some Nicorette. He placed his portable shortwave radio on the small table near his window and found some relaxing classical music. Then he got out his deck of playing cards and began to play Solitaire. As always after a fight, he re-played his moves in his mind and did a self-critique. He was satisfied how this one went. He recalled that the last time he did battle on a moving train was against Red Grant on the Orient Express, somewhere in the Balkans.

On Day Three, Bond saw his first glimpse of deep blue Lake Baikal from his bed, and he knew the train would soon arrive in Irkutsk. He hoped that Tanya had gotten off safely, earlier in Krasnoyarsk. By the time Bond showered and dressed and had breakfast in his room, Rossiya #2 had pulled into the so-called "Paris of Siberia."

He went outside for some fresh air and a quick jog around the station, but was not too surprised to find that the mid-October temperatures were about 20 degrees F. colder here than in either London or Moscow. He finished his short run, however, then popped inside to grab a wool sweater and some roubles before going outside again. He brought some smoked omul fish for snacking from a cheery, red-cheeked babushka platform vendor. As he turned to re-board Rossiya #2, Bond noticed an attractive, tastefully dressed blonde -- who faintly resembled the French actress Catherine Deneuve when she was about age 40 -- boarding the train with her suitcase. Their eyes met briefly, but that glance was enough to convince 007 that she deserved his further attention later if their paths crossed.

Back in #4, he read for about two hours, then did a series of push-ups and sit-ups. He wished that trans-continental trains would have a fully-equipped gymnasium car, but that was just a fantasy. Next, he practiced a few basic Korean phrases using his Smart mobile. But before long, his mind slipped into reverie. He thought about the hundreds of beautiful young women of so many nationalities that he had slept with over the years. His last bedroom escapade was about three weeks ago -- too long! -- and he needed some warmth. Almost all of his interactions were sheer animal release, and he heartily enjoyed every one (even those done in the 'line of duty' with female spies, who as expected betrayed him afterwards, as a matter of course). Yet he had been truly in love only once, to Tracy Draco, to whom he was married for less than 24 hours. She was fatally shot in the head by Ernst Stavro Blofeld's henchwoman, Irma Bunt, who was trying to kill James while he was driving with Tracy on his honeymoon in Switzerland. The shock had sent Bond into a deep depression, and he almost quit Her Majesty's Secret Service. Now, as he grew older, he realized he needed love and affection and lasting companionship with a woman, not merely endless casual sex.

Bond's mind next turned to killing Kim Jong-Un. He played various scenarios over and over in his mind, even what to do in the event of unforeseen problems or failure. So this would be his final job as 007. The reality was still sinking in, but it was what James had chosen and it was what he wanted. He realized that it was the careful planning and the exhaustive research and the minute details and logistics of the execution of the mission (and the 'escaping alive' part, with its adrenaline surge) that he relished most. A job well done, like a perfect-as-possible military exercise. Any actual killing and violence and destruction was usually somewhat of an anti-climax. In other words, Bond -- like most espionage field agents -- was not a natural born, blood-thirsty killer. Bond's mind then transitioned, so he took out his briefcase and studied the picture of his Vladivostok contact, Boris. Strong, heavy-set, full dark beard, probably mid-30s. Bond had no choice but to trust him when they would meet in just three day's time.

James was delighted when he saw the blonde woman eating alone in the dining car that evening. He tipped the waiter five Euros to ask her if she would like some company with her meal. She turned to meet Bond's admiring gaze, considered the proposition for a moment, then smiled and agreed. Bond introduced himself in Russian, but offered English, French, German, or Spanish if she preferred. She replied, "Oh, it has been long since I practice English, so let's try that. If bad, we can do Russian."

Her name was Larisa, and she was traveling from Irkutsk to Vladivostok to visit her parents. Her father was in failing health, so she tried to visit at least once a month. She had one younger sister, married, living in Vladimir, and a son running a computer software business in St. Petersburg. Larisa had lost her husband to a construction site accident three years ago. He had been an electrical engineer. Larisa had studied literature at University, then switched to Nursing School and had become a nurse.

Because Tanya was now gone, Bond was able to recycle his alias as Eric, a widower businessman from Frankfurt, on his way to sell machine calibration tools in Vladivostok. Dining with Larisa was easy and pleasant. Her soft eyes were the color of blue frost. Bond insisted on paying for her meal, but she revealed that her meal was included in her tariff. She likewise had a First Class ticket, but in the second car. Bond didn't press for her room number, even as he sensed a strong mutual attraction at play. Instead, he invited her for a nightcap in the First Class bar lounge car.

Larisa ordered a neat Drambuie, while James ordered a neat vodka. When presented with a choice between Smirnoff and Stolichnaya, he groaned, disliking both mediocre brands. He relented with the latter. When his drink arrived, he asked the bartender for a small dish of black pepper. Bond took a pinch of the pepper and sprinkled it onto his Stoly, to the puzzlement of both Larisa and the barkeep. "It attracts the harsh fusel oils and carries them to the bottom of the glass," he explained. "It actually lessens any hangover. An old trick I learned." He then used his index finger to remove any still floating specks of pepper, wiped them on a napkin, and drank. The pair talked some forty minutes more, then Larisa looked at her wristwatch. "I better get some sleep now, Eric. Thank you for the nightcap. I hope we can see each other again tomorrow, if you like." Bond paid the bill and tipped the barman, then escorted Larisa to her car. "I am in the next car, by the way. Perhaps sometime we can arrange a friendly game of chess? I have a small chessboard ready to play."

"Chess?" Larisa did not readily understand the word in English, so Bond repeated in Russian, "Shakhmaty."

"Oh, da, da...forgive me. Yes, we Russians love to play chess. I would enjoy the playing," Larisa smiled. "Until later then, Eric, Good Night." Bond returned to his Room #4 and listened to the BBC news on his shortwave for any new developments out of North Korea before retiring for the night. His mood was upbeat as he drifted off to sleep.

The morning of Day Four was crisp and clear, the scenery spectacular compared to the seemingly endless flatlands prior to Lake Baikal. Here were spruces, pines, and larches, with rolling hills, rushing rivers, and even mountains. They had passed Ulan-Ude, where many passengers got off and connected to the Trans-Mongolian Express heading to Beijing. Bond dressed and had his breakfast delivered to his room.

An hour later, there was a sharp knock at his door. His car attendant, Irena, flashed her silver tooth as she handed him a small sealed envelope, then went back to her cleaning duties. It was a note from Larisa, written in English.

"Good Morning, Eric -- If you would enjoy the playing of the chess now, my room is #11 in second car. Looking forward to see you. My Best, Larisa"

201

Bond smiled and grabbed his magnetic chess game and headed for her room. Larissa was comfortably dressed in a black cashmere sweater and dark slacks, with an amber locket on a silver chain around her neck. Her soft blonde hair complimented both her outfit and her smooth alabaster complexion. They played with skill and concentration, casually chatting between moves, for about ninety minutes, then took a break by ordering their lunches delivered to her room. The game concluded by late afternoon, when Bond fibbed and declared a draw. Dark clouds, meanwhile, had rolled in, and raindrops began to pelt the room's window. Bond removed the chessboard from the small table, got up, and stretched. Larisa asked if he missed his wife, and he said he did, but he was actually thinking of Tracy rather than his alias Eric's wife. Larisa confessed that she too got very lonely. Any new men that she was introduced to by friends turned out on dates to be typical Russian males -- heavy drinkers or crude dullards or both. Larisa then surprised Bond by asking if he knew any Russian poems or songs. Because he was supposed to hail from Frankfurt, Bond lied and said no.

"If you come here and hold me, I will sing you some songs and tell you some poems," she shyly offered, patting her bed. Bond gently joined her, and they snuggled up -- still fully clothed -- on her not-very-wide bunk. It reminded Bond of the more innocent, less randy female interactions he had during his younger university days before he joined the Royal Navy and later MI6. The rain streaking the window added to the mood, as Larisa spoke or sang her deeply Russian -- hence very melancholic -- repertoire. She then asked if she could take a nap in his arms, so he kissed her tenderly once and let her drift off. That he wanted her was undeniable, her lips electrifying, her body inviting. But now was not the time.

When Larisa awoke, it was nearly time for dinner, so the pair agreed to change clothes and meet at 19:00 in the dining car. Bond ordered borsht and Beef Stroganoff, while Larisa selected the goulash with a beet salad. They had a fair bottle of Georgian "bull's blood," which was simply a strong red wine, and split a berry tart dessert. Their conversation ranged easily from favorite books and movies to favorite foods and even childhood memories. Bond stayed in character as Eric. Larisa reached out and held his left hand, rubbing his fingers as the wine kicked in. They did not converse on current world events or recent incidents of terrorism. Too serious. Certainly not romantic. Bond made sure she did not accidentally touch the gold signet ring on his right hand. Thankfully, she never asked what the KR initials on it signified.

They were warm and relaxed as they walked back to Room #11 with their arms around each other's waist. The hallway car windows were steaming up, indicating the quick drop in the outside temperatures. The copper corner samovar would help make a lot of hot tea for passengers this evening. Larisa halted outside her door, stared dreamily into Bond's eyes, then leaned forward and whispered in Russian, "Eric, I need you...will you please spend the night with me?"

Their lovemaking was delightful. Her body was well-tended and alluring, her skin warm, soft and creamy, her nipples flushed pink, an arousing blonde triangle of hair between her legs. Although she had given birth to a son in her younger days, the couple found a sexual position on her bed that was snug and pleasing to both of them. Bond took his time as Larisa moaned with pleasure. When they were finished, both were happy and content. They fell asleep in each other's arms.

They made love again the next day -- Day Five -- this time moving to Bond's room, with ever-observant but discreet Irena giving Bond a knowing wink as the couple entered his #4. Afterwards, the spent couple greedily finished James' Latvian vodka and Beluga caviar (Larisa had even brought some crackers). Bond was genuinely attracted to Larisa, and he could imagine beginning a deeper relationship with her, but he was also on an important and dangerous mission, and he needed to be honest with her. They talked back in her room as the train pulled into the large city of Khabarovsk.

"Larisa, you know we must part tomorrow when we arrive in Vladivostok. You will see your parents, while I will conclude my business there, then transit on to Seoul and Osaka for more business," Bond explained, holding her hand. "I can make no promises, but I would really like to see you again. If you leave me your mobile number, I can call you once I get back home to Frankfurt." Bond gently kissed her. "I truly do care for you," he added with sincerity, for this was how he really felt about this woman. In fact, so far there was nothing he did not like about her. He kissed her again.

"I know," Larisa sighed. "It is sad and can't be helped. But here is my number," She opened her purse and took out a pen and a tiny notepad and scribbled the numbers and handed him the detached sheet. "Oh, Eric! Maybe we can have happiness in this crazy world. Knowing you since Irkutsk has made me very happy," she acknowledged. "Let us say good-bye here. Or I will cry on the platform in Vladivostok," she added, her blue frost eyes now teary and red-rimmed. "Spasibo, moy dorogoy," she murmured tenderly as Bond kissed her farewell and returned to his own room, her mobile number safely in his pocket.

The TSE pulled into Vladivostok Station amazingly only four minutes late, on Thursday, October 18th, a minute before midnight. Bond changed his Rolex from Moscow time to the correct local time. He tipped Irena twenty-five Euros as he left his compartment and stepped onto the platform with his Gladstone, his briefcase, and his garment bag. He had changed back into his earlier business suit. He kept his eye out for his Russian contact, Boris. He had carefully destroyed Boris' file photograph, and was now in full mission-mode. His very life depended on his focus and concentration now. He forced any thoughts of Larisa to the private back of his mind.

Vladivostok was built on a series of hills (much like San Francisco) on the western shores of the Sea of Japan. Because it was the home base of the Russian Pacific Fleet, it had been off limits to any foreigners for security reasons from 1958-1992. Bond noticed the temperatures had returned to like those in Moscow six days ago, for it was warmer here than in Irkutsk. Upon exiting the station, 007 noticed the brightly lit, modernistic, Golden Horn Bay suspension bridge, which was completed in 2012. He then spied bear-like, bearded Boris walking towards him, with an outstretched hand in greeting. "Dobro Pozhalovat, Mr. Rybeck. Come with me, my car is just over there," he continued in Russian, indicating an aged black Mercedes in the parking lot.

Boris stowed Bond's belongings in the boot, then outlined the next steps when they got into the car. "I already checked you in at the five-star Hyundai Hotel, just a few minutes from here." He produced the card key to Room 505 and handed it over. "You can ring up maid service to collect your laundry, and they'll have it ready in the morning. And I'm sure you'll enjoy at good night's sleep in a bed that's finally not moving! They have a fitness center and indoor swimming pool, which I'm sure you can use after six days on a train. They also have a fabulous inclusive breakfast buffet, the best in town. I'll pick you up at noon tomorrow in the lobby. Then it's a four-hour drive to Khasan, on the DPRK border. It's a small town with less than 800 people and no hotel, which is why you are staying here in Vladivostok tonight. I'm to drop you off at the Russian-Korean Friendship Rail Bridge at 17:00. That's all of my instructions, so I won't need to know any other details of why you are here or what you are doing. Well, here we are." Boris pulled into the deluxe hotel driveway, got out and retrieved Bond's belongings and handed them to him. "Have a nice rest and see you tomorrow. Dobroy Nochi."

Bond politely declined the luggage porter's help and took the lift alone to the fifth floor. Calling for laundry pick-up and placing the bag outside his door, he then placed the Do Not Disturb tag on his door handle. Finally, Bond washed his hands and face, brushed his teeth, closed the thick room drapes, stripped, and slipped between the cool sheets of his comfortable King bed. He was fast asleep in a few moments.

The next morning was cloudy and breezy, with welcomed patches of sun, as 007 threw open his room curtains and gazed out at the city. He collected his clean laundry from outside his door, then headed down to the hotel's fitness room for an hour of vigorous exercise. When he returned, he took a short, steaming hot shower, followed by a longer icy one, shaved, slapped on a nicotine patch, got dressed, and took the lift again down to the ground floor breakfast buffet. It was just before 10:00 a.m. He ate heartily -- steak and eggs, potato hash with diced green peppers, grilled tomatoes, toast with orange marmalade, grapefruit juice, and a large pot of black coffee. Using his mobile, he caught up on news from around the world after he finished eating. Then he returned to his room to continue reading his paperback for an hour until just before noon. He gathered his belongings and turned in his hotel key card at the front desk. His bill had already been settled.

Boris appeared right on time, and led Bond to the waiting Mercedes. The four-hour drive to Khasan was uneventful, with Boris doing most of the talking when he grew tired of listening to mournful classical music on the radio. Bond asked a few casual questions about how Russians felt about Putin. "Oh, he is probably the richest man in the world by now!" he exclaimed. "It is a well-known secret. He is very clever too. He wants to bring Russia back to its glory days. Most

Russians respect him for that." Bond then asked about the huge upsurge in organized crime, the dreaded Russian Mafia. "It's a terrible problem," Boris admitted. "When the Soviet State collapsed, opportunists took advantage of the chaos during the economic transition to a free market economy. Some got incredibly rich by working hard legally. But others began importing drugs and weaponry and sex slaves. They also hire young, skilled computer hackers to steal bank accounts and credit cards. The police and military try to crack down, but many are being bribed to look the other way."

The pair arrived in Khasan just past 16:30. "Well, Klaus, your next contact will meet you there at the front of the Friendship Bridge at 17:00," Boris announced, indicating ahead as Bond got out of the car. "This is as far as I go. Good Luck, my friend." They shook hands and 007 thanked him. Boris then headed back to Vladivostok.

Bond noted the border guards on the Russian side of the railway bridge, which spanned the rather narrow and brownish Tuman River. He could also see the first town on the North Korean side, Tumangang, and its border guards, in the distance. Bond was just turning around to inspect modest Khasan when a short man, grey-haired and probably in his mid-50s, approached him, produced an unlit cigarette, gestured, and asked in English, "Excuse me, friend, but would you happen to have a match? I'm just dying for a smoke." The stranger was dressed in ordinary clothing, but Bond had been previously trained to give the proper response to this carefully worded question. "Sorry, friend, but you'll be dying young if you don't give up the habit." The man smiled in recognition and acknowledgement. "Klaus Rybeck? I'm General Woon Ha Lee, at your service. Please wait here while I change into my uniform, then we will walk into the DPRK. My car is just across the river."

Ten minutes later, Woon Ha Lee returned from a nearby building, dressed in full North Korean General military regalia. "I also sent a coded text to London, informing them of our successful contact. After we cross the border, it is a ten and one-half hour drive to Pyongyang. The sun will set in a little more than an hour, so you won't see much until we reach the capitol. I brought some food and beverages in a picnic hamper for when we get hungry and need a break. Driving at night works to our advantage against suspicious, prying eyes!" Here he paused for a brief chuckle, then continued. "We will arrive around 03:30, and go directly to the DPRK's largest hotel, the Yanggakdo International. You can rest and prepare there until noon. We are scheduled to meet the Supreme Leader at his private residence in the Presidential Palace at 15:00 tomorrow, October 21. After you finish your assignment, we will get you away fast to Nampo. We made a decoy reservation on the 18:00 flight to Beijing, connecting to Dubai and then

Vienna. The drive to Nampo takes 44 minutes on the Hero Youth Highway. A fishing boat with six of my operatives as crew will meet us and take you west out into international waters. There, the British submarine HMS Triumph will rendezvous with you at 20:00 and take you to the Royal Naval Base at Gibraltar. Should take you about two weeks to get there if the skipper short-cuts through Suez. Questions?"

Bond committed all of Woon Ha Lee's specifics to memory. "No questions, General. I'm ready. Let's go."

The two men walked right past the Russian border guards, who saluted after Bond's passport was quickly stamped. Bond carried his briefcase and garment bag, while the General carried 007's Gladstone. It was somewhat tricky negotiating the tracks and ties on the Friendship Rail Bridge, because it was obviously not built for pedestrians. It took about five minutes to cross into North Korea. The DPRK border guards quickly snapped to attention and saluted their General. For show, he acted upset about something and yelled at them angrily in Korean. A large, vintage black Russian ZiL limousine was waiting for them. "A gift from our Marxist friends before the company went bust in 2012," Lee quipped. "For our privacy, I declined my usual driver. I will be at the wheel. Now, let them stamp your passport, and we will be on our way."

That task complete, the car sped away. Bond noticed a grey and brown land, dreary and devoid of trees. "All chopped down and burned for fuel in the winter," Lee remarked. The roads were pathetic, which was why it took more than ten hours to get to Pyongyang. The ZiL could never cruise at its top 125 mph speed.

As they drove in the fading light, they passed primitive, small villages looking like ones did a century ago. "30% of the people in North Korea live in poverty," Lee proclaimed. "Our 'free' universal medical care is abysmal, with out-dated equipment, alarming shortages of supplies and medicines, and rampant diseases still around that were eradicated decades ago in other nations. Naturally, the elites and the Party members and the Military get the best of everything while the rest of the country suffers. We continually have famine and food shortages. The Kim Dynasty started off well enough with the current dictator's grandfather, Kim Il-Sung. But it steadily went downhill with his son, Kim Jong-Il. Now, with Kim Jong-Un, it is a pure disaster. I put my life and the life of my family on the line and went 'mole' for MI6 to help save my country, Klaus. I went to school at Oxford, did you know? You must realize that there are no freedoms here in the Democratic People's Republic of Korea, and no human rights. Policy debates are outlawed, hence we live here in a nightmare world of total propaganda and press censorship, blocked access to the Internet, and secret police arresting any dissidents. Everyone is under constant fear and suspicion, with neighbors spying on neighbors. Meanwhile, The Chairman and Supreme Leader's will is absolute. All of his decrees are simply rubber-stamped and 'applauded'.

By now, darkness had fallen, and General Lee went silent. Bond looked out the window, deep in thought. About three hours into the drive, the two men stopped to piss and stretch their legs by the side of the road in a totally deserted area. The stars overhead were brilliant. The pair then broke out some cheese sandwiches, apples, and bottled water from General Lee's food hamper and ate by the car's running headlamps. In the ZiL's boot were several extra jerry cans of petrol, so Lee added five gallons to the limousine's tank after they finished eating. "It is so big and heavy that it only gets about 18 miles to the gallon. And the few service stations until we get to Pyongyang are all closed after dark," he explained. Bond noted that they have not seen a single car since they left the Tuman River area.

They drove until midnight, then stopped for another piss-food-petrol break. The General had talked about his family, and his hopes for the future once Kim Jong-Un was gone. "Like Hitler, there have been many plots to overthrow Kim or assassinate him. Obviously, all have failed.

The details have never been reported in the Western media, but of course the worldwide Intelligence community knows the facts," Woon Ha revealed. Bond then asked about education in the DPRK.

"One-third of the curriculum at all levels from pre-school to university is simply indoctrination about the Kim Dynasty. Students are brainwashed into believing that their leaders were (and still are) all-knowing, all-benevolent, and all-powerful. They are portrayed as near-divine gods who are more loving and more important than even one's own parents and family. Total insanity!" Lee added with disgust.

Three hours later, they reached the brightly lit outskirts of the capitol of North Korea. The road immediately became modern and smooth. Bond began to see tall, white apartment blocks and deserted parks and empty wide boulevards. "We will arrive at your hotel in about thirty minutes, Klaus. You can see it now in the distance. 1000 rooms, just like the Rossiya Hotel near Red Square in Moscow, only vertical instead of horizontal," the General laughed. Bond then remarked on a bizarre, huge, squat pyramid-shaped building in the center of the metropolis. "That will be an even larger hotel someday, but it has been under construction for many years now, with no completion date in sight. An absurd blight!" Lee commented.

Bond remarked on the many floodlit metal and stone statues and giant portraits of Kim's grandfather and father. There were no traffic jams or pollution here because the inhabitants walked or bicycled or took city buses to school and to work -- much like Beijing prior to 1990, Woon Ha explained. "There are also no homeless people, or graffiti or advertisements. Just heroic propaganda murals and banners." It was eerie to arrive in such a deserted capitol city, Bond thought, even if it was the middle of the night. "It is not much different in the daytime, either," the General admitted. You are looking at nothing but the grand facade of a would-be world power."

Around 03:30, they arrived as expected at the imposing Yanggakdo International Hotel. Bond grabbed his belongings, then General Lee got him checked in after his Klaus Rybeck passport was scanned. The lobby was devoid of any signs of other visitors, foreign tourists, or businessmen. The desk staff were all dressed identically in dull grey Mao-style suits, both men and women. Their faces were frozen in apathy, their eyes wary and suspicious. It was absolutely silent -- no lobby muzak, no gurgling fountains, no conversation. A sole flower bouquet on a marble table added a rare flash of color to an otherwise sterile setting of steel, glass and chrome.

The General leaned forward to subtly whisper in Bond's ear. "Have a good rest and a good breakfast, Klaus. Remember that your room is bugged and that you are under constant observation from now on. I'll come up to your room at noon tomorrow. You'll be in Room 1101. I'll be bringing you a change of clothes -- specifically a blue-grey, Mao-style outfit. Kim is uncomfortable around Western suits, and prefers his guests to dress more like him. I'll also bring a bottle of Johnny Walker Black Label, which you will present later as a gift to the Supreme Leader when you meet him at 15:00." Woon Ha Lee then turned and left.

The rest of the hotel stay was uneventful. At noon, the General returned with the two items he had earlier promised. He put his fingers to his lips, so there was no talking until they checked out and were safely back in the ZiL.

"Well, this is it, the Big Day...Are you ready, Mr. Rybeck?" Bond tugged at his Mao suit, straightening the polyester fabric a bit while seated. "Do I look ready, General?" They both grinned as professionals, but this would be deadly serious work coming up, and both their lives were on the line in the event of failure. The weather was cool and cloudy, adding to the pair's somber again mood.

"When we arrive at the Presidential Palace, you will be searched and frisked and put through a metal detector. Your briefcase will be carefully examined, but then returned to you. The gift bottle of whiskey will likewise be analyzed, then returned. You'll be asked to remove your Rolex for checking too, but your signet ring can stay on. We will then be served lunch while we wait for our appointment. I hope you like Korean food, but even if you don't, eat it anyway, because we will be constantly videotaped and monitored. You will go in alone to meet the Supreme Leader. He may or may not have either a male or female aide with him, I'm not sure. You can immediately speak English to him because I already informed him that you don't speak any Korean. Always formally address him as 'Supreme Leader'. You have only thirty minutes to present your offer and show him the pictures of your nuclear device and assure a deal. I will wait in an adjoining room. For God's sake get him to like you enough to shake your hand firmly for two seconds! We will then feign to leave for the airport, but instead race to Nampo. O.K., here we are."

The Presidential Palace complex was massively fortified with anti-vehicle cement pillars, high walls with electric barbed-wire, and throngs of security personnel along with monitoring cameras and several checkpoints. General Woon Ha Lee was saluted and quickly allowed access into the compound after his VIP passenger, Klaus Rybeck , was thoroughly checked out. Upon entering the enormous gaudy gold and marble hallways with their heavy crystal chandeliers,

Bond was reminded of Bucharest and the Palace of Parliament built by the crazed Romanian dictator Nicolae Ceausescu. Who do these pretenders think they are impressing? Bond wondered. Who exactly do they think they are fooling? Raping a nation's treasury and starving its population to build these shrines to twisted egos. The reality always sickened Bond.

Up grand marble staircases they trudged, their footsteps echoing in the vast, yet immaculate emptiness. Other than expressionless uniformed armed soldiers flanking the halls every two-dozen meters and saluting the General, Bond and Woon Ha Lee were alone. Finally, they arrived at a banquet room where an impressive luncheon meal for two was waiting.

Having dined years before in Seoul, 007 was familiar with basic Korean foods and habits. Koreans used stainless steel chopsticks, rather than wood or plastic as in China or Japan. The tips were scored to afford a better hold on slippery noodles and other dishes. The spoon was used for rice and for soups. One put the chopsticks neatly to the right of the spoon when finished.

A buffet line was set up, with both male and female white-uniformed servers. There was ox bone soup, short rib soup, and stuffed chicken soup with ginseng. Then came stir-fried Korean noodles, Mandoo dumplings, beef barbeque Bulgogi, Bibimbap with rice, assorted pickled vegetables, seasoned seaweed, bean sprouts, shredded carrots, and of course Baechu Kimchi, whose garlic smell oddly reminded Bond of battling Sergio back on the TSE. Both men passed on any beer, wine, or liquor and stuck with bottled mineral water and tea. Dessert was a variety of sweet cakes and sliced fruits. As ordered, Bond sampled a bit of mostly everything, even though his mind and appetite were elsewhere. He and the General made innocent small talk during the meal: comparing the Vienna weather to that in Pyongyang, or complimenting the food, which was actually quite good.

Shortly before 15:00, an aide to Kim arrived to escort Bond to his appointment. They first stopped at an ornate restroom and freshened up. Then the General was taken to one room -- with a gold-colored sofa in it -- to wait, while James Bond, clutching his briefcase and gift bottle, was taken past two armed guards flanking a heavy golden door which led into a formal reception room. Inside was a large, dark-wood executive desk with a tall leather chair. Behind it was an unlit fireplace, with two portraits arranged on the mantle: Kim Il-Sung and Kim Jong-Il. The DPRK flag was displayed alongside the desk. Opposite the desk were two modest chairs, presumably for visitors. A few feet behind were two blue sofas facing each other, with a low mahogany table between them. A huge chandelier provided the light. Although the room was vast, every piece of furniture was oddly crammed into only this one side. Bond remained standing, alone, studying the layout. Suddenly, he heard a commotion, and a panel opened, revealing a secret door. Three men rushed in, wearing identical black Mao suits. One of them was Kim Jong-Un. Bond recognized him instantly by his bizarre haircut, which helped make Kim the laughingstock of the civilized world.

"Ah yes, you must be Klaus Rybeck from Vienna!" He walked right up to Bond and shook his right hand vigorously. Bond was stunned, for he had been briefed that Kim never shook hands with strangers. James obviously had no time to activate the poison ring either. "I understand you have a special item to offer me for sale?" Kim continued. "Good, good. I see you have also brought me my favorite whiskey! Shall we share a glass now? Why not...glasses, bring me two glasses!" he barked as one of his aides sheepishly complied, quickly rushing to a wooden side cabinet. Kim opened the bottle himself and poured two fingers of whiskey into each tumbler. "Prost!" he toasted as he clinked 007's glass. "Bottoms up, but you first. I need to see if it is safe, you understand." Bond had no choice but to obey, with Kim eyeing him carefully for a long, silent moment. Convinced the liquor was legitimate, Kim then smiled and greedily gulped his drink. Then he surprised 007 again by asking out of the blue, "Say, Klaus, do you like karaoke? I love it! My favorite song is 'My Way' by Frank Sinatra. I'm sure you know it...can I sing it for you?" Bond looked at Kim in wide-eyed amazement. This man was a babbling idiot, a doughy-faced man-child...

"Ahem. Thank you, Mr.Park. Nice work, you can go now." Bond spun around and saw...Kim Jong-Un! He was dressed exactly the same, with the addition of thick, black-framed eyeglasses. "I see you already met my double, Mr. Rybeck. Just one of my many security precautions, I'm sure you understand. Mr. Park stands in for me at most public and media events. The resemblance is uncanny, don't you agree? Plus, he plays the fool so well. The West is completely tricked. Like that Dennis Rodman stuff. True, I am a basketball fan. But Rodman has never met the real me. Instead, he unwittingly parties with Mr. Park. I mean, who would actually want to spend time with that big ape?"

Bond's head was swimming, so he tried to stay focused on his only task. He was alone now with the Supreme Leader. Kim's black, Mao-style clothing stank of cigarette smoke. Bond then looked into Kim Jong-Un's eyes. They were the cold, unfeeling, dark eyes of a reptile. The eyes of a man who could kill millions of people without either justification or remorse. 007 had seen such eyes before. Meanwhile, the clock was ticking...

"Supreme Leader, it is a true honor to meet you. Thank you for inviting me. I have something here that I'm sure will interest you," Bond began, opening his briefcase.

"Yes, I know. General Lee told me all about your special little device. I assume you have photographs? Then we can discuss price and delivery details." Kim motioned to one of the blue sofas. "Let's see what you have. Spread it out on this table." Bond sensed that this man was intelligent, in command, and dangerous. But his pasty skin pallor and obesity bespoke underlying poor health.

"Certainly, Supreme Leader, take a look. A two kilo-ton device weighing only 28 kilograms. Fits neatly in a large suitcase. Easy to hide, easy to transport, easy to detonate. A fitting addition to your proud, ever-growing arsenal." Kim was carefully examining the photos as Bond lectured.

"Exactly where is the device now, Mr. Rybeck? Vienna?" Kim inquired.

"No, Supreme Leader, It is currently in Baku, in Azerbaijan. I purchased it from the Iranians there."

"I see...how long would delivery to me take? And how much are you asking for it?" Kim asked.

"If we can agree on the price, I can have it in Pyongyang within 48 hours by small private jet. I would want half of my payment deposited in my Swiss account now and the other half upon delivery. The price is $15 million U.S. This, I assure you, is an excellent price and is non-negotiable. If you are not interested I can sell to either the Russians or the Chinese. Of course, you can think about it for a day or two. If we are then in favorable agreement, General Lee will contact me and he will handle the financial arrangements in my absence. I must unfortunately leave for Vienna tonight at 16:00. I'm sure you understand, Supreme Leader. Business never sleeps where money is involved." Bond smiled, then went silent, watching his adversary. The body language. The breathing. The eyes. Bond leaned back on the blue sofa, casually placing his left hand over his right hand. A curled finger pressed the KR initials on the signet ring three times, as Q had demonstrated back in London. Bond detected a tiny movement on the underside of the ring. The micro-pin was activated. This was it. Bond slightly cupped his right hand so as to not accidentally inject his right pants, and hence leg, with mortal toxin. He willed himself, with every fiber of his being, to stay calm. The half-hour meeting time was almost expired.

Kim broke the silence. "I want this device, Mr. Rybeck. I want this because it will afford me still more power over my enemies, especially the Americans and the

Japanese. They mock me and my nation. But their time of world domination is almost over. You see, my nuclear test missiles are just a diversion. I have been secretly building a large nuclear arsenal underground. In another year, I will combine with ISIS and together we will detonate nuclear bombs all over the Western world! I suggest you move somewhere in the Southern Hemisphere soon, Mr.Rybeck, because once we start, Europe will be the first to be obliterated! America and her allies will attack both China and Russia, believing them to be behind the holocausts. They will destroy each other while I wait, don't you see? I swear I will outdo both my father and my grandfather to make myself adored by my people as the greatest ruler in history! We will co-rule the world at first with ISIS, then I will destroy them too!" Kim was now red-faced, his dark lizard eyes bulging, spittle forming on his lips like a madman. The man was insane, Bond realized. He had to make his move.

"Supreme Leader, I would be delighted in my own humble way to help you achieve your goals with my device. Just let General Lee know within the 48-hour timeframe. Can we shake on it? It is an old business custom that I still like to abide by," Bond emphasized.

Kim Jong-Un was still in his mental fantasyland as Bond approached him with an outstretched right hand and a friendly smile.

"Oh, yes, well...thank you and goodbye, Mr. Rybeck..." Kim was just distracted enough to slowly extend his pudgy hand, his mind elsewhere, already looking away, so there was no eye contact. Bond gave Kim's hand a firm grip and counted ...one, one thousand, two, one thousand...to himself before letting go. Kim's hand had felt like cold, moist rubber. The Supreme Leader turned and left the room through the hidden door. Bond hurried back to the low table and shoved the nuclear device photos back into his briefcase. He had to find General Lee fast and get the hell out of here!

In the hall, General Lee was waiting. Bond rubbed his nose, which was a pre-arranged sign to Woon Ha that the deed was done. The General said loudly, "Well, Mr. Rybeck, let's get you to the airport. You don't want to miss your flights back to Vienna."

The men walked in silence (knowing they were always being recorded) through the maze of the Presidential Palace compound, past still more saluting guards. Outside, the ZiL was already waiting. They quickly got in and left. Lee explained that they would head in the direction of the airport in case they were followed, but once he determined they were safe, he would drive the 58 km to Nampo on the fast Hero Youth Highway. Bond turned around in his seat and rummaged in his Gladstone for some Nicorette. He was aching for a drink too, but it that was not going to happen for a few more hours.

"You didn't mention that Kim had a 'double'," Bond said, examining the lethal ring on his finger that he prayed did its intended job.

"You actually saw a 'double'?" Lee replied, incredulous. "There have been several rumors among the top brass, but never any proof, so I had discounted that possibility." Bond then gave Woon Ha a detailed recap of the whole encounter, ending with the hopefully fatal handshake. The General was very excited. "Well done, Klaus!" I think we can exit here and head southwest for Nampo now. In 44 minutes we will be at the docks."

Nampo was the chief port for the capitol of North Korea, so it was large and busy with dozens of docked freighters. At a traffic light, Lee noticed the start of mournful music playing on mounted loudspeakers, which were set up in each intersection in every city and village in the DPRK to regularly blare either rousing martial music or monotonous spoken propaganda. He lowered his window to hear better. "It's funeral music!" he joyously exclaimed. "The last time that dirge was played was in 2011 when Kim Jong-Il died. This means that Kim Jong-Un is dead! You did it, Klaus!" The music was interrupted by an emergency news bulletin. The General translated. "We must sadly announce that our beloved Supreme Leader has left us to join his father and grandfather now in heavenly repose...all citizens of the glorious Democratic People's Republic of Korea are ordered to remain calm and await further instructions." Lee rolled up his window and sped off towards the docks. "A new day has dawned for my people, Klaus. I believe that with the right leadership, we will reunite with the South soon and once again become One Korea. I will stay to help with this transition. Just like with the Castro brothers in Cuba, there are decent people already in the wings who were just waiting for the Old Order to die. Those new leaders will now step out of the shadows and help our nation rejoin the modern world."

Security personnel saluted the General as he passed through several checkpoints at the central docks. He then wheeled his limousine and parked near the water's edge near a medium-sized fishing boat. "Here we are, Klaus. My crew will take you out past the 14-mile international waters boundary line. You can change out of your Mao suit on the submarine. It surfaces at 20:00. HMS Triumph. Appropriately named, don't you think? And don't forget your belongings." Lee handed Bond his briefcase, Gladstone, and garment bag. "If they don't give Kim a thorough autopsy, I should be in the clear. If they doubt he had a heart attack and do detect poisoning...who knows? I can face either execution or a medal.

I'm prepared for whatever happens. Good Luck, Klaus. And my nation -- in fact the whole world, I believe -- thanks you for ridding this planet of such a horrible human being." Overcome with emotion, the General embraced 007, then turned and drove away.

The six-man fishing boat crew helped Bond aboard with his gear, and quickly cast off. James soon realized that the men only spoke Korean. They smiled when he used a few words like "annyeong" and "gomawo." But Bond was exhausted and went to catch some sleep below deck.

When he awoke, it was dark, and the boat's motor was silent. He checked his Rolex. It said 19:48. Bond went up top. The crew was positioned, watching and waiting, one crewman with binoculars. They offered Bond some hot tea in a battered tin mug. It tasted wonderful.

Suddenly, huge bubbles and water wakes erupted nearby. A submarine blowing its tanks, like some kind of a metallic whale breeching. The huge greyish-black HMS Triumph surfaced about 100' away, the lettering 'S 93' on its conning tower. A hatch was opened, and an orange rubber dingy was released into the water. Two Royal Navy submariners skillfully motored the dingy over to the side of the Korean fishing boat and secured lines. Bond grabbed his gear, thanked his six friends (saying "gomawo" for the last time), then lowered himself into the dingy, and it shoved off. On Q's earlier instructions back at MI6, 007 removed the now inert signet ring from his finger and threw it into the Yellow Sea. The fishing boat started its diesel engines, turned about, and headed back towards the mainland.

When Bond climbed down the submarine's ladder, he immediately met Captain Merritt. "Welcome aboard, Mr. Rybeck. You will share my quarters. I just received a message from Fleet HQ with the good news that Kim Jong-Un is dead. My crew of 130 have strict instructions not to question you regarding your identity or why we picked you up. You have free run of the boat, of course. She is a real beauty, the last of seven Trafalgar-class nuclear submarines. We carry both Tomahawk cruise missiles and heavy duty Spearfish torpedoes. At 30 knots, she'll cover the 9479 nautical miles through Suez to Gibraltar in 13 days and 4 hours, according to our current GPS. The food is the best in the fleet too. So it should be a fine voyage. Anyway I can help you, please don't hesitate to ask. Any questions?"

Bond had to resist confessing that he himself was once a Royal Navy Commander. "No questions, Captain. Please call me Klaus. But could you send a coded message to MI6 headquarters in London? Just say: 'Package Delivered'. Now, where can I get out of this monkey suit?" 007

pleaded, referring to his Korean outfit. "And Captain? I could sure use a large, stiff whiskey."

Over the following days, James was relaxed. He read his own books and a few others from the Captain's library. He explored all aspects of the submarine, ate too well, played cards and chess with some of the crew on their off hours, and replayed his successful mission over in his mind. He found the slip of paper with Larisa's mobile number on it and daydreamed about her as well. He had made up his mind to contact her again.

Before the voyage became too wearing, HMS Triumph arrived at its destination, the fortified underground submarine base at Gibraltar. Bond sincerely thanked Captain Merritt and his crew. They made him an honorary submariner "Dolphin," complete with certificate and official uniform patch, as a parting gift. He was then driven to Malaga where a private plane immediately flew him to Palma, Mallorca. (James knew that he would use the Palma airport to fly to Monaco on occasion, where he could don his tuxedo and try his luck again at the Monte Carlo Casino baccarat tables.) From Palma, a car and driver took him to the new house that he had earlier chosen, overlooking the sea in Alcudia. The driver addressed Bond as "Mr. Weston," for now James was Alec Weston, and would be for the rest of his life. Meanwhile,

Bond thought about what kind of car he would be buying for himself soon.

The driver wordlessly handed James the keys to his new house, then sped away. When James walked in with his belongings, he saw that all of his clothing and the furniture from his Notting Hill flat had been carefully unpacked and arranged. A sealed manila envelope rested on his desk. It included his new passport as Alec Weston, along with various credit cards, his new Swiss bank account information, and other forged identity documents such as his birth certificate. (He had previously destroyed all remnants of his used identity as Klaus Rybeck.) James was pleased when he noticed that his refrigerator was stocked with fresh food, even including a bottle of Latvian craft vodka tucked away in a corner. He threw open the front curtains to enjoy the magnificent view. Then he opened all the windows, and smelled the sweet fragrance of flowers drifting in the warm, gentle air. The sunshine was almost overwhelming, in contrast to being under the ocean in a submarine for two weeks.

About six months later, Alec received a wrapped brown paper parcel. It was not delivered through the regular post, but simply had "Alec Weston" written on it in bold black Sharpie. There was no return address, stamps, or other markings. The package was simply on his front doorstep when he opened his door one morning.

Alec untied the parcel's string. Inside was a navy blue, Sea Island cotton short-sleeved men's shirt, size large. Also, there was a brief note:

"I was told you fancied these kind of shirts. Please enjoy it in good health and much happiness for many, many years."

It was signed: "With Our Gratitude,

Elizabeth R "

Alec called out across the room. "Larisa, come here, luv, and see what just came..."

THE END

by Jack Karolewski

September 17, 2017

WAGON TRAIN

The year was 1841. The Arbuckle family -- from St. Joseph, Missouri -- made the fateful decision to join an 18-family wagon train heading southwest on the Santa Fe Trail. With rest stops, the 800-mile journey from nearby Fort Leavenworth, Kansas to Santa Fe would take about 90 days. By leaving in mid-May, the 68-person party hoped to reach their destination by mid-August. Free land and a chance for a fresh start was the lure for most. For others, it was the opportunity to start a new business, and a new life.

The Arbuckles consisted of Chester ("Chet"), age 35; Rebecca ("Becky"), age 32; Rachel, age 14; Trent, age 12; and one-year old baby Leah. Chet and Becky had been married in 1826 in Independence, Missouri. Chet hoped to open a dry goods store in Santa Fe, to take advantage of the rapidly increasing trade between that town and Mexico City – long-linked by the Camino Real – as well as with Texas.

The 18 Murphy wagons assembled at Fort Leavenworth (established in 1832), and the various families got to know each other while loading their supplies. Each wagon could carry between 1800-2200 pounds of necessaries, but only essential equipment was allowed – hence, no heirloom music organs, heavy surplus furniture, or boxes of books (other than the Bible) would be coming along.

On May 16th, the group met their buckskin-clad Wagonmaster, Flint McCord, whose long ginger hair and reddish-brown beard gave evidence of his Scottish ancestry. He was tall and lean, in his late 30s, with a good six-foot frame of tough muscle. His blue eyes were penetrating and steady, his face and hands darkly sun-burnished. Flint had made this trip six times, he announced, and he began taking command by his opening remarks to his party.

"The Santa Fe can be a son-of-a-bitch even under the best of circumstances, if the ladies here will pardon my language. The Trail splits off into two sections: the Direct Route, and the Mountain Branch. The Direct Route will save us 100 miles – about 10 days of travel – but it leaves the Arkansas River and takes us across hostile Indian territory and a flat waterless area called the Jornada del Muerte. If you speak any Mexican, you know that means 'Journey of Death.' It's a 50-mile, 5-day ordeal with poor grass and no water. But after that, you hit the Lower Spring of the Cimarron River, and from there it's a better march into Santa Fe. The Mountain Branch, on the other hand, forces us to contend with the difficult Rocky Mountains. The good news with that choice is that we can follow the Arkansas River further for water, and we get to stop at Bent's Fort – the only supply depot and protection between here and Santa Fe. But that route also risks the danger of Indian attacks, rock avalanches, and busted wagon wheels. Both routes cross lands of the Pawnee, Kiowa, Osage, Kanza, and Kaw, but the worst tribes are the Apache, the Comanche, and the Cheyenne. I still have three arrowheads stuck in my back that the doc can't cut out, so I know from hard experience."

Flint paused a moment while he took out his pipe, packed it with tobacco from a small leather pouch, lit it with a smoldering twig from the nearby campfire, drew smoke, and continued.

"I've decided that with this group, the best course of action is to take the Direct Route. Three out of every four wagon trains do. If we fill our water barrels at the Arkansas and drink sparingly during our run across The Jonada – and schedule most of our travel for nighttime under a full moon – we should be fine. I've done it four times already, and never lost a pilgrim. If you object to my decision, then, hell, it's a free country, and you can join up with the next party tackling the Rockies. Anybody want to back out? Now's the time."

The 68 pioneers looked left and right at each other, some murmuring in discussion with their family for a few moments, but in the end, no one abandoned Flint McCord. The die was cast. Chet and Becky hugged their children, then grasped hands and solemnly nodded their approval.

"That's decided then," Flint boomed and slapped his large hands together. "Now, listen up, everyone. I want every wagon to have six strong, healthy oxen – four to pull at any one time, and two tethered to the back for rotation. We can make about two miles an hour -- roughly ten miles a day, so as not to exhaust the oxen --but some days we'll do a little more, and some days a little less. All depends on where we camp. Each family should also bring at least one horse or mule, to ride a bit when you get tired of walking beside your wagon. If you want to bring any cattle or a milk cow, no more than two. Our daily schedule will be like this: Up at 4 and leave at 7 after breakfast. Keep rolling until we stop for our mid-day dinner meal and some rest, then travel until 4 and set up camp. After chores and supper, everyone asleep right after sundown. As part of the deal, I take my meals with each family on a rotating basis. We'll also have rotated night guard duty, four men at all times, in two-hour shifts. For fresh meat -- and a welcome break from jerky and bacon – we'll try for pronghorn, rabbit, deer, and prairie dogs. But if we come across a stray herd of buffalo, we leave them be – Indians don't like you robbing their food. Also, everyone going outside of their wagon bonnet wears a hat. Too much sun on a bare head causes health problems. Another thing: I don't mind a man enjoying a little taste of whiskey at day's end, but I won't abide any drunks. Or card game gamblers. Anyone caught stealing, you'll deal with me, and when I'm finished with you, you'll be cast out. I aim to have peaceable travel for the ninety days or so that we are together. Any questions?"

A thin but ramrod straight man dressed in all black -- standing alongside a somber, pale woman also wearing all black – cleared his throat and spoke up.

"Mr. McCord, I am the Reverend Ezekiel Danforth from Connecticut, and this is my dear wife, Prudence. We ask your permission to have a brief Bible reading aloud after supper each evening at the campfire. We would also like to lead a hymn and a closing nightly prayer, if you are agreeable."

Flint leisurely scratched his beard, then replied, "Well, sir, I would never object to a fine man of the cloth doing his work. The Good Book tends to help calm people's fears when they enter a strange land, and that's a fact, so I'm sure everyone here will appreciate your efforts, Preacher. Consider it done!" he slapped his thigh and smiled, revealing a missing lower tooth. "Now, friends, each family has already paid me half my fee, so I remind you again that the other half will be due when we reach Santa Fe. We leave tomorrow at sunrise. Make sure the Fort blacksmith double-checks your wheel rims, axles, tongue, and yokes, and have the harness maker check all your leatherworkings and bindings. I bid you all a fond good-day. If you'll excuse me now, I have a bank deposit to make, and some final arrangements with the authorities before our early morning departure."

The Arbuckles checked the contents of their wagon again, for there would be no chance to re-provision until they arrived in Santa Fe almost three months from now. Most of the space in the twelve-foot long wagon bed was filled with food supplies (flour, bacon, coffee, tea, dried fruit, lard, sugar, rice, beans, corn meal, hardtack, salt, vinegar, baking soda), clothing, necessary tools, two lanterns, a few simple pieces of furniture, four wooden chairs, a laundry tub, soap, some basic medicines, a tent, blankets, pillows and bedding. In the wagon's side box were cooking pots and pans, tin plates and cups, and other utensils. Two 40-gallon barrels for water were lashed to each side of the wagon. Under the wagon seat was a coil of rope, a towing chain, a container of axle grease, two rifles, a pistol, and ammunition. Last but not least, a spare wagon wheel was attached underneath the wagon itself. After Chet gave his approval, his family went to the Missouri River to bathe and then dress in clean clothes. The six oxen were fed, as were the one horse ("Phineas") and one cow ("Sally") that the Arbuckles were taking with them.

Dawn broke clear and bright. Trent and Rachel were itching to get started, along with their parents and the other sixty-four pioneers. The 18 Murphy wagons were aligned in a neat column as directed. The Reverend Danforth gave a short blessing, worn black Bible in hand. Flint McCord gave the loud command: "Wagons Ho!" and off they went. The date was Monday, May 17, 1841.

The breezy, cool, mostly sunny weather cooperated nicely for the twelve days it took to traverse the green, hilly ups and downs of eastern Kansas, as the train then moved into the start of flatter terrain. The party had covered about 120 miles so far when they arrived at the Neosho River. Water barrels were replenished as the party camped in a fine mile-wide grove of trees. One huge oak in particular was pointed out to the group by Flint.

"Folks, that there is the famous Treaty Oak. In 1825, early emigrants paid the Osage Indians $800 worth of goods for permission to cross their lands in perpetuity, and both parties made that pact right here under this tree. And the peace with that tribe has held ever since. Both the Osage and their neighbors the Kaw are mighty peaceful. They generally won't bother us, so don't worry."

Trent Arbuckle then spoke up. "Mr. McCord, when do you figure we'll see our first Indians?"

Flint chuckled and replied, "I know that you and the others are curious, boy, but if we don't see any on this trip, consider yourself lucky." He mimicked a scalping, and winked.

The group was ordered to spend two extra days here (an area that would later be known as Council Grove), to rest the animals, bathe, and for the women to do their laundry. The following morning, however, broke cloudy and dark. Thunderstorms were rolling in from the northwest. Soon, lightning crashed and thunder boomed. "Sorry, folks, but we have to travel whether it's dry or wet. Let's move out." An hour later, the wagon train was miserable, soaked in wind-whipped, torrential rains. But the storm eventually passed, and they bravely rolled and trudged onward. The wet teased out the smells of sagebrush and mesquite, and brought forth abundant, colorful wild flowers.

Over the next thirteen days, it rained two more times but not as hard. Rachel Arbuckle first heard, then spied her first rattlesnake, which her father warily beheaded with a long-handled hoe. Meanwhile, several deer and antelope were spotted and shot by the hunters in the group, so fresh meat went gratefully into communal stew pots. Trent even bagged two jackrabbits. Becky attended to baby Leah and kept her family fed, trying her best to vary their diet despite the limited variety of provisions. She prided herself in making fresh biscuits every morning in her Dutch oven, and she faithfully milked Sally their cow every day – sharing the surplus milk with other mothers who had children but no cow. The group had adapted well to Flint McCord's daily schedule. No injuries, accidents, or wagon breakdowns had occurred as of yet. Each night, Reverend Danforth read aloud from his Bible, and offered up prayers to the Almighty for the group's safety and deliverance. All joined in, too, in the nightly religious hymns. But after their voices faded, there was absolute silence -- other than for a few crickets and the crackling of the large campfire in the middle of the encircled wagons. Not even a lone coyote howl was heard. The vast heavens above were inky black with wide splashes of twinkling distant stars – a constant reminder how far away the party was from any civilization, and that their former homes were just a memory now.

By now it was June 10, and they had reached the impressive Arkansas River. Flint explained that they would rest here for two full days, staying on the right bank, because they wouldn't have to cross the rushing waters until they reached the Direct Route cutoff point.

Chet Arbuckle rotated Rachel and Trent riding on their horse, Phineas, when they appeared tired of walking alongside their wagon. Sometimes, Becky had Rachel watch Leah when the baby was asleep, so that she could stretch her legs a bit from mostly sitting inside the wagon out of the sun.

Two days later, the wagon train saw the landmark called Pawnee Rock. It was a barren, grayish brown outcrop of sandstone – about 150' high -- jutting out of a huge green mound of earth. From the top, Flint explained, you could see many miles in every direction. Various Indian tribes used this unique rock as a lookout spot to sight game and to ambush enemies.

"Can we stop and climb it?" pleaded Trent.

"Sure, boy, but I think we should spend no more than an hour here. You can also carve your name or initials in the rock. It's pretty soft, and you can use your knife. Let me ride ahead and check out the perimeter first, though, to make sure that no hostiles are hiding behind." Flint swung into his saddle and galloped away.

About ten minutes later, he signaled with his hat that all was safe, and the wagon moved ahead, and met up with him. Flint singled out Trent. "You wanna know how this place got its name, son? It was in 18 and 26. A young Kit Carson – the way I heard it, he was about 17 at the time – was here with a scouting party, and it was his turn for night guard duty. Well, he was startled by a strange noise around midnight, and thought it might be an attacking Pawnee. So he snuck around a

242

rock corner and fired his rifle. But all he hit was his own mule, who had gotten loose in the night! Luckily, the critter lived. But Kit's group teased him non-stop for days, and they dubbed the spot where it all happened 'Pawnee Rock,' And the name stuck to this day." Flint flipped the brim of Trent's hat downward with his index finger, then added, "Now climb up there and make your mark!"

Trent excitedly scurried up the sandstone, and soon discovered a handful of other dates, names, and initials of people who had passed by this way before. He proudly carved his family name 'Arbuckle' with his buck knife and then quickly added '1841' underneath. The view from the top of Pawnee Rock was spectacular, the 18 wagons looking like miniature toys resting below at the base.

The wagon train continued nine more days before it arrived at the point where the Santa Fe Trail split in two. The date was June 23. Using their chains, the wagons attached themselves in pairs and carefully crossed the rushing Arkansas River guided by rope tethers. Once all were safe, Flint announced, "We will rest three days here. Have your stock drink all the water they can. Same for you. Then fill every water barrel and canteen to the brim. With my apologies to the Preacher, we will be going into Hell. La Jornada del Muerte. The absolute worst part of our journey. If you make it, you'll have quite a tale to tell your grandchildren. So get ready to gird your loins."

That night, Chet and Becky gathered their brood close and reassured them as best they could. Other families did the same, each in their own way. The Reverend Danforth recited Psalm 23, and offered up extra prayers in an attempt to bolster the group's courage. "God will be with us, as He was when He led the Israelites into the Promised Land," Ezekiel guaranteed his flock of pioneers. Prudence then led a final, solemn rendition of "My Faith Looks Up to Thee," before the group retired for the evening.

It was Sunday, June 27 when the wagon train started on La Jornada del Muerte. As Flint had hoped, the moon would be at 2/3 phase that night, increasing to 3/4 phase the next two nights, then full phase for the final two nights. Daytime temperatures were humid and in the upper 80s here at the river, but would climb as they headed across the shade-less and barren aridity of La Jornada. The 68 brave souls could see the merciless flat area ahead, and each was confined to their own private thoughts of dread. The sky was devoid of clouds, the sun unblinking. A hot wind from the west blew brown dust.

Flint's plan was to travel three hours in the morning, then rest in and under the wagons and tents until nightfall, when travel would continue for four hours between 10 p.m. to 2 a.m. No guards were needed for the next few nights now, because even the Indians avoided this place of relentless misery.

As time crept by, conversation was reduced to a minimum. The animals moaned and complained. The heated earth permeated the boots of everyone walking. Sweat evaporated quickly. The water barrel levels were slowly going down. Dehydration made appetites lag. Exhaustion came quicker. After day three, several pilgrims were prostrate in their wagons. The elderly and young suffered. Sally the milk cow stumbled and would not rise, and the Arbuckles were sadly forced to leave her behind. Soon, other cattle and horses dropped. Vultures appeared, circling their next meal. Flint had to be firm in his leadership and discipline. Keep going, almost there, don't stop...

After day four, the water was gone from all the barrels, most of it ladled out for the oxen and remaining stock. Only canteens held the remains of life-giving liquid. Fevers were breaking out among the weak. Eyes were listless and glassy. The party passed occasional piles of old bleached bones. Yet Flint McCord pointed ahead at the wagon ruts they were following, saying, "Look! The folks before us made it. And so will we! Don't give out on me now, we are getting close to

Lower Spring on the Cimarron River. Just one more day, you'll see it. Water!"

It was just after 9 a.m. on July 2 that the wagon train reached the safety of Lower Spring. Although the water was brackish, it was drinkable despite the taste, and the animals didn't mind one bit. The pilgrims put their rifles down and rushed in a panic to drink, and several even plunged fully clothed into the water, filling their hats and pouring the blessed contents over their heads and faces.

That was when tragedy struck.

A band of twenty hostile Comanches on horseback were waiting for just this moment of weakness and distraction to strike from their hidden location behind the numerous trees growing at the river's edge. Soon, arrows and spears were airborne, and the first man to get hit was Wagonmaster Flint McCord. A fatal arrow protruded from the side of his neck, which had sliced his carotid artery, causing blood to gush out.

Instinctively, Flint wheeled with his rifle and dropped one of the approaching attackers, then dropped another two using his revolver. He quickly issued orders to the pilgrim men to grab their rifles and fire back, but to also release three horses and then cease firing, in hopes that the Comanches needed those mounts more rather than risk losing their braves. Chet immediately cut loose Phineas, and two nearby trail mates likewise obliged. Sure enough, the Indians stopped shooting and chased after the horses. Soon, the warriors were gone, leaving seven of their dead behind. But Flint had since collapsed to the ground.

His voice growing weak and his breathing labored, Flint called out to the boy, Trent, who came running. "Fetch your Pa, boy," Flint murmured. Chet Arbuckle came and called out, "I'm right here, Flint."

Chet slowly knelt down next to McCord. Flint said, "I'm a goner, Chet. I'm making you the new Wagonmaster. I've been watching you. You're honest, brave, and smart. I know you can lead. Just keep heading southwest. Follow the wagon ruts. You'll cross nine other shallow rivers or creeks. You've got to bring the train safely into Santa Fe. We are more than halfway there from here. You can be there by mid-August. I'm trusting you with their lives, Chet…" Flint McCord, bleeding out, went into a spasm of coughing, stopped, closed his blue eyes, and died.

The whole party meanwhile had naturally assembled around their dying leader during this moment, and the Reverend Danforth offered up Flint's soul to God. Two other men had been wounded during the Comanche attack, one arrow shot in the leg and the other in the shoulder. Both wounds looked non-fatal, and given proper removal and time to heal, both men were expected to live.

Flint McCord was buried under a cottonwood near the Cimarron, with Trent carving a grave marker. Trent was solemnly presented with Flint's rifle and pistol, and Chet was given Flint's horse, saddle, and knife. Stones were then carefully placed over the dirt burial mound. Prudence sang "Rock of Ages" and tears were shed without embarrassment.

The wagon train settlers were still in a state of shock when Chester Arbuckle took up the reins of command.

"My dear friends, as you can see, we are on our own. There might be another wagon train a week behind us, or not. But we are close to our goal of Santa Fe. We can't just wait here and hope. The Indians will probably be back to collect their dead, so we need to be gone by then. There is no turning back, no giving up. Our children are depending on us. We must depend on each other. We have enough supplies. I want the night guards doubled until further notice. Let's fill our water barrels now and move on. The worst is over, I have to believe. Pray God we are spared any sickness, or injuries, or further hostile attacks. We will follow the right bank of this river, then we can expect nine other places to provide water along the way in the weeks to come. There will likely be grasses and game again, all the way into Santa Fe. I know this because I once talked with a trail guide named Linus Hunt when my family and I were back in St. Joe. He told me about four trail markers ahead on our route that we must look out for: Autograph Rock, Rabbit Ears, Wagon Rock, and Pecos Ruins. I have to believe that he told me the truth. Unless there are any questions, I say 'Move out!'"

Although no one could have known it at the time, Flint McCord had fallen near the spot where famous mountain man Jedediah Smith had been similarly ambushed and killed by a Comanche war party ten years earlier, at the age of 32.

The wagon train traveled for four days. The July 4 holiday came and went unheralded, for no one was in any mood for celebration. But fever hit many of the settlers now, including Becky Arbuckle, possibly from the brackish water at Lower Spring. The accompanying chills and diarrhea were not curbed by the usual medicines. Chet called for a halt of three days, because many in the party were too weak to travel. Fortunately, they were now at water, a place known as Middle Spring, near a large rock outcrop. Unfortunately, gnats and mosquitoes plagued the emigrants. Buffalo chips now had to be gathered for cooking fuel, because there were few trees for firewood.

During a routine chip gathering, Rachel came breathlessly running back to her father. "Pa, I just saw a horse in the distance. And it looked like someone lying on the ground next to it."

Because no one on the wagon train had a spyglass, Chet grabbed his gun and jumped on Flint's former horse (now re-named "Renegade") and rode out in the direction that his daughter indicated. There he found a painted pony and an Indian boy lying next to it. The lad looked to be around age 15, and he appeared to have fallen and badly broken his left leg. Chet knew nothing about identifying any Indian tribes, but he did notice that the colored body markings on the boy differed from those of the attacking Comanches from Lower Spring. The Indian pulled his knife to defend himself, because his quiver of hunting arrows and bow were out of reach. He spoke in a loud, threatening manner (which naturally Chet did not understand), but then winced in pain and shifted his leg and was resigned to silence.

Chet slowly put his rifle down and offered the boy a drink from his canteen and a piece of jerky from a pocket. The Indian was wary, but greedily took both offerings. Chet then pantomimed that he would help the boy and take him and his pony back to camp. Chet carefully lifted the lad and placed him face down on the saddle of Renegade, then grabbed the paint by its mane and walked both animals the mile or so back to the wagon train.

The settlers at the camp were startled at the sight of a young redskin. Some wanted him killed, as revenge for the death of Flint McCord and the wounding of their two comrades. Reverend Danforth calmly intervened, calling instead for mercy and Christian charity. Chet agreed with the preacher, and found a train member who knew how to set a broken bone and rig a splint. Chet then had the boy placed in his tent to rest after he was fed. "We can take him with us to Santa Fe. Someone there will know what to do with him," Chet announced.

Meanwhile, the two men who had been wounded at Lower Spring were unfortunately taking a turn for the worse. Both the leg wound and the shoulder wound were badly infected. Regrettably, little could be done. One settler mentioned that he heard that Indians routinely doused their arrowheads with dung or piss to hasten the death through blood poisoning of whatever they were hunting. The first man, Josiah Brown, died on July 8, and the next, Patrick Riley, died the following day. Both were properly buried and marked just outside the camp, their wives and children then comforted and aided by the group. The 68 pilgrim group were now down to 66. The party was rested, but those who were ill were still quite weak from their sickness. Yet Chet had no alternative but to keep moving the wagon train onward to Santa Fe.

For the next six days – one during a cold, severe hailstorm – the wagon train kept rolling, eventually crossing, then leaving, the Cimarron River. Morale was flagging, but Ezekiel and Prudence did their best to help brighten people's hopes. Chet Arbuckle proved a capable leader, supervising the replacement of two broken wagon wheels and making an inventory of group provisions. He also wisely and regularly checked that all oxen were rotated in their yokes.

The Indian boy, whom the group named "Pompey" -- after Sacagawea's son, who was born on the famous 1804-1806 Lewis and Clark Expedition – was gradually adapting to being with the party, and vis-versa. He rode in the Arbuckle wagon with a still prostrate Becky, and with Rachel, who was caring for baby Leah while her mother was ill. Rachel even named Pompey's pony "Lewis," and was plainly fascinated by the Indian boy. Communication between the two foreign races, though, was entirely done through slow pantomime.

Pompey was observant and appeared clever. He particularly noticed the debilitating fever sickness lingering among many of the group, especially as they stopped to relieve themselves periodically with awful bouts of diarrhea. He communicated with Rachel to help him down out of their wagon at one point, and he motioned for her to dig up the roots of a particular plant alongside the trail. He next pantomimed for her to boil the roots in water and make a type of herbal brew that those suffering should drink. Some feverish members refused, suspecting Indian trickery, but others were eager for any chance of relief and soon drank the pungent brew. Happily, by the following morning, those with fever who drank the tea were noticeably improved, causing the others to relent and likewise drink. Chet gave Pompey some sugar as a reward for his helping doctor the sick, and Pompey responded with the first shy smile anyone had seen him surrender.

On July 16, the train reached an area called Cold Spring, and more importantly, they finally saw nearby Autograph Rock, which confirmed that they were traveling on the correct trail. Unlike Pawnee Rock, this place was a thirty-foot tall sandstone cliff rather than a mound, but like Pawnee Rock, it had names, dates, and initials carved in it -- mostly around the base at ground level. Trent even spied one from 1806, from a "T. Potts," before adding another "Arbuckle 1841" to the rock face. Chet, meanwhile, called for a rest of two days here, due to its sweet, fresh water. The grasses were rich for the animals too, and the hunters lucked into shooting 15 prairie dogs – almost one for each wagon. A small herd of buffalo were also spotted in the distance by Pompey – who was undoubtedly disappointed that his still healing leg was preventing him from any pursuit. But Chet remembered Flint's former command to leave any buffalo alone, or risk the wrath of the natives. So the huge, majestic wooly beasts slowly went on their way, unmolested.

It was five more days of travel until they glimpsed a mountain on their left with two distinct peaks. "This must be the Rabbit Ears," Chet proclaimed. "Linus Hunt told me that from here it is about 200 miles or 20 days to Santa Fe. Let's rest one day here by the river." It was the afternoon of July 22, 1841, and the river the train camped by was the North Canadian River, which drained eastward into the Oklahoma Panhandle. The wagon train had covered almost 600 miles since May 17. It seemed like a long, long time since they had departed from Fort Leavenworth, but the group's health and spirits were both good now. They were optimistic that they could make it alive to their final destination. In fact, they had already crossed into New Mexico Territory two days ago, unknowingly.

After traveling eight more days, the distinct shape of Wagon Mound loomed straight ahead. Linus was right again! Chet thought with relief to himself, assured that they were on the right path. Sure enough, the small mountain resembled a Murphy wagon with its bonnet up. Other than one walking pilgrim twisting an ankle by unwittingly stepping into a prairie dog hole, there were no mishaps. Meanwhile, Pompey's leg was healing nicely, and he was anxious to get his split removed so he could ride his paint, Lewis, again. He wanted badly to return home to his Apache village tribe, but of course he could not explain the whole story to his rescuers of how he had become separated from a pronghorn hunting party of six young braves when they fanned out, and how he had been thrown off his pony when it got spooked by a rattlesnake.

On August 2, the second rest day, about 40 mounted Indian warriors suddenly appeared at the camp. Chet had every available firearm made ready, then bravely went out un-armed to meet an imposing brave whom he presumed was the leader. Chet made an attempt at sign-language, to let the band know that the emigrants were merely passing through and were peaceful. The leader, however, seemed unmoved and unimpressed and did not dismount. Chet quickly called for his son to bring a red wool blanket and Flint's old buck knife from the family wagon. When Trent complied, Chet formally offered the two items as gifts to the leader. The Indian's face, however, was a study in passivity. He was in truth simply thinking about how best to kill all these white invaders with a minimum loss of life to his braves.

At this dramatic moment, the stillness was broken when Pompey loudly called out a string of sentences in the Apache language, which shocked every person assembled. Rachel quickly helped Pompey out of her family wagon, and he hopped unaided on his good leg up to the war party. He and the leader then talked back and forth with vigor and apparently mutual understanding.

Pompey then turned to Chet and pantomimed that although this was not his family tribe, these warriors were also fellow Apaches, and that he would leave with them now, and that they would eventually reunite him with his village. He also had related to the leader that these white men were friends who had rescued him, thereby saving his life, and begged that they should be allowed to leave unharmed.

After this labored, lengthy exchange between Chet and Pompey, there was silence for a moment. Finally, the Apache leader grunted and raised his right arm in peace, and all looked well.

Pompey was helped on his pony with some effort by Trent and Chet, his left leg still awkward in its splint. He grinned and likewise raised his right arm in peace, and shouted something as a salute of sorts in Apache, then slowly departed with his forty whooping comrades. Chet breathed a sigh of relief, as did the other 66 badly-shaken pilgrims! That evening around the large center campfire, Reverend Danforth offered up additional prayers of thanks to the Almighty on behalf of the group.

The following day, the wagon train broke camp, traveled for six days, then rested for three. This would be their last rest break, so laundry and bathing were again attended to. In just five more days, they would hopefully reach Santa Fe! They had crossed two more rivers, and had just one more to go -- the south fork of the Pecos. They had also passed the intersecting junction where the Mountain Branch merged with the Direct Route. From there, the Santa Fe Trail was one road again. But no other wagon trains were in sight from the north.

At night by the communal campfire, families shared their plans and wishes for what they would do once they reached their final destination. Chet admitted looking forward to getting a new pair of boots. Becky confessed that what she most looked forward to was a long, hot bath with perfumed soap. Rachel wanted a fancy new yellow bonnet. Trent just wanted to eat an entire, freshly-made apple pie. And baby Leah simply gurgled and smiled.

On August 12, the wagon train resumed its course. Before long, they crossed their last water source, ironically during a hefty rainstorm. They camped the next night at Pecos Ruins, a large Indian village that had been abandoned three years earlier. What was left of the reddish adobe brick buildings was impressive, but what most interested the party were the circular underground kivas, which were accessible by climbing down thick wooden ladders. These cool, mostly dark rooms had been used for various ancient tribal rituals. And although the emigrants didn't know it, the Spanish explorer Coronado had been here at this very place back in 1541, exactly 300 years ago.

The final challenge for the wagon train was traversing the tricky Glorieta Pass through the Sangre de Cristo Mountains, the range which ringed the east side of Santa Fe. Chet supervised the 18 wagons one at a time as they carefully negotiated the Pass. Once through, the overjoyed pilgrims saw their first glimpses of the Palace of the Governors, the central Plaza, and the many churches of their long-sought goal -- Santa Fe!

Making their way single file, the party headed directly for the Plaza. At 7200' elevation, the town was bustling, the locals mostly a mixture of Mexicans and Texans. The air was crisp and scented with pine. Red chili peppers hung in woven strands on adobe doorways. Excited riders rode out to meet the new arrivals, shouting questions and yelling answers. It had taken the party 93 days to get here -- 75 hard days of travel and 18 rest days. They had traveled about 790 miles. In the decades to come, other wagon trains would be able to do the same route (later to be called the Cimarron Route) in two months rather than three, but this hearty band of 66 souls could be proudly counted among some of the earliest trail blazers. The date was Tuesday, August 17, 1841.

The Reverend Danforth assembled his flock together for one final prayer of thanksgiving at the Plaza, then each family said their individual goodbyes, some tearful. Chet went to the authorities to report the names of the three brave souls who had died on the trail, then he collected the mail and grabbed a recent newspaper. He returned to the group and delivered the eagerly expected mail -- one letter was from his own sister -- then suggested that everyone write a letter to their kin informing them that they had arrived safely. He read aloud from the newspaper about President Tyler and other stories while the important task of putting pen to paper was being attended to.

Chester Arbuckle was deeply moved by the thanks which each family gratefully bestowed on him -- the warm handshakes, the hugs, the kisses, the tears of gratitude. His last duty, however, was to collect the other half of the fee which each family owed their late Wagonmaster Flint McCord. When this was done, he called the group together one last time and decreed that these funds -- amounting to $900 -- be divided in half and be given to the widows of Patrick Riley and

Josiah Brown. The pioneers applauded this fair and charitable decision. In the years to come, those in the group who stayed in or near Santa Fe became life-long friends and neighbors.

As the group gradually dispersed, an exhausted but suddenly content Chet turned to his son, tossed an arm across his shoulder, and said with a big grin, "Now, Trent, don't tell our womenfolk yet...but let's see if we can find you that apple pie..."

THE END

by Jack Karolewski

August 8, 2017

LOTTERY WISDOM

So you think that winning the lottery will solve all of life's problems? Think again. Believe me, some things will get better and easier, but other things will throw you for a loop.

My name is Buckley Wesmore, and I'm twenty-nine years old. I was named after my great-great grandfather from Pennsylvania who fought in the Civil War. Folks just call me "Buck," which is good because I prefer that name anyway.

I hail from Mullan, Idaho, a small mining town with a population of 674 in the mountains off of I-90, about ninety miles from Spokane to the west, and six miles from the Montana border to the east. Like most other men in town, I worked in the Lucky Friday Mine. We dug out silver, lead, and zinc at a depth of 6000'. I started there in 2011. But in 2012, one man died underground in an accident in April, and in December, seven men were injured too. As a result, the mine was closed for all of 2013, and 100 of us miners were out of work. My wife of two years, Sheree, filed for divorce six months after that, complaining that we never had any money, despite the fact that I found work as a janitor at the U of M in Missoula, some 110 miles away. It was a long two-hour drive there and two hours back home, Monday through Friday. The gas bills were a killer on my old truck. Sheree said she never saw me.

Maybe she had a point. But what else could I do? We had bills to pay and needed to eat. Anyway, the mine reopened in 2014 and I was back underground. Living alone sucked, but in order to meet new ladies, you had to drive to either Coeur d'Alene or Spokane on the weekends and cruise the bars. I admit that I succumbed to several one night stands, but they were loveless and left me feeling empty.

Life chugged along until last March, when all 100 Lucky Friday miners -- along with 150 other men from the nearby Morning and Star mines -- went out on strike against the mine owners, the HELCA Company. We walked the line for five weeks, over pay and safety issues. They finally caved and we were back on the job.

At the local Mullan watering hole -- the Outlaw Bar & Grill -- I was shooting pool and downing yet another cold bottle of Rainier with my buddies, when Casey Keene started talking about how it would be if he ever won the Powerball lottery.

"I play the same numbers every week, so if I keep it up, I'm bound to hit it big eventually," he remarked. "Buck, you never play the lottery, do you?" Casey asked.

"No, it's just a waste of money. The odds are so steep that it would take a mathematical miracle for you to win. You are as likely to get hit in the head in the next second by a meteor as win," I chortled. "And remember: you're not even wearing your miner's helmet!"

"Aw, you should try it at least once in your life. Who knows? Someone has to win. It might as well be you," Dan Stegler added. "You can drop a dollar at the gas station on your way home tonight. Pick some lucky numbers. I hear the pot is up to $263 million now."

Well, I lost the pool game, so I had to pay for the beers. It was time to call it a night. I went out into the chilly, pine mountain air and passed by the Sinclair gas station. Just for fun every October, as the evening temperatures began dropping here at 3300' altitude, the outdoor, 8' x 5', green plastic brontosaurus out by the pumps – the symbol of the Sinclair Oil Corporation – was 'dressed' in a large purple sweater, a white scarf, and a purple stocking cap. These were the colors of our high school team, the Tigers. The station was owned by the Alatorre brothers, Juan and Carlos. Minding the store Tuesday nights was Juan's wife, Natividad, who went by the nick-name "Nati." The Dino-Mart flashed – along with several neon beer signs by its entrance -- a modest on and off Powerball Lottery sign, with a rainbow leading to a pot of gold. On a lark, I went in.

"Hey, Nati, how's it going?" I began. "Dan suggested that I finally buy my first lottery ticket. Got any lucky numbers for me?"

"Well, Buck, most people pick a combination of important dates, kids' ages, birthdays, addresses, scrambled social security numbers, you name it. If it was me, I would just let the computer do a random pick for you. The odds are so lousy that you can simply blame the machine then when you lose," she laughed.

I laughed too. "O.K. Give me a lucky one dollar ticket, computer generated. $263 million, here I come!" Although the drawing wasn't until tomorrow night, I wasn't anticipating anything other than losing $1.

I worked at the mine the next day as usual. When Wednesday night came around, I was watching an old re-run of The Twilight Zone, the episode where a sophisticated team of bank robbers go into suspended animation in a hidden cave for 100 years with their stolen cache of gold bars – only to discover that gold in the future is worthless as a form of money. At 7:59 p.m., interrupting the commercial break, the lottery drawing was announced. With meager excitement, I retrieved my single ticket from the pocket of my grubby jeans. The Powerball official was crowing about how the jackpot had rocketed to $377 million at last count. I got up from the couch, grabbed the last of my Chips Ahoy cookies from the kitchen, and returned to the living room. By now, all of the numbers had been drawn by a cute blonde assistant and were displayed on the screen.

Unbelievably, as I stared at my ticket, I realized that all of my six numbers matched. I couldn't believe my eyes. But it was true!

I turned the TV off.

Winners had 180 days to claim their prizes. I laid awake half of the night in shock. I called in sick to work the following morning. Then I found the state lottery main office phone number in Boise and called them.

"I...um...think that I won last night's Powerball. What should I do?" I asked nervously. A woman official told me to read the all of the numbers carefully off my ticket to her. After a long pause, she told me to get to Boise as soon as was convenient. "And whatever you do, don't lose that ticket!" she warned. I told her I'd drive down there tomorrow. I later also called in sick for Friday at work.

My head was spinning for the rest of the day. Who should I tell, if anyone? My coworkers? My parents and my two sisters? My boss, Ted Fisher, at the Lucky Friday? I paced the floor thinking and, barely eating any dinner, I went to bed early and suffered another fitful night's sleep. I left the next morning at sunup in my old truck for the lottery office in Boise, some eight hours and 500 miles away. I arrived around 3:00 p.m. after two restroom and gas stops, and a quick lunch at a Taco Bell.

Sure enough, after checking again, I was declared the winner. The sole winner. $377.4 million. I surrendered the ticket to the officials. I signed a bunch of legal documents and chose the 'one lump' payout option, rather than the 25-year monthly payment option. This dropped my winning amount down to $294.3 million. I was counseled to hire both an estate lawyer and a financial planner/accountant. To guard my privacy, if I requested it (and I did), my name would be withheld from the media. A representative from the IRS was on hand, however, and immediately took half of my winnings. But I was still left with over $147 million, given to me as a certified check. (Nati, at the Sinclair station, would also get 1% of the jackpot -- $3.77 million before taxes -- as the sole seller of the official winning ticket.) I shook a lot of hands, and was congratulated numerous times by all of the lottery office staff. I walked out the door in a daze as Idaho's newest multi-millionaire.

Not knowing what else to do, I drove back to Mullan. My town has an elementary school, a high school, the founder "John Mullan Museum," a small weekly town newspaper, a post office, one church (Emmanuel Lutheran), a modest City Hall & adjacent Fire Department, and a library – but no bank or police department. We had to drive eight miles west to Wallace for our main banking (where our mine paychecks were auto-deposited), although the Sinclair station had an ATM machine for quick cash. The nearest police were also found in Wallace, inside the Shoshone County building. I got home around 1:00 a.m. on Saturday and went right to sleep, having driven a thousand miles since Friday dawn.

The U.S. Bank in Wallace wouldn't open until 9:30 a.m. Monday morning, so I had to wait the rest of the weekend to deposit my colossal winning check. I was reluctant to go outside for some odd reason – even to surprise Nati with the stunning news at the Sinclair station – so I stayed in, and passed the time thinking, watching TV, leafing through old hunting and fishing magazines, surfing the internet, eating, and napping. Fortunately, none of my friends either called or stopped by. But I did call Ted at his home, and told him I would be well enough to be back at work in the mine on Tuesday. Strangely to you, perhaps, but I have to confess that I experienced no real joy or ecstasy at suddenly becoming very wealthy. Maybe I was still in shock or denial. It was like being in a surreal dream. Would I be better off in the long run, or was I unwittingly headed towards some unknown disaster?

Abe Fenton at the bank was speechless when I turned up to deposit my certified check on Monday. He even called his Western Division manager to make sure he was handling such a huge, new account correctly. "It wouldn't surprise me if you are now one of the richest men in the State, Mr. Wesmore," Fenton proudly declared. "On behalf of our whole family here at U.S. Bank, we are entirely at your service, day or night." He even offered me his personal home telephone number, but I said that wasn't necessary. He helpfully suggested that I pay off my 30-year house mortgage with U.S. Bank immediately, which I did. He also issued me one Gold and one Platinum-level credit card, either of which could purchase anything around the world instantly without question.

One thing I did want to buy was a new truck. A new 2018, Ford F-150 two-door, to be precise. So I drove further west to Coeur d'Alene until I found Mike White Ford. He had a beauty on the lot in Stone Gray, so I dumped my old 229k-mile beater truck on him and slipped behind the wheel of the new vehicle after we made a very sweet deal. By now, I was starving, so I stopped for lunch at the Cracker Barrel for my favorite meat loaf, then cruised home. The new 5.0 L, V-8 engine purred like a kitten. She handled like a dream too on the curving mountain roads. And the sound system was incredible! I actually began to relax a little, and enjoy the scenery. It was a superb, brilliant autumn day.

My next big decision was whether to quit my job at the Lucky Friday Mine or not. I mulled the pros and cons as I drove. I remembered that I also needed to hire an estate lawyer and a financial planner/accountant very soon.

My new-found reverie was shattered, however, when I exited I-90 at the Mullan Sinclair gas station. There were three local media vans with their satellite upload dishes, and a sizeable crowd outside the Dino-Mart. I pulled in to see what was happening.

Reporters and photographers were surrounding Nati and Juan Alatorre. I overheard an excited question as it was yelled aloud: "So, how does it feel to be a new millionaire, Natividad?"

Nati caught my eye and pointed to me, happily beaming. "Ask him! That's Buck Wesmore. He's the big winner! I got 1% of his winnings as the sole seller of his winning ticket. " She and Juan rushed over to me. Nati was crying tears of joy and hugged me, while her husband stood stunned but grinning from ear to ear.

The press immediately switched to me, like sharks in a feeding frenzy. I noticed from the corner of my eye several of my coworkers and other locals from around the town. Everyone started cheering and applauding my almost unbelievable good fortune. Cameras and cell phones clicked.

Microphones and television equipment were shoved in my face. Looking back, I can barely remember the questions they asked, not to mention my answers.

But one thing was certain: My goose was cooked. Everybody knew I won now. My life was headed for a major upheaval.

That night, multi-millionaire Buckley Wesmore's face was all over the TV news. My home phone and doorbell both seemingly rang non-stop. I was swamped with emails when I logged on my laptop, futilely seeking a little relief. Fortunately, I had no Smartphone, or I would have also been overwhelmed with text messages. Mostly, I was warmly and enthusiastically congratulated, or simply asked how I would spend the $147 million. I awkwardly confessed that I didn't know yet. Finally, I took the phone off the hook and went, exhausted, to bed.

The next morning, a special edition of the town's Mullan Examiner was published, its headline blaring, "Buck Wesmore Wins Mega-Bucks! Millionaire Homeboy Makes Mullan History!"

I called up Nati and congratulated her and her husband, but quickly added that I wished she had taken the lottery 'anonymity' option like I opted for. "I'm so sorry, Buck," she lamented. "I guess I wasn't thinking clearly when I got the shocking announcement call from the lottery people in Boise. Please forgive me. I hope I haven't ruined your life with my big mouth." I told her it was O.K., and that things would probably settle down after a few days anyway.

I went back to work with my dented lunch pail after breakfast like I promised my boss. At the Lucky Friday Mine, my coworkers ogled my new F-150 as I pulled into the parking lot. Casey quipped, "Hey, Buck...you've got enough cash now to buy all 100 of us a new truck like this beauty. How about it? That's what friends are for, ain't it?" Everybody laughed, but there was a peculiar feeling in the air as my squad went down the 6000' shaft in the elevator cage. "Man, I'd quit this mining shit tomorrow if I ever struck it that rich," was the general sentiment said by more than one worker, as we toiled hotly with drills and heavy equipment underground until quitting time. Truth be told, my mind was elsewhere during my shift, although I did my usual job. Ted asked me to stay behind to talk in private for a little bit after the other guys took off.

"Buck, what are your plans now? I read that other lottery winners usually come to work the very next day and tell their boss that they quit. I need to know if I should look for your replacement anytime soon. You can imagine that there are plenty of other men in northern Idaho who could really use a steady, good-paying job like yours," he remarked.

"Well, Ted, my windfall was as big a surprise to me as it is to you. I'm just not sure what I need to do – legally, financially, even morally. Can I keep coming to work until December 31, then give you my decision?" I asked. "I need consistency and routine now to keep my sanity. I hope you understand."

Ted agreed and said it was no problem. "If HELCA asks me, Buck, I'll relay the words you just told me. Now go home in that new truck and enjoy some filet mignon and caviar for dinner," he teased. "See you tomorrow."

Meanwhile that evening, Abe Fenton from the bank emailed me with some recommended contacts for both an estate attorney and a financial planner/accountant. I promptly emailed the first two names back and set up an appointment to meet with them on Saturday at my house. The lawyer's name was Richard Kane, and the financial wizard was Stuart Keyes. They were professional colleagues and even played golf together. They outlined various helpful plans for tax shelters and high-yield/low risk investments. I gave my consent a few days later after checking out some related books at our library and reading up on money management. I was only a high school graduate, and not really up on any advanced economics. I also talked more with Abe at the bank in Wallace.

Was I then surprised to hear from my ex-wife Sheree? Or from my parents and my two sisters? Not really. Sheree called and wanted to come back to me, explaining in a somewhat pleading voice that she still loved me, and that the only reason she divorced me was over money woes. "Now that you have plenty, Buck darling, don't you see that we can be a couple again? We could even have the children you wanted that we couldn't afford before. It's a sure sign from heaven, don't you think? Can't I just come over and see you for a little while, honey?" she offered in desperation. Her naked attempt at a cash grab was pathetic, and I told her so just before I hung up, saying, "No, thanks...Good-bye, Sheree. And please don't bother calling me again."

Next, I heard from my parents in Rapid City, South Dakota. My relationship with them was strained years ago, when I left and moved on my own to Idaho and got married. Dad was in the Air Force, and when his only son declined to follow in his strict military footsteps, a gap widened between us. Mom, meanwhile, went sheepishly along with whatever Dad said, forever siding with him. So I was virtually an outcast. In fact, I hadn't heard from either of them since my divorce five years ago. Not even a birthday call or card.

"We heard the good news on the television, son," Dad began. The last word was uttered with such phoniness, I thought, that I wanted to laugh. "Your mother and I are getting up in years, so naturally we figure that you might be inclined to share a nice chunk of your windfall with your dear old parents," he reasoned. "After all, we brought you into this world, and clothed you and fed you and gave you a roof over your head all those years."

I was filled with an uncomfortable mixture of sadness, anger, and disgust. "Don't forget to add the love and understanding and support that you both showered me with my whole life, Dad. That by itself is worth a few dollars at least," I added sarcastically. "Look...just leave me alone," I spat out before hanging up.

A few days later, my two sisters each made separate attempts to demand some of my winnings. If they hadn't been so obnoxious about it, I might have given them something, but their manner was so crude and harsh that I dismissed their entreaties, vaguely saying, "I'll have to think about it..." The fact that both of their husbands openly derided me and considered me a loser in years past also helped harden my resolve against ever being charitable toward them or their families. If only my sisters had been nice to me when we were growing up together, and had been supportive when I needed it most as we grew older, with no thought of any future material reward!

Meanwhile, I went to work as usual Monday through Friday, but the unspoken tension there was ramping up. First, Dan Stegler explained that because he had been the one who had urged me to buy my first lottery ticket, certainly he should get a reward. "A million dollars would be fair, Buck, don't you think? That still leaves you with $146 million. You won't even feel it. What do you say, pal? For old time's sake? I could really use that dough." I just looked at him in surprise and said nothing.

Casey and my other former friends gradually stopped inviting me for beers at the Outlaw and for poker games on the weekends. I was becoming estranged, against my will. My other coworkers looked at me oddly, or avoided eye contact, or suddenly stopped talking when I approached. It was as if we had nothing in common anymore, even though nothing had changed from my point of view. I sort of sensed that they were envious of me, or that they, too, wanted some of my fortune but were afraid to ask. Only my boss, Ted, related to me in a more normal manner, as he always did.

At home, things also got weird. Riley the mailman regularly brought me dozens of letters from strangers from all across the U.S.: Inventors needing a cash stake for their revolutionary new product. Real estate investors promising huge profits. Offers urging me to Buy Gold! Marriage proposals, many including explicit nude photographs. Former classmates from school needing money. Obscure so-called 'relatives' -- whom I had never heard of -- wanting cash. 'Sob story' cases who pleaded for money for life-saving operations for their children. Which were real and sincere, and which were fake? I couldn't tell. Unknown women claiming I impregnated them and wanting child support. Meanwhile, telemarketers called so often that I had my phone number changed to unlisted. Strangers even appeared on my doorstep, begging for dollars for this and that, some even forcing me to call the police in Wallace to come and get them moved off. I had to delete my Facebook account because of overwhelming 'friend' requests from total strangers. Even some of my lesser-known coworkers came quietly with hat in hand. And the pastor from Emmanuel Lutheran likewise came with a plea for some funds for a new church auditorium.

The usual snows had come to our area in early November, with on and off storms for the next two months. When Christmas approached, I was surprised that only my boss, Ted, invited me to join his family for dinner. I thanked him for his kindness, but explained that I had earlier accepted an invitation from the Alatorre brothers and their families. On a trip to buy gas at the Sinclair, I had fallen into conversation with Juan, and he confessed that Nati had similarly been badgered constantly for money from all directions. They planned to move to San Antonio in the spring and build a big new house there -- so as to be closer to her family in Texas -- while Carlos and his wife, Gabriella, would stay and continue to operate the Sinclair station in Mullan. The Christmas feast at their house was filled with spicy, traditional Mexican holiday treats. Although I wasn't much of a churchgoer, I even attended the Midnight Mass on Christmas Eve with them and their children the night before at St. Joan of Arc Catholic Church in Coeur d'Alene. The warmth of the devout service brought me a needed hour of peace and reflection. I really enjoyed the traditional songs too, and sang along.

Soon, the end of 2018 was in sight, and with it, my last day of work -- just a half-day, because of New Year's Eve. Ted Fisher called all 100 of us together, and gave a speech thanking everyone for an accident-free year at the mine, and concluded by saying that this was my last day and that I would be missed. Perfunctory applause was offered, I shook Ted's hand, and then waved good-bye to those assembled.

I went back to my house on Earle Street. I didn't feel like going alone to a bar for a drink at midnight, so I simply watched the Times Square 'ball-drop' on television, munching on some microwave pizza. When "Happy New Year, 2019!" was at last ushered in, an idea popped into my head as to what maybe I should do next with my life. Having never traveled overseas, I thought that going on an "around the world" cruise could prove both fun and interesting. So I went to bed with that curious thought on my mind.

The next day, January 1, I researched ocean cruises on the internet -- ports of call, dates, reviews, etc. I already had a valid U.S. passport, which I used on several hunting and fishing trips into British Columbia and Alberta. I also found a good travel agency in Coeur d'Alene, called Dream Adventures Travel. I called them when they opened the next morning on Wednesday. Their most experienced agent was a woman named Jana, a forty-year veteran of the travel business.

"You say your name is Wesmore? Buckley Wesmore? You wouldn't happen to be that recent Powerball lottery winner, would you?" Jana asked.

"Yes, I guess that's me...Well, I'm looking for an around the world cruise, leaving sooner rather than later. I need a long change of scenery and lots of time to think. Can you set me up?" I inquired. "And please, just call me Buck."

"Certainly, Mr. Wesm...I mean Buck," Jana replied. "I see on my computer screen here that the Cunard Line has a sailing from Southampton around the world on the Queen Victoria, departing on January 10 and returning on April 28...would that be agreeable? 107 nights visiting six continents, with 35 ports-of-call. It will be absolutely amazing!"

"Sounds great, Jana. Can you book me a nice cabin?" I asked. Although I was basically a simple, bearded bachelor who wore flannel shirts and blue jeans and work boots and liked country music, the exotic images of foreign places I had studied yesterday on the internet beckoned to me now.

"Yes, Buck, let me check...I have sailed on Cunard before, and I can assure you that every cabin is perfect, as is the service and the food and the included shore excursions. You will be treated like royalty, believe me," Jana gushed. "Oh...wait a minute...sold out? Every level? Just a minute...no, wait...yes, yes, I see a last minute cancellation...good, very good...I can get you on Deck 8...it's amidships for a smooth ride. Club Balcony class -- Looks like Room 8058. A little over $33,000 total. O.K. -- Do you have your credit card and passport handy, Buck? I'll need some numbers from you."

I gave her the information she needed. Jana told me that the Queen Victoria was christened in 2007, and that it carried 2061 passengers and 981 crew. "It's awesome, and you say this is your first cruise, Buck? You will be totally impressed," she added. "Now, let's get you flights to London Heathrow and back. Cunard will meet you at the airport and provide a V.I.P. transport to the docks at Southampton. Would like prefer First Class air seats, Buck? You'll fly from Spokane on Alaska Airlines to Seattle, then take British Airways non-stop to London."

I agreed. I had, however, a rather unique special request that I hoped Cunard could agree on. "Once I am aboard ship, Jana, I want to be listed under an assumed name. I don't want to be known only as the Powerball multi-millionaire Buck Wesmore for the entire voyage. I need anonymity. Can you understand and accept that? I would like to be referred to by all the ship's staff as "Nick Adams." He was the main character in a book by Ernest Hemingway that I once enjoyed reading in high school. I identified with his thoughts and his feelings about life...it's kinda hard to explain. Especially his simple love of the outdoors. Can you arrange this for me, Jana?"

Her voice had a smile in it when she replied, "Buck, you would be surprised how many wealthy people sometimes prefer to use a necessary alias for a while. I bet there are several dozen already on your cruise that made the exact same request. And Cunard knows how to please their clients in every way. Nick Adams it will be, for all of your 107 days with them. Not a problem. You are all set. Thank you so much for your business. Let me know if you ever have any other travel needs or questions. And as our office always says: have a real Dream Adventure! Stop by anytime and say Hello."

All of my travel documents arrived via FedEx the next day. I decided to drive to Spokane airport myself and park my truck there. Frankly, I was afraid of theft or vandalism by anyone twisted or jealous, should I leave it in my gravel driveway for more than three months unattended. I also contacted a home security company and had my house wired with an alarm system. By early morning on January 9th, I was all packed and ready to go. I informed Abe, Richard, and Stuart of my itinerary, and of my April 28 return date.

I had never flown First Class before, and I must admit that it was quite a treat, especially on British Airways from Seattle to Heathrow. My spacious cubicle converted into a flat bed when it was time to sleep. They even provided pajamas! The food and drink service was amazing, as were the movie and music offerings. I actually arrived in England -- after nine and a half hours in the air -- quite refreshed and excited. I adjusted the hands on my Timex as I stepped off of Flight #48. Local time was now just past noon, January 10. Jet lag would have to be dealt with eventually, but not yet.

A uniformed Cunard representative met me and my luggage after I went through customs. "Right this way, Mr. Adams," he motioned. He took my bags and escorted me to a deluxe V.I.P. van, and we drove on the wrong side of the road to Southampton, about 65 miles away. The weather was cloudy and chilly like back home, but there were no mountains like back in Idaho. Only rolling hills dusted with snow, with occasional brown patches of fields and pasturelands peeking through. Champagne and snacks were available to me as I comfortably sat in the back of the vehicle taking in the scenery.

The Queen Victoria was a massive ship, visible in the Southampton docks even from a distance. Once aboard past security and escorted to my #8058 stateroom -- which was supplemented with a large bouquet of fresh flowers, a fruit basket, and a chilled bottle of champagne, compliments of Jana and Dream Adventures Travel -- I stepped out onto my balcony. This will be nice, I realized, once we headed into warmer waters and balmy weather, which the majority of this voyage would provide. Then I inspected the ship's facilities.

The ship was a magnificent symphony of fine woodwork, gleaming brass and chrome, and sparkling crystal chandeliers. Jana had not exaggerated its splendor! A complete fitness center with spa, swimming pool, massage, steam room, and sauna. A hair salon. A two-story extensive library. A business center with computers, fax machines, and printers. Wi-fi throughout the ship. The Royal Court Theatre for Broadway-style stage shows, hobby and craft demonstrations, informative lectures, and movies. Several grand dining salons and intimate bars. On-deck sports facilities. A fully-equipped basic medical ward staffed with nurses and physicians. A multi-story atrium. Shops and an art gallery. A casino. And more.

After an obligatory lifeboat stations drill, we raised anchor and festively slipped away from the dock. As I continued my explorations, I noticed that I was probably one of the youngest passengers among the 2061 aboard. Most of the passengers were together as couples -- those retired and able to afford such luxury, with typical ages ranging from the mid-50's to the early 80's, I guessed. When I asked, a helpful hall steward ("Yes, Mr. Adams? How can I be of service?") informed me that there were always some divorced single men and widowed women aboard looking for a mate or at least for some romance, but that the ratio was 4-1 female to male.

I returned to my stateroom to change for dinner. My chamber had a flat-screen TV, a king bed, a desk, a couch, two end chairs, and of course a private bathroom with shower. A schedule of events had been delivered to my door.

I frankly felt somewhat underdressed in the casual elegance of the main dining salon, The Britannia, as I looked around at the other guests. I was seated at a table of eight -- three couples and another single like myself, a charming older divorcee. I was the sole American at our table. Everyone was gracious and put me completely at my ease. The service was excellent and the food was outstanding. During pleasant dinner conversation, I vaguely offered that I was in the mining business out West, even though nobody directly asked me what I did for a living, or any other probing personal questions for that matter. This was rather remarkable to me. I felt that I was completely accepted by seven total strangers with warmth and friendliness. I realized that we were all part of the same sort of social 'group.'

Over the next six days at sea, I relaxed by reading, watching movies, and working out at the Fitness Center. I also took long walks around the Promenade Deck for fresh air and further exercise. I was intrigued at mealtimes -- I ate with different groups -- how nobody was stressed or aggressive or egotistical or competitive. Similarly, the waiters and stewards and maids and officers and other Cunard staff were cordial and unflustered. They were, in fact, all perfect professionals.

Just before we arrived on January 17 at our first port of Hamilton, Bermuda, I got a serious email from Nati Alatorre back in Mullan. She apologized for disturbing me on my vacation, but thought I should know that my former mine boss, Ted Fisher, underwent emergency stomach surgery yesterday and needed to stay in the Kootenai Clinic hospital in

Coeur d'Alene for several days. He was resting comfortably at this point, and was expected to make a full recovery.

"The problem, according to his wife, Buck, is that even after his HELCA medical insurance pays out, their family estimates that they will still be over $343,000 in debt from all the bills. I thought you should know the whole story, seeing as you always spoke so highly of him. It's a sad, tough situation for them. We have been saying prayers for them. Anyway, I hope you enjoy your cruise, my dear friend. Juan and I might be moved out to Texas by the time you get back in late April, but you are always welcome to visit us anytime at our new house in San Antonio. Love and hugs, Nati."

There was no question as to what I could and should do. I immediately emailed Abe Fenton at U.S. Bank and instructed him to wire $343,000 to Ted Fisher, along with flowers and a sincere get-well card from me -- adding that he should mention that I would visit Ted when I returned to town in late April.

It was nice walking around Bermuda for the day, enjoying the sunny 70 degree weather, and strolling down the well-tended streets lined with attractive, pastel-colored shops and houses. The British colonial past was still evident, with the khaki, Bermuda shorts-clad, uniformed policemen directing downtown traffic.

Back on the Queen Victoria at dinnertime, I was seated at yet another new table, and was introduced to Miles Carrington and his wife, Ellie. They lived in Hamilton, and had just joined our cruise. They were going as far as Cabo San Lucas in Baja, Mexico. "We have never gone through the Panama Canal, so we thought it would be interesting," Ellie explained. She was an attractive, petite, platinum-haired woman in her late 50's, I estimated. Her husband, Miles, was tan and fit, tall and silver-haired, probably in his early 60's. He offered that he was a retired real estate developer from North Carolina. He met Ellie when sailing his yacht from the Caribbean to Bermuda thirty years ago. She was a Bahamian citizen, so when they married, she was granted dual U.S.-Bahamian citizenship, as was Miles. They had two grown sons.

As we sailed towards Florida, I kept bumping into Miles over the next two days, either in the Fitness Center, or walking the Promenade Deck for brisk exercise before breakfast. We started into conversation. I remarked how everyone I had met so far was remarkably pleasant, and how people didn't pry into each other's personal lives.

"Well, Nick, you've probably observed that most of the passengers onboard are rather wealthy. It is an unspoken rule among such society to never probe into another one's business in public. We never discuss any specifics regarding money, or politics, or religion. That is always done on a private, personal level among friends. For example, you said that you were in the mining business out West. That's all you need to say, ever, in public. People respect that rule. Now, you may have inherited vast wealth, or may be currently amassing it at your young age through brains and hard work. "Old" money or "new" money, as it were. You may have made a fortune gambling, or in the stock market, or in organized crime. You may be hiding from the authorities. You may even be traveling under an alias. No matter. You are completely accepted here -- as long as you 'blend in' and don't violate the established 'peace of the club,' so to speak."

I asked Miles how many Americans he thought were on board.

"Of the 2000 or so passengers, from what I have observed, and from past cruise experience at this level, I would guess about 200," he replied. "Of those, most will be from the East or West coasts: Boca Raton, Hilton Head, Boston, Palm Springs, La Jolla, Newport Beach. Some Texans from outside Dallas/Ft. Worth. A few from Denver, or Jackson Hole or Telluride. Maybe some from Hawaii. But most of the passengers on the QV are from Europe and the U.K., Australia, Canada, Singapore, China, the United Arab Emirates, India, or Saudi Arabia. Not that long ago, you saw many from Japan, but no more. Instead, you have the rich newcomers from post-Communist Russia -- but most of those have mafia money, and tend to mix only with their fellows."

The following day, we talked more while walking the top deck for exercise.

"Nick, I like you," Miles began, smiling. "You are friendly and curious. I wish my two sons had turned out more like you. But sadly, they both became lazy, wastrel playboys, throwing away a serious chunk of the money I worked so hard to earn over thirty-five years in the real estate market. Blew it at race tracks, or on booze, bimbos, even cocaine. Ellie and I finally disinherited them. We never talk with either one anymore. Maybe we spoiled them too much when they were boys, who knows? Anyway, if you don't mind, can I share with you a quick lifetime of advice that might help you with your own life's journey? I could take you 'under my wing' -- kind of like a father and son -- until we part ways when I get to Cabo and fly home. How about it? I daresay you might find my counsel useful to you one day."

I was both intrigued and honored, so I agreed and listened. Plus, Miles seemed cordial, honest, and sincere.

"O.K., well, Nick, let's start with some gentle advice regarding your appearance. You might consider getting a completely new wardrobe. (I was ashamed to admit -- and I didn't -- that I bought all my clothes at Wal-Mart, and that my cruise luggage was packed with nothing but.) When we get to Port Canaveral for Orlando tomorrow, let's take a few hours together without Ellie -- she'll understand -- and buy you some new clothes. Then, I would most respectfully suggest -- and please don't be offended -- that we take you to an upscale hair salon for a better haircut and the removal of your bushy beard. You will look so sharp when we get done, trust me! What do you say?"

I laughed and thought, sure, why not? Beards were a sweaty nuisance in tropical weather anyway, and being better dressed could make me in fit more easily, appearance-wise, with the rest of the ship's passengers.

Shopping the next day was actually fun. Miles knew which stores offered the finest clothing for the best prices. My gold American Express card provided extra special attention from each shopkeeper. I purchased various kinds of shirts, slacks, shorts, shoes and socks, along with two new belts, a wide-brimmed tropical hat, and a swimsuit. I also bought one dark and one light-colored sport coat. Miles explained that I wouldn't need a tie, but that I could rent a tuxedo on board our ship for any gala, such as the Captain's Dinner. Then we went and I had my first barber shave, just like in the movies. I was actually impressed after that -- and with my fine new haircut -- when a mirror was presented for my approval by the beaming elderly Cuban barber!

Back onboard later for dinner, I asked to be seated again with Miles and Ellie. The rest of our table remarked how handsome I looked, now clean-shaven and wearing a light silk sport coat over a navy Sea Island cotton polo shirt. I indeed felt like a new man! Someone at our table later brought up the topic of sailing. Miles soon talked about sailing with his wife from Hamilton to the Bahamas on his yacht, the "Miss Ellie," named both for his lovely wife, and for their favorite character on the "Dallas" prime time soap opera TV show from the 1980's, played by the actress Barbara Bel Geddes. "Of course, that was before Nick's time," Ellie added, and everyone smiled. I admitted in reply that I once saw the famous "Who Shot J.R.?" episode on YouTube, but that was all.

The next day we docked at Fort Lauderdale. Miles asked if I wanted to play an hour or two of tennis while Ellie and some of the new friends she made onboard went shopping. ("I know our ship has a tennis court on Deck 11, but this will be better," he assured me.) He had complimentary admission to an exclusive beach club through his American

Express Centurion card -- the so-called Black Card -- one of the most exclusive in the world, obtained only by referral from another Black Card member. I had to disappoint him by admitting that I had never hefted a racket. "That's O.K., Nick. And I know neither of us likes to golf, but how about we go find a good bookstore instead? I have a mental list of books I would recommend you read, some of which are not available in our ship's library."

At Miles' urging, I picked up some books by or about Andrew Carnegie, John D. Rockefeller, Charles Francis Feeney, Bill Gates, Michael Dell, and Warren Buffet. "Focus on how they made their wealth, then on how they gave -- or are still giving -- it away to noble causes or through foundations," Miles counseled. "With great wealth comes great responsibility. Many in the public have a dim view of achievers, clouded by envy and ignorance or the Media. They assume that we are all just greedy crooks, or dumb lucky, or that we were simply given our wealth, or that we made our fortunes exploiting the poor working classes. Yes, some of this goes on, but believe me, probably 80% of the rich today worked hard -- sometimes 60-80 hours a week for decades -- and worked fairly and honestly for their success. (Did you know that the top 1% of earners in America pay 55% of the entire nation's federal income taxes, Nick? The wealthy in our country pay their legal share and more, believe me.) Most ascribe to a strong moral and humanitarian outlook, whereby they provide needed jobs, products, and services for people everywhere-- while at the same time benefiting communities around the world through admirable relief charities and other philanthropies in science, education, medicine, and the environment.

Few need ever be ashamed of their wealth, Nick, providing they put it to good use for mankind. Capitalism is far from perfect, but it is still the best system we have at this time in history."

We continued on to the western Caribbean island of Aruba, then later stopped in historic, colonial Cartagena in Columbia, my first pleasing taste of the exotic continent of South America. Soon, it was time to transit through the Panama Canal. I read David McCullough's excellent history, "The Path Between the Seas" from the ship's library to better appreciate the experience. Miles and Ellie marveled at the amazing construction feat through the steamy isthmus jungle. The canal had recently been widened and deepened to allow for larger ships to pass through. It was quite impressive!

Miles and I agreed to meet for an hour a day -- either in the Fitness Center or walking the decks for exercise -- to continue my 'education' as a father might give to a son. Truly, this remarkable man took more interest in my welfare over just those many days than my own father had ever shown me over many years. I was very grateful! One day, I learned about what and how to order in a fine restaurant. Another day, I learned about wines and liquors, or what were the best cars, or how to tip graciously. He advised me about banking and investments (Move your money to either the Grand Caymans or Switzerland to avoid excess taxes, and avoid 'high risk' stocks in the stock market), or what were the best charities to donate to (Salvation Army was #1, but avoid both the United Way and the American Red Cross because of their high administrative overhead and recurrent scandals). He educated me on the subject of classic movies ("Citizen Kane and The Treasure of the Sierra Madre will both teach you well about the pitfalls of money, Nick.") and on classical music and opera (with no mention of either Johnny Cash or Shania Twain, imagine that -- ha!). Although he didn't hunt, Miles knew quite a bit about firearms, so we discussed that topic during one of our hours together. Later, we even talked about fly-fishing -- the only subject I actually knew more about than him! I learned about other cultures from Miles' many travels too, and what additional countries to visit someday after my around the world cruise was complete. Finally, he warned me about women and lawyers.

"Beware of the gold-diggers, Nick. If you marry again (I had earlier revealed that I was once divorced), be sure to get a signed pre-nuptial agreement. Check out her family background and her overall mental health carefully. Be in love, sure, but keep a clear mind at all times. As for lawyers, consider yourself lucky if you can find a good, honest one. Beware of estate lawyers and accountants that you may hire to financially plan and manage your fortune. They may try and skim off money for themselves that you are unaware of. Always check your receipts for any shady 'double-billing' or worse. Also make sure that they work independently of each other, not in tandem. They shouldn't be old friends who golf together, for example." At that last mention, I had a sinking feeling in my stomach, but stayed silent. I flashed back to Richard Kane and Stuart Keyes. Was I wise to trust them, on only banker Abe Fenton's recommendation?

      Our next port was Puntarenas in Costa Rica. We had a planned afternoon excursion to explore the country's famous rain forests. I decided to take all of my old Wal-Mart clothes -- except my winter coat -- and donate them to the first poor Costa Ricans I met that morning after we docked. I asked my stateroom porter for two large plastic bags. Taking the filled bundles with me, I wandered quite far from the docks to a local bus stop. Suddenly, I was back in the Third World, and the effect was jarring in both sights and smells. I offered one bundle each to a poor man and a poor woman waiting for the bus. They were dumbfounded at such generosity from a complete stranger, and thanked me profusely in Spanish. Then I returned to the ship and made myself ready for the rain forest activity -- my modest good deed done.

Cabo San Lucas was the end of the line for the Carringtons, so it would be farewell here to both Miles and Ellie. "Now if you ever get to Bermuda, be sure to look us up. We can even go sailing around the island on the Miss Ellie," Miles offered. We exchanged emails, and I thanked him heartily for all of his help and advice. "Oh, it was a real pleasure," Miles assured me. "Just remember that money is only a tool to use and not an end unto itself. Your health is the most important thing in this world, and next comes having enough time to enjoy it. Find the true love of your life and love her in return. Do what you are happiest doing for your career, Nick, if the mining business doesn't completely satisfy you. Be your own boss, if possible. Be independent-minded. Don't be suckered by politics. Strive for excellence in everything that you do! And give back what you can to help make the world a better place for your being in it." Miles and I clasped hands in a rather emotional goodbye, then I hugged and kissed Ellie. Lastly, Miles surprised me with a small wrapped gift that he had hidden behind his back. I was embarrassed that I hadn't gotten a gift to give them in return and said so, but Miles just laughed and winked and whispered: "Pay it forward." The wonderful couple then smiled and turned and walked away down the gangplank onto Mexican soil, where a waiting limo would take them to the airport.

Back in my stateroom before my snorkeling activity at Cabo's iconic sea rock Arch, I opened my gift. It was a new silver Omega SeaMaster wristwatch, the same kind I noticed Miles had worn. Included in the box was a note which said: "Make every day count, Nick, and thanks for sharing some of your time with me – May God continue to Bless you...Best wishes always, Miles" Wow. I would never forget this remarkable man, and all that he taught me...I took off my battered Timex from my wrist (saving it for sentimental reasons, and placing it in a desk drawer) and replaced it with the pristine Omega.

From Cabo, the Queen Victoria steamed up the western coast of North America to San Francisco, where we would arrive on February 6 and stay for two days. I walked the entire Golden Gate Bridge and back again, visited the de Young Art Museum, took in Fisherman's Wharf, and toured the infamous defunct federal prison on Alcatraz Island. Back at sea, I socialized anew with other passengers at mealtimes, or during the daily traditional 4:00 p.m. British tea time, or when I was simply strolling the decks or at the swimming pool. I likewise chatted with the ship's officers and was even invited to visit the Bridge, where the basics of sea navigation were briefly explained to me. I attended lectures in the Royal Court Theatre on the upcoming flora and fauna we would encounter in the Pacific, and also on the history of its many islands. (Inspired, I promptly borrowed a copy of James Michener's hefty novel, "Hawaii," from the ship's library, which the presenter eagerly recommended.) On one of many crystal clear nights, I even took in an expert astronomy lecture, complete with telescopes, sighting the various constellations of the Northern Hemisphere, all of which would later vanish once we sailed south of the Equator. Meanwhile, I surmised that about one-fourth of the guests were going on the complete circumnavigation like me, while the remaining passengers were getting on or off at shorter sailing segments. I spent many hours, too, on my room balcony in the sun and mild breezes, reading the books that Miles had suggested. Such inspiring and interesting lives these men led! I thought, as I poured over biography after biography.

Honolulu was our next port of call, as our good weather continued. In fact, we had only four days of rain so far since leaving wintery Southhampton. I could only imagine the cold and gray skies back in Idaho at this time of year. Mullan seemed such a distant memory now...

It was in port in Hawaii on February 11 that I first set eyes on the stunningly beautiful Loni Tang. She was tall and slim, about 5'10", with long black hair parted down the middle, long legs jutting out from under her short, flower-print dress, and fine, tapered fingers. Her dark eyes were alluring, and she had a dazzling smile which complimented her flawless, tanned skin. I found out later that she was twenty-four years old, and was a travel agent from Honolulu on a complimentary Cunard junket to Sydney. Would I be exaggerating if I said that she immediately caught every man's eye on the QV, and every woman's envy? Her blood ancestry was French Polynesian, Chinese, and Filipino -- a typical mixture common with many residents now living in Hawaii.

Over the next five days at sea, we ate several meals together and had long, pleasant, and meaningful conversations. I bet everyone on board sensed that romance was in the air whenever Loni and I were seen together, and that we would make a superb couple. I confess that our mutual attraction was positively electric, and I was very pleased when she finally invited me into her stateroom one calm, moonlit night...

Our lovemaking was incredible, her body perfect and responsive, unlike any woman I had ever known. Was I falling in love with her? Too early to say, but my heart was captivated by Loni's charms and by her tender, easy-going manner. She was smart and worldly too, perhaps surprisingly so in one so young. She allowed that she used a diaphragm for birth control, and that I needn't worry about using any condoms. Loni always slipped quickly into her bathroom and then skipped back into bed just before we made love. Total bliss! "Oh, Nick..." she murmured, overwhelming me with her kisses and caresses.

After crossing the International Date Line on February 14, the QV steamed south of the Equator -- and into the reversed season of summer -- as we visited Samoa and Tonga, then headed for three stops in New Zealand, including their capital, Auckland.

But time was running out on Loni and me, as we were now just two days out from Sydney and her departure back to Honolulu. I desperately wanted to continue to be with her, and directly said as much, as we prepared for another night together.

She went into her bathroom beforehand, as usual. I happened to accidentally knock over a stack of travel documents that had been placed on her nightstand beside her bed, as I moved them to place a water glass that I had been drinking from. When I gathered the papers back together, the bottom one fell out: it was an article about big Powerball winner Buck Wesmore of Mullan, Idaho -- along with my previously bearded photo!

"What the hell is this?" I angrily demanded, holding up the article, as Loni came out of her bathroom in the nude.

"Dammit, Nick! What are you doing looking through my private papers?" she answered. But I could tell she knew she was caught and guilty of something very, very bad.

I calmed down somewhat and asked her to sit down beside me on the bed. I took her hand, "Look, just tell me the truth, Loni. What's going on here?"

There was a long pause, then a big, exhaled sigh from her. "I'm very sorry, Nick...or should I call you Buck now? I used my special travel agent internet tricks to secretly find out which passengers were traveling on the Queen Victoria incognito, based on their actual passport names and numbers. I have actually done the same Honolulu to Sydney run on different cruise ships at my own expense the last three years. I look for wealthy single men to blackmail for my silence when I reveal that I know their true identities. I have also collected expensive gifts like jewelry or simply cash from men -- single or married -- whom I sleep with on these cruises. As for you, dear heart, I'm forced to shamefully admit that I hoped you would get me pregnant on this voyage, so I could sue you big for paternity. I was going to testify in court, if need be, that I 'forgot' to insert my diaphragm in a moment of reckless passion the last time we had sex. So now you know that I am both a liar and a whore. I'm really sorry, Buck, but I'm really not ashamed of the terrible things I do. A girl has it tough in this world, and only so many years before her freshness and beauty fades, and I'm just looking after myself because, well, nobody else does."

In disgust, shock, and hurt, I lowered my face into my hands, and closed my eyes, bewildered. After a minute or so, I got up and got dressed. "So all you did and said with me was just for money?" I asked, incredulously. But Loni had her back to me now and was getting dressed. She never responded. I walked in a daze to her stateroom door and went away, back to my own room. Loni Tang left the ship on February 27, and I never spoke with or saw her again...

The QV stayed docked in Sydney Quay for two days. The city's location was stunning, but I was so miserable that I couldn't appreciate any of its offerings. I even had some of my meals sent to my stateroom, because I was in no mood to socialize in public. It took me several more days to get over what Loni had done to me, but time heals all hurts, doesn't it? We had three more stops in Australia, then headed for beautiful Bali in Indonesia. From there, we went on to Singapore, then made three stops in Vietnam (where, on March 15th, I celebrated my 30th birthday in Ho Chi Minh City, with a complimentary cake aboard ship after dinner) as we worked our way north to Hong Kong. We enjoyed a nice two day stay in that amazing and exciting city, then went back south through to Malacca in Malaysia, on our way to Colombo in Sri Lanka. By now, March 29, I was feeling like my old self again. In another month, the stately Queen Victoria would arrive back at Southampton, and my 107-day epic circumnavigation would be over. I hoped that by then, I would figure out how and where I wanted to spend the rest of my life. Although I didn't bring a camera with me on this trip -- preferring to simply collect one memorable postcard from each of the ports we visited as my only souvenirs -- I did take in a nature photography lecture as well as two art drawing classes. I even took some tennis lessons on Deck 11, but have to confess that I wasn't very good. I also read still more books, this time on the subject of famous mariners and explorers, like James Cook, Ferdinand Magellan, and William Bligh (of "Mutiny on the Bounty" fame).

I really liked the Indian Ocean islands of the Seychelles, Mauritius, and Reunion. The coconut palm trees and crystal blue waters lapping on white sand beaches were intoxicating, as was swimming with colorful tropical fish and sea turtles. Later, when we finally set foot on South African soil, I realized I had now been on six of the seven continents of the world! I especially enjoyed our two days in Cape Town, a fabulous city in a magnificent natural setting near the historic Cape of Good Hope. Two more ports followed -- Walvis Bay in

Namibia, and Gran Canaria in the Canary Islands. At last, precisely on schedule on Sunday, April 28, we steamed back into the docks at Southampton.

As I was taken to Heathrow, the driver said upon our arrival, "On behalf of the entire crew of the Queen Victoria and the Cunard family, I would like to thank you for giving us the pleasure of serving you, Mr. Adams. As we now say good-bye, we wish to further award you with this special, inscribed Circumnavigation certificate, proving that you are one of our most exclusive passengers who have completely circled the globe with us. We wish you happy future travels, sir, and hope to see you again soon." He then escorted me and my luggage to the British Airways First Class lounge, where we crisply shook hands, and other BA personnel took care of my documents and tickets. What an adventure! The long voyage had really opened my eyes and my mind, yet I was anxious now to get back home to Idaho. Plus, I was back to being called by my real name again.

Upon my return at Spokane Airport, I was gladdened to see my Ford F-150 truck was still there, safe and waiting. I stopped in Coeur d'Alene on the way back home for Dream Adventures Travel and said a quick "Hi!" to Jana, thanking her again for setting up such a delightful cruise for me. Once back in Mullan, everything looked strange and foreign for awhile. I picked up all the mail at the post office that I had asked Riley to save for me, and went into my house. Dropping off three large bundles of letters, as well as my luggage, I called, then went right over to see how Ted Fisher was doing. He was fortunately in fine shape and great spirits, and had been given the green light by his doctors to go back to work as before. He noted my missing beard and tanned face. "You look terrific, Buck!" He then repeatedly thanked me with deep emotion for gifting him all of his unpaid medical bills. "You saved me, Buck, and I can never praise your thoughtfulness enough," Ted spoke, with tears in his eyes. I told him we would always be good friends.

I stopped next at the Sinclair Dino-Mart to pick up some groceries for my pantry and my refrigerator. Gabriella and Carlos rushed to greet me. "Where's your beard, Buck? Did you forget it on some tropical beach?" they teased. I shared some of the highlights of my trip. They informed me that Juan and Nati had moved out to Texas already, then they invited me to have dinner with them and their kids anytime I wanted, once I was resettled.

It took more than three hours to review my backlogged mail piles the next day. Probably 95% was either money requests or junk. The remainder was bills, bank statements, or other important documents. Taking Miles

Carrington's advice, I carefully checked the billings from both Richard Kane and Stuart Keyes. Sure enough, I found some 'padded' statements, some questionable hours billed, and some probably deliberate math errors. Each man appeared to have skimmed roughly $45,000 of mine over the four-month period. I immediately called Abe Fenton at U.S. Bank and angrily complained. He said he would investigate, but sounded nervous, like he too had something to hide. Meanwhile, I had already decided in my mind to fire both Kane and Keyes and to move my entire account to another bank, away from Abe's control. I would also pass on any further legal action against those two men, judging that the additional costs and time might not be worth the fight to prove malfeasance in court.

After another month, I was back to growing my beard again, and wearing T-shirts and blue jeans. I put my battered Timex back on my wrist, and placed my Omega in a drawer, to be worn again only on special occasions along with my finer clothes from the cruise. And although they whined and denied and complained, I fired both Kane and Keyes.

June came in with her usual warm weather and sunshine. Having never visited Glacier National Park in remote, northwestern Montana, I decided to drive up the 150 miles and check it out. Once driving through Kalispell, I instantly fell in love with the place, located just before the main Park entrance.

Rustic, not too crowded, beautiful scenery, nice people. I investigated land prices first, then home prices. There was nothing holding me back in Mullan, so I thought that building a deluxe log cabin on five groomed acres on the outskirts of Kalispell might be the ideal way to go. I scouted out the details and looked at possible home locations over the next three days, staying at a motel while I explored.

I eventually found a builder that I liked: Custom Cabins, Inc. The contractor offered a 2900 square foot, two-story gem. It featured 4 bedrooms, 2.5 baths, and came with a wrap-around front porch and huge stone fireplace for those rough Montana winters. Asking price was $879, 599. I told him I would give him $850,000 cash if he could start work right away. "Mr. Wesmore, got a deal, sir! She'll be ready to move in by September." He grinned as we both happily pumped hands.

The next task was transferring all of my money from Wallace to a new bank in Kalispell. I went with Valley Bank of Kalispell, in business since 1911. The manager, Roger Mann, took care of my saying goodbye to Abe Fenton, as my remaining $145+ million was electronically shifted to the new facility. I cancelled my two U.S. Bank gold and platinum credit cards and obtained new ones through Valley Bank. As for getting a new estate lawyer and financial planner/accountant, I would do my own research and hiring down the line when the need arose.

I then continued my planned trip into Glacier National Park. Spectacular! More than I expected. Nature's grandeur and majesty on raw display at every turn of the road, especially on the "Going to the Sun" Highway. Plentiful wildlife. Plus, I found something else here that was totally unexpected. A gorgeous, young Park Ranger by the name of Dawn Everett. I casually asked her out to dinner when she got off duty. Luckily, she accepted. We ate at the Ptarmigan Dining Room at Many Glacier Lodge. I had the Bison Tenderloin, and Dawn had the Wild Alaskan Salmon. We both drank craft beers and split a gooey dessert.

Dawn was twenty-eight, and had been a Park Ranger for three years. She grew up on a ranch in Billings, with three brothers. She had always been an outdoor person -- horseback riding, skiing, backpacking, mountain biking. Dawn even knew how to hunt and fish -- bonus! She was sturdy but very feminine and shapely, about 5' 7", with reddish-brown hair tied back in a ponytail, and a ruddy complexion from being out daily in the sun and wind. I can tell you that the chemistry between us was definitely there! Her park duties included doing Ranger trail walks, identifying the plants and flowers, spotting bears and mountain goats, doing night star hikes, leading canoeing excursions on the lakes, and attending to the 'junior ranger' kid programs.

Over several dates, our friendship developed into something much more serious. I drove back and forth from Mullan to Kalispell, checking on the progress of my new log house while then arranging to spend maximum time with Dawn. I explained that I had been a silver miner, but that now I wanted to try something else. I further allowed that I was building a house in Kalispell and that I had once been married, but I mentioned nothing about my financial situation. We finally made love for the first time at the Red Lion Hotel back in Kalispell, and it was truly very special. In fact, it was perfect...

I should note here that while all of this was happening, I was taking an increasing interest in the various kinds of carpentry going into the building of my deluxe cabin home. I asked to be taught some of the simple wood skills, and the dozen or so workmen I was employing were more than happy to oblige. Each time I dropped in to see their progress, I was allowed to do more and more carpentry. It was wonderful work that completely absorbed me. Truthfully, I liked it much better than mining underground. Because there were no restrictive union rules preventing anyone with experience to build houses in Montana, the men said that after this job was completed, they could easily set me up working with them on other construction projects. "The pay is good, too, but working outside in the winter up here is totally different than during the nice summer months, so be forewarned!" they advised.

I told Dawn the next time we met of my desire to become at least a part-time carpenter. "I may have found my new calling, sweetheart," I revealed. "How about you move in with me in my new house when it's finished in September, and you can help decorate and furnish it from scratch? Kalispell is close to your job. I can sell my old house in Mullan. We can try out our relationship for six months or so, and see if it's a 'keeper.' Then I want to meet your family...and if you agree...we can get married. You must realize by now that I love you." Dawn's eyes kind of popped out of their sockets, but she then replied without hesitation, "Buck, baby, I'm in! And I love you too, my special darling." We hugged and kissed all night, laughing and loving, back at the Red Lion Hotel...

As promised, my deluxe log home was completed in September, and Dawn moved in. I needed to make one last trip back to Mullan to sell my house on Earle Street. I decided as I was driving to simply offer my house for free -- with all of its furnishings -- to my good friends Carlos and Gabriella Alatorre, because they had been living in increasingly cramped quarters in the rear of the Sinclair station and Gabriella was expecting a third child in December. They were overjoyed in thankfulness as we later signed the transfer documents! I loaded up a few boxes of clothing and personal effects into my truck, and drove back to Kalispell after stopping by Ted's house to give him my new Montana address. As a final act for my old town, I gave the Mullan Public Library a check for $100,000, to encourage others to love reading as much as I had re-discovered on my epic ocean voyage.

It was fun choosing the new appliances and furniture and other accessories for our new cabin with Dawn over the next three months. Dawn continued working at Glacier, while I worked part-time learning and doing various carpentry jobs in the Kalispell area. Our relationship was strong and deepening. I wanted to spend the rest of my life with Dawn, and told her so. I also wanted to start a family after we got married. Regarding finances, I assured her that money was not going to be a problem, and that I would explain that cryptic pronouncement someday soon. "Trust me," I said, and that was the bottom line. And she did.

I'll never forget Christmas Eve, 2019. Dawn had to work late at the Park until 8:00 p.m., so I was alone as the sun set and it quickly got dark. I was up for some exercise, so I decided to take a walk around downtown Kalispell. Everything was either closed or closing, as people hurried home for the festive evening. A full moon was out, and snow was gently falling. By now, the streets were almost deserted. All was calm and peaceful. It was then that a heard the rhythmic ringing of some kind of hand bell. I decided to follow the sound down the street to see where it was coming from.

After a block, I saw a tiny old woman stationed by her Salvation Army kettle, which was hanging on a metal tripod. She was wearing her official dark blue uniform and cap with its red piping. The street appeared deserted except for her and me. "Merry Christmas!" she chirped and then smiled as I approached. Intrigued, I asked her name and why she was still out so late on this special night.

"My name is Grace, and I do this every year for any last minute donations. You ask me why I do this? Because it's the right thing to do. It helps other who need it. It's that simple, really. Ask yourself this one, all-important question whenever you wonder what to do next in your life, young man: What is the right thing to do? God will always give you the answer."

I was stunned at her revelation, and then at my own deep realization. I took several large bills out of my wallet and stuffed them into the slotted red kettle. "Thank you, friend! I guess I'll pack up now and go back. I think you are the last person I'll see tonight. Merry Christmas again, young man, and May God Bless You!" I asked if I could hug her good-bye, and she laughed and said," Sure...I can always use any extra warmth at my age!" Grace felt so tiny in my arms, but so good too. We then went our separate ways. When Dawn came home, I told her all about the transcendent encounter. "Wow, that sounded like something out of a movie...how cool is that?"

The day after Christmas, I contacted the Salvation Army Western District office. I then made plans with Roger Mann at Valley Bank to send them an anonymous wire transfer of $135 million. I thought of all I learned from Grace, and from Miles Carrington, back on the QV. This truly was the right thing to do...

My remaining Powerball winnings of just over $10 million would take care of Dawn and me and any future children of ours for the rest of our lives.

I sat down with Dawn on New Year's Eve and told her my entire life's story, and about my wealth and what I had done with it. In early 2020, I met her family in Billings, and we announced our engagement. She had no qualms about signing a pre-nuptial agreement, given the circumstances. In fact, she insisted on doing it. We got married on July 6th in a cute chapel in Missoula, and later honeymooned at Lake Louise in the Canadian Rockies.

When Dawn happily announced months later that I would soon be the father of a baby boy, my next thought was: Should we name our son Nick, or Miles?

THE END

by Jack Karolewski

December 6, 2018

I SAW THE LIGHT

I was nine years old in 1960, and was living with my family on the South Side of Chicago. Our house was small – around 875 square feet, built of wood for my maternal grandparents in 1898 – with one area used as a bedroom by my two sisters, one bathroom, one bedroom for my parents, and one tiny bedroom for me. There was a kitchen, a dining room, a living room, and also a basement. We lived a few blocks from both the steel mills and Lake Michigan.

Our house was sold -- with all of its furniture and appliances, for $8500 – after my Father died in 1974. (My Mother died in 1966.) The house then had a few different owners until it burned to the ground in 2007 when the neighborhood became a drug- and crime-riddled ghetto. Today, it is a weed-choked vacant lot, a dangerous area only viewable quickly during daylight hours from one's moving car, with its windows and doors locked. But back to my true tale.

Being the only boy in the family, I spent a lot of time either alone or with my school buddies. I sensed at an even earlier age that my family was largely dysfunctional, and that I was trapped in a bad situation. My parents argued like cats and dogs. Excessive alcohol didn't help matters either. There was always fear among us three children whenever we were home, either day or night. What would the next hour bring? The answer was always unknown until it happened. There were beatings and cursing, doors slammed, threats made. Cigarette smoke choked our childhood lungs. As for love and affection from our parents, it was so sparse that I can hardly remember any. The same went with encouragement, or praise, or guidance towards any kind of potential future careers. Sadly, there were few books in our basically non-intellectual household. As a result of this environment, I spent as much time as possible away from the turmoil at home. I rode my bike far away to the beach, or to undeveloped areas where I explored wild grassy fields. I often begged to stay overnight at friend's homes, where I was treated to refreshing glimpses of family normality. My dream, my goal was to get away and never come back. I had to get away, or my mind would shatter at the sad reality of the unfairness of my environmental circumstances. What had I done to deserve this? Why couldn't I have been born into a different family? How could I escape, even at age nine?

Meanwhile, I worked hard at school and got good grades, and enjoyed going on my bicycle to the closest neighborhood public library branch every Saturday to load up on my weekly limit of ten books. I absorbed everything, especially picture books of faraway lands and different cultures and scenes from ancient history. I would pour over maps and globes. I began reading encyclopedias, starting in alphabetical order. But I was always forced to go back home for food and work chores and a place to sleep.

When I got especially frustrated with my home life, I would play alone --in good weather -- outside at the front of our house. We had a tall wooden staircase which led fifteen steps to our front door. At the bottom, to the left, was a clump of two green bushes. That was my secret kingdom. There, I observed insects, and played with my toy soldiers and toy dinosaurs for hours. I would dig into the dirt with sticks and old pieces of metal. Sometimes I would flood the whole area with cups of water, or make miniature cities out of stones or cardboard. It was a peaceful activity, akin to building plastic model airplanes, boats, cars, and army tanks indoors on winter evenings.

As always, though, my respite was short-lived, and soon I was thrown back into the hectic maelstrom of family dysfunctionality. Meal times were tense and unnatural. There was little meaningful conversation, just unhappy people staring around the table. Unimaginative menus. No fun or laughter. What was I doing here? Where was the simple joy of living? Not here. That was a phantom. Nowhere to be found in this place.

Of course I secretly cried at night, lost and alone. My sleep was tormented too. Headaches and stomachaches during the day, nightmares at night. Trapped.

I forget the exact date, but I am sure it was in late August of 1960, shortly after my ninth birthday. School would be starting up again after Labor Day, in about another week. The day was especially stressful, filled with yelling and face-slapping for ridiculous, minor transgressions that were beyond my tender realizations. I fled the house and stood between our small house and the tall three-story apartment building next door, to the north (or right) of our frontage.

It was the golden hour of light, when the sun seems to flare up in magnificent splendor just before it begins its descent over the western horizon. The rays warmed my face as I stood on a narrow strip of cement which separated our meager city lawn with that of our neighbors. I was barefoot, wearing worn blue jeans and a soiled t-shirt. The shaft of light poured down on me, seemingly magnified by being squeezed between the two structures. The air was calm, but with the typical smells of summer. It was quiet. There were no other people around, which was unusual because many folks sat out on their porches after dinner to relax and chat with neighborhood passersby. I was all alone.

My heart was wounded, my soul was suffering, my spirit was in despair. I was at the end of my rope.

"Dear God, help me!" I pleaded, my eyes burning as I stared into the nearly setting sun. "I'm lost. I can't do this anymore. I don't know what to do. Please help me. I can't do it alone anymore." In my soul, I was at the edge of an abyss.

It was then that I felt an overwhelming sense of peace and reassurance flood my entire being. I didn't hear a voice as such, but I heard this thought clearly in my mind and in my heart: Don't ever worry. I am with you. I will always protect you. You are never alone. I will help and guide you. Trust me. All will be well. Forever.

That experience was immediately followed by such a feeling of love that my eyes filled with tears of relief and recognition as I looked down from the golden light. I was in awe. Maybe some would call it a feeling of God's grace or His blessing. Had something Divine happened? All I can attest was that it was so deep, rich, and beautiful! I – who was nothing but a kid, and undeserving – was now humbled beyond words. I stayed there in the same spot in mystified contemplation until the sun went down, then went back inside and slipped into my bedroom and closed the door. I felt I had been fully transformed by my encounter with The Light. I sensed that I was somehow reborn, and was perhaps touched by something Universal, something Infinite.

My interaction was so personal and intimate that I told no one about it until years later when I was an adult. Needless to say, my life changed at that point. I now had the support and confidence that I needed. I absolutely knew that I would survive. I was assured beyond any doubt that everything would be all right. Suddenly, my family life – though my parents were unchanged – was seen as something bearable, and as more of a temporary inconvenience rather than an endless tragedy. I could endure it and then transcend it. I then began to see my own parents as simply large, flawed children who were pathetically staggering through life, pretending they were mature adults. My anger and fear towards them gradually morphed into a kind of detached pity, a form of sympathetic understanding that they were in fact just lost and confused souls. Hence, I was now incapable of hating them. And as the years rolled by, I became a contented and successful adult, teacher, husband, and father. I am truly grateful for every day.

Whenever I remember that miraculous August moment, however, I wonder how it happened and why it happened. Did this phenomenon ever occur to other people? Does it still occur to those in need today? I hope it did, and I hope it still does...

THE END

by Jack Karolewski

July 29, 2017

A BROTHER'S LESSON

Marius and Georges Arnaud were brothers growing up in the town of Betton, in the Brittany area of northwest France. Betton -- with a population of just under 1300 souls, now in the year of Our Lord 1700 -- was about 8 km north of the larger cathedral town of Rennes. The River Ille bisected Betton, and the town was on the main road to both St. Malo and Mont Saint Michel. The boys' father, Gaston, was the town's only blacksmith, and his hopes were that someday one or preferably both of his sons would follow him into that worthwhile trade. Their hard-working mother, Renee, was equally proud of her sons, who were robust and intelligent, and were both turning out to become fine young men. Marius was born in 1701. About 12 cm shorter than his brother, he was gregarious and muscular, a lady charmer with his ready smile and curly brown hair, and he excelled in hunting and fishing as an enthusiastic outdoorsman. Georges was born the following year. He was tall and slender, with piercing blue eyes, but his temperament tended to be more introspective and analytical than his older brother's. Despite their differences, they were very close and devoted to each other. The only year of concern so far in their young lives was in 1718, when France went to war with Spain. But that conflict was fortunately short-lived, and the boys were spared any involvement.

Like most boys, Marius and Georges were restless and craved adventure. They heard exciting stories from travelers passing through Betton about the colony of New France in North America, specifically about its wild, savage Indians and the fortunes being made in the fur trade. They secretly wondered what it would be like to go there, but never shared their fervent interest with their parents. Neither boy wanted to become a blacksmith, but they were reluctant to tell their earnest father, who was increasingly insistent that they begin apprenticing that trade. They feared his wrath and his disappointment.

"There are said to be many different native tribes in New France," Georges shared one afternoon. "Some are peaceful and accept our civilized ways, but others capture and torture or even kill any white men who disturb them. Our brave holy missionaries in particular enter the dark forests to convert these heathens, but many never return if they fail to escape."

"Meanwhile, trappers are taking beaver pelts in great numbers, then loading them into their canoes for sale in Montreal and other trading centers," Marius added. "The pelts are eventually shipped to Europe to make those popular felt hats that only the rich can afford. A trapper can earn twice in one year what an average laborer or artisan can earn here in Betton. Even twice what our father earns at his forge. Just imagine!"

In December, 1720, a huge fire destroyed all the timber-framed houses in northern Rennes. Although the fire did not affect the lofty stone Cathedral de Saint-Pierre (where the Arnaud family attended Mass every Sunday), the rest of the city immediately began rebuilding its destroyed sections exclusively using stone. As a result, Gaston's services as a trained blacksmith were in urgent demand to both create and repair the needed metal stone cutting tools and related equipment. With Renee in understandable agreement, he moved temporarily to Rennes for five days and nights every week while his wife and sons remained in Betton. The family reunited in church every Sunday, then Gaston went home with them to Betton until each Tuesday morning, when he returned to work in Rennes.

It was while their father was away in March, 1721 that Georges got the sudden urge to make his first pilgrimage. There was a Benedictine abbey at Saint-Gilles-du-Gard, on the southern French coast. St. Giles, whose holy remains were venerated there, was the patron saint of blacksmiths, cripples, and infertile women. Coming originally from Greece, Giles lived in the late 7th- early 8th centuries as a holy hermit in the woods of southern France. According to legend, his main companion was a tame red deer. When the king's archers were hunting for fresh game one day, they chased a red deer to the entrance of Giles' cave and fired an arrow. As Giles moved to protect his animal friend, he took the hunting arrow in his own leg instead, crippling himself for the rest of his life. Years later, after Giles died and achieved sainthood (as prayers to him generated several miracles), the apologetic king ordered that an abbey be founded on the site of Giles' grave. So it was here that Georges would journey. He would give alms and hence accrue blessings for the continued good health and the immortal soul of his blacksmith father. Meanwhile, Marius would remain in Betton with his mother.

The pilgrimage from home to the abbey in Saint Gilles would take twenty-one days, walking unfailingly eight hours a day, barring any injuries or mishaps. He would sleep rough outdoors -- using his cloak as a blanket -- on his route whenever village churches were unavailable. Georges knew that churches would also provide free, simple meals to all sincere pilgrims, seeing as this road was well-travelled, being a main route in the opposite direction to connect with the famous medieval Camino de Santiago over the Pyrenees into northern Spain.

Fortunately, Georges was blessed with mostly dry -- but still rather chilly -- weather. There were no surprise confrontations with any robbers or rabid mongrel dogs, and Georges welcomed the generosity of strangers who shared their fruit, cheese, bread, and wine -- their only request in return being that a prayer be said by Georges for their souls once he arrived at his destination.

Finally sighting the Romanesque abbey after walking for three weeks, Georges Arnaud's emotions were unexpectedly stirred into a kind of religious ecstasy. This feeling was only further heightened when he descended into the subterranean crypt which held the sacred bones of St. Giles. He ultimately sensed The Lord, Jesus, calling to his heart as he prayed in the upper chapel before a large hanging crucifix. Georges felt the unmistakable silent summons of a true religious vocation. And he was further drawn to the realization that he surely must now become a missionary in New France, and attempt to save the lost souls of its savages. Next, the young Arnaud found and placed several livres in the abbey's alms box, and prayed devoutly for both his father and for those who helped him on the road, as intended. Finally, Georges cornered a nearby black-robed Benedictine monk and proceeded to pour out his glowing heart. The somewhat startled man gently directed him to see the Head Abbott.

"I understand your new intentions, my son," the aged Abbott declared, after carefully listening to Georges' passionate realization. "The Holy Spirit has indeed blessed you. But you are not destined for monastic life here with us. Instead, I will write to the Jesuit seminary in Paris recommending your admittance. It is they who are sending zealous young men such as yourself into the wilderness of New France -- but only after two years of rigorous preparation. You must return home now and await their reply of either acceptance or rejection. If you leave tomorrow, you should be able to reunite in Rennes with your family by Easter Sunday on April 13. Go with God, my son." The kindly Abbott smiled and blessed Georges, who in turn kneeled, then kissed the Abbott's wrinkled hand in joy and respect.

The 800 km journey back home was more difficult, due to muddy roads after many rainy days. But Georges kept to his daily walking regimen, and he made it back to Rennes Cathedral by Easter. His family was happy and relieved that he had returned home safely. After Mass, on the way back to Betton for their modest holiday feast, Georges shared his new religious convictions. His mother was pleased, his brother was surprised, but his father was wary and critical.

"I had been counting on you and Marius to take on my blacksmithing trade," Gaston groused. "Now you are telling me that you are possibly leaving for two years of Jesuit study in Paris, followed by a missionary placement in New France?" he remarked, hurt and confused.

Marius quickly spoke up. "Forgive me for interrupting, Father, but if you allow Georges to go, I promise I will stay here and learn your trade for the two years he is in Paris." Renee demurely added that the arrangement seemed fair and reasonable to her.

This offer placated Gaston somewhat, so the matter went undiscussed for the rest of the day. Yet later that night as the brothers lay in bed, Marius revealed to Georges that after those two years, he likewise planned the leave for North America. "I will learn to become a *coureur de bois*-- a 'runner of the woods' -- who will trap the beaver and trade its pelts. I plan on becoming very rich! And I will send half of the money I earn home to our parents. I hope that will satisfy our good father."

Several days later, a folded, red wax-sealed letter came from the Jesuit seminary in Paris. Georges had been accepted! All he need do now was to walk for 70 hours from Betton to the capital city by June 1. His room and board would all be paid for by the Church, in return for his lifetime commitment as an eager young Jesuit missionary in New France.

Giving himself an extra day in reserve so as to arrive in Paris a day before the deadline, Georges said an emotional goodbye to his family on May 21, seeing as his journey would take nine days. He promised to write home every two months. Renee washed and packed his two best blouses, and wrapped a fresh quiche in a clean cloth for him to eat on the road. The weather was sunny and warming, and life was full of promise.

Paris was a marvel, the largest city Georges had ever seen. The stained-glass windows in Notre Dame Cathedral were especially stunning and much more impressive than those in Rennes. Before long, he found the formidable building of the Jesuit seminary. He submitted his formal letter of acceptance to the reception priest at the front gate.

The following two years of his instruction were challenging yet fulfilling, and passed rather quickly. Georges Arnaud, now age 21, was granted permission to be called "Pere ('Father') Giles" as his new Jesuit name, in honor of the saint in whose abbey he first became aware of his vocation.

Pere Giles was called into the Director's office one morning for final instructions before leaving the seminary. His name was Pere Auguste. He was a powerfully built man in his early 50's who had served several years in New France, both in Quebec and among the Mohawk Indians. He needed to realistically point out the many dangers that North American missionary work entailed.

"Pere Giles, your teachers tell me that you possess a fine, clear mind and that you are sincere in your determination to save heathen souls as a member of our Society of Jesus. Your health is strong, and you have proved yourself pious in observing all the strict rules which our order imposes. Normally, it takes a ten years to become a full Jesuit. But because of our urgent need in the New Colony for priests, we are sending you for just two more years of training to the Jesuit College in Quebec before you will be ready to work among the Mohawks. After mastering the various Indian languages, you will be sent to the settlement area called 'Kahnawake,' which means 'place of the rapids.' It was founded by us in 1719, and it's located on the south banks of the St. Lawrence River near Montreal, extending outward in a very large area about the size of Portugal," Pere Auguste explained.

Then the Director cleared his throat. "But you need to know, Pere Giles, that fully half of our priests are killed by the heathen during their first year of service. Other manage to escape back to civilization, but only after suffering horrible tortures and mutilations. Some even go mad and simply disappear completely from our priesthood. Others, however, return to France, like myself." At this, Pere Auguste extended both hands out of the cuffs of his robes, revealing a left hand missing two fingers and a right hand missing three. Then he pushed his thick, long grey hair aside, revealing a missing right ear and a burned-scarred right side of his face -- the flesh resembling hardened melted wax. "I assure you that my chest and back were likewise rendered...unattractive," he added. "True, the Mohawks are members of the Five Nation Iroquois League, and are pledged to being peaceful. But in the hinterlands of Kahnawake, there are those sub-groups who torture and kill any unarmed white men who intrude on their lands. Bringing them the Word of God is crucial to saving their poor souls from everlasting torment, so we continue undaunted in our missionary efforts, even if it means our own martyrdom, like that our beloved Pere Isaac Jogues. Our native conversion and baptism rate is pathetically only around 10%, most of those women, as best as we can determine. So it is this challenge -- this 'cross,' somewhat related to Our Savior's burden -- that you have accepted," Pere Auguste concluded. After saying a solemn prayer together, Pere Giles was formally dismissed, and was allowed to head home to Betton, this time by horse-drawn coach. He was given papers to present at the port of Brest by the end of June, allowing for an official paid passage across the Atlantic to Quebec, in the colony of New France.

When Pere Giles arrived home, his family found that it took a little time for them (and the rest of the town, for that matter) to get used to seeing him in his black priestly robes. One afternoon after the mid-day meal, Marius asked to speak to his younger brother in private.

"Don't worry, Georges...I mean, Pere...I won't ask you to hear my confession, nor will I ask you how difficult it is to maintain your new vows of poverty, chastity, and obedience. But I wanted to confide in you that I intend to leave with you when you sail to New France. I told you two years ago that I wished to become a fur trapper and trader. Well, the King of France signed an edict way back in 1681, which limited the granting of *conges* -- legal licenses -- to only twenty-five new fur traders per year. I learned that I must go to Montreal in person to apply and obtain one. I have earned a bit more than the cost of a ship's passage of 150 livres by working with our father these past two years as promised at his forge, as he continued his role in the rebuilding in Rennes. My real problem now is that I have yet to disclose my specific plans to our father and mother."

Pere Giles remembered their old conversation on this topic, and how Marius intended on sending half of his earnings back to his parents every year. He declared they should tell their father together about Marius' decision that very Monday evening.

Over a mushroom soup and pork roast supper with wine and fresh bread, the brothers informed their parents of Marius' plans. "We will take a coach to Brest, and sail together across the ocean on a merchant East Indianman. Then we will proceed up the St.Lawrence to the city of Quebec, where I will disembark and stay for two years of further study at the Jesuit College. Marius will of course continue on to Montreal, " Pere Giles explained. Marius then spoke up. "And I pledge to send half of my earnings back to this house, my father. This is a golden opportunity to make the Arnauds quite wealthy. I humbly ask for your blessing."

Gaston Arnaud pursed his lips and scratched his beard for several silent moments. "I see that your mind is made up, Marius. I sensed long ago that neither of my sons had a true devotion to my trade -- an honorable skill that my own father taught me when I was young. Well, you are a grown man now. I suppose you must make your own path in life, as your younger brother has already decided for himself. One of our neighbors, Marcel Aubert, has a twelve-year-old boy, Maurice, who has shown keen interest in apprenticing as a blacksmith. So it appears I must turn to him instead..." Gaston's voice trailed off as he looked down at his strong, gnarled hands resting on the wooden table top. "You therefore have my permission. Do you have enough money for this trip, my son?"

Overcome with emotion, Marius leapt up from his chair and embraced his father. "Oh, Papa, yes I do, and thank you! I will make us proud, as has Georges...I mean, Pere!" The family all chuckled at this reoccurring slip of the tongue from the older brother. Renee then stood proudly and gave all three of her men hugs and kisses. Pere Giles then led his family in a solemn prayer for God's guidance and safety.

Arrangements were made for the Church to pay the coach fare to Brest for the priest and his 'guest.' After the brothers said an emotional farewell to their parents, they departed. Who knew when -- or if -- they would ever meet again as a whole family?

The westerly trip by mail coach to the Brittany coast took four days -- saving them fifteen long days of walking. The brothers arrived at the harbor in Brest on June 13, 1723. There were several merchant ships ready to set sail, while others were just arriving with their cargos from ports throughout Europe. A sturdy, Dutch-made, three-masted, forty-five-meter long East Indianman immediately caught their eye.

She was called Le Renard, and a large, brown fox was suitably carved on its bow as a figurehead. She ran the French flag, was manned by a crew of twelve, and was under the command of Captain Jacques Soubret. After proper introductions and the presentation of Pere Giles' documents and Marius' cash payment, Soubret showed them to their tiny shared cabin. The vessel's cargo hold was loaded with 200 barrels of fine Bordeaux wine and another 100 barrels of brandy, as well as 75 barrels of hard cheese and 50 of dried peas. The 2614 nautical mile trip to Quebec would take 25-30 days, depending on the winds and the weather. The Captain hoped to cover 160-225 kilometers a day at a speed of 4-6 knots. On his return run from Montreal, he would load up his ship with as many bales of North American beaver pelts as he could pack. Such was the fur's value and demand back in France and the rest of Europe that a handsome profit was thus assured for the ship owners -- not to mention a hefty bonus for both Captain Soubret and his crew upon successful and timely delivery.

Le Renard weighed anchor on Tuesday, June 15. The brothers took their meals with the Captain and his First Mate, Jean-Baptiste, and were enthralled with their tales of adventures from around the world. Every Sunday at sea, Pere Giles said Mass and distributed Holy Communion to the faithful. He used a compact 'traveling altar kit,' which included a small stand-up silver crucifix, a modest silver chalice, a leather flagon of blessed wine, a simple white altar cloth, and a silver container for the blessed wafers. The altar was always set on a long wooden board positioned between two large empty barrels. In his concise sermons, Pere Giles preached passionately about the necessity of forgiveness and mercy in this imperfect world, and for compassion, and for loving one's enemies as Christ decreed. The crew was attentive and respectful, because the Captain had chosen his twelve sailors carefully. They were all disciplined family men -- not the usual dregs of humanity who drifted from port to port and ship to ship as their fancy or needs dictated.

Luck was with the ship as she made steady progress westward, for the weather was favorable. After twenty-six days, the Gaspe peninsula and Perce Rock came into view, leading into the entrance of the St. Lawrence River. Three days later -- Tuesday, July 13, 1723 -- the two brothers arrived at the fortress city of Quebec, high and imposing on an immense cliff above the water. After carefully docking, while some of the ship's supplies were being unloaded, the brothers said their emotional goodbyes, kissing both sides of each other's clean-shaven cheeks.

"Because I will be out in the wilderness trapping most of the time, I cannot promise to write regularly," Marius confessed. "But whenever I send money home to our parents, I will let them know how I am doing, then they can relay any news about me to you here in Quebec." The black-robed priest agreed that it was a good plan, at least for the next two years. Then they shook hands one last time. Pere Giles said, "Go with God, Marius," then finally turned and walked down the gangplank with his modest luggage, returning a final friendly wave from Captain Soubret. He immediately asked for directions to the Jesuit College from the nearest bystander once his sandals touched the land of New France.

Two days later, Le Renard arrived by mid-morning at the docks in Montreal. The summer winds from the north brought the sweet smells of the New World -- North America! After asking directions, Marius Arnaud made quick time to the Governor's Office, so as to obtain his all-important conges, his legal fur trading license. But he was dismissively given an appointment time of tomorrow afternoon at 3:00 p.m. instead by a snobbish clerk at the department in charge of such matters. After an evening meal, Marius found an inn nearby for the night and waited. He wondered how long his 73 livres would last, for both expenditures thus far were more than he would have thought.

But when Marius arrived at his appointed hour the next day, he was stunned to discover that all twenty-five conges had already been assigned for the year! Suspecting that this was a classic ploy by the administrator to casually obtain a bribe, Marius offered 20 livres as a 'gift' to the bureaucrat for his checking a second time to see if there was a chance that "just one conges might still be available." But the man simply frowned wearily and shook his head.

"Monsieur Arnaud, I assure you that you must return next January, with 300 livres, and wait in line like the others to purchase your conges. They will all be sold in a matter of hours, I warn you, such is the high demand," the man advised him coldly. "Please, put your coins away and go now."

Marius was crestfallen as he left the grey stone government building. His dreams of freedom, adventure and wealth were shattered! He had failed before he had even begun! It would probably take two years to earn the required amount just to purchase his conges. Depressed, he entered the first tavern he spied for a glass of wine. He needed time to focus and consider his grave circumstances.

Sitting alone at a corner table with his drink, Marius was approached after several minutes by a short but powerfully-built stranger, perhaps ten years older than himself. He was darkly bearded and long-haired, with a weather-beaten face and rough, strong hands. His brown eyes, however, were alert and intelligent. He was dressed in greasy, dirt encrusted buckskin with fringes to wick off any moisture, and he carried a musket, a powder horn, and a large knife in a leather scabbard on his waist-belt. On his feet were soft deerskin moccasins. His head was topped with a bright red wool toque. He grinned with stained teeth and then introduced himself as Claude LaBoeuf, originally from Marseilles. He declared that he was a premier beaver trapper. He carried a half-empty bottle of cognac and a pewter tankard.

"You look new in town, young man! If you prefer to drink alone, just say so and I'll leave. If not, I'll stay and we can a nice sociable chat. What's it to be?"

Marius politely offered Claude a chair. He was intrigued to meet an actual fur trapper. He introduced himself and told Claude about his family and where he grew up in France. Then he told him about his bitter disappointment upon not being able to buy a conges this year.

"Well, my friend, many have been stuck in your position. The selling of those damn licenses is just a lot of *merde*, a crooked way for the government to tax our hard work. But there is still a way to trap furs and sell them for much money," he winked, then lowered his voice. "You can sell them illegally. I've done it for several years now. I know all the tricks," he confessed, his cognac breath wafting in Marius' face. "If you care to team up with me, I'll teach you everything you need to know. I learned from Pierre de La Verendrye himself. Perhaps you have heard of him? Anyway, my companion of the past five years just returned to France unexpectedly with his substantial earnings, so I am looking for a new partner. You look willing and capable. And you say you can use a musket, and that you can hunt and fish, and that you thrive in the outdoors -- all the better! I sense you are honest, smart, and trustworthy. Think it over and let me know. But do it fast before I head out next week for the woods again. I know where all the beavers hide!" he roared boastfully, pouring some cognac into Marius' empty wine glass.

Not knowing what else to do other than trying to find work somewhere as a blacksmith's assistant, Marius agreed to Claude's intriguing offer. They toasted their new partnership, then shook hands on it. Marius then collected his belongings at his inn, and joined Claude at his ramshackle lodgings down near the river. "True, it could use a woman's touch," Claude explained as Marius settled in amid the dirt and clutter. "I have two squaw wives and two mixed race children out west, plus a wife and three children back in France whom I last saw eight years ago. But I am so rarely here that the mess doesn't really bother me."

Next, Claude got down to specifics. "The first year, we must split our profits 25% for you and 75% for me. This is only fair, seeing as I will be training you and hence doing the bulk of the planning and supplying. But in all the following years, the split will be even, 50-50. I can tell you have never paddled a canoe or set a beaver trap or portaged two 40 kilogram pelt bundles at the same time. And you certainly can't speak any Indian dialects yet. But your short, strong body build is perfect for the main task you will need to do, like kneeling in a canoe and paddling 12 hours a day at 50 strokes a minute with me. I'll show you how to set beaver traps, and how to trade cleverly with the Indians for their finished 'made' pelts."

"Speaking of the Indians, they come in all temperaments. Some, like the Algonquin, are peaceful and cooperative, as are the Oneida, the Onondago, the Seneca, and the Huron. But the Mohawk and Iroquois are mostly murderous bastards who will slit your throat if you ever let your guard down. They prize bravery and physical strength above all things, so be prepared to fight hard or even kill without hesitation if we ever have to. Never, ever show them fear! They torture, then slowly kill any unarmed white men who come uninvited into their hunting grounds -- especially missionary priests, the 'black robes,' whom they believe bring a bad magic which upsets their nature gods. Their butchery is done merely for their own twisted amusement and to test the courage of their captives. (Upon hearing this, Marius shuttered, instantly thinking about his younger brother.) They will trade their furs, however, if you have something they really want, like guns and liquor." Claude remarked. He paused and took out a pouch of tobacco and a clay pipe, filled then lit it, puffed contentedly for a few draws, then continued.

"Tomorrow, we will enter the wilderness to begin your training and to collect the remainder of this year's pelts before the rivers and lakes freeze in late September. Our season usually begins in May. We will go west then north down the Ottawa River, then turn left at The Forks and proceed into the *Petite Riviere,* the Mattawa. That will next take us through 14 kilometers of *La Vase Portages* to Lake Nipissing. All the greats took this same route from Montreal into the interior: Champlain, Lallemant, Radisson, and Groseilliers. But we will proceed to my new trapping grounds to train you for a month, then see to my stored furs with my Nipissing Indian friends. You will meet my wives and my two Metis children at their village before we head back to Montreal next May to begin our new season." La Boeuf went on to explain that by staying the winter with his Indian family and tribe, they would save much money, rather than spending a more expensive several months in the big city. "The winters are much more brutal here than back in France, however," Claude warned. "But you'll get used to it -- you'll have no choice!" he laughed. "Remember: soon you'll be earning 500 livres or more a year!"

Marius contributed his share of 25 of his remaining 73 livres to help purchase supplies with Claude. They bought sugar, salt, dried peas, dried beans, salt pork, and dried hard biscuits. To this, they added gunpowder, two dozen steel fish hooks, and brandy. For his squaws, Claude selected some colored buttons, ribbons, sewing needles, spools of thread, and beads of various sizes. La Boeuf already had a large, six-man birch bark canoe and twenty-four beaver traps. "Next, we need to buy you a *capot* -- a thick hooded coat made of wool for the winter, a waist sash, and a red toque cap," Claude announced. "We will make your first buckskin outfit and moccasins in the field. You already have a good musket and a knife. But you need to stop shaving and grow out your beard beginning now, *mon ami*, to protect your face from sun, cold, and insects."

At first light the following morning, they carried their canoe with their supplies across the city to the Ottawa River. With Marius in the bow and Claude steering in the stern, they set out. La Boeuf taught Arnaud his three favorite French paddling songs, which helped them keep the rhythm for their required fifty strokes per minute -- "A La Claire Fontaine," "Voici Le Printemps," and "La Belle Lisette." Marius confessed that the third song had special significance for him, for Lisette was the name of the pretty blonde milkmaid whom he had lost his virginity to a few years ago in a haystack back in Betton -- a sin he had never openly revealed to anyone. Claude bellowed with laughter at Marius' admission, remarking, "You must then sing out lustfully and with fond memory whenever that one comes up! Making love is always a delight, *n'est-ce pas*? And where we are going, the Nipissing women are ready and willing!"

Hour after hour they paddled in the hot summer sun. Soon they were sweating and stripped bare to the waist. Claude showed Marius how to rub bear grease on his skin to thwart sunburn. Marius' hands were sprouting painful blisters too, but Claude promised that calluses would form eventually. The pair avoided the river banks in the early morning and evening hours to dodge the persistent plague of mosquitoes and biting black flies. By staying in the center of the water current, they were granted relief. At nightfall, they slept under their canoe, but had to keep a smoky fire going to help keep flying insect pests away.

Often, the men paddled in silence for long periods when they were not singing, each lost in their own world of thoughts or in the observations of their surroundings. At other times, they would talk about everything. Marius found out that Claude had a rough past.

"My mother was a whore in the slums of Marseilles," he revealed one day. "I never knew my father, so technically I'm a bastard. I grew up near the docks, and learned to fight and steal. I have killed men too when I had no other choice. I probably have some brothers and sisters, but who knows? I chose the name La Boeuf because I liked the sound of it. I eventually found work by becoming a sailor, and later I got married to a plain, simple woman named Claire and sired three children. One day, I heard about a merchant ship sailing for New France. I was told that I could make a fortune as a fur trapper and trader there, so I jumped at the chance. I told my family I would return within three years. But now it has been eight and I'm still here. Of course, I send them money and write once a year. But I like the freedom here, and the adventure. To be honest, I can't say if I'll ever leave. I love the challenge and I love the life of being my own man. I believe in God but not in the Church, so maybe someday I'll wind up in Hell."

Marius had listened intently to Claude, but offered no judgment on his remarks. "We are partners and friends, and I trust you, and that is all that counts in the end," young Arnaud finally proclaimed, with sincerity. Claude nodded and smiled.

The men stopped to fish and hunt when they needed fresh meat. They spied foxes, martens, minks, bear, muskrats, and even an elusive lynx in the dark forests beyond the river, but didn't take them. ("Another time," Claude advised, "because their fur is also valuable.") They shot three deer, skinned them, then dried the hides after scraping them clean. Claude showed Marius how to make a buckskin shirt, pants, and leggings, as well as moccasins. He taught his young partner the names of various useful plants and trees, and which roots were edible, and which leaves could be brewed into tea, and he explained how to identify different species of birds by just their song, and also how to read the sun and the stars to find directions. Then he outlined the all-important survival necessity of making pemmican.

"To stay healthy and keep up our strength, we need to eat about 3-4 kilograms of meat or fish every day, along with our peas, cornmeal, beans, and hard biscuit. Yet just one fourth of one kilogram of pemmican will provide equal nourishment to all of that fresh meat. Made properly, good pemmican can last a whole year. If you take about 180 kilograms of fresh meat -- deer, bear, elk, or caribou -- it will render down to about 25 kilograms of pemmican and about 20 kilograms of dried meat."

To show Marius the technique, the pair set up camp in a clearing for several days. First, they shot two deer and a black bear. After dressing the animals, they made drying racks for the meat, with smoky fires underneath to discourage the flies. Then Claude instructed Marius in the art of pounding the meat between two flat stones while pouring melted fat into the mixture. Next, bones were cracked open and the marrow was extracted, then melted and added. Finally, various wild berries that the men collected were blended in, until, when hardened, the pemmican was cut into regular sized and weighted bars. Marius was allowed the first taste, and found their rich creation satisfying and filling!

Meanwhile, over time, Marius was hardening in both muscle and in his determination to become an expert woodsman under the skilled tutelage of Claude La Boeuf. Young Arnaud's skin was darkening to the color of walnut shells from his long days in the sun and fresh air. He even began sampling Claude's clay pipe, finding the tart tobacco refreshing. His soft brown beard was coming in too, matching his curly brown hair.

When they arrived at The Forks and turned left into the Petite Riviere of the Mattawa, the men had been gone for more than a month from Montreal. Now, Marius would be taught the tricks of trapping the wily beaver as they gradually approached the La Vase Portages -- the connecting series of streams, small lakes and ponds, and three portages which led for 14 kilometers to Lake Nipissing. Even though they had yet to see any other trappers, they set up a hidden camp about a kilometer to the west, and there they would stay for about a month until finally ending their journey at Claude's Nipissing family's longhouse village.

Taking out his two dozen well-used steel traps, Claude explained the procedure: "It takes 44 adult beaver pelts to make one 40 kilogram bale, known as a *piece.* We will stay here long enough to make one bale and construct one fur press to make the bundle tight. Beaver fur is thickest in the Spring after the long cold winter, but trapping is still good now in late August. We will look for dams and lodges in watery, marshy areas where the beaver work and live."

With six traps at a time, the pair went out every day. Claude showed Marius how to place the traps.

"The key is in this bottle. It is taken from the sex gland of the female. It's a liquid called castoreum, or just 'castor' for short." He gave Marius the uncorked bottle to sniff. "Ugh, that's awful!" young Arnaud exclaimed, gagging in disgust. Marius grinned, then continued. "You carefully place your open trap 50 centimeters under the water near where beavers travel. Mark it with an upright stick. Pour a few drops of castor on the stick. It attracts the male, who thinks a female is near and ready to mate. He goes underwater to investigate. Ideally, you hope he triggers the trap with his larger rear foot, because if it gets him by the smaller front paw, he will often twist and rip out his own paw to escape. But if the trap works well, the beaver quickly drowns underwater. We come and collect him the following day. You can also set your traps near their dams at the point where a trail is worn by them going back and forth. Lastly, you can also set your traps by a 'castor mound,' which is a small hill made of sticks in front of their water lodge. The beavers spray these mounds with their own castor so as to warn rival beavers away."

Marius interrupted and asked a question: "Why don't we just storm the beaver lodges and shoot them? Wouldn't that be quicker and easier?"

"A fair question, *mon ami*," La Boeuf replied. "But there are two problems there. One is you put a shredded bullet hole into the pelt, mostly ruining it. Secondly, the beavers would quickly escape through their underwater entrance tunnel at the first sign of any danger or attack. Thus, we must trick and trap them instead."

The two trappers systematically went about their task each day -- setting their traps, checking their previous traps, and recollecting their traps. Marius was warned to be extra careful setting the vicious, sharp, steel-toothed traps, for Claude had seen trappers lose fingers or even whole hands if they had an accident. Sometimes the traps were empty, so they were moved and re-baited with the pungent castoreum. But the majority of the traps did their intended job, and soon the men were skinning and 'fleshing' (scraping any flesh off of the pelt) and stretching the furs on circular, woven tree branch frames, and leaving the pelts to dry in the sun. The pair rarely ate the left over beaver meat, both finding it too unpalatable , so they merely left the denuded carcasses in a pile far away from the camp for scavengers to consume. But they saved most of the special glands which contained a fresh supply of castor.

By now, it was mid-September, and the early mornings and evenings were increasingly getting colder. The men had built a crude wooden fur press, for they had collected their forty-four pelt goal. The furs were stacked fur end to fur end, then squeezed, wrapped in deerskin, and tightly tied into a 'piece' bale. Marius felt very proud of what he and Claude had accomplished, and Claude was likewise proud of his new, very capable partner. Claude had Marius hoist the heavy bale on his back for practice. "Now remember, you will need to carry two of these bales stacked on your back at the same time, for miles at a stretch, with a leather forehead strap on the top one for stability, when we go out next season," he warned.

They broke camp the next morning and loaded up their canoe, and paddled the remaining distance to Lake Nipissing. They carried their canoe over the three portages, then went back each time for their supplies and their fur bale. Soon, the streams and ponds would freeze up, for up north, winter could never be stopped from coming.

Upon arriving in the Nipissing village, Claude was greeted with familiar warmth and excitement. The whole 63-member tribe assembled as he introduced Marius to the group, using their native tongue, which he promised to teach his companion in the months to come. Of course, they were welcomed to spend the winter! the tribe exclaimed. Claude presented the keg of brandy, the keg of gunpowder, and the steel fish hooks to the village elders as gifts. They, in turn, showed him his three fur bales which they had stored in trust since his last visit -- when Claude's former partner had unexpectedly quit in mid-season and left early.

The thriving village consisted of six large longhouses, made of wood and bark in the style used by most of the Five Nation League tribes. Claude had Marius follow him into the nearest one. "Come...I want to introduce you to my wives and children!" he added eagerly. Marius then met Laughing Turtle and Moon Woman, followed by Claude's four-year-old son, Running Fox, and his three-year-old daughter, Asking Sparrow. They rushed to happily hug and kiss Claude over and over. He then formally presented both wives with his gifts of beads, buttons, spools of thread and sewing needles. To his delighted children, he allowed each the rare treat of a handful of sugar apiece. La Boeuf explained that his children would always remain with the tribe, and never be taken by him to Montreal. "The Nipissing prize and treasure Metis children, so they are best simply staying in the Indian world. In so-called 'civilized' society, mixed-race children are merely sinful outcasts in the eyes of the government and the church, and are frowned upon, as are mixed marriages. But, my friend, it is a good practice to take a squaw or two in our business, because it helps to build peace and trusting relationships when we come each year to trade for furs."

Marius noticed a shy Indian maiden staring at him from around a corner. She seemed amazed at seeing a white stranger, yet was smiling. She was perhaps fifteen years old. She had clear eyes and a fine, ripening body, long dark hair, and an open, eager expression.

"Ah, *mon ami*, I think she likes you already!" Claude remarked, noticing her interest in his companion. "Her name is Singing Wind. I think maybe you will take her to wife during our upcoming long and cold winter nights!" he laughed.

The next seven months were a revelation to young Marius. He learned all about the Indian way of life and found that he enjoyed it. He marveled at how cleverly the tribe both used and respected the natural world around them. Everything was so different than in France! Over time, he grew to appreciate the native foods and how they were seasoned and cooked. The winter's frigid cold and winds were -- as Claude had warned -- harsh and bitter, as were the periodic snow blizzards. Marius met each morning with Claude for language lessons -- beginning with universal Indian sign language, then proceeding to the spoken languages of various

Indian groups after he mastered the tongue of the Nipissings. Marius then learned how to make a new canoe out of wood and birch bark, and how to repair one if it suffered a hole or leak. Next, he went on hunting and fishing forays with the young braves of the clan. They likewise taught him new winter skills (like how to walk using snowshoes, and how to fish by cutting holes in the ice) and new techniques in both stalking game and in reading animal tracks and spoor. Although the tribe had several muskets, they still relied mostly on their traditional bows and arrows and spears for both hunting and protection. So Marius practiced with them too.

Young Arnaud also got to know Claude's family better, finding his two children delightful, and both his wives charming and industrious. (Claude slept with each of his wives, alternating each week, and Marius noticed neither rivalry nor jealousy between the two women, who acted almost like close sisters to each other.) And not surprising -- as Claude had foretold -- Marius was soon sharing the warm fur bed of the attractive and energetic Singing Wind, though making love with a dozen other people in the longhouse noticing and murmuring took some getting used to! By January in the new year 1724, she joyfully announced that she was with child. Marius proudly married his Indian maiden in a festive Nipissing ceremony and joyful feast, and he already looked forward to returning in September to see both his bride and their new baby.

When May arrived and the streams and ponds were once again free of ice, the two trappers set out with their now four fur bales to return to Montreal. Singing Wind had made her husband a surprise additional complete buckskin outfit plus two extra pairs of moccasins to take with. After an emotional farewell to their families and to the entire village, the men headed over the three strenuous portages and made it back to the Ottawa River. It would take a month from here to get to the city.

Claude La Boeuf explained to Marius about their next steps when the church spires of Montreal finally came into view. "Because we have no conges, we must beach our canoe and goods just outside the city. You will guard both while I fetch my illegal trader friend, Francois Tremont. Under cover of darkness I shall return, and he will bring his helpers and a wagon, retrieve our bales, and pay us our cash. Now, *mon ami*, you need to know that while you are alone guarding our pelts, there may be robbers and bandits lurking about, just waiting to steal our treasure. So if you must fight to protect our goods, you must fight to kill. Use your knife like so," Claude demonstrated, unsheathing his large blade, "and go for the throat or slash at the sides of the neck. If you are in close to the body instead, slab deeply between the ribs so as not to hit bone, then twist your blade sideways before pulling it out. This will make your enemy bleed out faster because the wound won't close up so quickly. I've only had to fight and kill once in my eight years doing this work, so odds are unlikely you will be bothered this time. But be on your guard at all times until I get back."

When they arrived at the designated spot, Claude left once it got dark. Marius watched and listened, but no other souls were around for the two hours that his partner was gone. La Boeuf returned with Francois and three of his helpers, along with their horse and wagon. After introductions, the deal was smartly concluded and the agreed upon money was exchanged. The illicit trader and his crew skillfully slipped back into the darkness.

Carrying their canoe, the men made it back across the city to Claude's unkempt lodgings near the St. Lawrence. The money was divided between the partners according to their prior arrangement. Both men then wrote letters back to their families in France. The next day, bank drafts were likewise written up and added to the letters, which were then posted for delivery on the next outbound ship. Marius sent his promised half-earnings, but neglected to say that he was now trapping and trading illegally, and excluding the fact that he was now married to an Indian squaw who was expecting his baby -- their first grandchild. He ended his letter saying that he was in good health and that he would be earning and sending much more money this new season. Writing to his parents made Marius wonder how his younger brother was doing with his studies at the Jesuit College in Quebec. What stories he could tell Georges if they could meet now!

The regular routine now for the duo would be re-supplying, then traveling, trading, and trapping from late May to late September, then wintering near Lake Nipissing with their families until the following early May. The men loaded up their canoe first with their required foodstuffs, then with trade goods -- bolts of broadcloth and linen, wool blankets, knives, kettles, hatchets, gunpowder, glass beads, mirrors, liquor, ammunition, and assorted firearms. New Indian settlements of various tribes in different locations would be carefully approached to trade these goods for 'made' beaver pelts. The men would of course trap their own furs as much as possible, because that was the cheapest way.

Claude and Marius did well in their first full season together. Before the first freeze, they were back with their Indian families near Lake Nipissing. Claude's children were growing strong, and Marius had a new daughter named

Starlight on the Water. The wives were happy that their husbands were back healthy and safe, and life was good.

For the next three years afterward, the routine was unaltered. Much money was earned, and a sizeable portion was sent back to France with a yearly letter. During this time, Laughing Turtle gave Claude a new daughter, Blue Flower, and Singing Wind gave Marius his first son, whom they named Flaming Sunset.

It was now May, 1727. The two trappers had returned to the outskirts of Montreal yet again, this time with six rich bales of pelts. But as they were unloading their canoe in the dusky evening, they were suddenly attacked from behind by five land pirates. In the fight that ensued, two robbers were killed by Claude and one by Marius -- the first man he had ever killed. The other two attackers, badly wounded, fled. In the dim light, Marius saw that one of the men fleeing was missing his upper two front teeth, while the other had a thick scar on his clean-shaven chin. He would remember them both. But Claude had been mortally struck in the back of his head by a large rock. Marius went gently to his old friend and partner. There was nothing to be done. Claude La Boeuf could say nothing in farewell with any last words. Instead, he looked at Marius helplessly with his eyes, then slowly closed them, groaned deeply, and died.

Arnaud dragged the three outlaw corpses to the river and dumped them in the swirling current. Next, he hid Claude's body in a nearby grove of trees away from the bank, along with the six fur bales. He carefully removed and saved his companion's musket, power horn, knife, and red toque. These he would present to Claude's young son, Running Fox, the next time Marius would return to the Nipissing village with the awful, sad news.

Recalling that their illegal trader contact frequented a tavern in town called the Old Cannon, Marius waited, in exhaustion dozing on and off until dawn. At first light, he noticed a teen-aged boy baiting his hook to fish at the riverbank, a relatively short distance away. The trapper casually walked over and made a simple but lucrative request.

"My friend, I have 5 livre coins for you this lucky morning if you go to the Old Cannon tavern and ask for Francois Tremont. Tell him that Claude is ready for him at the usual meeting place and to come at once. Leave your fishing gear here with me and I'll wait," Marius directed.

The boy, happy with his unexpected good fortune, readily agreed. Two hours later, he returned with Tremont and his crew and their wagon. The boy was paid and told to leave right away -- and to tell no one what he did or who he saw. He obeyed. When the lad was out of sight, Marius explained all that had happened the turbulent night before.

"*Mon Dieu*, what a tragedy!" Francois wailed. "Claude was such a fine and trusted friend for the last twelve years. We must bury him here in secret so as to avoid a lot of questions by the Montreal authorities. Then you will paid for the six bales right here now. Think about if you still wish to continue to do business with me on your own, or maybe with a new trapper partner someday. You know where to find me. You are an honest man, Marius, and I believe in you."

The grave was dug and Claude La Boeuf was solemnly laid to rest. No marker was left, for obvious reasons. Marius said goodbye to Tremont and his men and said he would be in touch -- explaining that he needed time to think about his future plans. With his new payment, Arnaud carried the canoe and the remainder of his belongings back to Claude's ramshackle lodgings. Upon entering, it was odd and sad to think that Claude would never be there again with him.

Finding an old letter in the dusty clutter with La Boeuf's wife's address in Marseilles on it, Marius wrote a brief note explaining the tragedy, then added a bank draft for the remainder of all of Claude's money -- including his past savings, which Marius found hidden in a secret cache in a discarded moccasin under his bed -- and posted the packet the following day. (He similarly sent his own parents their annual 'half of his earnings' bank draft, but excluded adding any updated personal news.) Then, Arnaud thought about how he would tell his Indian family the bad news when next he went to Lake Nipissing. How he wished he was with Singing Wind, and his adorable son and daughter, right now! What should he do next with his life? Continue trapping and trading alone? Try to find a new partner? Move to the Nipissing village permanently? Go back to Betton? Somehow get in touch with his brother, Georges -- Pere Giles -- and ask for his advice? Marius was sick at heart. He went to sleep in sheer exhaustion. He dreamed fitfully about the recent attack and the killings at the river, and about Claude's dying eyes looking at him. When the sun finally rose, Marius Arnaud was a changed man -- but not in a good way. He was severely depressed and angry and bewildered at life's sometimes senseless and unfair ways. And he wanted to strike out at somebody. How could God allow this evil to coexist with all that was good in His Creation? The absurdity was too much to fathom. Marius became mean with black hate, his heart numb. He wanted revenge. He would find the two wounded bandit bastards that escaped the fight. And he would kill them.

Arnaud soon started drinking heavily at various taverns in Montreal, day or night, it mattered not. He started gambling at cards and dice, and picked fights when he lost, which was often. He often slept with whores when he got drunk enough and needed release. He was becoming familiar to the city police for his assorted trouble-makings. He forgot about his Indian family. He forgot about trapping and trading. He forgot about many other things -- except about his revenge for his friend's death.

About five weeks after the deadly attempted fur robbery attack, Marius unmistakably noticed the clean-shaven man with the scarred chin exiting a well-known brothel one night. He quietly followed the man down an alleyway. Waiting until he was sure he was unnoticed, Marius carefully slipped behind the man and slit his throat, muffling his cries until the victim stopped moving. Dragging the body to a trash pile, he crudely piled assorted refuse on top of the victim, after taking the man's paper money so as to make it appear that a random fatal robbery had occurred. Marius then discreetly cleaned his murder knife and walked home by a longer route, casually tossing the small handful of worn livre notes onto a nearby conveniently burning trash fire.

Four days later, Marius spied the second robber, the one missing his upper front teeth, as he staggered one night drunk out of the Wharf Rat tavern. Arnaud secretly followed the man as he wandered unaware down by the shadowy docks area. Hiding behind a stack of wooden cargo crates, Marius waited patiently until just the right moment. He grabbed the surprised man from behind by the throat, first choking him into weakness, then sharply snapping his victim's neck sideways then backwards with his muscular arms and hands. Making sure he was unseen, he then dumped the body into the rushing St. Lawrence. The corpse, if ever found, would probably be seen as a typical accident by yet another unfortunate drunkard.

Because Montreal was still a rather rough and wild place and not yet a peaceful metropolis, unexplained disappearances, unidentified corpses, and unsolved crimes were not uncommon. Marius felt his two murderous deeds would probably go officially nowhere and be dropped from any serious lengthy investigations after just a few days. So now I have killed three men, he mused. One was necessary in self-defense, but the other two were deliberate and done in cold blood. Maybe I'll go to Hell if it exists, like Claude, he briefly thought. But in reality, he really didn't care anymore. Life was an empty, meaningless wallow of *merde*!

Going back to his now favorite tavern -- The Raven -- the following day, Marius sat alone as usual at his corner table with his bottle of brandy, puffing on his clay pipe between drinks. Both the regular customers and the proprietor learned to leave him be, due to his erratic temperament and his willingness to fight anyone, anytime, over anything.

A strange trapper, however, came in, and peering carefully at Marius from afar, eventually made for his table, carrying a large glass of cognac.

"Mind if I join you? My name is Guy DuChamp. I bet you are Marius Arnaud. I heard about what happened to your partner, Claude La Boeuf. I met him out in the wild northwoods a few times when we were both trapping beaver. He was a good man and he will be missed."

Marius stayed silent, looking at Guy without much interest. He gestured apathetically to a chair. DuChamp took it. The man wanted company and to talk, but he picked the worst choice in Marius for both. Guy covered many topics for about twenty minutes, with only a few grunts in reply from Arnaud. Suddenly, the trapper's talk turned to the recent killings of several Jesuit missionaries in the vast Kahnawake settlement area south of Montreal. Marius perked up.

"It was pretty brutal, from what I heard. None of the priests escaped. It was the Mohawks that did it. Tortured then killed six...or was it seven? I remember one telling that was particularly savage. The priest had each of his fingers chewed down to the bone after his fingernails were torn out. Then he was stripped of his black robes and made to run

The Gauntlet, beaten with clubs and sticks between two long rows of the assembled tribe. Next, the poor priest was staked to the ground and hot coals were applied to his face, chest, stomach, and cock. All the time he stoically said nothing except the words "Father, forgive them, for they know not what they do...' again and again, but soon his prayer grew weaker and weaker. Then small strips of his skin were peeled off one at a time -- hundreds of them. It takes about three days to die like that, in horrible, terrible agony. After he died, the Jesuit's body was hacked into bits and fed to the dogs. It was all supervised and encouraged -- and most acts specifically done -- by a sadistic Mohawk warrior named Fearless Wolf. The trapper who told me all of this got there the day after the killing took place, when some of the Mohawk braves shared the grisly details with him. Said the priest's name was something like Pere Gilbert, or Pere Gerard...something like that. Oh, and I think he was young and had blue eyes."

Instantly alert now, Marius slowly asked, "Could the name have been Pere Giles?"

"Giles...Yes! Now I remember...that was it...Pere Giles," Guy replied.

Marius was stunned. his mind in a daze. His only brother, Georges. Dead! Martyred. Killed by a butchering Mohawk savage named Fearless Wolf. This appalling news pushed Marius into a boiling rage, then over the edge. He would find this monster and rip the life out of him with his bare hands if it was the last thing he did in this miserable world. His teeth clenched and his eyes on fire, Arnaud quickly thanked DuChamp and paid for the trapper's drink and his own, then abruptly got up and left The Raven.

Marius left Montreal and went south the next day. Over the next three weeks, he traveled throughout the Mohawk settlement lands, asking villages the whereabouts of a warrior named Fearless Wolf. Because Marius showed no fear -- and was apparently completely willing to fight or kill anyone who challenged or impeded his quest -- the braves he encountered did not molest him. Instinctively, they knew he was very dangerous. Bad medicine. Maybe even crazy.

The day finally came when Marius got the news he had been relentlessly searching for: by following a nearby stream, some helpful but suspicious Mohawk villagers explained, he would eventually find the tribe of Fearless Wolf. With black hate and the thirst for revenge in his heart, Marius set out to fulfill his destiny. He cared not if he lived or died by this day's end -- only that he be allowed to kill the Mohawk who had orchestrated the killing of his beloved only brother.

Arnaud soon found the village, and his surprise appearance shocked the Mohawk tribe living there.

Marius was quickly surrounded by a band of hostile braves ready to fight, but he boldly and fearlessly shoved them aside and shouted out loudly in their tongue so everyone could hear: "I would see Fearless Wolf alone and do battle with him, for he killed my brother, the Jesuit priest called Pere Giles!"

From the central longhouse, a tall, bronzed, muscular Indian emerged in a deerskin loincloth, wearing feathered leather bands on his biceps and calves. His hair had been plucked from his scalp, with the exception of a tuft still growing on the crown of his head, from which three dark hair braids extended. He looked mean and fierce, his eyes dull from many killings. "I am he," the Mohawk proudly proclaimed.

The tribe immediately formed a large circle, with Fearless Wolf and Marius in the center. Marius declined the use of lethal tomahawks as weapons when offered. Seeing as he was the formal challenger, his choice of knives in this fight was permitted. As a result, Fearless Wolf casually tossed his tomahawk aside and was given a knife instead. The formidable Mohawk then loudly decreed that should he fall, the white man trapper would be allowed to leave unharmed as a matter of tribal honor for his courage. Marius stripped off his buckskin shirt. And so, the deadly battle began.

Circling each other, the men entered into fierce combat. The shorter Marius was quick and agile compared to the Mohawk, yet both successfully slashed each other's chests and arms with deep, bleeding results. They grabbed each other and wrestled to the ground, rolling in the dust and dirt, then got up again, over and over, up and down. The tribal observers were silent in their concentration at and knowing appreciation of the bloody, gruesome spectacle. Both men emitted grunts of effort and groans of pain.

Although Fearless Wolf was powerful, he was also perhaps ten years older than Marius. Thus, his strong energies were slowly getting tapped out as the minutes passed, his breathing becoming more labored now and heavy. His attempted slashings were missing more and going wide, so Marius calculated and waited until he saw his opening. When the Mohawk moved forward suddenly in a desperate lunge to stab, Marius dodged and swung around and slashed his opponent's back, then immediately kicked his opponent's legs out from under him, knocking the warrior down hard backwards. Caught unawares, Fearless Wolf's knife flew out of his hand when he landed. Marius, like a man possessed, instantly went in for the kill, diving atop the Indian's heaving, sweating chest, his own knife in both hands at the defeated Mohawk's throat. Fearless Wolf knew he was done, and his eyes stared wide at the strange and wild trapper who was about to take his life.

Suddenly, a lone woman screamed. The tribe of spectators turned to see the wife of Fearless Wolf running toward the combat circle, holding a silver crucifix. She yelled, first in her own language and then in French: *Misericorde au nom de Jesus!* Mercy in the name of Jesus!

She was weeping as she approached Marius with the crucifix, the shocked crowd parting for her. Marius froze as he recognized the silver object with its attached stand from his brother's traveling altar kit that he had used whenever he had said Mass on Le Renard as they sailed to North America. The squaw whispered her plea again and again, looking down at her helpless husband under Marius' killing blade. She then offered the crucifix to Marius with her left hand, kneeling before him as he still sat atop Fearless Wolf. Looking down in supplication, she carefully and slowly made the Sign of the Cross with her right hand.

A powerful light seemed to be triggered inside of Marius during this supremely dramatic act, a distant light of remembrance and recognition. He remembered his brother Georges --Pere Giles -- sermonizing aboard ship about forgiveness, and mercy, and compassion, and about the need to love one's enemies as Christ had taught. This realization made Marius slowly lower, then drop his knife and grab instead the crucifix with both of his hands. He pressed its cool silver against his flushed forehead, and felt all of his hate and anger and lust for revenge melt away. His brother was right. Marius then got off of the beaten Fearless Wolf and stood up, holding the silver crucifix high overhead so all could see it.

He repeated the Indian woman's phrase in a loud, clear voice, his heart and mind finally at peace, with tears streaming down his face. "Mercy in the name of Jesus!" He circled the crowd with the sacred object depicting the suffering Savior. "Mercy in the name of Jesus!"

One by one, every native fell to their knees in respect, understanding what Marius had incredibly done. A stunned Fearless Wolf then covered his face with his hands, and -- kneeling too -- realized the awesome, true power of this God. The Mohawk warrior went on from that position, and humbly prostrated himself, and even pressed his brow low into the dust...

THE END

by Jack Karolewski

April 25, 2018

THAT VOODOO THAT YOU DO

He met her on Facebook.

Cutter Kendrik, age 31, was a Samsung cell phone sales associate living in St. Paul, MN. After the recall of the Galaxy Note7 model -- which became a disaster after its battery repeatedly exploded or caught fire and was now banned on airlines – Cutter was continuing to have a tough time convincing new customers that the new Samsung 8s phone models were safe.

One Saturday morning in May, while checking his Facebook news feed, Cutter had a new friend request pop up from an unknown person. Her name was Charlotte Stiles, age 29. Cutter discovered that she worked at the Mall of America (celebrating its 50th anniversary this year, with 520 stores) in nearby Bloomington, as a women's apparel clerk at Nordstrom's. She lived in Minneapolis, practically next door to St. Paul. Furthermore, her profile pic looked promising. Charlotte had brown eyes with dark eyebrows and long brown hair. Her face and skin tone looked faintly Central American, from what Cutter could guess. Maybe she was from El Salvador or Costa Rica? Other photos showed her smiling in a variety of feminine dresses, looking slim and fit. Nice body, fresh, attractive. But why did she choose him to 'friend'? A real mystery. Cutter thought for several minutes, then took a chance and accepted the friend request. What could be the harm?

The following morning, Cutter was granted the usual Facebook access to Charlotte's more complete profile. (Of course, his profile was also available now for her to view.) By that afternoon, he was receiving posts from Charlotte, first thanking him for friending her, then revealing that she was relatively new to Minnesota, having been here for just under a year. The winter was a real shock – so cold and snowy! She had come to the U.S. on an immigrant visa from Panama looking for work, so she was accustomed to tropical weather. She was still trying to make some American friends, and she had chosen Cutter because he was not married and was living relatively close by. Plus, she thought he looked handsome in his profile pic. "You had a kind face, and I sensed that I could trust you," Charlotte confessed. "Your eyes told me everything I wanted to know."

Cutter was intrigued. He waited a week before asking to meet Charlotte for a date. She quickly agreed. Cutter had been on several blind dates over the years, some fun and repeatable, others rather disastrous – 'one and done.' But nothing long-term stuck, even though the sexual aspect of any brief relationship – if he got lucky -- was always thrilling. Cutter truly wanted genuine romantic love, yet he seemed to be slipping slowly and unwillingly into sustained bachelorhood.

The pair met at a local Chevy's Mexican restaurant for lunch. When Cutter first saw Charlotte in person, he was impressed. She was slightly taller than he imagined, maybe 5'8", but he liked tall girls because he was tall too. She wore a subtle but colorful floral-patterned dress with comfortable shoes. Cutter was further impressed when she ordered off the menu in Spanish, but quickly switched back to English when she realized that their perky young waitress was not bi-lingual. Charlotte smiled sweetly and was relaxed, which in turn made Cutter relax. She affected a calm, natural appearance, avoiding the typical female first-date tendency to overdo her make-up, nails, hair, jewelry, and perfume.

While enjoying their spicy enchiladas and cold beers, they talked about their jobs and their families and their hopes for the future. Although Cutter had graduated from a community college with a business degree, Charlotte wanted to ultimately continue her education in the U.S. and to pursue more job opportunities than were currently available to her in Panama. After dessert, Cutter paid the tab, and was sufficiently confident and comfortable to offer Charlotte another date.

Over the next several months, the pair became a couple. Before long, they were sleeping together, alternating at each other's apartments. The harsh Minnesota winter was perfectly designed for cozy, warming lovemaking, they laughingly agreed. Cutter's mood was on the upswing, and even his sales quotas were being surpassed as his commissions likewise rose. He even visited Charlotte on occasion at her job at Nordstrom's, and met her boss and coworkers, who raved about her energy and her potential.

One day, the happy couple got on the topic of where to go on vacation, for they had both earned a week off of work. Charlotte suggested that they visit New Orleans, for she had always wanted to experience that unique American city. Seeing as Cutter had never been there either, the couple decided to select the Big Easy as their upcoming destination. Goodbye, ice and snow! Spanish moss and bayou, here we come...

It was pleasantly warm in New Orleans in April, but not yet miserably hot and humid as it would get later in the summer. Charlotte and Cutter enjoyed strolling through the French Quarter and Jackson Square, rode the old-fashioned streetcar/trolley through the magnolia-scented Garden District with its beautiful mansions, dined on fine Creole and Cajun cuisine at legendary restaurants such as Brennan's and Antoine's, and even had some requisite evening drinks on Bourbon Street (with throngs of other similar tourists) while listening to traditional Dixieland jazz.

One morning, over beignets and chicory coffee at Café du Monde near the Mississippi levee, Charlotte mentioned an interest in going to the Voodoo Museum on Dumaine Street. "Some friends of mine in Panama went there a few years ago, and said it was very interesting," she elaborated.

So finishing up, off they went. It was but a short three-block walk under bright sunshine. After paying $7 each, they entered the darkened museum building, which had first opened in 1972. They learned from their wizened black female tour guide, Sister LaVeau – who claimed was blood kin to the legendary voodoo priestess Marie LaVeau – all about voodoo: the history of zombies, what gris-gris were (good luck/protective amulets in tiny pouches), the use of special voodoo altars and rituals, and who some of the famous voodoo queens of New Orleans were and where their festooned graves were in nearby cemeteries. The last museum section was all about voodoo dolls and curses, and how they were used by some devotees even to this day. The gift shop here was also something to behold: Beads, scented candles, crucifixes, medallions, different kinds of special incense, posters, 'holy cards' with portraits of priestesses, 'blessed' lotions and creams, perfumed oils, charms, crystals -- even plastic bones and skulls. And, of course, small hand-made generic voodoo dolls stuffed with corn husks.

Back at their hotel swimming pool, Cutter and Charlotte worked on their tans as they relaxed in their lounge chairs and got into a broad discussion about religion and spirituality and primitive beliefs in superstitions. They found out that neither had had any church upbringing as children. Their talk then drifted into political beliefs and finances – two topics they had never previously discussed – which was usually a sign that a relationship was getting more serious and possibly committed.

Over a superb shrimp etouffee washed down with NOLA Blonde ale that night for dinner, the couple was enjoying their final night in Louisiana before returning to frosty Minnesota. Out of the blue, Charlotte said, "Hey, how about we play a game? It's called Tell Me a Secret. Let's flip a coin to see who goes first." Cutter laughed and rolled his eyes, then dug out a quarter from his pocket and tossed it. Charlotte called out "tails" and won.

"O.K. my darling, here goes: Ever since I was a little girl, I have had a really strong belief in reincarnation. I also believe in certain aspects of the Occult. I have read a lot of books on these subjects. I hope that doesn't disturb you. I don't talk about it much. I won't embarrass you by bringing up the topic in front of other people, so don't worry... Now, it's your turn! Tell me a deep, dark secret about yourself." Charlotte giggled, just a tad nervously.

Cutter thought for a moment, took a big breath, and then let out a long sigh. "Well, you asked for it, so here goes. I'm going to tell you something that only I and my doctor know. I'm taking a chance here with you, Char, because I care deeply about you and you have a right to know." He reached over with both hands and lovingly held hers as he looked into Charlotte's eyes.

"Oh my God, don't tell me you have a STD, or terminal cancer, or something else horrible!" Charlotte interrupted fearfully, her face a pained expression.

"No, no, nothing like that! Please, you can calm down." He tenderly kissed both of her hands, one after the other. "No… What I have are periodic panic attacks. They are very common in both men and women. It's simply a psychological problem, like being hypochondriac. I know when I am having a panic attack, and understand what triggers it, and hence I can take steps to control it. It started a few years ago when I read a magazine article for the first time on the subject of heart attacks. Well, I got so freaked out that I imagined any kind of chest pain as a precursor to having a massive, fatal heart attack! Naturally, the more I thought about it, the worse the panic attacks got. Although these attacks are physically baseless, they do cause actual physical reactions such as sweating, shortness of breath, dizziness, sleeplessness, and so on. It is linked to the 'fight or flight' reflex of our human nervous system. When I told my doctor about all of this, he gave me a though cardiac work-up and found absolutely nothing wrong with either my heart or my overall health. You can imagine my relief! He went on to explain how panic attacks occur and how to thwart them. So I rarely have them now. But sometimes, a new fear or susceptibility to imagining the worst outlook regarding my health comes up, and I have to deal with it, and grapple with the coping steps from the onset until I can control myself again. It is my only flaw – my Achilles Heel, if you will. Other than that, I am in great shape in every other aspect of my life to the best of my knowledge. Now, I hope I didn't freak you out, Char. I thought you should know."

Charlotte looked at Cutter for a long time without speaking. Then she smiled, and – seeing as they were still holding hands -- kissed both his hands, and said, "I'm glad you told me the truth, Cutter. It is something I needed to know. Now, how about some dessert? That Grand Marnier sponge cake with fresh strawberries looked good."

Later, back in Minnesota, Charlotte caught a very bad cold, and Cutter did not see her for an entire month at her request. "I can't see anyone yet, I'm contagious" she insisted.

"Please be patient with me until I get better, and don't call or text me, O.K.?" Cutter ordered a down quilt for her on Amazon, and had it delivered to her apartment to keep her warm, even though it now May. "Maybe you can pretend you are toasty again in Panama until you recover," he gently messaged on the surprise gift card.

During their month apart, Cutter had a serious realization. He went to a long- established jewelry store in downtown St. Paul and purchased a tasteful sapphire engagement ring. He decided he wanted to marry Charlotte.

When she had fully recovered from her illness, and was back to work at Nordstrom's, and had her regular appetite back, Cutter picked Charlotte up at her place and took her to the venerable St. Paul Hotel, a city landmark built in 1910. They had dinner at the fancy and expensive St. Paul Grill, because in Cutter's mind, this was to be a very memorable occasion.

After the meal, Charlotte began acting somewhat odd and appeared distracted and upset about something. Cutter hoped that the engagement ring secreted in his pocket might change the mood. "Charlotte, I have a big surprise for you. I realize that I love you, as I hope you love me. I have thought about us for a long time. I want to be with you for the rest of my life. Will you marry me?" He paused, shyly smiled, then offered her from his sport coat pocket a little purple velvet case with the sapphire engagement ring.

The look she offered him back was totally shocking, even deadly. Charlotte didn't even touch the case to open it.

"No, I cannot marry you, Cutter. Do you want to know why? Because I have to kill you. That's right, you heard me. Kill you." She looked at Cutter with pure hatred and loathing, her dark eyes boring into his.

A stunned Cutter choked out a feeble, "What...what are you talking about, Char? Are you feeling all right?" He felt dizzy and lightheaded, his meal sitting in his stomach like cement. Cutter's heart pounded and he began sweating.

"I never felt better, so let's get it all out now," she spat out in barely contained fury. "Three years ago, in Panama, I went to see a famous psychic reader on a recommendation from some friends. I was plagued with insomnia and horrible nightmares about dying, and was desperate for any kind of relief. Remember when I told you about my secret interest in the Occult? This gifted woman went into a brief trance, then hypnotized me and took me back to a past life in an age regression. I discovered that I was part of a pioneer family going west across the Great Plains in the state of Kansas in the 1840s. We were attacked by a band of hostile Indians and everyone was massacred. You were one of the murdering

Indians. Your face was burned into my mind. I could never forget it, especially your eyes. I swore revenge before I was raped, gutted, scalped and died. After coming out of the hypnotic trance, the psychic woman told me that my soul would never rest until I found you and killed you, because you were alive now somewhere in Minnesota. So I moved here and got a job and an apartment. I searched on Facebook every day for weeks until your face showed up. Your face was slightly changed, but your eyes were exactly what I remembered. That's the real reason why I sent you a 'friend' request. And the rest of our 'relationship' was nothing but an act, a lie. Even when we made love, I hated you, and lived only for the day when I would get my revenge. Well, the day of reckoning is here now, you bastard. And my name isn't Charlotte Stiles either, just so you know, so don't try to run like a coward to the police."

This all-of-a-sudden, completely transformed woman looked at Cutter with disgust -- like a cold, unfeeling reptile. "So, you brought me a present? Well I brought you one too." From her purse, the woman removed a voodoo doll with Cutter's face pinned on it; it had been cut out of a photograph of him they had once taken together. "Yes, it's you...filled with some locks of your hair, and some fingernail parings, and other tiny personal objects of yours that I secretly gathered. I went back to New Orleans during the month I was pretending to be sick. This voodoo doll is the real thing, officially cursed by a real voodoo priestess. I'll stick it with pins every day until you die in agony. Only then can I rest and have relief in this life." The enraged woman quickly shoved the doll back into her purse and bolted from the table.

"Wait, Charlotte, no, no... you must be crazy. You're out of your mind. Stop, stop! I'll get you help. Please, no Charlotte, wait..." Cutter ran after her, and caught up just as he saw her roar away in a taxi. He returned to the dinner table in a daze, and sat alone in disbelief for an hour after he paid the bill.

A week later, her furnished Minneapolis apartment was found vacated when Cutter checked. She had similarly abandoned her job at Nordstrom's. The woman who once called herself Charlotte Stiles had simply disappeared.

That's when Cutter Kendrik's pains began.

Sudden, piercing, stabbing pains in the stomach, the heart, and the lungs. Burning spinal pain. Blinding headaches. Insomnia. Nausea and vomiting. Cutter called in sick at work so frequently that his boss at Samsung Cellular insisted that he see a doctor, which Cutter did. But nothing physically wrong could be diagnosed. When Cutter tearfully told his doctor the whole bizarre saga, the doctor recommended that Cutter see a psychiatrist as soon as possible. Cutter took a leave of absence from his job, and was thankful that they granted him a full month off.

In his misery, Cutter went on-line and searched for anything on Charlotte Stiles. He found many women with the same name, especially on Facebook, but not his intended. Next, he poured over web sites and linked articles about voodoo dolls and their effect – particularly how to remove their dreadful curse. At last, in final desperation to rid himself of relentless, pain and agony, he booked the first non-stop flight to New Orleans he could get.

His destination was the Voodoo Museum. Cutter was frantic by the time he got there by cab from the airport. He quickly sought out Sister LaVeau and asked to speak with her briefly in private after the museum closed for the day. "Yes, I can see you needs my help," she murmured, peering carefully into his eyes. "You got a very, very bad curse on you, cher. I can see de black cloud on you. You gonna die, boy, unless de spell is broken. Come back at six o'clock, we go to my place. Not too far from here, jes' around de corner."

Cutter had two hours to kill until the museum closed. He thought about going into the nearest bar for a Sazerac or a Hurricane to help him relax, but his stomach was in such pain that he vetoed the idea -- plus, he needed to be clear-headed. So instead, he walked nervously around the

Vieux Carre, ignoring the colorful old French and Spanish colonial buildings, many with traditional wooden shutters and cast-iron balconies. By the time church bells chimed six o'clock, Cutter was back to meet Sister LaVeau.

When they arrived at her place and went inside, Cutter noted that her rooms looked similar to the Voodoo Museum, dark and cluttered and smelling of incense, with plenty of candles and gaudy altars and priestess pictures. Sister flipped off her shoes with a grunt ("Lordy, my dogs is beat!), then offered her guest some sweet tea, which he took out of politeness. They sat on a worn teal sofa and Cutter told her the whole sordid story of his relationship with the woman who once called herself Charlotte and its bizarre aftermath. Sister LaVeau listened intently.

"Cher, I'm afraid you is up the creek, sho'nuf. Dis be de blackest of magic here, de work of de Devil." She quickly made the sign-of-the-cross. "But I think I knows someone who can break dis spell. Dat be Madame ZuZu. De most powerful voodoo priestess in Haiti. You gots to go to Port au Prince right away and see her. Only she can stop yor pains and end yor sufferin' forever. You don't needs no address 'cause everyone knows her house. Now you gots to go, cher, and God bless you." Sister rose slowly from the sofa and led Cutter to the door. Cutter pulled out his wallet and gave her a twenty for her help. She winked and shoved the bill in the cleavage of her ample bosom. "Y'all take care now," she finally said as Cutter left. His stabbing pains were back again and getting worse. At this point, he was eating non-prescription painkillers as if they were candy, as well as antacids. He was an anxious, nervous wreck.

At his New Orleans hotel, Cutter Kendrik used a computer in its business center and booked a flight to Haiti and a room at the Marriott in Port au Prince. What else could he do? he thought, pathetically. But why did it have to be Haiti! The absolute hellhole of the entire Western Hemisphere. Unbelievable squalor and poverty, rampant crime, political corruption, and still recovering from its disastrous 2010 earthquake. A total national basket case, among the worst places to visit -- and tough to make it out of alive and healthy. Oh God...

After reading the multiple travel warnings on health and safety from the U.S. Department of State website the following morning (basically screaming: DON'T GO!), Cutter boarded his American Airlines flight to Miami, then continued on to Haiti's capitol, Port au Prince (PAP). He was warned by Marriott not to take a taxi or to talk to anybody once he arrived at PAP, and that a hotel shuttle would identify him and pick him up. Cutter had no luggage other than a carry-on bag, good for three days.

Arriving at Aeroport International Toussaint Louverture , he was quickly spotted by the Marriott hotel driver because Cutter was almost the only white man in the arrival hall. Once on the road with locked van doors, Cutter realized that PAP was worse than he feared as he looked out his window: chaos, noise, filth, heat and humidity, crumbling infrastructure, burning garbage, crowds, nightmarish traffic, mongrel dogs, and the eerie sense that uncontrolled anarchy could erupt any minute. Jacques, the black Marriott driver, warned Cutter about going out after dark alone in most parts of the city: "Just don't do it, man, because crazy people will kidnap you and then kill you just for your shoes." But the hotel was safe and the rooms and food were very good, he boasted.

Cutter checked in and ordered room service, took some more painkillers, then showered and listlessly watched some TV before dropping off exhausted to sleep. As was now usual, he suffered nightmares most of the night.

After breakfast the following morning, Cutter got down to business and asked the front desk where he could meet up with Madame ZuZu. The young female clerk made a quick telephone call, and about ten minutes later, a rough-looking older black man strode into the hotel lobby and came up to the female clerk's station. They spoke briefly in French in hushed tones, then the woman announced that this was Pierre, and that "he will drive you to see Madame ZuZu and bring you back here safely. You must pay him $100 U.S. cash now, however, for this service." Cutter complied, then followed Pierre out to his battered wreck of an old blue Chevrolet.

There was no conversation in the car, mostly because Cutter could speak neither French nor Haitian Creole, the two official languages of the island. Pierre steered his Chevy through dangerous neighborhoods, and Cutter was nervous, fearing violence or worse. The locals were milling about, seemingly looking for trouble, unemployed, restless. The car was hot and stuffy inside, naturally without air-conditioning, the windows rolled up and the doors locked to prevent crime at road intersections and traffic lights.

After about 45 minutes, on a hillside on the outskirts of the city, Pierre stopped at a large shanty made of cinderblocks and a tin roof, shaded by palm trees. He gestured for Cutter to get out and go in. Cutter turned to see the ocean in the distance behind him as he walked up to a red wooden door and knocked. Suddenly he panicked: What if Madame ZuZu doesn't speak English? But instead the door opened and a cheery, barefoot girl about 8 years-old wearing faded orange shorts and an old yellow t-shirt said, "Bonjour! Or do you prefer Hello?"

Cutter replied with relief, then introduced himself and asked to see Madame ZuZu if she was available. "She is taking a nap, but I'll see if she is awake. Please wait and I'll tell her you are here."

A few moments later, the girl reappeared and said solemnly, "Madame will see you now. Follow me."

Cutter was led into a darkened, large room dominated by lit candles and the now familiar voodoo paraphernalia and its associated odors. In the center of the room was a big bed with purple sheets and many pillows, and propped up in the center of that arrangement was a huge, formidable, 400-pound black woman -- the legendary Madame ZuZu, the supreme voodoo priestess here in the voodoo capitol of the world. She was wearing a green paisley silk bathrobe and was barefoot. Her hair was covered by a matching kerchief. She extended her fleshy arms out towards Cutter, offering him an embrace of greeting.

"Yes, yes, I know of you, Cutter Kendrik. I have dreamed about you and know of your sufferings. Someone bad has done evil to you and you need my help. Madame ZuZu is at your service! Come and hug me, then we will talk. Camille, bring this poor man a seat." The door greeting girl reappeared

386

directly with a somewhat rickety wooden chair. Before Cutter sat down, however, he did as he was asked, and went up close to Madame ZuZu for an embrace. She stank of earthy body odor, and one of her eyes looked milky and appeared to be sightless. Her breath was likewise foul, as her teeth were mostly rotten. She had multiple chins. She is probably fifty years old, Cutter guessed. He stifled a gag after the fast, mandatory hug, then sat in the chair several merciful feet away from her bed.

"I see you noticed my bad eye. Yes, I am blind on that side. So was my late mother, a powerful voodoo priestess from Ghana. It is a divine gift, really, because it protects me from the Evil Eye both day and night. Yes, yes, my sainted mother taught me all of my skills. And she taught me the most important secret magic spell in the world too. It is the name of God, backwards. I am the only person alive on this earth who possesses this terrible knowledge. It is terrible because if I ever say the word aloud, the world will instantly cease to exist. I am telling you the truth! Of course, I hope that day will never come. I never married or had children, so this secret will hopefully die with me. Now, you must know that I alone have the power to cure you, and to end your sufferings forever. Do you believe me?

Having no alternative, Cutter meekly replied, "Yes."

"Good, good...I have the potion ready and the necessary spell to break the curse. But these things cannot be shared freely. There is a price, of course." She smiled blandly. "The cost is $50,000 U.S., in cash."

Cutter almost fainted.

"Don't worry, my friend, you Americans can always afford what at first appears to be a shockingly large amount of money. Think about what you are getting in return: freedom from pain for the rest of your life! You are young, with many soon-to-be comfortable years ahead of you. You will likely marry and have a family. You will undoubtedly enjoy much health and happiness. Certainly, you can re-earn your savings!" Madame ZuZu cajoled. "But my offer is for today only, my friend, good until sundown. Pierre can safely escort you a large, well-known bank branch with the ability for same day international cash transfers. I therefore recommend the Banque Nationale de Credit on Route de Delmas. The whole transaction should take no more than two hours there and back. Then Pierre will return you safely to your hotel. Now, do we have a deal, Monsieur Kendrik?"

Cutter was simultaneously in a state of shock and in pain from the continual phantom stabbings all over his body.

His mind and will were at the breaking point. There was nowhere to run. He was trapped. "Deal," he agreed weakly.

Later, at the bank, he realized that $50,000 was almost 90% of his liquid assets. He would be nearly broke after this action. Dammit! He tried to push his economic future out of his mind for the time being. He had the required cash placed in a zippered canvas bag, and was escorted by armed bank guard to Pierre's beat-up Chevy. Pierre looked unimpressed at the added fortune and was again silent as he drove back to Madame ZuZu's.

Camille let them back in through the red front door. Madame ZuZu beamed from her bed and said, "There,there, that wasn't so bad, now, was it? I trust you, my friend, so I won't need to count the money and take up any more of your time than is necessary. I have written down the instructions and the healing spell which I guarantee will lift the dreadful voodoo doll curse."(At this point, she called him near and handed him a brown paper bag with all the necessary supplies, and read aloud off a piece of notebook paper.) "Here it is:

* 3 candles (1 each of purple, blue, and white)

* Myrrh oil

* Mint oil

* Sandalwood Oil

* 3 pieces of quartz

* 3 small pieces of paper

Anoint each candle with all three oils, then place them in a triangle shape in a sacred altar area. Anoint the stones similarly and place them in front of each candle. Next, write your name on each piece of paper, then place them under the stones. Say the following spell three times --

"Magick mend and candle burn

Illness leave and health return."

Leave the candles burn for three hours, then snuff them out. Do this for three nights in a row. Believe, and your pains will vanish forever. Trust me. God bless you -- Madame ZuZu."

Cutter, exhausted, took the paper bag with the supplies and folded and placed the instruction paper inside. He thanked Madame ZuZu -- mercifully avoiding a hug, instead shaking her pudgy, oily hand with its claw-like red fingernails -- and fled to Pierre's car. Cutter relived the horror of the entire day thus far in his mind as they once again motored through the chaos that was Port au Prince without any conversation, arriving safely back at the Marriott at sunset.

Cutter checked out of the hotel the next day, anxious to get home to St. Paul and break the damn voodoo doll curse once and for all. Jacques drove him to the airport without incident, and they said goodbye. Goodbye, you pathetic excuse for a country, Haiti! Cutter thought with disgust. I'm never coming back to this shithole again, he swore. But he felt sorry that Jacques was probably stuck here for life.

The AA flight was an hour late, but when it finally arrived, the passengers all had to be bussed out to the plane on the tarmac in the steamy heat and humidity.(Cutter had to check his carry-on bag because of the liquid voodoo oils it now contained.) As he was mounting the stairs, he turned around at the top of the ramp for a final look at dismal and depressing PAP.

That was when he saw a young woman near the terminal building catch his eye and give him a single, almost dismissive wave.

It was the woman who had once called herself Charlotte Stiles, and as he took his seat in stunned disbelief on the aircraft and fumbled with his seatbelt, he realized with sickening certainty all that had just happened...

THE END

by Jack Karolewski

June 4, 2017

SHERLOCK'S CHALLENGE

It was a cold and drizzly November day in London in 1898. The world's most famous consulting detective, Sherlock Holmes, was seated in a burgundy velour armchair, smoking his favorite pipe while staring into the dancing flames of his fireplace at his lodgings at 221-B Baker Street. As usual, he was deep in thought. He was wearing a loose, dark green, quilted silk smoking robe with a wide curled-back collar.

At age 44, under the strict urgings of his colleague, friend, and medical doctor, John Watson, Holmes had given up occasionally injecting himself intravenously with a 7% solution of cocaine whenever he was overwhelmed with despair and ennui. This nasty habit was born out of a need for mental stimulation, for above all things, Sherlock loathed boredom. Nowadays, Holmes only satisfied his bodily cravings with tobacco, which he kept loose in the toe of a Persian slipper on his mantelpiece.

The man himself was a bachelor, tall and thin, clean-shaven, with piercing dark eyes, a prominent nose, a sharp jawline, and a handsome head of dark hair swept backward away from his brow and ears. For relaxation, he enjoyed playing the violin. He was still quite strong and fit, and was proficient in several of the Eastern martial arts, as well as in boxing, sword-fighting, and marksmanship. Sherlock Holmes always carried himself with supreme confidence and fearlessness. His legendary mind was an international marvel – keen and sharp as a Sheffield saber. Yet he was not a pursuer of publicity or accolades, preferring only the personal pleasure of solving complex and challenging crimes when others had failed.

Sherlock's Baker Street apartment was on the first floor up. It was filled with the usual crowded Victorian furnishings – Oriental carpeting, potted ferns, thick velvet curtains, two sofas and three padded armchairs, some painted nature scenes framed and hanging on the walls, and an impressive marble fireplace. Lighting was provided by gas lamps. But Holmes' lodgings was also cluttered with a prominent laboratory table (burdened with glass beakers, test tubes, an alcohol burner, various pungent chemicals, and a microscope), stacks of old The Times newspapers, bookshelves groaning to overflowing, and even a jackknife stuck into a wall, holding up papers and correspondence that the great detective was reluctant to discard. Tossed upon a desktop near one of two large windows was Holmes' deerstalker cap and his magnifying glass. Inside a drawer of the same desk was a lethal pistol with a box of cartridges. In the adjoining bedroom, Sherlock kept a portrait of Irene Adler on his bed stand. She had been the only woman that he admired and felt tenderly towards.

Mrs. Hudson, a widow, was Sherlock's long-time matronly Scottish landlady and housekeeper. She tried, often in vain, to keep his rather messy living quarters tidy, but she was treasured by Holmes as a splendid cook and manager, and she knew when to stay quiet and how to be discreet and unobtrusive.

Now, she knocked loudly on Holmes' door and announced that a messenger had left an important note. "Something assuredly of interest, I presume Mr. Holmes," she offered, eyes twinkling, holding out to her lodger a silver tray with a wax-sealed letter upon it.

"Thank you, Mrs. Hudson. We can only hope. Please bring the morning post when it arrives. That will be all," Holmes curtly dismissed her.

He took the letter over near a gaslight and broke the red seal. He read the letter once quickly, then a second time slowly and carefully. It was from his arch-enemy, Professor James Moriarty, the evil villain Sherlock had once dubbed The Napoleon of Crime!

Moriarty was a criminal genius, starkly feared throughout Europe. Once an esteemed professor of mathematics at a major German university, he had instead twisted his formidable intellect away from academia and towards the development of the most elaborate and diabolical crime syndicate that both the Continent and the British Isles had ever seen. He, like Sherlock, had never married. Holmes had oblique confrontations with this singularly dangerous foe and his minions throughout the course of his detective career, but had never met Moriarty face-to-face. Sherlock knew in all seriousness that one day, the two opposites must meet and battle, and only one man would ultimately survive. Would this be the day? Here is what the letter said:

"Dear Mr. Holmes,

I wish to invite you to dinner at one of my rented residences here in London this coming Sunday, 13 November, at 1:00 p.m. I will arrange a hansom cab for your convenience at half-past noon, so my specific address need not be of your concern.

Please come alone and unarmed. I pledge my honor as an English gentleman that you will be safe and unharmed while in my company at this particular meeting. After our meal and chat, you will promptly be returned to your Baker Street flat.

I felt it was time that we met in person. I have some important information which should interest your 'particular talents'.

I am, sir, your obedient servant --

(signed) J. Moriarty"

The following day, a Thursday, Dr. Watson arrived for a short, casual visit. The two friends saw each other less frequently since Watson took a wife, Mary, nine years earlier. Watson was still powerfully built, with a square jaw, muscular neck and a thick, tawny mustache. A medical doctor, he had served Her Majesty in both India and Afghanistan, and had been wounded once in his right leg, which caused him to limp slightly. Holmes discussed Moriarty's invitation at length with his trusted companion. Both men agreed that Sherlock should be extra cautious, but that he should go, if only to find out more information regarding this mysterious and foul criminal mastermind.

Sunday arrived cloudy and blustery cool, but dry. The detective dressed in his brown suit for the occasion. A cab picked Holmes up at 12:30 p.m. as promised. After a half-hour negotiating the crowded and noisy streets of the city, Sherlock found himself deposited in front of a typical non-descript white apartment block behind black-painted wrought iron fencing. He noticed that a busy, fancy restaurant was across the street at the corner, filled with families and couples who had recently exited church services and were now about to partake in the traditional British Sunday dinner. His keen eye also noted three, tough-looking chaps scattered at random down the block, watching him intently. Probably his host's henchmen, should their services be needed, Holmes suspected.

Moriarty greeted Holmes at his apartment door. He was wearing a somber black suit over a white shirt, resembling nothing less than a mortician assessing a corpse. He was thin, about three inches shorter than Sherlock, with a pale complexion. His cheeks also suffered some pock-marking, probably from childhood smallpox. The man standing before him was a few years older than Holmes, perhaps near the same age as my brother Mycroft, the detective surmised. But the most striking physical feature of the professor was his large head with its thinning hair and its enormous, domineering forehead. Moriarty's dark eyes were dull and reptilian, however, their lizard-like components reinforced by the man's anxious habit of licking his thin lips as would an iguana. His facial expression was oddly blank, neither welcoming nor hostile. Holmes was on his highest guard.

"Forgive me if I decline shaking hands, Mr. Holmes, but I have a peculiar aversion to germs which I fear touching my fellow humans helps promote. But please, sir, do come in and make yourself comfortable. I have a fine meal which was just delivered from the establishment across the street, which I'm sure your sharp eye already noticed. As a result, we are assured complete privacy, without the annoying possibility of eavesdropping by any in-house cooks or servants," the host announced.

The spacious apartment itself was rather drab and sterile. 'Utilitarian,' was Sherlock's one word first impression. He doubted Moriarty spent much time here, for it was uninviting and looked little lived-in. The dining room, however, was immaculately set up, the table sparkling with fine china and crystal and silverware, with even a simple floral bouquet of young ferns as a centerpiece. He had really made an effort to be gracious, Holmes deduced, but what is his ultimate game here, he wondered? On the sideboard, expensive covered silver serving dishes held a generous sliced roast beef, Yorkshire pudding, roasted potatoes, a medley of peas and carrots, and a glass dish with celery stalks and sliced radishes. A fine ruby claret in an elaborate decanter was offered, along with some bottled mineral water from Baden-Baden.

"Thank you for coming today, Mr. Holmes. Please help yourself. I assure you that the food is excellent, though I think that neither you nor I care much about what we consume in regards to nutrition. It is simply fuel for the body and, more importantly, the mind -- don't you agree?"

The two rivals slowly and quietly ate without resorting to any banal conversation. They watched each others' eyes intently, however. Sherlock was struck by a cold reality, that across this table sat a living monster who personally arranged the murders of dozens of mostly innocent human beings that opposed his vile designs -- a man given to extortion, bribery, robbery, kidnapping, torture, and worse. A man without guilt. A man without normal emotions. A man without mercy. A misanthrope and sociopath.

Dessert was treacle tart, offered with silver tips Chinese tea. Brandy and cigars concluded the meal.

The two men finally sat in opposing comfortable armchairs near the fireplace while they smoked. Then Moriarty spoke.

"We are the last titans in this weary world, Mr. Holmes. You represent the forces of light, and justice, and redemption – whereas I embrace the darkness. I am one who lives off misery and greed and betrayal and hatred. I see the world as it is, not as it pretends to be. I use my power and money to ascend to the heights of my chosen profession. You may see me as evil, a madman, a kind of wicked demon. But I and others like me are those who are secretly admired by most people for our fearlessness and bold cunning, not you and your sense of law and morality and virtue. The world is a violent place, Mr. Holmes. Evolution has bred us for war and mischief, not flowers and mercy! Darwin knew the facts. All religions are absurd, a mockery of our essential nature, don't you see? Police forces around the world and detectives like yourself represent the last gasp of a soon-to-be extinct species, Mr. Holmes. Did you know that I run a vast international network of spies, traitors, bankers, politicians, and newspapermen who all do my bidding without question? I manipulate national elections and stock markets, direct specific assassinations, and steal gold and many currencies across Europe to finance my ever-expanding empire. I 'own' quite a few judges, lawmakers, and even clergy and police when necessary. My sinister cohorts sit undetected on the boards of important and influential businesses and corporations. You have heard of the Freemasons, the Illuminati, the Priory of Sion, no doubt? My reach goes even further. My grasp is tighter, and my goals are even more ambitious!"

Moriarty paused to lick his lips like a demented lizard, his dull eyes suddenly animated with pure hate and greed. Sherlock listened intently without interrupting, and was certain the deranged former professor was mad, and had to be locked up in an asylum, or -- preferably -- destroyed, sooner rather than later.

"Did you know that I have had you watched every moment, both day and night, Mr. Holmes, for years? I could of had you killed anytime with a mere wave of my hand on a dozen different occasions, or eliminated forever your beloved brother Mycroft, or your closest dear friend Dr. Watson. I could have easily poisoned this meal which you just enjoyed – but don't worry, I didn't. Truly, one of us must die someday so that the other can go on. But the time is not right yet. We must still grapple with our wits, tooth and claw, like it is an enormous game of fate. You see, Mr. Holmes, you alone are my only true equal, in both intellect and determination. But it remains to be seen who will be the winner in our little contest – who will be the final survivor. It might take years, or it might end tomorrow – who can say?"

Moriarty paused as he tossed the remains of his cigar into the fireplace, then clapped his hands together in a gesture of transition. His eyes reflected the flickering log flames, and resembled those of a deadly viper or cobra.

"Now, my esteemed guest, I would like to share some fascinating information with you. Do forgive my bragging about my newest project, Mr. Holmes, but perhaps only you and I can appreciate its unique brilliance? I aim to tease or perhaps actually trigger a war between France and England, the eternal rival nations. Only this time, the conflict will become more global, due to various interrelated alliances with other European nations. I have used forgery, blackmail, and bribery to accomplish my mission. In an effort to recompense French honor for their humiliating defeat to the English at the Battle of Waterloo in 1815, the French government will demand that the British government pay them the amount of 1 million pounds sterling in gold bullion. If the British fail to pay the bounty by the prescribed deadline, the French will be forced to pour large quantities of fatal arsenic into the River Thames, killing thousands of hapless citizens. This act of aggression will thus trigger a new Great War in retaliation. It will be in the British self-interest to pay, as the lesser of two evils. Rest assured, I already have the massive arsenic supply if they don't comply. And even if a large-scale war does break out, I will still make a fortune selling armaments -- to both sides, of course! Here, Mr. Holmes, let me show you the carefully forged French ransom document."

Sherlock knew of the dangers involved here from reading the recent news, because a mere ten days ago, the Fashoda Incident between the two world powers was resolved in southern Sudan. But it was a humiliating defeat for France, forcing them from the region, and leaving the British in sole control of the area, including the important colonial prize of Egypt. Tensions were high, and any provocation, such as Moriarty was planning, could easily spiral out of international control. British-German relations were also strained at this time, over who would have world naval supremacy on the high seas.

Holmes was then offered the document, and he read the explicit demands.

"I would give you a copy for your files, sir, but I'm afraid this is the sole copy. My skillful master forger -- who must remain unnamed -- is unfortunately serving time in a French prison at the moment. You are looking at a letter purportedly written by the French Minister of Finance, Paul Peytral, under the auspices of current French President Felix Faure. Peytral will take the Channel ferry soon to England, then proceed by train to London, and personally deliver this document to Queen Victoria's Chancellor of the Exchequer, Sir Michael Hicks Beach. Both men are under my considerable influence, one through blackmail, the other through bribery. One man will be paid 5,000 pounds sterling, and the other 25,000 pounds sterling for their roles in the plot. President Faure will never know about my extortion plan, unless the British foolishly refuse to pay and actual war is declared on France after my arsenic is released. Sir Beach will need to inform Her Majesty, of course, but with the understanding that the press and the public never learn of the one million pound secret gold payment."

Holmes then spoke up, after carefully rubbing the paper between his fingers and minutely inspecting it for a few moments. "This document forgery is quite good, but two significant errors were made. First, the paper weight feels to be a Bond 28, whereas I happen to know that all official French documents utilize the thicker and thus heavier Bond 36. And secondly, the female Liberty headdress on the Great Seal of France at the top of the letterhead has only six projecting rays, whereas the actual Seal has seven. However, the average recipient of such a document would probably neglect to notice either mistake."

Moriarty drew in a deep breath and frowned, and appeared disappointed with the minor flaws in his precious, pivotal document. But he simultaneously gave Sherlock some offhand praise when he said, "I see your reputation as a master sleuth is rightly deserved, Mr. Holmes. Your training and experience is indeed commendable. I would expect no less of you."

In the distance, Big Ben tolled the four o'clock hour. Seconds later, the rather plain clock on Moriarty's mantelpiece likewise struck the hour. The professor instinctively reached with his left hand for his own vest pocket watch and popped it open, while also licking his lips again. Sherlock noticed a small, dark, rounded mole on Moriarty's left wrist past his thumb when his white shirt cuff lifted up in the movement. Then his host announced, "I fear our visit must conclude now, Mr. Holmes, for I have other pressing business to attend to. Your hansom cab is waiting outside as I speak. Surely, we will meet again, but be aware that I have many residences throughout the British Isles and Europe. I rarely sleep in the same bed twice in a row. Should you find your way back to this apartment, for example with the police to arrest me, you will find me already long gone. I also employ several 'doubles' who resemble me. They do my bidding precisely as I dictate. These measures are for my personal safety and freedom, for as you know, I have never spent even a minute behind bars in any prison."

The detective grabbed his formal hat and silver-capped black walking stick (which concealed a thin, razor-sharp sword), and turned to leave. "Common courtesy requires me to thank you for this afternoon's invitation and meal, Professor. Therefore I do. But I would be less than honest if I did not tell you outright that I consider you a twisted, poisonous blight on the whole of humanity, and that I will fervently dedicate myself to thwarting all of your dastardly designs until you are either permanently institutionalized or in your grave. That is my blunt and solemn pledge, sir. I bid you farewell." Outside, a light rain began to fall on the world's largest city.

Through his open front door as Sherlock stepped out, Moriarty replied, "All will be as it should be, sir. I have the substantial resources and the manpower. You are alone, and have only your wits. That will be your challenge. As they say in the sporting arena: may the best man win! Good bye, Mr. Holmes, until we meet again."

Sitting in his cab as it trotted back to Baker Street, Holmes replayed the entire afternoon encounter in his mind, committing to memory every detail. Certainly, his first task was to ascertain exactly which day Paul Peytral intended leaving Paris for London to deliver the forged ransom demand.

Three days later, Sherlock learned through his police connections in France that all foreign diplomatic courier deliveries were done on the last business day of each month. That would be Wednesday, November 30, he noted. Holmes got a physical description of Peytral and some other details -- the Minister had a trimmed white beard with mustache, was fluent in English, and counted bird-watching as his favorite hobby -- and waited. Sherlock had to intercept and destroy the sinister forged demand. Meanwhile on Sunday, the detective was invited to Dr. Watson's house for afternoon tea.

Mary put on a grand spread of Darjeeling and Earl Grey -- and the traditional tiny sandwiches and dainty cakes -- and soon left the two friends to their privacy. Holmes relayed to Watson every aspect of his dramatic, three-hour encounter with the infamous Napoleon of Crime.

"Nothing short of amazing, Holmes," Watson snorted as he lit a cigar. "The man is clearly insane. A vile menace to all that is civilized. Have you thought of how to stop him? And may I be of any assistance?"

Sherlock told his good friend that, while he truly appreciated the offer, the fact that Watson was now a married man precluded him from sharing in any situations which might jeopardize his safety. "Best to stick with your medical practice and stay by your dear wife, old chum," Holmes gently declared. Then he shared his detailed plans with the doctor. "One thing I will require of you, Watson. A small vial of liquid chloral hydrate. I need to secretly sedate the French Minister, aged 54, for about three hours. He is of average weight and build, for purposes of the dosage." The good doctor said he would have it delivered by courier to Holmes' flat within twenty-four hours.

On Monday morning, November 28, the great detective received a hastily scribbled note from a woman he had never met before named Christine Beryl. She gave her address in Kensington, and said that she had been blackmailed and urgently needed help. She pleaded for Sherlock to come. Seeing as it appeared to be an uncomplicated domestic request and that he had some unscheduled time until Wednesday, Holmes decided to take the case.

When he arrived at the indicated address a few hours later, Sherlock was met at the second floor apartment door by a striking young woman in her late 20's. Her hair was honey-colored and fashionably swept up, her eyes were emerald green, and her face and complexion was exquisite. Her lavender silk gown was sumptuous and flattering. The only feature which was off-putting was her runny nose, which had turned red from recent crying, as she clutched a white lace handkerchief after dabbing it in embarrassment. Holmes introduced himself and was invited into the flat, which was finely arranged and richly decorated. "Christine Beryl, Mr. Holmes," she spoke, offering her hand. "Thank you for arriving on such short notice. Please forgive my appearance, but I have suffered some disturbing news and my emotions have been shaken." Sherlock was invited to make himself comfortable while Miss Beryl (for the woman was not wearing a wedding ring) retired to an adjoining room to bring back what she claimed was a blackmail demand regarding her brother in Cardiff, Wales.

After more than a few minutes, however, Holmes was called aloud by Miss Beryl from her bedroom to please come in and assist her. But when the detective walked over and through the bedroom doorway, he was totally surprised to see Miss Beryl in a state of near nakedness. She had removed her formal lavender gown and was now wearing an open, floor-length, pink French silk negligee. Her flawless flesh was like alabaster, and Sherlock thought that he felt the soft warmth emanating from her body, even from three feet away. He was momentarily speechless.

"Come now, Mr. Holmes. Surely you have seen an eager young female in a state of desire and undress? I have asked you here for an hour at least, strictly for our mutual pleasure. Or perhaps you have never had a woman before, being so cerebral and always busy with your many detective chores?" Christine appraised him seductively, showing her fine white teeth as she smiled.

Sherlock's disciplined mind, however, directed his eyes to sweep the room instead, until they fell upon the toe of a single brown boot slightly protruding from the bottom of a thick blue bedroom window curtain.

"Ah, yes...the old entrapment game...well, well...what have we here?" Holmes leaped toward the curtain and pulled it back with a jerk. A frightened middle-aged man, holding a Kodak No. 1 Box Camera, was caught there, hiding. "You are certainly no Irene Adler, Miss Beryl...nor are you a lady!" Holmes spat out with disgust. "Trying to smear my reputation with a scandal photo for the lurid London tabloids? How dare you! Did Professor Moriarty put you up to this tawdry farce?" Sherlock hotly demanded. The man with the camera quickly rushed past Holmes and fled out of the apartment, having failed in his assignment. Holmes ordered the woman to get dressed as he stormed out of the flat and hailed a cab.

The very next morning, Mrs. Hudson informed the detective that a Miss Christine Beryl was downstairs and pleaded to see him. Surprised yet still annoyed from yesterday, Holmes nonetheless ordered her sent up. Now what does she want? he wondered with distain.

"Do forgive this intrusion, Mr. Holmes, but I just had to see you in person, and humbly beg your pardon for yesterday's pathetic charade. I need to explain everything," Miss Beryl cast her emerald-green eyes downward and her cheeks flushed with embarrassment. Holmes offered the distraught woman a chair. "I am truly no strumpet, sir. My brother, Miles, in Cardiff, was indeed being blackmailed by James Moriarty, who had damning evidence of financial misfeasance regarding my brother's business dealings in Wales. Moriarty approached me and offered Miles a reversal of fortune if I cooperated by attempting to seduce you, then be caught and photographed in a compromising posture. I am so very sorry, Mr. Holmes. Please believe me!" Christine pleaded.

Sherlock was struck by the female's sincerity. "You have verified my suspicions, dear lady, that Moriarty was behind this play. I will contact the Welsh authorities at once and have your brother's safety guaranteed, although he must of course make any fiscal recompense to his business associates. In the meantime, I suggest that you stay here for the next forty-eight hours, so as to be unavailable to Professor Moriarty's wrath for having failed in your role as my seductress. Mrs. Hudson will see to your needs and comfort, and provide you with a spare room, until I return from abroad." Miss Beryl agreed, and thanked the great detective profusely with tearful eyes as she was ushered out by the matronly landlady.

Next, Sherlock Holmes packed his leather Gladstone bag (including Dr. Watson's chloral hydrate vial) and took the night train to Dover, the Channel ferry then to Calais, and from there, on to Paris. He had a fitful sleep for a substantial portion of the journey, but it was enough to sustain him for the important tasks which now lay ahead. It was Wednesday, November 30. Holmes stayed watchful at the Gare du Nord until he spied the French Minister of Finance with an overnight bag and a briefcase boarding the 7 a.m. train to Calais. The 236 km. trip usually took just under four hours. The detective was currently in disguise, costumed as an elderly white-haired pensioner returning to London from a pleasant fortnight's bird-watching holiday in France. Naturally, he was ever-vigilant for any of Moriarty's possible henchmen lurking about.

Both Sherlock and his prey boarded the First Class carriage. An hour into the trip, breakfast was just being served in the dining car. The detective nimbly followed directly behind the Minister, who kept his briefcase by his side. Holmes was thus seated with Peytral, as was his intention, and they were soon joined by two other strangers, both French, both going only as far as Lille. Sherlock made a show out of shuffling his birding guidebook and his worn binocular case after placing his order of croissants with quince jam and milky coffee with sugar. "Forgive me, gentlemen, but I'm afraid my French is quite poor. *Parlez-vous Anglais*? My name is Reginald Fitzhugh, from Dorchester," Holmes offered sweetly and innocently.

The two Frenchmen ignored Sherlock with a negative shake of their heads, but Paul Peytral spoke up, saying, "Yes, I speak English. And I notice you are interested in bird-watching? By coincidence, it is also a fine hobby of mine," the Minister revealed. He then introduced himself -- by first name only, not revealing his official government title. The other two diners at the table did not recognize Peytral, regardless.

As the men ate, Holmes made casual conversation about the train, the food, his home in Dorchester, and even mentioned his late wife (no children). But Sherlock became quite animated when discussing the new birds he had seen on his French holiday. "Amazing! So many species not common in England: Caspian tern. Alpine swift. Sardinian warbler. Spotless starling. Even some coming in from North Africa, assuredly. Tell me, Paul, what are your favorite bird-watching spots? And where are the best migration flyways in France? I would really like to know, from your experience."

The two men talked excitedly for another thirty minutes or so after the silent French pair left the dining car. Holmes then gently apologized for taking up so much of Peytral's time, adding, "But if you happen to be taking the Calais to Dover ferry, Paul, I would enjoy inviting you for a drink in their lounge." Peytral admitted that he was indeed on his way to London, so he would welcome talking more about birding with Reginald again. "You know, the Languedoc region in southern France offers the finest birding in western Europe, home to over 40% of its species. England is smaller and more densely populated than France, so it has much less open lands for bird populations. But we can continue our delightful talk once aboard ship. I will find you in the lounge once I get settled," Paul promised.

At 10:44 a.m., the train pulled into Calais station, near the Channel ferry dock. All ongoing passengers boarded "Le Nord," a large, paddle-wheeled French Channel steamer which held up to 500 passengers. There were 140 private, two-bed cabins, for those who wished to pay extra for privacy on the typical four-hour and forty-five minute crossing. Holmes had earlier booked a cabin for himself. When he approached the steward on the gangplank checking all the passengers in, Sherlock carefully glanced at the manifest as his own name was being verified, and saw that Paul Peytral was going to be staying in Cabin #117. Sherlock would be in Cabin #92.

The ship cast off promptly at 11:15 a.m. Holmes went directly to his cabin and freshened up, also checking his white-wigged disguise in the room mirror. Satisfied, he then removed the vial of liquid chloral hydrate from his Gladstone bag and slipped it into his vest pocket. He headed down to the lounge and waited. Fortunately, although the weather was cold and cloudy, at least the Channel was not rough, for the winds had not whipped the waves up as they were sometimes apt to do.

Just past noon, Paul showed up in the lounge and greeted Holmes, who was seated in a discreet corner near a window. Sherlock ordered two large Bristol Milk sherrys, with Peytral's approval. They settled back into easy, even more friendly conversation, except that when Paul was asked if he had any children, he allowed that he had a son, Victor, age twenty-four. As the Minister of Finance confessed this fact, however, Holmes noticed that Peytral's eyes looked away, in an expression of sadness or perhaps worry. The canny detective surmised that Moriarty had blackmailed Peytral, and that Victor was somehow involved. The Minister did not appear in any way to be a dastardly, evil man eager to tease a war between England and France. Sherlock artfully turned their conversation back to their mutual fascination with birding, and he saw Paul visibly relax. They settled on the topic of flamingos, and how these birds could be found, improbably, even in Chilean Patagonia!

Holmes casually put his fingers in his vest pocket and uncapped the hidden chloral hydrate vial and waited until the right moment to slip the sedative into Peytral's sherry. The barkeep was occupied with another customer. The lounge was sparsely populated. No one appeared to notice the two men in the corner.

Suddenly, Sherlock exclaimed, "I say, Paul, I do believe I just spied a male Rutland Osprey catching a fish! Look there!" Holmes pointed out the window. As Peytral obliged the command, the detective deftly poured the sparse contents of the vial with his left hand into the other man's drink. His motion was undetected. Holmes knew the tasteless sedative would react about ten minutes after ingestion, and would be good for three or so hours of deeply drugged sleep.

"Sorry, Reginald...I'm afraid I must have missed it," Paul replied. "Such a magnificent breed. I know it...dark brown top with a cream underbelly...and a distinctive 'highwayman's mask,' like a bandit, across the eyes. Perhaps we'll see another, though they seldom travel in flocks, being a more solitary fowl." Peytral took a long quaff from his sherry tumbler.

"If you ever get to Dorchester, do look me up, Paul. Ask for me at the Red Stag Inn. They'll direct you to my house. You know, there is some good coastal birding nearby if you have a free afternoon, especially in the spring." Paul said he would remember, then excused himself, saying that he felt very tired and would retire to his cabin for a nap, and rest up for the final leg of his journey – the 68-mile train trip from Dover to London, which took just under two hours. "If we don't see each other again before England, it was a pleasure to have met you, Paul. Pleasant journey," Holmes offered, and the men shook hands, with a now exhausted-looking Peytral thanking Reginald for the drink as he drained his glass, then walked with heavy legs out of the lounge.

Holmes waited a half-hour for the drug to fully take effect before slipping off to Cabin #117. Casually looking both ways in the hallway so as not to be seen, the detective removed a lock-picking tool from his inner coat pocket and noiselessly entered Peytral's room. The curtains were drawn so the room was quite dim, but there was enough light for Sherlock to accomplish his mission. Paul was in bed, loudly snoring, his face turned toward the wall. Holmes spied the Minister's briefcase in an overhead luggage rack, so he slowly brought it down and quietly opened it. He quickly found the crucial forged French ransom document that Moriarty had previously shown him. Slipping it into his inside jacket pocket, Holmes replaced the briefcase and tip-toed to the door. Peering out, he saw the back of a ship's steward walking away down the hallway. Sherlock waited a few seconds, then checked the hallway again. It was empty, so the detective was safe to exit the cabin and return to his own room #92, which was on a different deck.

Once inside his cabin, Holmes removed the document and studied it one last time before lighting a match and burning the letter to cinders, dropping it in his room ashtray. Then Sherlock relaxed and had a smoke. About an hour later, he headed downstairs to the dining room and ate a light lunch before returning to his room for a much-needed but brief nap. The ferry Le Nord would later arrive on schedule in Dover at 4:00 p.m.

Holmes noticed Paul Peytral eventually exit down the ship's gangplank, but kept out of sight by blending in with the milling, departing crowd. Sherlock deliberately missed the next train to London's St. Pancras Station so as not to encounter the French Minister again. Instead, he took the following train, which arrived fifty minutes later. While he waited, in the Gents Toilet at the ferry terminal, the detective skillfully removed his effective white-wigged disguise and clothing costume. So far, all had gone well, he felt, with ample relief.

But Holmes' train to London suffered some unexpected mechanical difficulties, and was forced to stop at Ashford for two and one-half hours of repairs. The passengers were allowed to exit their carriages in the town while waiting, so Sherlock took advantage of the delay and had a much-needed hearty evening meal, and purchased a newspaper to read afterwards.

Taking a hansom once he arrived at St. Pancras at 8:50 p.m., Sherlock Holmes was back at 221-B Baker Street by 9:15. But he was met by a frantic Mrs. Hudson, with Christine Beryl standing behind her, also looking tense and disturbed. Mrs. Hudson relayed that Holmes' older brother, Mycroft, had just come from the Diogenes Club and then departed, but left alarming and dire news that Dr. Watson had been abducted nearly three hours ago! She pressed the terse note that Mycroft had left into her famous lodger's hand. Sherlock read it with shock, and was crestfallen. Here is what it said:

"To Mycroft Holmes --

Please inform your meddlesome detective brother that I have kidnapped his dear friend, Dr. Watson, and will hold him for twenty-four hours until my valuable document, which was stolen, is returned intact.

If my demands are unmet by then, Watson will die.

(signed) M"

"Should we inform Mary at once, Mr. Holmes?" Mrs. Hudson asked, with a somber and unsteady voice.

Sherlock thought deeply for a moment, still clearly shaken, then replied after taking a deep breath and exhaling while rubbing his chin, "Not yet, Mrs. Hudson. I must formulate an effective plan of safe rescue for our good doctor. We have roughly twenty-one hours left. I believe that both my brother and Scotland Yard can be mustered to help me deal with this dastardly and heinous development."

But just then, a large man, red-faced, obviously struggling to catch his breath from running, and with a bleeding right hand wrapped hastily in a red-soaked handkerchief, burst into the room.

It was none other than Dr. Watson himself!

"My friends, quick, a stiff brandy, if you please!" Watson ordered. In an instant, Mrs. Hudson stepped to a sideboard and complied, pouring a generous draught of the restorative liquor from its decanter into a glass.

"My good fellow! Are you injured? Your hand...you must tell me what happened," the detective cried. "But first you must sit and recover yourself," Holmes urged. Watson did as he was directed, clearly exhausted. He drank the brandy with care but with eagerness and gratitude. "Mrs. Hudson, please send word to Mary that her husband is well and is here with us, and that we will explain the complete details later," Holmes directed.

"Oh...forgive my manners, Watson. This is Miss Beryl, whom you have not yet met. She is staying with us here for the moment, for she has also suffered some unsavory dealings with Professor Moriarty," Holmes explained. Watson nodded in greeting to the woman, for he was asked by her not to formally rise for the introduction, given his condition.

"Please, doctor, do let me attend to your injured hand. Allow me first to loosen your collar and unbutton your waistcoat," Christine suggested. She then darted away, and returned carefully with a basin of warm water, a small towel, a cake of carbolic soap, and some fresh bandaging which Mrs. Hudson helped her assemble. "Now, doctor, it is your turn to play the patient, so please relax...umm...yes...your bloodied knuckles were badly scraped, sir, but no bones appear to be broken," Miss Beryl announced, after examining, then cleaning, disinfecting, and expertly bandaging his injured right hand. She also wiped some of the sweat and grime that had accumulated on Watson's face during his ordeal. "My mother was a nurse, you know, so I learned a few first aid tricks from her," Christine acknowledged.

Having mostly recovered by now, Dr. John Watson next dropped a bombshell.

"Holmes, I have shot and killed Professor Moriarty..." the doctor confessed. "With his own pistol, in a life or death struggle, within the past hour or so. First man I ever had to kill who was not an Indian or Afghani rebel soldier. We need to go to Scotland Yard immediately and identify his body."

It was almost December and biting cold outside as the two men hailed a cab. During the ride, Watson explained to his friend how he was grabbed from behind by two thugs and chloroformed into unconsciousness by a third as he left his medical office after hours.

"When I awoke, I was tied to a wooden chair in the middle of a freezing, derelict warehouse somewhere near the Thames, for I could smell the foul odors of the river through the broken windows where I was imprisoned. Two unsavory characters were guarding me. But one of the scoundrels left to purchase a pint at a nearby alehouse. The remaining man told me how Professor Moriarty would be arriving within the hour, and that he was very angry, and that he would first torture and then probably kill me on account of your actions, dear fellow. Fortunately, the ropes restraining me in the chair were crudely tied, so as I listened, I covertly loosened my bindings. When the guard came close with a cup of water that I requested, I broke free and we struggled, fists to face, boots to body, blow by blow. That is how my hand became injured. Then I got a lucky punch in, and knocked the loathsome rascal unconscious. When I got up to flee, however, Moriarty had arrived alone, with surprise on his face. I knew it was him by your recent description, Holmes. He reached inside his coat to withdraw his revolver, but it dropped to the ground in his haste. We both dove for it. We reached the gun at the same time and struggled. The pistol went off right in Moriarty's stomach. A fatal arterial wound. He bled to death rapidly, right in front of me. I fled for fear that the other henchman would return from the alehouse, and perhaps likewise be armed. I ran as far away as I could, then hailed a hansom. In the distance, I could hear alarmed police whistles, for someone had heard the gunshot and alerted the proper authorities." Watson paused and looked at Holmes. "I had the cab drop me off two blocks away in case I was being followed, and then ran here -- my old leg war wound aching with every step. The whole incident was nightmarish, Holmes. I feel I will never be able to write it up for publication, as I have dutifully done for most of your other criminal cases and adventures, which have brought you such deserved recognition and acclaim."

Sherlock marked his dear companion with renewed regard in his eyes. "I say, well done, Watson! And thank heaven that you are again safe and sound after such a harrowing encounter and escape. Your wits and skills are truly commendable, old chum. Do you realize that you have just rid the world of one of its worst villains? Outstanding! And rest assured that you had no other choice in killing him, my friend. Your conscience can be quite clear in such a circumstance."

When the cab dropped them off at Scotland Yard, Holmes and Watson were met by Inspector Lestrade, a long-time police colleague in the seemingly endless fight against crime. However, the inspector had always been both jealous and in awe of the great detective, for Sherlock had the remarkable knack of cracking many of the tough cases that Lestrade and his department had failed to solve. He took the pair directly to the basement morgue, where fresh or unclaimed crime victim corpses were stored.

"Looks like Dr. Watson has impressively beaten you this time, Holmes!" Lestrade crowed. "Moriarty himself dead at last. All of England and the rest of Europe will sing your praises and sigh with relief, Doctor, once the press hears about this one. Could well be the 'victory-over-crime' story of the year!"

Sherlock easily ignored most of the inspector's ramblings, and instead ordered with a tired sigh, "Let's just identify the body now, can we, gentlemen?"

The new corpse had just arrived and was waiting for them, laid out on a wheeled metal cart and covered with a fresh white sheet. The stark, clinical room smelled of antiseptics, formaldehyde and finality.

Holmes was the first to peel back the sheet. Watson and Lestrade peered closely over Sherlock's shoulder. Moriarty lay there -- pale, cold, and lifeless. There was the formidable brow, the cruel, thin lips, and the pock-marked cheeks. The dark, reptilian eyes were now closed forever.

But Holmes continued to peel back the shroud until his gaze halted abruptly upon the left wrist of the dead body. The great detective slowly frowned in bitter realization. Where there should have been a small, dark, rounded mole near the base of the thumb, there was none!

Shaking off his shock and disappointment, Sherlock announced with a saddened voice, "I'm afraid, gentlemen, that we are examining nothing more than the remains of one of Moriarty's many 'doubles', or lookalikes." He then explained the specific detail. "Our man is still at large, somewhere, maybe even laughing at us this very minute. He has once again outwitted us and given us the slip. But I swear to you both on my honor that I will pursue this evil villain Moriarty and bring him to justice if it is the last thing I do on this earth."

"Come, Watson! The game is still afoot!" Holmes cried as he strode, with renewed confidence and singular purpose, out the door, the good doctor, forever faithful, close by his side...

THE END

by Jack Karolewski

June 30, 2019

KLONDIKE

Enoch Powell, age 29, was not a happy man.

He lived in Galesburg, Illinois, and worked as a brakeman for the Burlington Railroad. Although he longed to marry and start a family, Enoch's short stature -- at 5'3" -- made the ladies largely ignore him and turn elsewhere. Powell, however, was tough and hard-fisted (he even took boxing lessons for a time), because he had to deal with persistent hobos and vagrants who tried to ride the rails for free. He despised being called "Shorty," but the nickname stuck to him like flypaper his whole adult life, so he finally accepted its reality. Maybe if he somehow got rich, everyone would finally treat him with respect.

The Klondike Gold Rush gave Shorty his longed-for opportunity. Two ships -- the Portland and the Excelsior -- arrived in Seattle on July 17, 1897, bringing ecstatic miners who had unearthed over $1 million in gold nuggets from Bonanza Creek outside of Dawson City in the Canadian Yukon. The news spread quickly -- not just across the country but around the world. Soon, a stampede of hopeful men headed for San Francisco or Seattle to steam north for what they felt was their rightful share of the riches. Many left their jobs and/or their families after just a few day's notice. Virtually none had any experience in either mining or living outdoors in harsh conditions, including Shorty Powell. Many were clerks or farmers or salesmen, or new immigrants from Europe who had moved into American cities. As soon as he settled his meager affairs, Shorty left Galesburg and took a Burlington train (using his employee 'free rail' pass) to Seattle. Powell would later telegraph his boss from there, informing him that he had quit his job as brakeman.

The wharf at Seattle was bedlam when Shorty arrived. Thousands clamored for the mere hundreds of steamer berths. Frantic men pushed, shoved, and bid for tickets, often paying several times their standard price. Shorty was forced to hang around the docks for three days, trying in vain to catch a ship. While he waited, he spent his time purchasing some of the necessary warm clothing, sturdy boots, and digging tools he was told he would need -- the prices of which were steadily increasing by the day. Luckily, he found a man who had seriously taken ill and was willing to sell his berth on the new steamer Vanguard for only twice its original $40 cost. Powell was relieved to be finally sailing north the following day.

Steaming up through the Inside Passage to Alaska was a somewhat frightening revelation for the Illinois flatlander. Gloomy, gray mountains (some with snowy peaks), chilly rain and drizzle, damp forests, fog, and bitter winds assaulted Shorty's senses -- even though this was still the season of summer. He saw scant signs of any human habitation on shore. Orcas, seals, otters, and bald eagles abounded, but lonely silence was the area's chief impression. All of the stampeders on board, however, tried to make light of the eerie experience, with the usual animated male group boasts and brags. The favorite topic at mealtimes was naturally how much gold each expected to find and how they were going to lavishly spend it. And of the 355 passengers on board, Powell noted only three women, and those females were accompanying their husbands. There were also some sled dog teams, and a few large, single dogs.

After stops in Juneau and Skagway, the steamer Vanguard arrived at last in Dyea. This was where Shorty would disembark. His decision was based following a detailed discussion with the ship's crew about which was the best of the two routes to the goldfields: the longer (45 miles) but less steep White Pass route -- which began in Skagway -- or the shorter (33 miles) but more arduous Chilkoot Pass route, which began in Dyea. Both trails ended at Lake Bennett, where a boat would need to be constructed from felled trees to sail down the Yukon River 550 miles to Dawson City and the nearby lucrative diggings.

Dyea was a muddy, ramshackle tent city with a few crude wooden buildings, basically set up to supply the miner's needs, especially for food supplies. The prices were outrageous, but the stampeders had no other recourse. Shorty learned that he had to pack 2000 pounds of food and gear (enough to last a year) to the Canadian border, which began at the crest of the Chilkoot Pass. There, it was strictly checked by the Northwest Mounted Police. This One Ton Rule meant that the average man had to carry fifty pounds on his back at least forty times, making the trip not just 33 miles from Dyea, but rather an exhausting ordeal of backpacking a total of 1350 miles! In addition, no weapons or alcohol was allowed to cross over from the Alaska side. If a newcomer -- called a 'cheechako' (later to be known as a veteran 'sourdough,' after he had spent at least one full year in the Yukon) -- had enough cash, he could hire native Tlingit packers to carry some or all of his required load. But that option was very expensive, and the Indians wisely took advantage of the situation by continuously raising their rates.

Powell loaded up on beans, bacon, oatmeal, coffee, flour, baking powder, lard, sugar, salt, dried fruit, split peas, dried potatoes, butter, and rice. Next, he purchased a 6" buck knife, a small tent, a rubber mat, two thick wool blankets, some cooking equipment and eating utensils, an axe, a saw, a 200' coil of rope, a hammer and crate of nails, a kerosene lantern with extra fuel, two bars of soap, and a simple medicine kit. Shorty then made a wooden frame with shoulder straps for carrying his big canvas supply pack, as he saw others do.

Mentally spent by now, the former railroad brakeman sat down to eat a meal. He was shyly approached by a fellow cheechako wearing grimy, worn clothing who asked if he could join him. The stranger appeared to be in his mid-40's, and was accompanied by a large, seemingly friendly dog.

"Howdy. I'm Ben Naylor, a barber by trade from St. Paul. This here's Samson. He's a beauty, ain't he? He's a Bernese Mountain dog. The breed is originally from Switzerland -- at least that's what the man who sold him to me in Seattle told me. He's bred strong for hard work, yet he's calm and good-natured. Samson's perfect in many ways for the Yukon, but I sadly found out that I'm not. I marched over to the area they call the Scales -- that's where they first check your supply load -- then I climbed the so-called Golden Staircase up to the Chilkoot Pass. The ascent is only 3/4 of a mile, after the 15 mile trek from Dyea, but the 45 degree angle is so steep, and the rock and scree are so sharp and loose, that it just about killed me. And heaven help those who attempt it in slippery ice and snow! I made only one trip up carrying another man's fifty pound load for two dollars as a trial to see if I could do it. Brutal ain't the word, friend! I called it quits right then and there. I ain't cut out for this place. My feet and back are still aching. And they say the winter cold up here is beyond belief, minus 50 or even minus 70 -- even worse than Minnesota. No sir, I'm heading back home. Getting gold this way is plum crazy. I'm glad I checked it all out in person before I purchased my ton of gear and supplies. But somebody robbed my poke while I was sleeping last night in a bunkhouse, so now I'm flat busted. You see, the law is lax here in Dyea, so I'm out of luck with ever getting my money back. Now, I just need enough cash to buy a boat ticket back to Seattle, and then take the train back to St. Paul and my barber shop. Shaving chins and cutting hair suits me way better. Anyway, you seem like kind of a nice fella, Enoch...maybe you would like to buy my Samson? He's all I got that's worth anything. He's only five years old, and I was told his breed can live to ten. He can help you carry some of your gear over the Pass, which is the reason why I bought him along in the first place. So...whatta ya say? Can we make an honest deal right here and now?"

Samson had a long, silky coat of black fur, with a white chest, rust-brown legs, and white paws. His noble head was an attractive mix of black, white, and brown. He was about 28 inches at the shoulders, and weighed about 115 pounds. His dark eyes bespoke both intelligence and loyalty.

Shorty Powell was frankly smitten. He thought long and hard, then made Ben a fair cash offer, which was eagerly accepted with a firm handshake. Naylor took his leave after giving Enoch his heartfelt thanks and his St. Paul address. "Write me if you ever strike it rich, Enoch! I'd like to know at least one person who actually found some nuggets in this God-forsaken wilderness!" Then the Minnesotan lovingly hugged and petted his dog one more time ("You be good to Enoch now, Samson. He's your new master.") before walking away in the drizzling rain toward the big boat dock and its tiny ticket office.

The dog at first looked confused, but then he went to Shorty and licked his hand, and wagged his tail, and got a good petting in return. Powell went with Samson back to the mercantile and bought a full case of tinned corned beef for his new canine companion. He also later fashioned a kind of canvas saddlebag for the back of his dog, which could carry about twenty-five pounds of supplies. Together, they would journey on to the rich Yukon goldfields. The date was August 3, 1897.

It took Shorty and Samson forty-five torturous days -- averaging thirty miles of backpacking a day -- to move their one-ton of supplies first, from Dyea to the Scales, then up and over the Chilkoot Pass to Lake Lindeman, which was connected to Lake Bennett. (There, the White Pass Trail merged, bringing fellow gold stampeders from Skagway.) The ordeal was truly agonizing -- monotonous, initially wooded and muddy, then rocky and often wet and slippery -- all while being plagued by ferocious mosquitoes. The narrow trail was too rough to allow any kind of sledge or wheeled cart. Shorty noticeably lost weight (the waist on his pants was now baggy and loose), but he also gained muscles he never knew existed. Similarly, the blisters on his feet and hands had turned to thick calluses. Samson was still robust, and was allowed to forage and catch any small mammals -- largely gophers, squirrels and mice -- to eat at each day's end to supplement his diet of canned meat. He was probably pleased to see several dozen other dogs, too, here at Lake Bennett. The nights, meanwhile, were getting colder, so man and dog slept together under thick wool blankets in their tent. Powell heard rumors that of the 100,000 souls who tried for the Klondike, only 30,000 made it this far. Now, a boat had to be made somehow and launched before the Yukon River froze up, which typically started in mid-October and went to the end of May. (Shorty had no experience in boat-building; he assumed would carefully watch others, then try to imitate their skill.) But because it was already September 17 -- and the boat building would take at least another month to build and test, and because the river journey from Lake Bennett to Dawson would take another twenty-eight days -- Shorty realized with no small frustration that he was out of luck for this year. He and Samson would have to winter here -- with 30,000 other men -- after building his boat, then wait for the Yukon River ice to thaw so that the estimated 7000 homemade vessels could sail for the Klondike diggings in the spring.

But unexpected things can happen in this life, even in the strangest places, without warning. Shorty had just set up his tent and was preparing a hot meal for himself and his dog when three strangers approached.

"Nice dog! What's his name? You wouldn't want to sell him now, would you, pardner?" asked a tall man by the name of Dick Kincaid. He then introduced his two partners, Bob Thompson and Jim Rogers. All three men were from Denver, and were university students in their early 20's studying mining. Their elderly professors actually insisted that they leave their classes and head north to gain some practical field experience while having a historic, manly adventure."We just finished our boat -- such as it is -- and we aim to shove off for the gold fields tomorrow at first light. Gotta get there before all the rich claims are staked. Sure could use a good strong dog, though."

Shorty simply smiled and said that Samson was not for sale.

"Well, how about selling us some of your foodstuffs instead? Supplies here are even more expensive than in Skagway. We are running kinda low, because we are always hungry and we underestimated our stores," Thompson explained.

"You fellers are welcomed to share some of my bannock if you want," Powell offered. "It's still warm from the fry pan. And I've got some leftover coffee too, but you'll need to go and bring back your own tin cups. But I likewise won't sell any of my food supplies. They have to last me through the coming winter and then into Dawson."

"Fair enough," said Rogers. "We'll be right back." While Shorty waited, he made a mental note that Samson was content and wagging his tail when the three strangers first showed up. Powell noticed over the past weeks that the dog would always growl if he sensed anybody was a bad person, or if he expected any harm to come to his master. This intuition helped Shorty decide that he could indeed trust these college men.

When Kincaid, Thompson, and Rogers returned, the four cheechakos gathered around Enoch's fire for the fresh bannock and coffee. After a sociable half-hour of random conversation, Kincaid spoke up.

"Enoch, my friends and I have been talking. We like you and trust you. How about you throw in with us and sail on our boat to Dawson tomorrow? All we ask is that

Samson joins our merry party, and that we can share your foodstuffs on the journey. You help us, we help you. Once we arrive in Dawson, we can split up and go our own ways again. How about it? Is it a deal?"

Shorty Powell was momentarily flummoxed, then jumped up and said, "Sure...you bet! I wasn't very happy at the prospect of staying here alone over the winter anyway. Let's shake on it!" The quartet pumped handshakes all around and grinned. Samson barked along with the excitement too.

Dawn broke the following morning with rare blue skies and sunshine. Naming their boat 'The Denver,' the four men and one dog went to register their craft with the Northwest Mounted Police. This was required by law to keep track of the occupant's names for next-of-kin if the boat and/or crew was lost to the Yukon rapids, or simply sunk due to leaky construction. The Denver was given number 239, which was then painted on its bow by the Mounties.

The boat appeared well-made to Shorty's casual eye, its seams double-caulked with hardened pine resin. It had two side oars, a canvas main sail which could be raised and lowered depending on the winds, and even a steering rudder. It was quite ideal for four men, a large dog, and all of their food and equipment. Their goal was to arrive in Dawson City in twenty-eight days before the river froze solid. They would travel 550 miles of the Yukon's 2000 mile length, intending to average about twenty miles a day before beaching her each night on shore to rest.

The worst dangers they were warned about were three sets of rapids: White Horse Rapids, Miles Canyon, and Five Finger Rapids. No one on The Denver had ever navigated a boat through white water, so the men knew they were taking a gamble and had to count on their own good luck. Still, everyone's spirits were high, and even Samson settled in with his new friends well. In the evenings around the campfire, the four men took turns reading aloud from three books that the college chums had brought with them from Colorado: Charles Dickens' "Great Expectations," Robert Louis Stevenson's "Treasure Island," and Jules Verne's "Journey to the Center of the Earth." Shorty Powell, who was only educated to the sixth grade, was thrilled by the tales from such fine novels, each filled with interesting characters, plot twists, and suspense. Their routine by now was established, and the four men had plenty of food rations too.

The first few days went by -- either cloudy and grey, or rainy, or cold and windy, or a rare one featuring glorious sunny skies. Soon, they saw their first set of churning, roiling rapids -- the dreaded White Horse. It was frankly terrifying! The boat sped up tremendously, bucking up and down like a bronco, the chilled waves soaking them with spray as they dodged huge boulders and sharp stone outcrops. Enoch laid down on his belly in The Denver's bottom for ballast, holding Samson tightly for safety, with Bob and Jim at the oars, and Dick at the rudder. Fortunately, the crew had wisely lashed down all of their equipment with taut ropes, so nothing went lost overboard. Days later, Miles Canyon -- mercifully not as ferocious -- was similarly met and survived.

But at Five Finger Rapids -- on Day 14, about half-way to Dawson -- disaster struck. Four wicked reddish basalt islands in the center of the river divided the waters into five racing channels, like the fingers on a flat inverted hand. Not knowing which channel to run, Dick pulled their boat's rudder and steered to the left instead of the far right, which (they would later learn) was the correct course. They soon rammed into the basalt cliff walls, shattering Jim's oar and catapulting him out of his seat and into the frigid, racing waters. Dick tried to jump overboard in an attempt to rescue his friend, but Enoch leaped up and held him back, shouting, "No! Throw him a rope instead, or we'll lose you too!" But it was already too late. In horror, the three men helplessly watched the fourth man slam into jutting rocks at full force, his body twisting and flipping like a limp manikin. Jim's head finally popped up -- gashed and bleeding, visibly unconscious -- before he went under the unforgiving waves for the last time and disappeared.

The three shocked survivors, soaking wet, beached their craft on the next calm sandbar downriver. The made a quick fire, changed into dry clothing, and dried out their wet outfits. Dick blamed himself for the tragedy, but Bob reassured him that it was an accident and nobody's fault. Kincaid offered to write to Rogers' family, explaining the awful circumstances of their son's death, once they arrived in Dawson. The boat was inspected for damage, and other than the lost oar and its oarlock, and a chunk of wood split off of The Denver's bow, the vessel was intact. They decided to spend the night where they were, and make up the lost hours the following day.

The rest of their time sailing down the Yukon was uneventful, as the gold boomtown at last came into view around a bend on October 16, 1897. Dawson City! The vast shorelines of the mighty river were just starting to ice up as the daily temperatures had continued to drop and the current slowed, so the men had made it just in time. They only wished that Jim Rogers had lived to be there with them now -- hence, their triumph was understandably tinged with much melancholy. The Denver was met by a curious crowd of well-wishers, who were also eager for any news from the outside world. And two Mounties were there too, waiting to register the safe arrival of boat # 239. Kincaid then told the red-uniformed officials about the tragic loss of their companion at

Five Fingers. Afterwards, he went to the postal service to pen a heart-breaking report to Jim's parents while Powell and Thompson stayed behind, guarding their boat and its gear.

Next, Enoch, Dick, and Bob divided up their remaining supplies and easily sold their boat to the first bidder, likewise splitting the money. "Well, looks like this is where we say our good-byes," Kincaid announced as they enjoyed a farewell whiskey toast in the first saloon they spied. "As you know, Bob and I have our mining plans already laid out. So we both wish you good luck with your diggings, Enoch. Write us back in Denver if you strike it rich, and we'll send word to Galesburg if we do the same!" Samson barked his adieu as the two college chums walked off with their gear towards Bonanza Creek, which was several miles south of town.

Dawson City lay on the right bank of the Yukon, in a large flat area beneath a high mountain to the north. The town was noisy, smoky, chaotic and crowded with over 8,000 people so far -- and more were arriving every day. The streets were largely seas of mud, but there were some wooden sidewalks on Front Street, the main thoroughfare adjacent to the river. Ramshackle wooden buildings and crammed tents offered meals, lodging, mining supplies, mail service, whiskey, and gambling. There were banks, assay offices, dance halls, a few doctor's offices, and even an opera house -- but no schools or churches yet. Everything was for sale (even imported champagne and caviar), but the prices were heart-stopping. A single egg first cost a dollar, then two, then three. A 20-cent gold pan could be sold for $8. The town's preferred currency was gold dust or nuggets, and every establishment had its own table scales to weigh it. Prostitutes even had their own area called Paradise Alley, its lane of one-room 'cribs' sporting distinctive red doors, and offering all manner of carnal pleasures for a price -- in a place where lonesome, lusty miners outnumbered women by almost a hundred to one.

But newcomers were stunned and dismayed to learn that all the rich claims had already been staked out and dug in the several months immediately following the 1896 Discovery Strike, and that they would either have to look farther away for any gold or simply abandon their quest all together and go back home -- their back-breaking, dangerous, and costly ordeal utterly fruitless. Yes, a few hundred lucky miners had gotten fabulously wealthy, but most of the stampeders would come up empty-handed -- with nothing but a good adventure tale to tell their grandchildren. The people making money in Dawson now were all of those who "mined the miners," that is, shrewd entrepreneurs selling the diggers all the goods, services, and pleasures that they needed and relied on.

Shorty Powell, however, was still stubbornly determined to make his fortune in the Klondike. He would never go back to Illinois in shame and defeat. With his faithful dog by his side, he set out to familiarize himself with his strange, new environment and its wild, assorted inhabitants. That being done, he would then do everything possible to capture his share of the precious, elusive yellow metal in the gold fields.

Seeing as he had not had a hot bath since leaving Seattle, Enoch made that his first priority. While he soaked in comparative luxury in a dented tin tub in a bath tent, he had a boy run his pile of filthy clothes over to a Chinese laundry to be boiled clean. Then Powell headed for a haircut and a beard trim in the barber tent next door, recalling Ben Naylor while he was being attended to by an cheery Italian who spoke little English. Shorty then treated himself to warm indoor lodgings for the night, but Samson still had to sleep outside -- rules of the house.

The next day, Enoch went to retrieve his clean clothes, changed, and left the dirty ones he was wearing to be washed by the Chinamen. He walked around the town with his dog, making casual conversation with fellow gold-seekers while asking questions. Shorty declined persistent offers to sell Samson. He also noticed some of the dog sled teams and their masters anxiously waiting for the first snowfall, which was soon expected. This far north, Shorty noted that the hours of daylight were shrinking fast each day. The sun rose at 8 and set at 6, but in another month it would rise at 10 and set at 4. Time to find and stake a claim and start digging -- before the annual coming darkness covered the land for months.

Powell headed for dinner at Joe Ladue's Saloon, with a perky Samson at his heels. While he waited for an open seat, Enoch saddled up to the long bar with his dog and ordered a beer. That was when a large bully from Texas named Snake-eyes Malone accosted him.

"More over with that mutt of yours, half-man," Snake-eyes growled. "Make some room for a genuine Sourdough." The obnoxious man had already been heavily drinking and smelled it. He was dirty, bearded, and ugly, with tiny, beady eyes -- which gave him his peculiar nickname.

Shorty tilted back his hat, examined Malone for a few seconds (his harasser was well over six feet tall and sixty pounds heavier than him), then shifted over a bit to his left at the bar rail. "How's that? Got enough space now?" he asked plainly, but in a low voice tinged with annoyance.

"Look, you runty cheechako, why don't you just shove off with your smelly cur and give me some real elbow room?" Snake-eyes snarled. Then Malone whapped

Powell's hat off his head with a sharp swipe of his fist. Samson sensed the evilness of the other man, and became fully alert, and would attack this enemy if ordered by his master.

The commotion quickly grew a crowd around the two men, already sensing a good, head-busting fight. Shorty knew he couldn't back down from this bully in public, or his newcomer reputation would forever be as nothing but a lowdown coward. He then remembered what his old boxing coach had once told him: When faced with a sure fight with a bigger bully, always get the first blow in, then add as many more punches as you can before your opponent can respond. So Enoch slowly stooped to retrieve his hat, and turned to his dog saying, "It's O.K., Samson," as he patted his furry head. But as he rose, Powell bounded and powerfully rabbit-punched his left fist twice into Malone's nose, followed by a strong sharp right to his opponent's slack jaw. Snake-Eyes was caught unawares, and reflexively took a step back as his nose began to ooze blood. The crowd murmured its approval as still more miners put down their drinks or dinner forks and came to witness the action. Some were even ready to place fast bets on who would win.

"Why you little son-of-a-bitch!" Malone bellowed. "Now you're gonna get it!" Snake-eyes unsheathed his big waist knife, and wielded it with menace.

Shorty went for his buck knife, but a massive hand from behind covered his fist and froze it there. Then he heard a deep voice say, "Hold on there, friend. I'll settle this."

Shorty turned and saw a mountain of a man -- 6'6", 250 pounds -- a huge, bearded Paul Bunyan-esque character in a brown plaid flannel shirt and a red toque on his head. His name was Big Mike Mercer, and he was a Cajun from the bayous of Louisiana, which accounted for his distinctive Southern accent. He had worked the docks in Shreveport before coming North. He gave Powell a small smile and a quick wink.

"I think y'all should pick on someone your own size, Snake-eyes. You know...someone like me," Big Mike now glared at the bully with intense anger in his cool blue eyes.

Foolishly, Malone licked his lips and made a forward step, and thrust with his knife. But Mercer had already grabbed a chair sideways, then lifted it with both hands and crushed it into the startled face of his opponent. Snake-eyes went down, his blade spinning out of his hand. As the drunk slowly climbed to his feet, Big Mike towered over him, and punished Malone with a brutal right uppercut that reeled the bully backwards and into the dark land of unconsciousness. The fight was over. The inert body of the loser was dragged out the saloon door and dumped into the mud. The crowd loudly cheered the victor with hearty claps and whistles.

"Can I buy you fellows a drink?" asked a genial 21-year old, clean-shaven stranger, approaching the pair. "I'm Jack London, from Oakland, California. I came North for the gold like you, but I'm also a writer. I'd like to get your names and all the details correct when I write up the story of what just happened. And what a magnificent dog! What's his name?" He warmly rubbed Samson's head.

The trio was offered a vacated table, and they talked for two hours and drank while Shorty also enjoyed a delicious -- but pricey -- sirloin steak dinner. (Samson, meanwhile, was given a large cow leg bone to gnaw.) Jack told his new pals about his adventurous life so far: he had been a fish cannery worker, an oyster pirate, a fur seal hunter, and a penniless tramp who had once spent a rough month in jail for vagrancy. London -- who smoked cigarette after cigarette as he animatedly spoke and gestured -- later generously picked up the meal and bar tab, after excusing himself to leave the saloon for another appointment. "Her name is Esmerelda, and she's a real fine gal down in Paradise Alley...sure don't want to keep her waiting!" Jack laughed as they shook hands. "See ya around, boys!"

And that was how the friendship -- and later partnership -- of Enoch Powell and Mike Mercer began. After talking more into the wee hours, Shorty learned that Mike's digging partner had contracted scurvy and had headed home to St. Louis to regain his health. Would Powell like to throw in with Mercer, he asked? Big Mike had a claim he was working off the Klondike River, not far from Bonanza Creek. "No big strike yet, but it yields an average day's wages in gold dust. How about it?" Enoch said he would certainly like to join him, with but one simple caveat: "Just don't ever call me Shorty, alright, Mike?" Mercer agreed, and they shook on it. Soon, Dawson City was used to seeing the oddly-matched mining pair -- one a diminutive 5'3," the other a towering 6'6" -- when they came into town for supplies or a drink.

"Did y'all happen to buy a bear whistle yet?" Big Mike asked Enoch one morning when they came in from the bush for supplies.

"No...why?" replied Powell.

"Well, we are in the wilderness, and in bear country too, and when y'all are hiking through the brush, you need to regularly blow a whistle, or clap your hands, or otherwise make a lot of noise so you don't surprise a bear when coming around a blind bend. If you come face-to-face with an unsuspecting male bear, he will charge you and attack.

Likewise, if you run into a she-bear, she'll fight to protect her cubs. So let's get you a good bear whistle at the nearest Mercantile. It's also handy if y'all ever get lost or injured. Just keep blowing three blasts until help arrives." Mercer then pulled out his silver whistle on a leather lanyard from under his shirt and demonstrated. "Of course, in the swamps of Louisiana, we Cajuns only need to worry about alligators sneaking up and biting your ass!" he added with a grin. So they bought Powell a metal whistle, and his first pair of snowshoes, and a used Winchester rifle for hunting and protection against claim jumpers.

Over the following three weeks, Powell learned exactly how hard it was to actually dig for gold. You put shovel- after shovel-full of soil and gravel into a wooden cradle, then poured buckets of water over the pile, rocking it back and forth, searching for any glimmering flecks of color. The water was icy cold, and one's fingers grew numb as each tough day progressed. The ground was frozen with permafrost just a few inches under the topsoil, so fires had to be used to melt the ice in the digging trenches. While Enoch was initially thrilled with discovering his first gold flecks, both he and Mike yearned to find a rich 'pay streak' in the rocks that would yield actual nuggets. Meanwhile, the weather was increasingly snowy and getting bitterly colder by the day. Many cheechakos threw in the towel in disgust and defeat at this point and sold their claims at a loss. But they were trapped by now by the solidly frozen Yukon River, and could not leave Dawson until next May when the ice usually broke up. Only then could they sail by boat north and west downriver on the Yukon all the way to Mt. Michael, a small town on the coast of the Bering Sea, and connect there with steamers going back to Seattle or San Francisco. Living back in Dawson City for the dark winter was also expensive, so most newcomer's money belts were getting thin and light. Patience waned and tempers flared. Veteran Sourdoughs called it 'cabin fever,' and it would get worse in the coming months of forced inactivity. Drinking, fighting, murders, and suicides all increased during the strange, dark wintertime.

One morning in mid-November, coming back from a short hunting trip looking for fresh game, Mike told Enoch that they had some serious trouble to deal with.

"Some nearby diggers confronted me a few hours ago and said that my claim here is invalid, and they threaten to take me to court. They say their boundary extends into my property. I lost my legal title papers in a camp fire accident about six months ago, and never thought I would be challenged and need to prove my rightful ownership of our diggings. I need to go to the official NWMP office at Forty Mile and get a duplicate document of the original that I filed there when I first came North. It's about 55 miles from here one way.

I need you and Samson to stay behind and guard our claim and our camp goods until I get back. I'll travel on the frozen river in my snowshoes. It's three days/two nights to Forty Mile, one day rest there, then three days/two nights back. So I'll be gone a full week. I know the way, so I won't get lost," Mercer assured Powell with confidence.

Big Mike packed up his necessary gear and headed out at first light -- which wasn't until 10 a.m. -- the following day. The thermometer in Dawson registered a numbing 15 degrees below zero Fahrenheit.

But Mercer did not come back on schedule a week later. The weather had worsened -- a freezing Arctic blizzard was brewing. Temperatures had fallen now to minus 30, with bitter winds. Powell was worried that something terrible had happened to his partner. He asked a trusted neighboring miner, Amos Baskin, to watch his claim and goods while he was away. "I should only be gone a few days, heading on the river towards Forty Mile." Enoch promised. "I have to find out if Mike ran into any trouble."

It was now that Powell made his worst mistake. Old-timers tried to warn each green cheechako of one hard rule -- never to go out into the bush alone in the winter. But in his haste, Enoch rushed off north with his faithful dog on the frozen Yukon in his snowshoes and backpack. It was hard traveling. Even with his warmest clothes, he was still cold and had to keep moving to generate enough body heat. By just after 4:00 p.m., it was already getting dark, the skies slate gray and blowing both snow and stinging ice pellets. No moon would be visible tonight. Even the moisture in Enoch's eyes was icing up, and he had to repeatedly squint and blink and close his eyelids to thaw them out. He realized that he had to make a shelter fast for himself and Samson, and wait until tomorrow's dim light. He headed towards the forested area above the left side of the snow-covered river bank to make camp.

That was when Powell thought he heard something amidst the howling winds. Faint man-made sounds of some sort. Was it a whistle? He listened carefully, with all of his concentration. Yes! Weak and distant, but clearly -- three blasts. He pulled his own whistle from his pocket and blew as loud as he could. But the simple act of taking his mittens off for a few moments caused his bare fingers to begin freezing up. He left the whistle clamped in his mouth and quickly put his mittens back on. The metal froze fast to his lips. He regularly blew three blasts as he hiked ahead.

Enoch kept going downriver towards the sound. It had to be Mike! It was night now, but Powell was able to light his kerosene lantern after striking several matches, blowing on his mitten-less fingers as they numbed with the cold before replacing them back in their warm coverings. He held the lantern aloft as he snow-shoed forward, and blew his whistle at regular intervals, pausing between reports to listen for any acknowledgement.

Twenty minutes later, Enoch found his friend, aided by Samson's alert barking. Alarmingly, Mercer was barely alive. He had fallen up to his waist through an odd patch of thin ice near the shore, and had somehow dragged himself up out of the water. He had a compound fracture of his right leg, his tibia sticking out at an awkward angle under his solidly frozen pants. Mike was ghostly pale and miserably freezing to death from hypothermia. Powell removed his whistle from his lips so he could talk, but some skin ripped off where it had frozen to the metal, and his lips were suddenly raw and painful.

"Enoch...is that you? Oh thank God! I couldn't make it into the woods and make a fire. I made it O.K. to Forty Mile and got our claim papers. But then this happened. I'm so cold... I just want to go to sleep...but if I do, I don't think I'll ever wake up again...Enoch, y'all got to make a fire quick..." Mercer weakly insisted, his once mighty strength fading fast.

Powell tried to remain calm and keep his mind clear from the shock of their dire situation. He carefully went with his lantern up the river bank and into the forest to get some kindling sticks, but he had to push away the snow from under the trees to find any. After a few minutes, he had a small bundle of wood and placed it on the river bank closest to Big Mike. He would first go and inform his friend of the plan. Enoch would then go back and get the fire going, and drag his partner to its blazing, life-saving warmth.

Horribly, it was too late. Mercer was dead by the time Powell returned. Enoch was all alone now, his own life precarious in a merciless, murderous Yukon snow blizzard.

Another disaster came next, when Powell tripped over a hidden tree root as he climbed back towards his wood pile and fell, shattering his lantern and extinguishing its beam in the process. Plunged into sudden darkness, Enoch then lost both mittens when he frantically removed them to find his matches in his pack to light a fire. The bare flesh of his fingers burned in an instant with rapidly approaching frostbite. He could hardly move them. They were freezing into numb, alien, claw-like appendages. His only hope of staying alive was to light a match and start the kindling on fire. Oh dear God, please don't let me die here like this, he prayed, he pleaded...

He looked into the steady dark eyes of his faithful companion, Samson. Then he had a final, desperate, appalling idea. Bringing his beloved dog close to him in a hug, with his fingers now barely able to hold anything, Enoch pulled his buck knife out from its waist-belt leather sheath. "I'm so sorry, Samson, my old friend..." he, murmured, choked with emotion. The dog gave a sharp whine as his master slit its throat, letting the steaming hot blood soak onto his frozen fingers, giving their blessed circulation back. Then Enoch gently slit the great dead canine's belly open, and placed his hands fully inside the body until they were warm enough to find his life-saving matches and start a fire. The last chance gamble worked, and soon orange flames ignited and spread. More wood was then gathered and added. Shorty sat as close as possible to the fiery warmth.

Two hours later, Powell heard gunshots fired in regular rounds of three, and he saw swinging lanterns in the distance approaching his fire shelter. It was his trusted claim watcher and diggings neighbor, Amos Baskin, along with a seasoned search party of five men from Dawson. "When I realized that you had gone looking for your friend by yourself, Shorty, I knew you might get into serious trouble, especially in this weather. So we came looking for you," Amos explained. The Dawson men soon saw the corpse of Big Mike, his still blue eyes frozen open, as well as the sliced-open body of brave, mighty Samson. "Too bad, Shorty, but you had no alternative. As heart-breaking as it is, always remember that dog saved your life." Enoch Powell said he knew, then broke down and wept uncontrollably for a time, wailing in grief for both Samson and Big Mike. Their remains would be brought back to Dawson for burial once the weather improved.

Enoch recovered from his near-death ordeal in Dawson for the next six months. He was praised for his selfless bravery in trying to save his partner's life. He was also lauded for his survival skills and his smart -- though regrettable -- action involving his dog. But he was also seen as foolish for going out alone in the bush in the winter, a dreadful mistake he admitted with shame, and he told every other cheechako who would listen to heed his hard lesson. Shorty's experience made him an honorary Sourdough in the eyes of the gold rush town.

Powell ran into Jack London twice during his months of recuperation, but he found out that the young writer had unfortunately contracted scurvy. London suffered bleeding gums, the loss of four front teeth, and had terrible muscle pains in his legs and hips. So a Dawson doctor sternly advised him to give up the Yukon and head back to sunny California -- and its healthy citrus fruits -- when the river ice finally broke up on May 29th. Jack reluctantly left Dawson City on June 8, 1898, after saying farewell to Shorty and others.

Five days later, the Yukon Territory was officially established. Civilization had finally claimed the wild boom town. Dawson's population, however, briefly swelled to more than 30,000 by mid-June, as the 7000 homemade boats from Lake Bennett -- that had been waiting for the Yukon River ice to finally melt -- arrived at last. But to the surprise and dismay of the eager newcomers, every gold claim had already been taken. After all of their brutal toil and cost to get here, it was too late.

By now, Enoch had enough of Dawson as well. He wanted to go back home to Illinois, if not to Galesburg, then to somewhere else -- maybe Springfield or Peoria. He sold his mining claim to Amos Baskin after a few final weeks of meager digging, and at last took a passenger boat downriver to St. Michael in mid-September. He had been in the Klondike for a full, amazing year. Other stampeders were leaving too, for the Gold Rush was basically over, with hydraulic mining and corporations now moving in. The adventure and its dreams of wealth were rapidly fading away for the tens of thousands who had come North.

But fate or luck has a funny way of appearing when one least expects it. When Shorty arrived in St. Michael, word came from the city of Nome, 110 miles north up the coast, that three Swedes had found gold at Anvil Creek there. What was different this time was, incredibly, that the gold was lying right on the ground in nuggets in the black sand beaches! So Enoch headed up to Nome on the next boat to see for himself.

Powell found over $58,650 of gold in just two months, and then left Nome just before the usual frantic hordes of new stampeding miners overwhelmed the town and exhausted the Strike. Enoch took a boat back to St. Michael, then a steamer back to Seattle and a train back to Galesburg. He was settled into a fine new house there by New Year's Day, 1899. He then wrote to Dick Kincaid and Bob Thompson in Denver, informing them of his windfall of riches, as earlier promised, and invited them to visit anytime. He also wrote to Ben Naylor in St. Paul. More than anyone, Ben deserved to know the full story of noble Samson, including the great dog's sacrifice which ultimately saved his master's life.

Nobody teased Enoch Powell or ever called him Shorty again. He cleverly decided to invest in several property areas in the busy Illinois real estate market, and soon expanded his fortune considerably. Before long, he met an attractive and sensible young lady, Virginia Longworth, who -- at age 24 and 5'2" -- was truly honored to accept his proposal of marriage. Over time, their home would resound with the laughter of their four children. Powell was also pleased when he read in the newspapers how his old Dawson pal, Jack London, had become one of the most famous and wealthy writers in the world, getting his start by penning true or fictional stories about his days during the Yukon Gold Rush.

Enoch had come a long, long way in a relatively short time. He had been severely tested -- physically, mentally, and spiritually -- but had come back a wiser and hopefully a better man. His deep Klondike memories lasted him until the end of his days, after a long and happy life...

THE END

by Jack Karolewski

December 8, 2019